Also by Belinda Bauer

Blacklands
Darkside
Rubbernecker
The Facts of Life and Death
The Shut Eye
The Beautiful Dead

FINDERS KEEPERS

Belinda Bauer

Grove Press
New York

First published in Great Britain in 2012 by Bantam Press,
an imprint of Transworld Publishers.

First Grove Atlantic edition: March 2017

Published simultaneously in Canada
Printed in the United States of America

FIRST EDITION

ISBN 978-0-8021-2643-6
eISBN 978-0-8021-8940-0

Grove Press
an imprint of Grove Atlantic
154 West 14th Street
New York, NY 10011

Distributed by Publishers Group West

groveatlantic.com

17 18 19 20   10 9 8 7 6 5 4 3 2 1

To Dr Robert Bracchi

PART ONE

MAY

1

It was late in the season to go hunting. Although Jess Took wasn't hunting really, just watching.

If you could call it even that.

Jess was thirteen, and over the past year 'going hunting' had become a euphemism for sitting in her father's horsebox, deafened by hip-hop and blinded by the mist that formed quickly inside the windows in the early chill of a spring morning.

Although it was May, Exmoor had been prettied overnight by a sheen of sparkling frost that made it look gift-wrapped and Christmassy. The rising sun washed the hills with gold, making glittering gems of the dew. Tourists came from all over the world to see such sights. Sights like the one Jess Took was currently ignoring in favour of the sensory underload of opaque glass, an alien beat, and the faint smell of horse shit that she'd sucked into her wet lungs with her very first breath, and which none of her family had ever tried to clear from their nostrils.

John Took was the Master of the Midmoor Hunt. *Joint* Master,

Jess was fond of reminding him. Since the divorce, Jess only spent the weekends with her father, and it had given her the distance to develop a critical eye and the almost uncanny ability to hit him where it hurt. In return for his having an affair and leaving her mother, Jess had stopped riding to hounds with him. She missed it but was determined to make him suffer.

In return, John Took refused to allow her to stay home alone on the Saturday mornings when he was scheduled to hunt, and instead loaded Blue Boy and then Jess into the box with equal brusqueness, then took the horse out and left *her* there on whatever gravel pull-off or grass verge they chose to park on that day. He always made some lumpy sandwiches for her, and – to teach him a lesson – she never ate them.

Now, as she turned the key so she could direct some heat on to her feet, Jess squinted against the new sunshine diffused through the misted windscreen. She was dimly aware that somewhere beyond her senses, her father would be shouting and bossing people about in that way she hated; pulling too sharply on Blue Boy's mouth in his bid for the spectacular turns and stops that he thought made him a better rider.

She sighed. Sometimes she felt like giving up their battle of wills. She was beginning to suspect that it was hurting her more than it hurt him, and it certainly required more effort than she really wanted to expend on anything apart from texting her friends and craving Ugg boots.

She wondered whether 6.45am was too early to text Alison and tell her what a shit life she was having.

Probably.

The flat white glass of the passenger window was filled with the darkness of sudden approach, and the door yanked open. Jess flinched and opened her mouth, prepared to be rude to her father for scaring her. Then left it gaping in shock as a faceless man reached in, wrapped his arms around her – and simply dragged her out of the cab.

It all happened so fast.

Jess felt her feet smack the gravel and the cold hit the small of her back as her sweatshirt bunched up. She squirmed and kicked and tried to turn her head to bite the man's strong arms, but all she got was a mouthful of the bitter grease of his waxed coat.

Jess felt herself being dragged across the dirt, half trying to find her feet, half trying to make herself heavy and hard to hold. Her earphones pulled out of her ears but she could still hear the beat – tinny and feeble – somewhere around her neck, along with the scrape of gravel and the squeezed sound of her own breath. Her father's horsebox left her vision and she saw the early-morning clouds like puffs of cotton wool in a pale-blue sky; Mrs Barlow's trailer flashed briefly and she grabbed for the loop of baler twine attached to the side. Her fingers burned as she was torn from it. She yelped.

This was real.

This was *really happening*.

The yelp reminded her that she had a voice and she said 'help', in a way that sounded both experimental and petulant.

She was embarrassed to be shouting for help like a victim in a movie, when she was Jess Took, who was just a normal girl in a boring place. Still, she said it again more loudly and the man's hand banged across her mouth and nose hard enough to make her eyes water. She felt instantly violated in a way she hadn't while being dragged from her father's horsebox and across a gritty patch of moorland. The hand was woollen and smelled of dirt. She tried to shake it off but the man gripped her face tightly now – pressing her teeth into her tender lips, shutting off her airway, his overwhelming strength sapping what was left of hers.

He spoke calmly in her ear. 'If you scream, I'll shoot you in the head.'

The bone went out of Jess's legs and she felt terror warm her thighs.

She sobbed fear and shame in equal measure.

He turned her, and pushed instead of pulled; something hard caught her across the buttocks and she tumbled backwards and landed just a couple of feet down on what felt like hard carpet.

Her legs were picked up and hoisted after her, and she just had time to register that she was in the boot of a car before the lid fell and cut off her cry, her light – and every idea she'd ever had of how her world was going to be – with a single metallic bang.

The hunt drew a blank.

The dogs followed the trails laid by terrier men on quad bikes to their anti-climactic conclusions and never had a sniff of an accidental fox to liven up the day. Blue Boy stumbled after jumping the stream at the bottom of Withypool Common, and by the end of the day he was uneven. The huntsman wasted fifteen minutes cutting a hound out of a barbed-wire fence. And that over-horsed fool Graham Gigman kept overtaking the field *and* the Master on his white-legged, wall-eyed beast that should have been shot as it slid out of the mare, in John Took's not-so-humble opinion.

All in all, by the time they got back to the foot of Dunkery Beacon, where they'd left the boxes, Took's mood was foul.

'At least it didn't rain,' shouted Graham Gigman as his nasty animal skittered sideways past Took for the last time. Until the next time.

Took ignored him and slid sullenly from Blue Boy's back. The bay's near fore was swollen at the knee.

Great. He'd have to ride Scotty on Monday, and Scotty was not half the horse Blue Boy was.

Took banged the tailgate shut on Blue Boy, removed his sweaty helmet and opened the door of the horsebox.

'Not a bloody fox in sight,' he told Jess.

Except Jess wasn't there.

Instead there was a note on the steering wheel. A yellow square. John Took's mouth tightened. Bloody Jess and her teenage rebellion. She used to be such an easy kid before the divorce. Where'd she buggered off to now?

He reached up and peeled the note off the wheel. As he read it, his frown of annoyance became one of confusion. The note consisted of four words that were both simple and utterly mysterious.

You don't love her.

2

There was a place between light and dark – between life and death – where Jonas Holly lived after his wife died.

He was split into the physical and the psychological – a keen division which saw him wake every day, get up, get dressed, move his arms and legs, blink, while all the time his mind just sat there as if on hold in the great switchboard of life. His mental processes stretched no further than the immediate and the practical. It got dark, he switched on a light; the milk arrived, he took it in; he had thirst, he drank water. On the rare occasions when he hungered, he ate. It took him almost two months to pick his way through what was left in the freezer, the larder, and Mrs Paddon's doorstep donations. His already long frame became stretched; he ran out of notches on his belt. Finally, canned tomatoes over kidney beans marked the end of food and the start of starvation or shopping. It took Jonas three days before he walked into the village to choose the latter.

He was pared down to the primitive. Animalistic. He barely spoke. Every few days he would answer Mrs Paddon's neighbourly inquiry with a mumbled 'Fine, thanks' and then immediately go indoors. For an hour once a week he was probed by the psychologist and managed to tell her virtually nothing. The only reason he went to Bristol for their sessions was because he had to be passed fit before he could go back to work, and the only reason he planned to go back to work was because he had absolutely no idea of what else he might do with the rest of his life. Or much interest in the subject.

Kate Gulliver, the psychologist, seemed OK but he didn't trust her. Nothing personal – Jonas didn't trust anyone any more, not even himself.

Especially not himself.

Occasionally Jonas would look hard into the bathroom mirror. He never saw anything but his own brown eyes staring back at him quizzically, doubting even his own memory of events. He remembered the knife. He remembered the blood. He remembered how one had led to the other. At least, he thought he did. His memory had always been shaky, and the lack of horror that accompanied these images made him wonder whether they had happened that way at all, or whether they were all his mind could cope with for now. Maybe the gaps would be filled in later, when he was better able to deal with another truth.

He hoped not.

It was already enough truth for Jonas that every time he went upstairs in their tiny cottage, he had to cross the flagstones behind the front door where Lucy had died – and where he had almost managed to follow her.

Sometimes he pissed in the garden and slept on the couch.

Truth was overrated.

Kate – who encouraged Jonas to call her that – talked about the stages of grief and wanted him to explore his feelings. Jonas thought that would be a bad idea. He knew his feelings were in there somewhere, on a high shelf in the wardrobe of his psyche, but he was wary of fetching the stool that might enable him to reach them.

He was worried about what else he might find there.

Denial, anger, bargaining, depression and acceptance. Jonas knew the stages of grief by now. He knew them backwards. He could juggle them like plates. It didn't mean he knew how they *felt*.

So instead he had done his best to demonstrate the appropriate emotions at what he guessed were appropriate intervals over the eight months they'd spent in each other's sporadic company.

'Do you ever feel guilty?' Kate would ask.

'Of course,' he'd answer. 'I should have got there sooner. In time. To stop it.'

She'd nod seriously and he'd look at his hands.

He'd spent three sessions in total silence, gazing dully at the cheap carpet in her stage-set office while she'd asked careful questions at long intervals. It had been calming and, he imagined, would be construed as depression.

Soon he would have to find the energy to have a go at anger. He kept putting it off.

In one way he hoped that affecting emotions might magically give rise to the real thing, but all he had felt since the death of his wife was a strange numbness that was a smoked-glass barrier to reality.

Only in his dreams did Jonas feel anything at all. In his dreams he often found Lucy. It was always somewhere unexpected. He would catch the Tiverton bus and find her sitting up front with shopping bags at her feet; he would steal a trinket in a foreign bazaar and then turn to find her at his shoulder. Once he saw her through the slats of Weston pier, and they kept flickering pace with one another – he above and she on the wet sand below – until they reached the beach, where they embraced.

Always they embraced.

Always they wept with joy.

I found you. I found you. He repeated it without moving his lips – a song sung by his heart that made his flesh tremble with happiness.

Always it ended the same way. Lucy sobbing in his ear: 'You shouldn't have come looking for me, Jonas.'

And he would realize for the first time that her body was cold when it should be warm, and – even as that horror struck him – he would feel her turn into a slab of dead meat in his arms.

He would wake, still groping for her, his pillow soaked in sweat and tears, calling 'I love you' into the darkness or the dawn.

Jonas didn't tell Kate Gulliver any of that.

He also didn't tell her how time slipped away from him. How he would fall asleep on the couch and wake in the kitchen with a knife in his hand. How the impulse to put the glittering blade into his mouth and jab and stab at his tongue and palate and cheeks until the blood ran from him like a hose was almost overwhelming. Or how, more than once, he'd watched his own hands twist a pair of his uniform trousers into a noose. They were an old pair, and missing a button – no good to anyone who wasn't handy, or who didn't have a handy wife.

He lost whole days – disappeared inside his head just as surely as if he'd been abducted by aliens. He would be returned to find that nothing had changed but the clocks.

Sometimes the calendar.

These were all things that his new, animal self knew were better left unsaid. Better not explored.

And so Jonas Holly said nothing, felt nothing, and hovered between the light and the dark – between life and death – until such time as he might be allowed to return to work as an Exmoor village policeman.

3

Steven Lamb wasn't sure exactly what he'd expected for his £300, but this definitely wasn't it.

Ronnie had told him the bike was not a runner. 'We'll get it going though, no bother,' Ronnie had assured him as they drove to Minehead. And Steven *was* assured. Ronnie Trewell could get *anything* going – countless Somerset drivers who'd had cars stolen despite locks, alarms and immobilizers could attest to that.

But what Ronnie *hadn't* told him was that the 125cc Suzuki was in what looked like a thousand bits. Two wheels and the frame were identifiable, but everything else – engine parts, cables, lights, tank, levers, nuts and bolts – was jumbled into two giant plastic boxes.

'It's all there, mate,' said the greasy-looking man with the shifty eyes whom Ronnie had introduced as 'Gary'. 'Top bloke,' Ronnie had added – as if that was all the insurance Steven should need to trust someone he'd never met with all the money he had in the world in exchange for a collection of random mechanical parts.

'There's the exhaust,' said his best friend, Lewis, peering into a box – as if that proved that the rest of the bike *must* be present.

Steven thought of all the mornings he'd got up in darkness to trudge through rain and snow with a bag of newspapers on his hip, to earn the money he had in his jeans pocket right now. Since he was thirteen. Four years' worth of numb fingers, blue toes and shooting pains in his ears, which stuck out beyond the protection of his dark hair. He'd bought other things along the way – a skateboard with Bones Swiss bearings, a necklace for his mum's birthday, a new shopping trolley for his nan, and even the occasional quid for Davey when his brother needed bribing. But a motorbike had been the goal for the past two years and Steven had been devoted to its acquisition. The thought of being able to leave Shipcott without relying on lifts from Ronnie or the Tithecott twins, or lurching country buses filled with blue-haired ladies and men who smelled of cows, was all the motivation he'd needed to keep walking, keep working, keep waiting.

'Deal?' said Gary, and stuck out his hand.

Steven looked at Lewis, who avoided his eyes – the bloody coward – and then at Ronnie, who gave him an encouraging nod.

'OK then,' said Steven miserably, and tried to shake the man's outstretched hand, only to be embarrassed to realize that it was held out palm-up for the money, not to seal the deal like gentlemen. Gary laughed as he fumbled, and Steven felt like a boy among men.

Feeling slightly sick, he took out the envelope stuffed with notes and – like Jack handing over his mother's cow for a handful of magic beans – gave it to Gary.

He wanted desperately to ask for a receipt, as his mother had insisted he must, but Gary had already stuffed the money into his back pocket and was picking up one of the boxes.

'Give you a hand,' he said, as if he wanted rid of the evidence as quickly as possible before anyone rumbled his scam.

Lewis took the frame, which was the lightest thing on offer, Ronnie picked up the other box despite his limp, and Steven took a wheel in each hand.

They loaded what Steven desperately hoped was a complete motorcycle into the trailer Ronnie had borrowed from some-where, and got into the Fiesta. Lewis in the front, Steven squashed up behind with an old greyhound, which was obviously used to stretching out on the back seat – and which gave way only grudg-ingly, before flopping back down across his legs.

They drove back to Ronnie's home in Shipcott too fast, and with the dog's bony elbows sticking into Steven's thighs round every precarious turn.

4

Detective Inspector Reynolds was worried about his fringe. He was worried about the girl as well, of course, but his fringe was a constant and the girl was just a case, like those that had come before and many that would follow. She had probably run away. Most of them had. If not – if she *had* been abducted – then she would be found or she would not; she would live or she would die – or she would live the rest of her life in a way that would make her wish she *could* die.

It sounded callous, but that was just the way things were with missing children. Naturally, Reynolds would do everything in his power to find her, but right now the girl's fate was an open-ended question. His fringe, on the other hand, was here to stay.

He hoped.

He examined it in the mirror and pushed it first to one side and then the other. It was a chilly morning and so he'd chickened out and worn a woollen beanie in to work. But he couldn't hide for ever. Somehow the plugs looked more obvious here under the cold fluorescents of the gents' toilet at Taunton police station than they had in his bathroom at home.

He pushed the fringe back the other way. It made no difference. He sighed. Maybe he shouldn't have let them cut it so short, but the spectre of Elton John's moptop had made him uncharacteristically macho.

Fuck it.

He'd spent almost four thousand pounds of his hard-earned savings on the bloody things – he couldn't hide in the bogs all day.

DI Reynolds took a deep breath and banged out of the toilets to take charge of the hunt for Jess Took.

*

You don't love her.

Reynolds had the note with him in an evidence bag for safe-keeping. He'd ordered its presence at the possible crime scene not to be made public. If Jess Took had been abducted, then it was a detail that could be useful in trapping her kidnapper in a lie. Alternatively it could weed out the weirdos who might like to claim the crime as their own.

He'd looked at it a hundred times as they drove from Taunton to Exmoor. Jess Took had only been missing for thirty-six hours and the graphologist hadn't wanted to commit himself without further investigation, but had told him that, due to the care taken with the lettering, the note was unlikely to have been written by a person who wrote every day. Very helpful. That really narrowed it down. Who the hell wrote every day – or *any* day – using a pen and paper? Reynolds himself couldn't remember the last time he'd picked up a pen with any real purpose other than to jot a few notes or to click the end of it while he mused. It was all keyboards now. Words were created and disappeared into a box and then you switched them off and back on again and hoped that they were still there. Reynolds was all for the paperless office, but for some reason the Taunton Serious Crime office seemed more paper*ful* by the week. It was an enigma, he thought, wrapped in endless reams of A4.

He smiled inwardly and wished he could have said something that clever out loud and to an appreciative audience. Detective Sergeant Elizabeth Rice was far from dull, but she did not share his erudition.

Rice *was*, however, a conscientious driver and Reynolds always handed her the keys. Then he could think, instead of being plagued by the *mirror, signal, manoeuvre* mantra that had been driven into his head so hard by his father that it had never found its way out again.

The roads started twisting the moment they left the motorway. There was no transition: one minute they were in the twenty-first century, the next in what felt like the 1950s. Thorn trees and hedges squeezed narrow lanes between them like black toothpaste curling out across Exmoor, and Reynolds knew that in his pocket his mobile phone would already be casting about for a signal.

'It feels weird to be back.'

Rice could not have mirrored his feelings more accurately.

Reynolds had not been back since a killer had cut a brutal swathe across the moor. Not since he'd driven Jonas Holly home from hospital just over a year ago and sworn to him that they'd catch the man who'd murdered his wife.

That hadn't happened.

But he had phoned Jonas on three separate occasions – each time more suspicious than the last that the man was screening his calls, and guiltily relieved by it: he was never phoning with any positive news. The few skinny forensic leads they'd had had dwindled to nothing and, although the case was still officially open, Reynolds knew that it would take a huge stroke of luck or another murder to see it shuffle its way back to the top of Homicide's must-do list.

He remembered that as recently as this January – a year after her death – Jonas Holly's answerphone still had his wife's voice on it. *'Hi, you've reached Jonas and Lucy. Please leave a message and we'll call you back, or you can ring Jonas on his mobile . . .'*

The voice of a ghost.

It gave Reynolds the creeps.

'It does,' he agreed with Rice. 'Very weird.'

It also felt strange to be in a grubby white van instead of an unmarked pool car. The van was a genuine one from RJ Holding & Sons Builders in Taunton. Roger Holding was a cousin of the desk sergeant, and had offered the loan of one of his vans so they could approach the Took family without revealing their identities. Kidnapping for ransom was virtually obsolete now outside some Eastern European communities, but it was best to follow procedure until they were sure. However, Reynolds thought Elizabeth Rice looked suspiciously attractive to be behind the wheel of a builder's van, even in jeans and sweatshirt, and with her straight blonde hair tied into a utilitarian ponytail. He should have brought Tim Jones from drugs, who looked and smelled like a navvy.

The van was littered with fast-food wrappers and underfoot was a dirty magazine, in every sense of the word. Reynolds had spotted it as he climbed into the cab, and had spent the whole journey trying to cover as much of it as possible with his feet, so that Rice would not be offended or – worse – make a joke about it.

He put the note back in the folder on his lap labelled JESSICA TOOK, and stared at the photo of the girl.

When it came to vanishing teenagers, the word 'runaway' was always above the word 'abducted' on the list of possibilities. Even an ostentatious liberal like Reynolds knew that if they treated every teenage disappearance like a kidnap, they'd spend their lives winkling sulky kids from under their best friends' beds or throwing a big net over them in London bus stations. The truth was that most kids simply went home, and – unless there was clear evidence of abduction – there was an unofficial 24-hour period when it was assumed that that was exactly what would happen.

It hadn't happened in this case. Yet. The file told Reynolds that the local community beat officer had been called and had cautiously started the ball rolling – calling friends and family, searching woods and outbuildings near Jess's home. If she'd been eight years old, the Seventh Cavalry would have been dispatched at once. But thirteen? There were different attitudes to teenagers. So Sunday had been a 'wait and see' day. *Wait* for Jess to get cold or bored or hungry or forgiving, and *see* her walk up the driveway to either her father's home or her mother's. When she didn't appear at either by Sunday lunchtime, Taunton was alerted, Reynolds was assigned and the case took on an official urgency.

Now – on Monday morning – it would begin in earnest: the formal interviews with friends and family, the organization of the searches and of the scores of volunteers who were sure to come forward. The discreet but close examination of every single one of those volunteers, in case one might be the kidnapper trying to insert himself into the investigation. Or *herself*, Reynolds thought. Best to keep an open mind about these matters. Although, of course, women who stole children generally took babies, out of some kind of primal desperation. Men who stole children, on the other hand . . .

Reynolds didn't bother completing the thought. Imagining what might be happening to Jess Took was counterproductive to the point of madness. He needed to keep a little distance from the nitty-gritty of such an investigation to maintain any sense of perspective.

Rice hadn't said anything about his hair.

Reynolds wasn't sure whether that was a good thing or not.

Rice gave a low whistle as they swung round a bend in John Took's driveway. 'Nice,' she said, and it was.

A whitewashed longhouse covered in great clumps of wisteria faced the wide gravel drive. Alongside was a block of half a dozen stables. The large garden was mown and edged to within an inch of its life. There were three cars on the driveway – none worth less than a year's salary to a Detective Inspector.

Reynolds immediately put 'ransom' up to number two on his chart of possible motives for the kidnap of Jess Took.

Inside, the house was furnished with a surfeit of money and a dearth of taste. There were several overstuffed tartan sofas, a dozen garish hunting scenes, and a brass and glass coffee table straining under the weight of a bronze horse almost big enough to ride.

John Took was a broad man with the florid complexion that comes from drink or weather. Reynolds wondered which it was. Possibly both. There were two women in the house, too – Jess's mother, Barbara, and Took's girlfriend, Rachel Pollack, who with her large blue eyes and long blonde hair was just a younger, slimmer version of Barbara.

Slimmer *and* dimmer, Reynolds gathered from just a few minutes' discourse with them both. Perfect for a man in the throes of a mid-life crisis. Reynolds had never been married but was pretty sure he'd be better at it than most men. He'd once seen a bumper sticker that said A WIFE IS FOR LIFE, NOT JUST THE HONEY-MOON. Too true.

The dynamics of this threesome were interesting. Although Rachel clutched John Took's hand throughout in a show of sympathy bordering on custody, it was plain to see that the real connection here – the *blood* connection – was between Took and his ex. They shared the same shaky tension, the same brittle hope, the same disregard for anything that was not Jess-related. More than once, Reynolds saw Rachel's mouth tighten petulantly as she watched the interplay.

They hadn't had any contact from anyone claiming to have abducted Jess.

'If we had, we'd feel better,' said Barbara Took, and Reynolds felt the same way. Knowing was always better than not knowing. And they'd have somewhere to start.

'Does Jess have a boyfriend?' he asked, and both parents shook their heads vehemently.

'She's only thirteen,' said Took.

'I would know,' said Barbara.

Reynolds put a question mark next to the word 'boyfriend' in his notebook.

He asked to see Jess's room – the best one in the house, and messy in the way that only teenagers know how to pull off. It set Reynolds's teeth on edge and made him happy he didn't have kids.

'Mr Rabbit!' said Barbara Took tearfully, picking a floppy old toy off the floor. 'She would *never* leave Mr Rabbit.'

That was complete rubbish, of course. Even Reynolds knew that. Teenagers were a selfish bunch and unlikely to be anchored by a childhood toy if they had a boyfriend waiting in the wings.

Barbara's ex-husband turned to give her a comforting hug and Rachel reached out and stroked the other woman's shoulder awkwardly, with a hand that was tipped with bright-red talons.

'Where's her phone?' asked Reynolds.

'I found it next to the horsebox,' said Took. 'She must have dropped it. Your lot have it now.'

'What about her make-up bag?' asked Rice.

'She doesn't wear make-up,' said Barbara and then looked at John Took questioningly. 'She doesn't when she's with *me*, anyway.'

'Nor me,' countered Took immediately, and let her go.

The bedside table held a little mirror on a stand but the drawer underneath revealed nothing but junk – bits of costume jewellery, keyrings with cartoon characters on them, coins, creams, a broken phone, and about fifty different kinds of hair clip.

Rice noticed a backpack at the foot of the bed. 'Is that her school bag?'

'Yes. John takes her on Mondays and I pick her up.'

Rice rummaged inside and quickly came up with a small pink make-up bag containing strawberry lip gloss, mascara and two five-pound notes. Barbara Took glared at her ex-husband, but Reynolds and Rice exchanged another kind of look entirely. If Jess Took had simply run away, make-up and money would have been the real essentials, whatever the hell Mr Rabbit said.

They filed back downstairs and Reynolds went through procedures with them. How things would work: how the search would be organized; arranging a similar visit to Barbara Took's home; assignment of a family liaison officer; and, finally, what to do in case of a note or call demanding ransom.

'I don't have any money,' said Took. 'The horses take it all.'

This was such a ridiculous statement that – in the circumstances – everyone in the room did him the courtesy of ignoring it.

Reynolds asked Took and his ex-wife whether they had any enemies. It was a standard question and rarely elicited a positive response.

Barbara shook her head, but John Took said breezily, 'Sure, who doesn't?'

Reynolds was taken aback. So, apparently, was Barbara.

'Not anyone who'd kidnap *Jess!*'

Took shrugged. 'Nowadays who knows? People are such fucking arseholes.'

And the mystery of the enemies is quickly solved, thought Reynolds.

*

At the foot of Dunkery Beacon, John Took's horsebox stood alone. The entrance to the makeshift car park had been barred with a strip of police tape. A few cars and an empty police Land Rover were parked on the verge. There was no sign of the matching officer.

After a minute stood turning aimlessly on their own axes, Rice pointed out a DayGlo flash behind some nearby gorse and they watched as a portly policeman zipped up and then emerged to return to his car. His pace picked up as he realized he was no longer the sole representative of the Avon & Somerset force on the Beacon.

Reynolds introduced himself and Rice but pointedly declined to shake hands.

'If you're going to relieve yourself in public, take off your hi-vis, will you? People can see you taking a leak from bloody Wales.'

'Sorry, sir.'

'When was the scene set up?'

'Last night.'

Shit. Almost forty-eight hours after Jess disappeared. The forensics would be a joke.

'You have the girl's phone?'

'I don't know about that, sir. You'd have to speak to the beat officer who called it in.'

'Jonas Holly?'

The man looked surprised, then careful. 'No, sir. He's on leave.'

Still? Reynolds said nothing. He'd rather not have to explain how *he* was the man who'd failed to catch the killer of Jonas's wife. *Ipso facto*: if he'd done his job, then maybe Jonas would have made it back to work by now. Even so, Reynolds couldn't help being relieved that he hadn't. He didn't need a reminder of past failures. Or of that hug – God forbid. The last time he'd seen the man, Reynolds had hugged him in an embrace that had been all him and no Jonas. Hugged him and promised to catch his wife's killer. Reynolds couldn't decide now which empty gesture he was more embarrassed by.

Reynolds told the patrol officer that forensic teams would be arriving within the hour. Until then no one was to cross the police tape. Obviously.

'Whose cars are these?'

'Walkers. I've been getting flak all morning for the car park being closed.'

Reynolds almost smiled at the flat dirt area being described as a car park.

He was keen to take a look inside the horsebox, but their leads on this case might be few and far between, without him and Rice adding their footprints to the dust alongside it.

They'd wait.

Reynolds had always prided himself on his patience.

5

There was a new girl. Emily Carver.

Steven tried not to look at her, but even the act of looking away from her made him self-conscious. When it was safe, he stared at the back of her head, where her thick brown hair was caught loosely in a green velvet ribbon.

Mr Peach had to call his name twice before he confirmed that he was present.

However, Emily's sudden appearance in class caused barely a ripple, due to the equally sudden *dis*appearance of Jessica Took.

The school was alight with *that* news. Excitement crackled through every class like cinema sweets. The ADD kids and the ADHD kids, and the kids who were simply angling for a label so they'd have an excuse, took the opportunity to be extra 'challenging'. Knots of girls stood around outside classrooms, tearful and hugging each other as if they'd all known Jess personally – and daring the boys or the teachers to question that sisterhood. In retaliation, the excluded boys took refuge in ghoulish speculation. Words that were too harsh for girls or adults to say out loud were common currency for the boys – worst-case scenarios shouted down corridors, and kicked about freely on the daisy-strewn playing field.

'They'll never find her.'

'She's dead already.'

'I bet her dad did it. Jess always said he hated her.'

Steven did not join in. He kept his eye on the ball and scored twice, thanks to the inattention of the opposition. He didn't want to speculate about a missing child. Many years ago, he'd almost been one himself. Up on the moor behind the houses, a man named Arnold Avery had once done his best to murder Steven Lamb, and it had left him wary beyond his years.

That didn't stop his friends.

Lewis was the most voluble, naturally, and had a million ideas about what had happened, how it had happened, *why* it had happened and what the police should do now. Lalo Bryant told them his sister wasn't allowed out on the moor alone any more, and those boys with sisters nodded agreement that this was a sensible precaution, and that they would immediately take on the role of warden once they got home. The Tithecott twins looked particularly keen, as their sister was a notorious pain in the arse, and definitely ripe for draconian controls disguised as brotherly love.

Only once the bell had gone and they were trailing back to class did Lalo Bryant say, 'You see that new girl, Emma?'

'Emily,' said Steven.

'Whatever. She's hot.'

'I'd give her one,' agreed Lewis.

There was barely a woman alive that Lewis wouldn't give one to; for a seventeen-year-old with flaming acne, he had remarkable reserves of self-worth. Even so, Steven felt a prick of anger and a defensive surge towards the brown hair and the green velvet ribbon.

'Yeah, but would *I* give *you* one?'

They turned to see Emily Carver a few paces behind them.

Steven blushed all the way down to his toes and the others shuffled and looked away.

Always the rubber ball, Lewis bounced back sufficiently to bluster lamely, 'Yeah, I bet you would.'

Emily Carver stopped, looked him slowly up and down with a curious expression on her face, and then burst out laughing.

It was devastating. Nothing she could ever have said could have destroyed Lewis more completely, and his acne positively glowed. Steven was a loyal friend, so he looked away to hide the fact that he was grinning.

Still giggling, Emily walked between the boys and towards the classrooms.

Lalo shoved Lewis in the shoulder. 'She got *you*, dickhead.'

Lewis shoved him back, harder. 'Thanks for telling me she was there, wanker.'

'I'm not your *mummy*.'

'Piss off.'

Steven stayed out of it. Lewis was his best friend, but it was nice to see him get taken down now and then. He needed it. Without it he would be *insufferable*. Insufferable was a good word. Steven had just learned it and was trying to work it in everywhere. This was a perfect place.

He watched Emily Carver walk on ahead of them, aware that by unspoken mutual agreement his little group had slowed so they wouldn't catch her up. It was a sure sign that she'd defeated them.

To Steven, it didn't feel much like losing.

By the time he got home, Davey had already told Mum and Nan about Jessica Took.

Typical.

Davey was the baby and spoiled – a double-whammy that meant he sailed through life with little regard for the feelings, thoughts or desires of other people.

Steven had that regard. Regard for the fact that his nan's son, Billy, had been stolen and murdered and lost for a generation out on the moors. And regard for the fact that he himself had almost died trying to find his body.

And so *he* would have told them slowly. Would have skirted the subject to see whether they knew already or whether he was going to be the bearer of bad tidings – then would have told them just enough so that they were not badly surprised by neighbours' gossip, or by seeing the papers in Mr Jacoby's shop. Although Steven delivered those papers around Shipcott every morning, he didn't deliver to his own home. His mother, Lettie, was too busy working to read, and Nan bought flimsy paperbacks filled with impossible crosswords, which she said were the only thing she ever wanted from a newspaper.

Steven would have been subtle.

But Davey didn't have a subtle bone in his body. Steven knew how Davey imparted news – he'd seen him do it a hundred times. Banging the front door, slinging down his schoolbag, shouting *Mu-um! Mu-um!* Rushing into the kitchen, and then stumbling over himself to get the words out. The vital news of his goal at soccer, his earth-shattering B in computer studies, his inside knowledge of the kidnap and murder of Jessica Took.

Steven knew how it went down.

So he wasn't surprised to walk into the kitchen to find his mother smoking furiously over the sink, his nan staring blankly into space over a half-finished puzzle, and Davey happily spraying tomato sauce over what looked like more than his fair share of fish fingers.

They knew.

'Hi,' he ventured.

'Hello, Stevie.' His mother's voice was husky.

Nan looked up at him, her eyes watery with memories.

Steven loved his brother, but – *shit* – sometimes he wanted to punch him so hard!

Nan reached out faintly and, when Steven took her hand, she drew him to her and squeezed his waist.

'Glad you're home,' she said, and then released him. Steven stayed by her side though, and rested a hand on her shoulder.

That night Steven and Davey watched *Top Gear* with the sound lower than usual, Nan frowned at her clues and Lettie laid what she called their 'valuables' out on the coffee table: an electroplated teapot and four mismatched candlesticks. She rubbed them all with Brasso until her fingers were black.

No one had asked him yet about the bike. That suited him fine. Nan had said she'd buy him a helmet as an early birthday gift. Steven didn't think she knew how much they cost. He couldn't in good conscience let her spend money on a helmet before he had a bike to ride. She'd expect to see him wearing it. Expect to see him *in* the helmet *on* the bike.

Which he didn't have.

If anyone *had* asked, he'd have had to tell them that he'd bought two wheels and assorted ironmongery.

So, at the end of the day, the news of Jessica Took's kidnap had saved him from an awkward situation.

Sick.

*

Because they knew Shipcott better than anywhere else on the moor, Rice had booked them rooms at the Red Lion.

It was a mistake on every level.

Cheap but noisy, and with mattresses that had been almost folded in half by years of heavy sleepers, and then turned upside down in a misguided attempt to redress the balance; it was like sleeping on the peak of a Toblerone. On the first morning, Reynolds rolled over, lost his grip – and slid down the west face to wakefulness.

They met in the deserted bar for breakfast – full English for Rice, croissant for Reynolds. None of it enough to disguise the country-pub whiff of stale beer, dogs and old crisps trodden into the carpet.

Reynolds wished they'd stayed somewhere else. He stood up before Rice could start mopping up baked beans with her fried bread. She was passably pretty and had many pretty habits, but that wasn't one of them.

'Meet you at the car,' he said.

Outside, the sun was already squint-worthy. How different. Last time he was here it had been in the middle of winter – a bitter January when snow had started and then continued in a way that had made him think it might never stop. The skies had been white or charcoal or pale blue by turn – none of them any indicator of how the weather might be even half an hour later.

This fresh, brilliant scenery brought with it little pricks of guilt, like pins left in a new shirt.

The pub was where they'd bickered and clutched at straws, while the killer went about his work unmolested. Less than a hundred yards away was Sunset Lodge, where four people had died while the police had dithered. Reynolds could even see the first-floor window where the killer had forced the latch. There, beside that doorstep, the killer had washed his hands of blood in a pile of snow, and there he had hidden in the alleyway beside the shop.

The village was a mosaic of memories he'd rather forget. Nothing had gone right for them then. The team – led by DCI Marvel – were behind from the start and never caught up. The killer had come softly, slain silently, and disappeared, like a snowflake which had been unique as it fell but was now just part of the whole once again. The only evidence that he'd ever existed outside the bloody crime scenes had been the notes that he'd left Jonas Holly – taunting him over his inability to stop the killings. And he'd taken Jonas's own wife as his final prize – a cruel punishment for the young policeman's failure. Reynolds had never felt more lost or beaten by a case, by a crime, by a place.

His hair had come out in handfuls.

Now he touched his fringe almost unconsciously, seeking the reassurance of soft strands instead of patchy scalp.

Reynolds turned his back on Shipcott and looked instead at the moor, which rose behind the pub and beyond the stream where Jonas Holly had found a body held motionless in the ice. It all seemed like an empty stage where a murderous play had once been performed, because on a day like this it was almost impossible to imagine anything bad happening here. The azure sky, the dew glittering on the bright gorse and the sheer silence made it feel like the set of a film – one of those Jane Austen things that were always on BBC Four. Their scenery always seemed as fanciful to him as their plots, but Exmoor in early summer was just such a place, captured in time. A rock moved just below the close horizon, and Reynolds's eyes adjusted to pick out the small group of deer grazing close to the skyline.

Calmed by the sight, Reynolds felt the jigsaw take shape in his mind. Now that he'd met Jess Took's father, he was leaning towards the personal revenge motive, rather than the sexual. That was good. *Really* good. If Jess Took had been stolen for ransom or revenge, the chances of getting her back alive were vastly improved. And success instead of failure in a kidnapping case would look so much better on his record.

Yes, revenge was the most likely scenario *and* the one that was liable to have the most positive outcome. On a day like this, one couldn't help being optimistic.

Rice walked across the car park towards him, and was opening her mouth to say something when her phone suddenly latched on to a passing signal and burst into life.

She took it from her pocket and frowned at the caller ID, then waited until it stopped ringing and put it back in her pocket.

Must be Eric.

Reynolds thought Rice had broken up with Eric. He wasn't sure, but a few months back there'd been a time when he'd noticed she was often red-eyed in the mornings and she'd taken some personal days. This was not the first time since then that he'd seen her fail to answer her phone.

He was glad that signals on the moor were so appalling. The last thing he needed was Rice being weepy and distracted by boyfriend troubles while they were trying to find Jess Took.

The deer moved off over the rise, each silhouetted briefly against the sky before dropping out of sight. At the summit, the big male turned and looked over its shoulder, straight at him. Detective Inspector Reynolds felt himself unexpectedly moved. It felt like a benediction – like a promise of success.

This would be different. This was *already* different. A serial killer of the old and infirm was not a kidnapper of children. And *he* was in charge now – not some throwback who didn't even have a degree.

He would work it out; Jess Took would be found; he would be a hero; he would lay to rest the hoodoo of the killer in the snow.

*

It turned out that John Took didn't have any money after all. He was simply very good at spending other people's. Of the nine people on the list he'd given them, eight were creditors – four of whom had made actual threats, ranging from 'Watch your back' to 'I'll burn your bloody house down.'

By Tuesday lunchtime, Reynolds and Rice had spoken to all four of those. Three had alibis that were easy to check. Early on Saturday mornings, even country folk were trying to lie in past 7am, and most had partners and/or children to prove it.

The fourth, Mike Haddon, was a local blacksmith. He was not tall, so his muscles had nowhere to go but outwards, giving him the appearance of a body-builder stretched to fit a widescreen TV.

He flicked through a filthy hardbacked diary with hands so huge and gnarled and ingrained with blackness that Reynolds almost admired them. They were Hulk hands, only not green.

'Two on the twelfth, another two on the twenty-second,' Haddon was saying, as he turned the pages to show them his dense writing. 'Three on the second – and that included that bloody Scotty I always charge extra for 'cos he kicks *and* leans. Another two on the sixteenth and one more on the twenty-third—'

'I see what you're saying,' Reynolds interrupted. He could tell that if he didn't stop him, Haddon was going to take them through every unpaid set of horseshoes, and they still weren't out of January. 'What does he owe you in total?'

'Eleven hundred and ninety pounds.'

'Bloody hell!' said Rice. 'How much are the shoes?'

'Sixty-five quid for a standard set, more if they want studs or bars, and they're replaced every six or eight weeks.'

Rice's mouth dropped open and Reynolds was amused to see her groping for some grasp on the sheer waste of shoe-money. As for himself, he wondered whether it was really enough to motivate abduction.

'That doesn't seem like an awful lot,' he mused.

'Is to *me*,' said Haddon with a disparaging look. 'Would be to you too, if you'd earned it in the snow with a half ton of horse on your bloody back.'

He had a point.

'So you threatened Mr Took?'

Haddon was still for a moment, then shrugged. 'Yur.'

Reynolds looked at his notes. 'He says you told him you'd break his bloody legs if he didn't pay you.'

'Yur,' said Haddon defiantly. 'And I still will.'

'I'm sure you could find a better way to resolve the dispute, Mr Haddon,' said Reynolds sharply.

'Maybe better. Not faster.'

'You do know that we could arrest you right now for making threats, don't you?'

Haddon simply gave Reynolds a baleful stare.

'And you do know that Mr Took's daughter is missing?'

'Well,' said Haddon, looking a little uncertain for the first time, 'I'd wait until she were back, like.'

Rice snorted with laughter and tried to turn it into a cough. Reynolds frowned but Haddon looked at Rice and winked. The laugh had relaxed him.

'Look,' he said, 'Took is an arsehole. Ask anyone. He owes money right across the moor, but he's driving around in those big bloody cars and keeping six horses while my van's falling apart. Gets up your nose, that's all. And I know his type – whoever scares him best will get paid first. That's all it is. You ask Bill Merchant up at Dulverton Farm Feeds – Took owes him thousands but he never makes a fuss, so he can whistle Dixie for *his* money. Before you know it, Took'll say he's bankrupt and we'll find out everything's in his girlfriend's name or some bollocks, and where will we all be then? Up the bloody creek without a bloody paddle, that's where.'

Haddon stopped, looking surprised at his own loquacity, and stared from Rice to Reynolds and back again – daring them to challenge his truth.

They couldn't.

'So you have no idea where Jess Took might be?' said Reynolds a little weakly.

Haddon looked genuinely surprised. 'You think I took his kid to make him pay up?'

'It's just a routine question, Mr Haddon.'

Haddon frowned and shook his head. 'Not me,' he said. 'But I tell you what – I bet *that'd* bloody work!'

Of the four less obviously threatening creditors on John Took's list, all were exasperated but seemed resigned to having to wait for their money.

'Other creditors have threatened Mr Took,' Reynolds told Wilf Cooper, who had supplied nine hundred pounds' worth of timber to Took to repair his manège.

Cooper smiled. 'There's no need for the Mafia. I just started small claims proceedings against him, like I do with all my late payers. One month, one letter and then they get notice of proceedings. He'll pay now or then; I'm not worried. Happens all the time with men like him.'

'What do you mean, "men like him"?' asked Rice.

'Men who get divorced and get a younger girlfriend. Suddenly they start to spend money like it's going out of fashion. Took's girlfriend – what's her name?'

'Rebecca,' said Reynolds.

'Rachel,' said Rice.

'Yur, well, whatever it is, she wants to ride, see? Not to hounds, like – which would be sensible, given he's the Master – but in shows, doing dressage and the like. So suddenly he's got to get a new *type* of poncey horse and a new *type* of poncey saddle, and he's got to build a manège and employ a poncey trainer and blah-de-blah-de-blah, you see? Just so's she'll keep tupping him and pretend she's liking it, pardon me, Miss.'

Rice shrugged it away.

'And it's not just the horses,' Cooper continued. 'You seen what he wears now? Come into the yard a few months back wearing *cowboy* boots!' He laughed at the memory. 'Trying to be young, see? And trying to be rich. It'll work for a while, I reckon. And then it won't, and he'll sell the dressage horses and fire the trainer and the girl will leave him and everyone will get paid. That's how these things happen.'

Cooper seemed so affable that Reynolds was confused as to why he was on the list at all.

'Who knows,' Cooper said with an expansive shrug. 'Took's a right paranoid tit.'

*

To the surprise of both Reynolds and Rice, the ninth person on Took's list was not a creditor. It was Jonas Holly's elderly neighbour, Mrs Paddon.

'She must be eighty if she's a day,' said Rice. 'How's she an enemy?'

'He said she was a leader in the campaign to get the local hunt disbanded.'

'Good for her,' murmured Rice.

Reynolds remembered Mrs Paddon. A tough old bird. They'd speak to her first thing in the morning; he had no doubt she was an early riser.

'Let me handle the interview,' he told Rice. He fancied he got on well with old folk. His mother's friends adored him.

Mrs Paddon didn't.

Mrs Paddon was as wary of Rice and Reynolds as if they'd been Jehovah's Witnesses – only reluctantly opening her door wide enough for them actually to enter her home, instead of conducting the interview on the stone doorstep.

Inside, the cottage was dark but clean. Every available surface was crammed with nick-nacks. No, not nick-nacks, Rice thought as she looked more closely; nick-nacks implied miscellaneous bad-taste china kittens and Spanish holiday souvenirs. Mrs Paddon's collection was a more unusual mix of chunky, practical objects and delicate glass animals. Brass barometers and copper kettles towered over dainty fauns and cut-glass hedgehogs. The mantel-piece held a parade of carnival glass ponies and a pickaxe handle. The ornaments gave the room a schizophrenic feel – as if a man and his wife warred constantly over the available space, and yet Mrs Paddon was a spinster, Rice remembered.

She offered them tea, then warned quickly that she had no milk. 'Or sugar,' she added discouragingly.

'We're fine, thanks,' said Reynolds. 'It's nice to see you again, Mrs Paddon. How have you been?'

'Well enough,' she said brusquely.

The old woman had remained standing in the middle of the front room, and did not offer them a seat.

'And Jonas? How's he now?'

'You'll have to ask *him* that.' Mrs Paddon took a string bag from the back of the front door. 'I was just off to the shop, actually.'

Reynolds ignored the pointed invitation to leave. 'We're here about Jess Took.'

'Oh.' The old woman seemed a little taken aback, and then her tone softened. 'Poor child.'

'We asked Mr Took for a list of people who might wish him harm, and we were surprised to find your name on there.'

Mrs Paddon snorted. 'I'm not! I certainly *did* wish him harm. Wished he'd fall off his horse into a pond, the fat buffoon.'

'But not any more?' Rice asked.

Mrs Paddon waved the very notion away with a flap of her string bag. 'The Blacklands hunt's gone. That was all I wanted. Of course, there's another one, and another one, and another one after that, but we did what we set out to do, and I'm too old to start sabbing all across Britain.'

'Sabbing?' asked Reynolds.

'Sabotaging. Being a hunt saboteur. You know,' said Mrs Paddon. 'Waving banners, blowing whistles, laying false trails.'

'Damaging property, personal injury,' added Reynolds dryly.

The string bag flapped again. 'Oh, I did nothing like that. That's for young folk and strangers. I just made life difficult for them, that's all. Made life difficult for *him*. And it worked, and the hunt's gone and I tell you what, being on that list is a badge of honour, far as I'm concerned.'

She winked one pale-blue eye at Reynolds, leaving him momentarily discombobulated.

'I can't wait to hear who else is on it,' she continued.

'I'm afraid that's confidential information,' said Rice.

Mrs Paddon snorted again. 'Rubbish! Nothing's confidential on the moor! Let's see. Mike Haddon the blacksmith. Bill Merchant at the farm shop, Andy Coutt at the Star in Simonsbath, that timber fella – Cooper, is it? I bet he's on there. Am I right so far?'

Reynolds shifted and cleared his throat.

'And however many are on there, they're just the ones John Took *knows* about.' She laughed again. 'Arrogant people are always surprised by how much they're hated, don't you find?'

Reynolds certainly *did* find. But he was reluctant to agree with Mrs Paddon when she'd hijacked his interview so completely. John Took's list was being reduced to garden-fence gossip before his very eyes.

'Well, thank you for your help, Mrs Paddon,' he said stiffly.

'Oh, don't take it personally,' she said. 'I don't mean to ruin your day, Mr Reynolds. I'm just saying that if someone has taken that poor girl to get back at her father, it's probably someone John Took can't even *remember* offending, that's all.'

'Do you have anyone particular in mind?'

The old lady seemed to give it a good deal of thought before shaking her head.

'I wish I could help,' she sighed. 'But who knows what goes on in people's heads?'

'Curiouser and curiouser,' said Rice as they got into the unmarked Peugeot they'd swapped the van for.

'Indeed,' said Reynolds.

They sat in silence for a minute or two, outside the twin cottages where eighteen months earlier their investigation had ended in abject failure.

'She seemed almost relieved we were only there about Jess Took,' mused Rice.

Reynolds nodded. 'Must have thought we were there about the murder. She probably feels protective towards Holly.'

'Can't blame her after what happened, I suppose.'

Reynolds nodded, then sighed. 'At least we know now that John Took seems to be universally hated – by more people than are on his list. That's good news for us. It means it's looking less and less like a random psycho, and more and more as if Jess was taken by someone in revenge.'

Rice nodded. 'And *that* means there's a good chance of us getting her back alive.'

Reynolds smiled at Rice and she smiled back. On a case like this, such sparks of optimism were few and far between, and to be enjoyed whenever they appeared.

Rice switched the engine on and put the car into gear. Reynolds's phone rang.

It was the desk sergeant at Taunton.

'Sir,' he said, 'I think we've got another one.'

6

Tarr Steps was beautiful at any time of the year. Early on a May morning, it was magical. The wide stone slabs that crossed the river at this point looked as if they'd been placed there by storybook giants. Under a tunnel of trees, the sunlight dappling through the broad expanse of dark water made the pebbled river-bed glow like Tiffany glass.

The only sounds were the river and the songs of a thousand birds.

And the faint wailing of Mrs Knox up at the car park.

She'd been wailing when they'd arrived and was still wailing now, almost half an hour later. From his time with Homicide, Reynolds knew she might keep wailing for a good while yet. Quite possibly a lifetime, on and off.

Very annoying, when he was trying to think.

PC Colin Walters, the local officer who'd been first on the scene, stood silently beside him as if waiting for instructions, his already weathered complexion further lined with concern.

Reynolds sighed and turned away from the river, and they both trudged back up the hill to the car park where nine-year-old Pete Knox had vanished from the family car and been replaced – as if by some slick, sick magic – by a square yellow note on the steering wheel.

You don't love him.

'But we *do*. We *do* love him! What does it *mean?*' sobbed Mrs Knox, whose husband was trying to wrap his arms around her – trying to smother her grief and his own – while she was floppy and frantic by turn. Suddenly she thrashed out of his arms and turned back on him with her teeth bared. 'It's your fault!' she screamed, making him wince in shock. '*Your fault!* You sent him back to the car. How could you do that? He's nine years old! He's a baby! You *stupid. Stupid. Bastard!*'

She rushed her stricken husband and started flailing at him – beating him about the face and head, before Reynolds and Walters prised her away. She collapsed face-down beside the six-year-old Golf in which her family had driven from Swindon to spend a week communing with nature. Reynolds and Walters both looked instinctively to Elizabeth Rice for help, and she rolled her eyes, but crouched beside Mrs Knox. The woman had deflated like an old lilo on the dusty tarmac, weeping herself out for a little while. Rice patted her back three times before Mrs Knox stopped throwing her hand off, and then settled down to talking to her as if she were a hurt child – soft words of calm and hope that Reynolds couldn't have managed if his life had depended on it, and which he was almost as surprised to hear coming from Rice.

At least it was quiet enough now to think.

'She doesn't mean it,' he told Mr Knox. 'She's upset, that's all. It's understandable.'

Jeff Knox nodded dumbly, but looked unconvinced – as if his wife's words would never leave him now, whether they found their son or not.

'I *did* send him back to the car,' he said miserably. 'For a towel. He fell in the water. Just one foot up to his knee. Mucking about on the stepping stones, you know?'

Reynolds nodded and Mr Knox looked down at his slack wife again before going on – staring at the opposite side of the valley as if he might yet spot his son. As if there still might be a happy ending.

'It's only a couple of hundred yards and he's a sensible boy. I thought he would be safe. There were other cars here. Other people. We were only five minutes behind him. It's nine o'clock in the morning, for God's sake!'

He halted angrily, and Reynolds knew that if God were here right now, Mr Knox would flail at him with the same hopeless, helpless terror as his wife had done.

'I've got all the other car numbers, sir,' said Walters. 'A couple of them look to have been vandalized.'

Reynolds turned to him in interest.

'Not much. Just a couple of windows broken.'

'Anything taken?'

'Not that I know of so far, but not everyone's back at their cars, so we'll find out then.'

'Maybe he was disturbed.'

Walters led him over to a Toyota RAV4 with a hole the size of a tennis ball punched in the back window. Reynolds stooped and cupped his hands so that he could peer into the dark interior. He jerked backwards as a flurry of fur, teeth and saliva slammed against the glass an inch from his face.

'Shit!'

His heart racing, Reynolds banged the glass in retaliation at the German Shepherd that took up most of the rear of the car.

He glanced at Walters to see if he was laughing, but the PC looked concerned, if anything. Thank God.

Reynolds scanned the car park. Unlike the scene at Dunkery Beacon, this was a proper car park – maybe thirty bays, and a new toilet block made carefully rustic. The day was young. There were perhaps a dozen cars. A few of them had bored-looking owners standing or sitting close by. People in hiking gear, children in shorts, dogs on leads, bikes and backpacks.

'OK, Walters. Don't let anyone come in or leave.'

'Yes, sir.'

'And the note on the steering wheel. We're keeping that back.'

'Yes, sir.'

Reynolds's optimistic mood had gone. John Took might be besieged by arseholes, but the hopeful theory that one of those arseholes had kidnapped Jess Took out of personal revenge had just been blown straight out of the water.

The promise of the stag had become evil voodoo. He looked at the moor, which rose around them on all sides. The birdsong and dappled sunlight were an alluring veil. Underneath, something smelled rotten.

Reynolds sighed and stepped over Mrs Knox's slack legs to peer into the Golf. It was filled with the usual detritus of a holiday – maps, water bottles, sandwich wrappers, coolbox, beach towels.

But once you knew it was also supposed to contain a nine-year-old boy, it seemed very empty.

*

Look at them.

Now they care. Now when it's too late. Where were they when he needed them? Arsing about down on the steps, thinking nothing could go wrong with their lives. Not thinking of how much they got to lose. Not thinking of *consequences*. And now consequences is all they've got.

It's funny really, in one way. And not in another. Not if you're the mother down there bawling like a calf. She *should* cry. She's a disgrace. They all are.

Ah well, reckon they'll just have to get used to it. Amazing what a person can get used to. Or what they'll do if they *can't* . . .

Anyway. There it is. I need him more than they do.

And I'll love him more, too.

7

Two children had disappeared in four days, and the press descended on Exmoor like gulls on a freshly ploughed field, screeching and flapping and pecking each other for the best bits.

Peckiest of them all was the formidable Marcie Meyrick.

Three things made Marcie formidable. First, she was thirty-nine – which was so far beyond thirty that it might as well be fifty. In terms of newsgathering, she was a dinosaur, a fossil, a dodo. A dodo who used her sharp little wings to prod rivals out of her way, and trampled them under her prehistoric dodo feet as she rushed headlong towards a story. Having rejected both her boyfriend and her biological clock for her work, Marcie Meyrick was not about to stand aside for the bouncy pre-teens who passed for journalists nowadays.

Second, Marcie was a freelance reporter, which meant she got paid by column inches, not because she'd signed some namby-pamby employment contract that included four weeks' holiday and a pension plan. Her whole aim in life was to sneak copy into newspapers past news desks that already had their own reporters, the Press Association and the might of Google at their fingertips. Pickings were increasingly thin, and so was Marcie Meyrick.

The third thing that made her formidable was that she was Australian – to which there was no defence. It made her bold enough to doorstep the most hostile of targets, thick-skinned enough to deflect the most brutal of insults, and so whiny that unfaithful politicians, lifelong criminals and hardened police press officers routinely crumbled before her – preferring exposure, censure and even jail to another minute of her nasal, mosquito-in-the-ear wheedling.

Two winters back she'd attended a press conference about the murders that had left Shipcott in tatters. The police had been insisting that they remained hopeful of an arrest.

'This year, next year, some time, never?' Marcie had drawled at that particular briefing – further endearing herself to one and all.

Now – with two children stolen in a week, every news outlet in the country wanted another bite of the Exmoor cherry. Pete Knox had disappeared on the Wednesday after Jess Took. By Thursday morning, more than fifty reporters, camera crews and photographers swarmed across Exmoor – each chasing the breakout story that would get them on to *Newsnight*.

Being ancient, Marcie Meyrick knew that only two things really mattered in a story involving both murders and children: scaremongering and a catchy headline. Scaremongering was simple in this case: children missing on a moor where a killer had been at large promised much in the way of repeat performances – and a ready-made climate of fear and suspicion. It was a climate that suited Marcie just fine.

She wrote the story fast, rather than well, and spent every additional second she could thinking of her headline. It was vital to capture the imagination of first the news desk, then the nation. Nothing was set in stone, of course, but she'd been around long enough to know that no sub-editor could resist a good pun-based headline, even if it did come from a lowly stringer.

She wasn't thrilled with it, but she finally punched the Send button on 'New Terror on Murder Moor' and then – confirming her status as dinosaur – she reached for a cigarette.

8

For some reason, the paperboy had stopped bringing Jonas's copy of the *Bugle*. Instead he delivered it to Mrs Paddon next door, who sometimes took several days to push it through Jonas's letterbox.

Not that he cared. He never read the *Bugle* any more, but cancelling it required thought processes and actions, so it was easier merely to pick it off the mat once a week and walk it through to the kitchen bin, along with all the junk mail.

On this day he stopped between the hall and the kitchen to look at the school photo of Jessica Took on the front page. Straight straw-coloured hair, slightly buck teeth, her school tie tied fashionably and ridiculously short. She looked familiar; he probably knew her by sight – one of the hundreds of children who would pass him every day in that same school uniform as he walked or drove through the seven villages that made up his patch.

What used to be his patch.

MISSING. That was what it said. But the report seemed vague

and full of holes, and Jonas's imagination filled those holes with dark and fearful things.

That night he found Lucy again. This time she had a child with her. Not Jess Took, but a child of her own. A child she'd always wanted and which Jonas had always denied her. When they finally embraced, the child was between them, awkward and annoying and demanding attention.

When Jonas got up the next morning he took the *Bugle* from the kitchen bin and carried it to the outside bin. When he threw it away, he made sure that Jessica Took was face-down.

＊

Steven didn't take the *Bugle* to Jonas Holly's house any more, but he still had to pass Rose Cottage to see if he could get an order from the new people further up the hill.

He flipped his skateboard expertly up into his hand and tucked it under his arm. Skating past the house where Mrs Holly had died seemed like the wrong thing to do, and so Steven never did it. But there was another reason. The deck made a loud rumbling noise on the rough tarmac and he didn't want anyone to know he was passing.

He didn't want *Mr Holly* to know he was passing.

Because Mr Holly had murdered his wife. Steven was sure of it. Almost sure.

He had no proof, of course, or he'd have told the police who were in the village two winters ago, hunting another killer altogether.

And what could he have told them anyway?

That he'd seen Mr Holly slap his wife's face? That he'd looked into his eyes and seen nothing human there? That it had scared him so badly that his legs had turned to jelly under him and he'd almost lost control of his bladder? Even now he squirmed at the memory and pushed it away. Pushed it *all* away.

He had no evidence. And anyway, who was *he*? Just a boy.

And who was Mr Holly? A man – a *police*man. A policeman who had nearly died trying to save his wife from a brutal killer. Supposedly.

Once, Steven had made the mistake of confiding in Lewis about his suspicions.

'You're mazed,' Lewis had said, tapping his own temple. 'You're just paranoid 'cos of nearly being murdered and all that. You need to get over it, mate. Lalo's aunt says Mr Holly's got wicked scars. I wish I had wicked scars. Awesome.'

Jonas Holly was a hero to everyone but Steven Lamb.

He sighed. He *should* try to let it go. Or at least shut up about it. It was the past, and if Steven had cared to live in his past, he would never have been able to enjoy his future, so he'd become a master of moving on. He often imagined he was swimming the breaststroke – sweeping great handfuls of blurry bad stuff behind him so he could reach the shores of a much better life. He'd had lots of practice and he was pretty good at it by now. His life *was* better, and *he*'d made it that way. When Steven thought about that, a little flame of happiness warmed his core and lit the way for him.

But it still didn't mean he could bring himself to deliver the *Bugle* to the home of a killer.

Steven watched the cottages approach. Rose and Honeysuckle cottages – their names on their respective wooden gates – almost hidden behind the high hedgerows that bordered the lane. It was only their top windows and roofs that were really visible from the road, but as he passed their gates he could look in and see that the little front garden of Rose Cottage, which had once been so well tended, was struggling to survive the weeds. Mrs Holly used to do the garden, even though she was sick. The summer before she'd died, Steven had arrived with the paper just in time to help her barrow a pile of greenery through to the compost heap at the back of the house. She knew all the plant names, and he'd told her about the vegetable patch he'd grown with Uncle Jude. His carrots and beans – and how even Davey would eat salad, now that it was made up of their own lettuce and tomatoes and little new potatoes which tasted more like nutty cream than like plain old spuds.

Mr Holly never came out any more. If he did, Steven hadn't seen him, and for that he was grateful. It meant he didn't have to think about him too much. Delivering the *Bugle* to Mrs Paddon once a week was as close as Steven ever wanted to get to Mr Holly again.

His glimpse of the gardens was over and he walked on, head down, until he figured he was at a safe enough distance to drop his deck once more and push himself up the hill.

Old Barn Farm was just about a hundred yards past the entrance to Springer Farm – or what was left of it. Steven's mother had forbidden him and Davey to go there since it burned down. She said walls would fall on them, rafters might plummet at any second, charred floorboards could give way under their feet. Steven had never been to Springer Farm anyway, but suspected that Davey often went to play there, now that his mother had made it seem like such an exciting place to be.

Old Barn Farm had new gates to go with the new residents. Big black iron ones that wouldn't open when Steven pushed them. He stood for a moment, undecided. The gates were so new that the mortar used in their brick posts was still dusted across nearby brambles. He wondered how far down the driveway the farmhouse was – whether it was going to be worth his while getting this order if he had to mess with the gates and then walk a mile after that every week. Or every day, if he could get them to take the *Western Morning News* from him.

'Hello.'

Steven looked around at the voice and noticed a shiny steel intercom built into the gatepost. An intercom! In Shipcott! There was a button marked 'Talk', so he pressed it, feeling like 007.

'Hello. Umm. I want to know . . . I wanted to know if maybe you want a newspaper delivered.' He released the button and then fumbled it back down and added 'please' – then pressed it again and said 'thank you'.

Double-O Dickhead.

There was a short silence, and then a spurt of laughter.

'I'm *here*, dopey!'

Emily Carver was on the grass verge behind him on a horse.

It took only a split second of mental panic for Steven to realize that nothing he could say right now would save him from looking like a complete idiot, so instead he just waved his arms in a gesture of vague resignation, and hoped his face wasn't as red as it felt.

She wasn't wearing the green ribbon. Her brown hair was plaited over one shoulder and held in place by a plain black band.

'I'm in your class,' said Emily, as her horse – a smallish, golden-coloured animal – put its head down and started to crop the grass of the verge.

'I know,' he agreed. 'Emily.'

'I don't like Emily. My friends call me Em.'

'OK then.' Steven nodded, but wasn't sure whether she meant that *he* should call her Em.

'What's *your* name?'

'Steven.'

She gave him a sly look. 'And your friend with the red hair?'

Steven's face fired up again, just as it had been cooling off. 'Lewis,' he said. 'Sorry about that.'

She gave a pretty little shrug and a wave, which Steven interpreted as his having been absolved of responsibility for his best friend's manners.

'Do you want to come in and talk to my dad?'

'What about?'

'The newspaper thing?'

Of course. That was why he was here.

'Oh, OK. Yes. Please.'

Em pointed a small remote control at the gates, which swung open silently, and tugged the horse's head out of the grass.

They passed through the gateway together and started down the stony driveway to the unseen house in silence. Steven was grateful Em was being so nice to him, but he also couldn't think of a single thing to say to her that didn't sound strained and fawning to his inner ear.

I like your horse.

Where did you live before coming here?

Where's your green ribbon today?

All rubbish. He wondered how anyone *ever* started a conversation with a girl. Not a girl you had to talk to because she was your home-ec. partner, or a girl who looked at you and giggled and said stuff to her friends that made them giggle too. But a *proper* girl, and a normal conversation. In that regard, Steven was at a complete loss.

Behind them the gates clicked quietly shut and he glanced back over his shoulder. 'Why do you have such fancy gates?'

'Oh,' said Em dismissively, 'somebody stole our trailer.'

9

Jos Reeves at the lab in Portishead called to confirm that green wool fibres that had been found stuck to the gummed note at the Pete Knox scene nearly matched fibres found clinging to the door handle of John Took's horsebox.

'Nearly?' Reynolds asked. He'd been about to get in the shower – or try to. He was not a stocky man, but he'd examined the cubicle with a mathematical eye and was dubious about every single dimension.

'Well, the fibre itself is the same,' said Reeves, 'but the ones at the second scene have traces of butane on them.'

'You mean lighter fuel?'

'That's the stuff.'

Reynolds thought of the old Zippo his father had used. Reynolds's parents had been married for fifty-two years – a whole three of them harmonious – but his mother still had no idea her husband smoked. The smell of a Zippo always made Reynolds think of huddling behind a barrier of cobwebbed terracotta pots in the garden shed while his father lit up, and inevitably brought with it the medical tang of the Fisherman's Friends he would then chew like Smarties to disguise the smell.

'So he's a smoker,' said Reynolds.

'Maybe,' said Reeves. 'Or a camper. Or just a man making bonfires.'

'Hoodies use it to get high, right?'

Reeves laughed a bit too hard for Reynolds's liking. 'I don't think it's for the exclusive use of hoodies, but yeah – it's a cheap high. For kids.'

'Could it have been used to disable a victim?'

'Sure. Wouldn't knock them out, but it would make someone woozy, disorientated, you know?'

'But it wasn't at the first scene,' Reynolds reiterated.

'Nope.'

Reynolds sighed. That meant the butane could be significant or simply a red herring. It could mean the wool was deliberately impregnated with butane, or it had been accidentally spilt. But if it was deliberate, then why wasn't it present at the first scene?

'And you have no idea what the wool fibres might have come from?'

'Not so far, but we're still working on them, obviously.'

Reynolds thanked Reeves and hung up, more frustrated than before. The Jess Took scene had been a mess of tyre tracks and footprints, while the Tarr Steps car park was tarmac, and had therefore yielded few samples for comparison. What little trace evidence they did have was more tantalizing than helpful.

Only the notes made the connection certain.

You don't love her.

You don't love him.

He thought of Pete Knox's mother wailing in the car park and understood the depth of her despairing cry: *What does it mean?*

*

Jonas pointed at the wall behind Kate Gulliver and asked, 'Is that new?'

Kate Gulliver was surprised. Until now, this session had been like all their others – difficult and mostly silent. Most clients were tough at first, but slowly opened up until they gained some level of comfort in this strange new context. After a few sessions, she was used to those clients coming in, sitting down and picking up exactly where they'd left off the week before – shedding their reserve as they warmed to their examination of self. After a while, many of them enjoyed it. They found themselves fascinating.

Not so Jonas Holly. He seemed to be as interested in himself as he was in everything else – which was not at all.

Usually.

Now she turned to follow his finger and pushed her dark hair behind one ear. It was a habit she'd once cultivated to appear girlish but couldn't break now, even though she was closer to forty than thirty.

Jonas was pointing at the small cross-stitched sampler over her desk. SUFFER THE LITTLE CHILDREN TO COME UNTO ME.

'No, it's been there for years,' she said.

He dropped his hand back on to the armrest where it usually waited, ready to propel himself off the chair at the end of the hour.

Kate wondered why he'd brought it up. 'What do you think of it?' she said.

'Nothing,' said Jonas, too fast for it to be true.

'Have you only just noticed it?'

He shrugged.

'Interesting,' she mused.

He said nothing, so she went on, 'That you've never noticed it before, but suddenly not only do you notice it, but you feel strongly enough to ask me about it.'

He shrugged again.

Kate Gulliver had seen more of Jonas Holly's silent shrugs than she cared to count.

Although it was her job to work him out, she *couldn't* work him out. Struggling through the aftermath of his wife's death with Jonas had been one of the toughest things she'd ever done as a psychologist. Sometimes she got the feeling that he hadn't progressed one iota from their very first session. The memory of that session was still branded on her consciousness – the way the sadness rippling around him was almost tangible, while he sat numb at its centre, like a black hole. She had treated many police and services personnel in her time – men and women who had seen terrible things, *done* terrible things – but she remembered that first session with Jonas Holly vividly – that feeling that reaching out to help *him* might instead suck *her* inexorably into his compressed misery. The whole experience had left her off-kilter and depressed. Afterwards she'd sought out her own therapist and had agreed that it would be best to keep a more-than-professional distance from the tall young policeman with the bottomless eyes.

So she'd gone through the motions with Jonas. No, no! That wasn't true . . . She knew her stuff. She did her best. But she wanted nothing more than to be able to tick the box marked 'Fit to return to duty' and never see him again. The fact that she occasionally suspected that he might be going through the motions with her in return was something she didn't want to examine too closely.

And yet here he was – eight months into their work – clearly disturbed by the sampler her grandmother had stitched as a girl.

'What is it that bothers you about it?'

Instead of shrugging, Jonas shifted in his seat. Another first – usually he was as still as a summer pond.

'I don't know,' he said, when he clearly did.

That was good though. It was an admission that it *did* bother him, which – in Jonas Holly terms – was hugely confessional.

'Did you ever want children, Jonas?' She hardly thought about the question. She asked it more to keep the conversation going than because she expected a response. Indeed, it was not an unusual question, but Jonas struggled to answer it. For a long time she thought he wasn't going to, but finally he said 'No.'

'Did Lucy?' she asked more carefully.

He got up, making her jump a little.

He walked across to the sampler, his hands dug into the pockets of his jeans. 'Did you do it?' he asked.

She watched his eyes run over the cross-stitch as if seeking answers. He'd already answered *her* question by ignoring it.

'My grandmother did. When she was thirteen. I think it's lovely.' She wasn't supposed to express personal opinions to clients, but whatever – this was *family*.

He stared at the sampler so long it became uncomfortable.

'There was a girl kidnapped near me.'

There was a long silence while Kate adjusted to the sudden change of subject.

'That's terrible. Do you know her?'

'Maybe. I don't remember.'

Kate had heard 'I don't remember' a lot from Jonas, too. But, unlike many of her clients, when *he* said it, it often looked as if he really *couldn't* recall the salient detail. Still, she was always suspicious of 'I don't remember', just as her ears pricked up at 'It wasn't my fault' and 'This has nothing to do with my mother.' She let this one go.

She was mentally couching her next question for maximum probe when Jonas carried on without prompting – again.

'People hurt children,' he said bluntly.

Kate hesitated. She had to be careful here; they were breaking new ground. 'Sometimes they do.'

He opened his mouth to say something, then closed it again.

'How does that make you feel?' she ventured, with little expectation of a reply. Another standard, stalling question. She wasn't sure where this was going.

She watched his throat work as he stared at the sampler; noticed his hands ball into fists in his pockets.

And suddenly, as surely as if she'd opened a window and felt the breeze, Kate Gulliver felt a wave of threat hit her from across the room. He was about to smash the sampler – strike it from the wall and grind it underfoot – then turn on her. She knew it in her gut. Panic rose in her like mercury, and she jerked in her seat from the sheer rush. She glanced at the door. If she had to, could she reach it before him? She didn't think so. There was an alarm button, but it was under her desktop and Jonas Holly was between her and the desk. If she screamed would someone hear her? Would they come running? Or would it just provoke him? Would she be dead before help came? Choked and lifeless on the carpet? Her throat slashed with a shard of glass from the broken frame?

All this flashed through her mind in the blink of an eye and left her feeling kicked in the heart.

Then she got a grip.

Ridiculous! She was being ridiculous. She was an experienced psychologist and Jonas was her client – a man of the law, who'd suffered a terrible loss and who needed help. Not some raving lunatic who might murder her over a bit of cross-stitch! She must be completely mad to have thought it, even for a second.

Jonas had not moved.

Kate almost laughed, but stopped the sound before it came out of her mouth because she thought she might appear as crazy as she felt. It was not like her to be irrational. She'd never done a single thing on impulse – always considered the consequences of every action. Now she tried to analyse where that feeling of danger had come from, how it had seized her – her physical responses to that flash of overwhelming fear.

It made her feel better to dissect it like this, but in her belly she could still feel the terror fizzing slowly away. A seltzer of instinct. Her body insisting that this *thing* had been real.

She concentrated on her breathing. She made herself wait longer than she needed to before she spoke – just to show herself that she could.

'I think that's the hour, Jonas.'

He looked round as if he'd forgotten she was there. 'OK. Thanks.'

He gave her a shy half-smile, and left without another glance at the sampler.

Kate released all her tension in one long, jolting breath. Her hands shook and she felt the corners of her mouth tremble downwards like a grazed toddler's. She felt tears close to the surface and made a giant effort to get a grip.

Stupid. You're being stupid. Stop it!

She cleared her throat and sat up straight. Something had triggered her fear response. More than likely it was something inside her – nothing to do with Jonas Holly at all. Maybe something to do with her grandmother, who had been a right old cow, if truth be told. Living in that gloomy house with the curtains always drawn. She'd been creeped out then; no wonder she was creeped out now. It was something she should be exploring with her own therapist, not something she should be blaming on a client.

She pressed a tissue to her eyes. She'd have to check her make-up before the next appointment.

Kate took a deep breath and felt everything inside her returning slowly to normal.

Jonas had shown his anger at last – albeit confined to a fist in his pocket – and had been fine by the end of the session. Calm. That was a kind of acceptance, wasn't it?

The missing pieces of his grief jigsaw.

You're scared of him.

She ignored the voice in her head. It wasn't logical or professional. What *was* logical and professional was to know when she had done all she could for a client and to allow him to move on. To get on with his life.

Kate Gulliver opened his file and ticked the box that cleared Jonas Holly to return to duty.

10

Steven Lamb was right about his brother. Their mother's dire warnings about the deathtrap that was Springer Farm had made it a magnet – and Davey and his best friend Shane played up there among the ruins whenever they could. The farmhouse was black and filthy and open to the skies through a skeleton of charred oak beams, with the stone chimney sternum piercing them like a monument to the dead. The row of cottages across the courtyard had been so vandalized by local children (Davey and Shane prime among them) that anyone could walk in and set up home – the few remaining sticks of furniture were so decrepit that the estate of the deceased had failed to assign any value to them. There was even an old bed, complete with mattress, in one of the rooms – where small black handmarks on the ceiling bore testament to the fact that the springs still worked.

The boys loved to sift through the ashes of the main house, looking for treasures, while sniffing chunks of charcoal, or using them to draw crude graffiti on the cottage walls.

D + S CrEw
This propEty bElongs to Lamb and Collins. KEEP OUT.
Mr PEach is a COCK.

They did occasionally find what they considered to be treasures in the ruin of the house. Once a green marble egg, another time a fox's mask, only slightly blackened down one side and mounted on a wooden shield. They'd wrestled over the mask and – from within a stiff headlock – Shane had decided he didn't want it anyway. He'd got the egg.

Once, when they were seeing how far up the chimney they could climb before getting stuck, Shane's foot dislodged an old biscuit tin that had been wedged there. Disappointingly, it contained nothing but a few dozen fuzzy and faded snapshots of boys and ponies. Davey said it was Shane's turn to keep the treasure, but Shane resisted; he didn't want to waste his turn on gay junk. So they just jammed the tin back where they'd found it.

Davey got furthest up the chimney – over twelve feet, according to the twine tied to his ankle, which was their judge and jury. He came down looking Victorian, and spent that night marvelling at the additional treasure of black snot that he discovered in his nose.

Of course, the boys weren't supposed to be at Springer Farm at all – or anywhere vaguely interesting. Davey blamed Steven, who'd ruined it for everybody by almost getting killed a while back. Davey was hazy on the details – he just knew that his nan loved Steven better than she loved him, and that that was why. Now *he* had to pay the price of his mother only working in the mornings so that she was there when they got home from school. Luckily, both Davey and Shane felt that lying to their mothers in order to be able to play properly was hardly lying at all, and so did it routinely. Davey's mother was told they were in Shane's back garden, and Shane's was told they were at Davey's. Once that lie had been told and believed, it was a simple matter to go anywhere they pleased for as long as

they liked. And, more often than not, they pleased to walk up the
hill until they reached Rose and Honeysuckle cottages. Then they
always ran, because everyone knew that a woman had been murdered in one cottage and that a witch lived in the other. Once she
had been at the gate and had asked them if their parents knew where
they were. They'd run past her, laughing with self-imposed fear, and
Shane had turned and – from a safe distance – had given her a V
sign. They weren't sure she'd seen it – and Davey secretly hoped she
hadn't – but it was exhilarating none the less.

Today they'd found nothing at Springer Farm, despite hours
spent sifting the ashes looking for treasures and the bodies of the
kidnapped children. Davey was adamant that it was the coolest
place to hide a body, but their search had run them a merry dance
through the gamut of anticipation, excitement and boredom – all
in the space of about three hours. The sun had gone, although it
would remain light for a good while yet.

They ran downhill past the cottages, then slowed to an amble,
talking – as they always did – about nothing at all. Both had hazel
sticks with which they whipped the heads off the cow parsley that
lined the ditch along the base of the hedge. They were merciless,
but the cow parsley seemed to come back as fast as they destroyed
it. Before this it had been dandelions; later would come docks.

Davey sliced through several fronds at once and Shane chortled
his approval. The foamy heads fell into the road in a pile.

'Nice one!' Shane took a penalty with the little pile of green-
white flowers, which fountained off his toe, then plopped to the
ground a few feet away.

'And Collins scores the winner for England!' He raised his arms
and made a rushing sound that was supposed to be the roar of
the crowd.

Davey didn't answer.

He was standing over a slip of paper revealed by the dispersal
of the clump of cow parsley.

Not a slip of paper at all. He bent to pick it up.

'What's that?' said Shane.

Open-mouthed, Davey straightened up and showed him a twenty-pound note.

'You. Are. Fucking. *Joking!*' Shane hurried back up to where Davey stood. The note was grubby and faded, but undoubtedly a twenty. More money than either of them had ever had at one time in their lives. Combined.

They stared at the note, and then at each other, then laughed, then stared at the note again.

'It must have been in the hedge,' said Davey.

'Maybe there's more!' said Shane.

The boys set about the cow parsley like Dickensian schoolmasters – whipping, slashing and beating the vegetation into green and white hay on the tarmac.

'There's another!' Shane reached in this time and retrieved a twenty.

'Fuuuuuuck!'

They laughed like drunks and then went back to their destruction of the hedgerow.

Three more notes came to light before the witch leaned over her garden gate and shouted, 'You boys leave that hedge alone!'

Giggling and giddy with wealth, Davey and Shane ran down the hill to home.

*

The thought of seeing the pile of crap that he'd spent his life savings on made Steven's heart sink. But, because of Em's trailer, he walked up to Ronnie's house after tea.

Ronnie Trewell – popularly known as Skew Ronnie, because of his lifestyle as much as his limp – lived in a scruffy bungalow at the end of a cul-de-sac that clung to the side of the moor. There was a garage almost the size of the house, where Ronnie hid his stolen cars.

Used to hide them.

Ronnie had been rehabilitated, apparently, by attending a course in Tiverton where young car thieves were allowed to tinker with karts and then race them. Steven would have given his right arm to race karts, but it seemed he'd have to be pretty dedicated to a life of crime before he could hope for that kind of reward.

He knocked and Dougie opened the door. Dougie was Steven's age. They skated together.

'All right, mate?'

'Yeah. All right? Ronnie in?'

'Hold on.'

Dougie yelled for his brother while Steven stood in the dank hallway that smelled of old dog and chip fat.

Ronnie appeared in trackies and bedroom slippers, and the three of them went out to the garage.

The trailer was still there.

'You want a hand taking that back?' Steven said casually.

Ronnie shrugged. 'They got plenty. They won't miss it.'

The bike was still there too – in bits. But Ronnie's enthusiasm for all things mechanical was infectious, and Steven was soon imbued with a sense of complete optimism about the task of reconstruction. Ronnie pointed out that the engine was largely intact, the tyres not perished, and the tank almost rust-free. The much-mentally-maligned Gary had, in fact, put all the smaller parts into plastic boxes and labelled them, and with Ronnie's experienced eye for what went where, the three of them were soon making a bit of progress.

As night approached, the greyhound wandered in and out and peered knowledgeably at parts with its soulful marble eyes, and Ronnie passed round a can of Carlsberg. Although he knew it was nothing really, Steven felt it was a night he'd always remember – the harsh fluorescent lighting, the blue-green dusk framed by the black garage door, the machined metal between his oil-stained fingers, and the bitter bubbles on his tongue that tasted like the future.

At nine he stood up reluctantly and said he should be getting home before it got too dark.

Ronnie and Dougie spent a few minutes ripping the piss out of him for being a mummy's boy, but he just smiled and rolled his eyes and brushed the garage dirt off the seat of his jeans.

'Thanks,' he told Ronnie.

'Come up any time you want to work on it. You know where the key is.'

'Cheers.'

'Get home safe now!' Ronnie and Dougie had a final laugh at his expense and then went inside and whistled for the dog.

Steven waited until everyone was asleep. Just after midnight he dressed quietly, took the torch from under the kitchen sink where his mother kept it for when the electric went out, and walked back through the silent village to Ronnie Trewell's house.

The garage key was where Ronnie had told him it would be; the up-and-over door opened with barely a squeak, and the trailer rolled easily out on to the driveway.

So far, so good, thought Steven, as he closed the door and put the key back in the hanging basket that contained a bouquet of dead weeds.

The trailer was made of aluminium and was well balanced on properly inflated tyres, so Steven made good time down into the village, towing it behind him. But he'd hardly gone fifty yards up the hill towards Em's house before he started to sweat and his hands to hurt from gripping the awkward metal so hard. He swung the trailer sideways so that it wouldn't roll back down the hill, and stopped.

He had never considered that he might not be able to tow the trailer all the way to where it belonged. Now, if he couldn't, he had blown it. If he couldn't get it up this hill, he would be unlikely to get it back up the similar hill to Ronnie's house. He couldn't just leave it on the street. Anyone might hitch it up and tow it away and then it really *would* be stolen, instead of just 'borrowed'.

Stopping and thinking had allowed Steven to get his breath back, and so he tugged the trailer another twenty yards before halting again, his hands burning. He was fit but slim – not a bulky young farmer like the boys who inhabited the YFC discos he had been to once or twice. The hill was long and unrelentingly steep, and the road was broken up in places that he knew from dodging them on his skateboard by day, but which he couldn't see by night, making the trailer bump and lurch now and then. But Steven Lamb was not a boy who gave up easily. He'd been through more in his seventeen years than most people had in a lifetime, and that was a well of experience he often drew from when faced with a difficult situation. Sometimes he thought that was all he really had – this determination. Other boys were great at soccer or cross-country running or chatting up girls. Steven was just plain *dogged*. He hated to give up. It wasn't a spectacular talent, but it was better than nothing.

So he turned the trailer so that he could push rather than pull it, and found that was better – he could get his weight behind it. Even so, it was only another fifty yards before he had to stop again, wiping sweat from his forehead with his arm.

He hoped no cars came up or down the hill. The trailer had no lights and he was in jeans and his black school jumper. He wanted to return the trailer, but he didn't want to get squashed doing it. Plus, if he were run over and killed right now, nobody would know he'd been returning the trailer. Everyone would think he'd been the one who'd stolen it in the first place. He'd die a thief, and that would be seriously unfair.

Spurred by that thought, Steven put his back into it once more.

The lane suddenly brightened, and he realized a security light on the eaves of Honeysuckle Cottage had picked up his movement.

Feeling horribly visible, Steven pushed on. He hadn't been up here at night for a long time. Well over a year. The last time had been in the snow, with his newspaper bag on his hip. He didn't want to remember that night – not now, while he needed to keep going on past Rose Cottage.

The memories crowded in anyway.

The night Mrs Holly had been murdered.

She'd made him tea; she'd given him money. She'd hugged him so fiercely that she'd squeezed tears from his eyes on to her blue shoulder.

And he'd given her nothing. For all the time they'd spent together – for all the interest she'd shown, and all the quiet little moments of kindness, he'd given nothing back. Not even when she needed him most.

A hundred times since that night, Steven had been burned by the shame of cowardice. It made him feel weak and unworthy of love.

Come with me.

That's what he could have said. *Should* have said. It would have been so simple.

But come with me *where*? He was just the paperboy and Lucy Holly was a real adult with a proper life, who was used to making grown-up decisions, despite her weak legs and her crutches. Something had told him that she would not consider that battling through a blizzard on the arm of a boy to his mum's house in the middle of the night was a sensible decision. Even *he* had known it would have sounded a bit nuts. Asking her if she needed help would have meant acknowledging the danger she was in, and he'd had no idea how to speak to her about that.

So instead he'd left her there to die.

The thought sent a chill through Steven.

He had to stop thinking of this. He had to be strong and focused, or this bloody trailer was going to run him over on its way back down to the bottom of the hill. He had to be *dogged*.

Steven gritted his teeth and locked his aching arms and shoved as hard and as fast as he could. He felt sweat trickling between his shoulder blades and snaking down his back.

The security light went out and he breathed a sigh of relief.

He was almost past.

Beyond Rose Cottage's box hedge, the coarse lane hedge took over again and matched its opposite all the way up to Springer Farm and Old Barn Farm beyond that.

But he had to stop, just for a moment – or his arms were going to drop off. He did, turning and leaning his backside against the back of the trailer to keep it from rolling, his legs braced against the road, trying to keep his panting as quiet as possible.

The security light came back on again.

'Hello, Steven.'

His heart stopped.

Silhouetted in the bright white light was Jonas Holly.

Only the thought of the giant effort he'd already made kept Steven from just leaving the trailer and running.

Jonas looked even taller than he'd remembered him being. So tall and thin within the bright white light that Steven wondered whether he was imagining him.

'You want a hand with that?'

It wasn't what Steven had been expecting him to say. The last thing he wanted was to spend time in the company of Jonas Holly. Especially alone in the middle of the night.

The silence unfolded smoothly between them, with a low whisper all of its own. He almost declined, but thought how weird it would look to say 'No, thanks', then turn and continue his snail-like progress under the invisible eye of the silhouette.

There was no option.

'OK.'

The man walked towards Steven with the light splayed behind him, as if he were emerging from a Tinseltown version of a diamanté heaven. The light clicked off and for a horrible second Steven lost sight of him completely.

Then Mr Holly was beside him and bending to grip the edge of the trailer. Steven did the same and they started up the hill together.

So much faster.

Jonas didn't speak to Steven at all. Once he muttered 'Shit' under his breath as they hit a pothole and they both hurt their wrists. Then they continued in silence broken only by bumping and panting and the occasional grunt of effort.

They went past Springer Farm, with its B&B sign barely visible through the bindweed, until they reached Old Barn Farm's shiny black gates.

'Here,' said Steven, and they steered the trailer off the road and straightened up.

'New gates,' said Jonas.

'New people,' said Steven.

He went over to the intercom panel and shone his torch at it. Then he pressed in the code. 1204. Em's birthday, she'd told him, so it was easy to remember.

The gates opened almost silently.

'They gave me the code so I could take them their paper,' said Steven – and then remembered that he didn't take a paper to Mr Holly's house any more and wished he had just shut up. What would he say if Mr Holly asked him about it? Silence was the only form of lying he was even halfway good at. But Mr Holly said nothing about his paper, and together they pushed the trailer inside the gates and left it there.

Steven closed the gates and they walked back down the hill in dark silence.

Steven felt the questions that waited to be asked just under the surface, like the big gold and white fish in the Austins' pond. The fish followed him from one end of the dark water to the other when he delivered the *Bugle*, and then did the same on his return journey down the path – hoping to be fed. Thus the unasked questions followed him and Jonas Holly down the hill from Old Barn Farm all the way back to Rose Cottage, hungry for answers.

It was enough to make Steven shake with tension.

But nothing was asked and nothing was told. Nothing of the mystery trailer, and nothing of the night when Lucy Holly had been murdered.

Instead Jonas Holly murmured 'Good night,' and peeled off at Rose Cottage, while Steven muttered 'Thanks,' and jogged home in a world that had just got that little bit stranger.

11

Jonas woke to a dawn that promised everything.

It was a week since Jess Took had disappeared, and May had become almost fictional in its brilliance – the kind of balmy weather that only Enid Blyton really seemed to have believed possible.

During the night Jonas had thrown off the sheets, and now he looked down the landscape of his own naked body to the moors beyond the cottage window.

They were spectacular. Under a sky that was already pale Wedgwood, Exmoor had burst into life. Heather that had made the hills look scorched and black through the winter had magically revived and now mottled them green. Grass that had been muddy just a month before had become like straw, while the yellow sprays of gorse and broom hid countless birds, betrayed only by their summer songs. Foals tripped along behind sleek mares, and lambs that imagined themselves lost bleated plaintively – a sound that carried for miles on a still day. Buzzards and kestrels looked down on it all – poised to bring sudden death without disturbing the peace. Jonas's parents, who had lived in the house before him, had never bothered with pictures or paintings. These windows on to Exmoor were all they'd ever wanted by way of decoration, and on a morning like this, Jonas understood them better than he ever had when they'd been alive. Van Goghs and Gauguins would be drab by comparison.

A starling darted up under the eaves outside the window and he heard the chicks clamouring like crickets, almost overhead. They were probably in the attic. When they'd flown he would go up there and block the holes and put up nesting boxes instead.

Maybe he would. He hadn't been up there since . . .

Lucy died.

Jonas sighed and looked down at the narrow plank of flesh that his body had become. His genitals seemed ridiculously large, jutting uselessly between his sharp hips, and thrown into relief by the early sun his ribs looked like ripples on a flat sea. On the plain between the two, even the scars on his belly seemed worse than usual – red and ridged and twisted and puckered.

They'd told him they would fade to white with time.

Time.

He looked at his alarm clock – something he hadn't done with any good reason in over a year. It was almost six thirty.

Jonas swung his legs to the creaking floor and headed to the shower. One bathroom window framed a picture of the edge of Shipcott and the towering moor behind it. The thought of going back to the village he'd let down so badly made his gut ache, but he almost welcomed the feeling. He deserved it.

The other window displayed the burned-out farmhouse on the closest hilltop, charred rafters piercing the sky. He stared at the remains of Springer Farm as if into a mirror, while he slid his soapy fingers over the slats of his own ribcage.

He sat silently on the bed until he was dry, then he put on his uniform.

*

Reynolds mustered his troops in the car park of the Red Lion. They were due to start the search at 8am. Reynolds was in the empty car park by seven fifteen and nervous by seven thirty. The only other people there were the press and TV crews.

Memories of his thirteenth birthday worried at the back of his mind. His primary-school classmates seemed to have taken the move to various secondary schools as an opportunity to abandon him as a friend. His mother told him it was because he was too clever for them and he was sure she was right. But he was also sure that many boys would still come to his party – if only for a magician called El Gran Supremo, complete with top hat, wand and rabbit.

But they hadn't come.

At least, only two of them had, and they didn't count: the wispy Digby Furnwild – who went everywhere with an asthma inhaler and a handkerchief impregnated with Olbas oil – and the giant Bruce Locksmith, who would have braved a pit of wolves for free cake, let alone a child's party. Bruce had eaten almost all the cake, but only made it halfway through El Gran Supremo before announcing that it was shit and he was leaving. He'd taken several going-home bags with him. Reynolds and Digby had sat in moribund silence at either end of the day-bed until Digby's mother had come to fetch him. After Digby had left, Reynolds's mother had gone ballistic because she'd found rabbit droppings on the lounge carpet.

He'd never hosted another party.

Until now. And now the thought that nobody would show while the nation's press bore witness made Reynolds sweat. He'd Google-mapped the middle of the moor and divided the resulting print-offs into numbered grids. He needed fifty people, at least, to cover the area properly. He wished he'd asked Rice to take the lead on this one; then it would look bad for *her* if nobody came.

But by 7.45am there were a dozen or so police officers, including four dog-handlers, and eighteen Shipcott residents. It was better than nothing.

He took the officers aside and briefly ran through where they were right now. Forensics on the horsebox and the Knoxes' Golf had been poor. The lab was checking out the green fibres found at both scenes, along with tiny traces of a sticky white plastic found in the broken car windows from the Pete Knox scene. They had no idea yet what that was or how – or even if – it was connected to the kidnap, and they were keeping these details from the press for now. He made no mention of the notes. They were his ace in the hole.

His men were already looking warm in their dark uniforms. It was going to be a scorcher. One asked if they could work in shirtsleeves and Reynolds was about to say 'No' when Elizabeth Rice said 'Of course.' He'd speak to her later.

With five minutes to go before the official start time, cars began to swing into the car park and disgorge dozens more occupants from surrounding villages. By 8am there must have been eighty people, all told, most of them ruddy-faced men and burly teen-aged boys, several with dogs on bits of rope. Touching flat caps in greeting, leaning over to shake hands, voices curtailed and low out of respect for the reason they were here. There was an excited undercurrent of common purpose. They reminded Reynolds of a lynch-mob, and he could have kissed their feet just for showing up.

Rice moved through them, taking names and addresses and ignoring banter about taking down *her* particulars. There was always the chance that the kidnapper might join the throng of searchers – either to gain an insight into how the investigation was being conducted, or to throw them off the scent if they got too close. Or just for the thrill of being right there, shoulder to shoulder with the desperate and the needy, in a warm cocoon of knowledge and control.

Reynolds climbed on to a chair from the bar and from there on to the low roof of the coal bunker, so that everyone could see him and – hopefully – hear him.

He patted the edges of his notes together and ran through his opening lines in his head.

Ladies and gentlemen. You all know why you are here and I thank you for it. (PAUSE.) Someone has come among you and stolen your children. (PAUSE.) Our job today – YOUR job today – is to find them and return them to the bosom of their families . . .

It was a good speech. And thank God there were now people to hear it. What might have sounded too grand for an audience of twenty was going to sound positively Churchillian to a crowd of nearly a hundred. And on TV too . . .

He cleared his throat, and as he opened his mouth to start, a murmur of surprise, then welcome, ran through the group, and Reynolds looked up to see Jonas Holly.

His heart sank.

Isn't he supposed to be on leave?

He watched people turn to shake Jonas's hand or carefully pat his shoulder. It seemed as if they'd seen about as much of him over the past eightteen months as Reynolds had. There was certainly less of him to see. Despite his irritation, Reynolds was taken aback by how much weight Jonas had lost, when there'd been so little to lose in the first place. His cheekbones were too high and his eyes too big. He looked haunted.

Hi, you've reached Jonas and Lucy . . .

Reynolds wondered whether the message was still on the answering machine, growing less tragic and more plain *weird* by the day.

*

Jonas had stopped shaking.

Walking down the hill into the village – into the midst of the people he knew must despise him – had been an unnerving experience. This was not like driving to Mr Jacoby's shop to pick up baked beans, when he could hide behind jeans and jumper and his father's old fishing hat that he'd found in the cupboard under the stairs. This was him very publicly in uniform – once more assuming the mantle of authority that had so spectacularly failed the village where he'd been born and bred.

He'd stopped at the playing field on the way to the Red Lion. The playing field with the skate ramp and the swings, and the little stream where Yvonne Marsh had died. To stave off the moment when he would have to rejoin society at the Red Lion, he'd crossed the field. The grass had crackled almost as loudly from drought as it had with frost two winters ago. He'd stared into the rill under the old blackthorn and remembered the pain in his legs where the icy cold had seeped into his very bones as he'd bent over the half-naked woman . . .

Jonas had had to stop again in the bus shelter and breathe deeply. He watched his hands tremble like a drunk's, and fought down the panic that had swelled into a great bubble in his chest. He couldn't do this. He needed to go home.

Bob Coffin passed by in his crumpled green Barbour and gaiters, despite the weather, and touched the front of his flat cap at Jonas.

'Mr Holly,' he said, as if they'd just met yesterday.

Jonas nodded shakily at him.

Bob Coffin stopped. He'd been the Blacklands huntsman for nigh on forty years, and his legs were bowed but sturdy from the hard labour of walking hounds. His eyes were deep-set and bright blue, and watched Jonas like those of a small, careful bird. He barely reached Jonas's chin, and yet when he inclined his head briefly towards the Red Lion and said, 'Coming?' Jonas only hesitated for one more second – then followed him like a lamb.

And so he'd got to the car park late, just as Reynolds was about to start speaking, and had been embarrassed that he'd been noticed and that people had turned to him and made a fuss. They were kind. So kind. Shaking his hand and grasping his shoulder and murmuring good wishes. Elizabeth Rice had put an arm around him and surprised him by pulling his cheek down so she could kiss it hello. Nobody had made a joke about it. For Lucy's sake, he guessed.

He'd been relieved when they'd all turned back to listen to Reynolds and left him alone, and he'd been able to breathe again.

When he had calmed down enough to actually look properly at Reynolds, he noticed he had hair.

All over his head.

*

Reynolds put up his hand to call for silence so that he could speak, but nobody was looking at him, and before he could clear his throat again there was the metallic sound of hoofs and at least thirty horses clattered up the road and milled at the entrance of the car park, to a spontaneous cheer from the volunteers.

The Midmoor Hunt had turned out in support of John Took, even if he *was* only joint Master. They were led by the other Master, Charles Stourbridge – the *real* Master, most agreed – who held up his hand for silence and got it in a heartbeat.

'Good morning,' he said in a voice that would have sounded well at the Globe Theatre. 'I believe we have some children to find.'

Once more the volunteers cheered and clapped and turned to face him, so that Reynolds found himself looking at a hundred shoulders. Even his own officers were showing him their epaulettes.

Proles.

'We're just here to help.' Stourbridge nodded at him modestly, and Reynolds disliked him instantly. Of course they were here to help! What did Stourbridge *think* they were here to do? Run the show? *He* was the one with the bloody Google maps!

When the search party finally turned back towards Reynolds, he started. 'Ladies and gentlemen, you all know why you're here and—'

'Can't hear you at the back!' said a gruff voice. 'Speak up!'

'Ladies and gentlemen,' he started again.

'Yes, we got *that* bit!'

Reynolds felt sweat beginning to form at the base of his plugs. Suddenly his speech seemed a bit flowery and superfluous. Wasted on a crowd of earthy farmers like these.

'I have some maps here!' he shouted. 'I've split the moor into twelve squares around a five-mile radius of Dunkery Beacon!'

Charles Stourbridge's horse opened the crowd like the Red Sea as he rode over to the coal bunker and held out his hand for a map with such expectant authority that Reynolds could do nothing other than give him one. He rested it on his horse's neck and studied it.

'What I want us to do,' shouted Reynolds, 'is to concentrate on outbuildings, barns and copses. Places where the children might be hidden!'

Reynolds hoped they'd all understand the subtext – that right now they still hoped to find Jess and Pete alive.

'What if they're dead?' said the same gruff voice. Reynolds searched for the speaker in annoyance, but couldn't pick out the culprit. He looked at Jonas Holly – easy to spot because of his height – but the man was looking at him attentively.

The crowd had gone quiet at the question, and there was no need for Reynolds to shout now. 'There's no reason to believe that Jess and Pete are dead. This is not a hunt for bodies, ladies and gentlemen, it's a search for two scared children desperately in need of your help.'

There was a smattering of applause, and Reynolds felt the balance of power swing back towards him.

'Good,' said Stourbridge immediately. 'Then let's not waste time making speeches. Let's crack on!'

Another cheer and suddenly the coal bunker was rocked by people clamouring and snatching at maps, even though Reynolds had worked out a careful system of small groups of volunteers, each under the supervision of a police officer. Instead, Stourbridge said, 'Right. My lot will take squares one, two, three, five and six. Lots of ground to cover and we'll be faster over it.' Before Reynolds could disagree, he'd ridden out again through the sea of people, and the hunt was moving off at a rattling canter.

If Reynolds had had a gun, he'd have shot him in the back.

*

The search took more than a hundred people three solid days. They concentrated on outbuildings and barns, simply because concentrating on open moorland would have taken a thousand people a year and might still not have turned up any trace of Jess Took or Pete Knox.

The weather was spectacular. *Too* hot, if anything. There was no sign of rain – or even of the chill mists that usually crept off the sea like pirates and smothered the summer moor under little puddles of winter.

The force helicopter criss-crossed the search area using thermal imaging cameras, and its noise – a distant whirr or an overhead cacophony – became the soundtrack to the operation.

Charles Stourbridge controlled the riders and Reynolds settled for controlling those on foot and in cars.

Rice continued discreetly to check the volunteers against the sex offenders register, and on the second morning they quietly removed a man from the team at Landacre Bridge. Thirty-six-year-old Terry Needles had travelled all the way from Bristol with his flask and his sandwiches and his conviction for download-ing child pornography. He spent the next twenty-four hours in a police cell at Minehead. Four hours while the police checked out his disappointingly solid alibis, and another tearful twenty just to remind him of how tentative his grip on freedom really was.

Reynolds had divided eighty-five volunteers into groups of twelve plus one of thirteen – each under the command of a local officer. They covered the seven squares Stourbridge had graciously left them. Progress was slow and sweaty but Reynolds couldn't help but be impressed by the stamina and determination of the searchers, who provided their own lunches and local knowledge.

Jonas found himself not leading a team that started in Wheddon Cross – the highest village on the moor. The officer whom Reynolds *had* put in charge was a desk sergeant from the neighbouring Devon & Cornwall force.

'Jim Courier,' he told his group. 'Like the tennis player.'

It dated him; Jonas was only vaguely aware that there had ever been a player of that name. Either way, he was uninterested in Courier. He was more concerned that the Reverend Julian Chard was among the searchers. Without once looking directly at the vicar of St Mary's, he was aware of his every movement. And soon that movement was in his direction. The Reverend Chard grasped his hand and shook it firmly in both of his, looking deeply into Jonas's face.

'So good to see you back, Jonas. How *are* you?'

Jonas could barely look at him. Not without seeing the face of the Reverend's father, Lionel, the deep sockets of his dead eyes twin puddles filled with blood. The killer had struck on Jonas's watch, and yet Lionel Chard's son was here now, holding his hand and welcoming him back. Forgiving him.

That was his job, of course. He was a man of God; what else could he do?

Jonas knew what *he* would have done. He mumbled something that apparently satisfied convention, and the Reverend

Chard nodded, smiled and patted him on the shoulder as they walked on.

They started out in the hamlet itself – checking sheds and out-houses and coal bunkers – and moved out to the north-west across fields and through farmyards and barns and hay stores and milking sheds. People came out and helped while they were close to their homes, then waved them off and wished them luck as they went – as if they were troops off to war, not a small and increasingly sweaty search party. Jim Courier took off his uniform jacket and slung it over his shoulder and Jonas did the same.

As they headed up into the heather, Jonas squinted into the sun. It seemed like years since he had felt its heat on his face – years since it had seeped through the layers of his skin to warm the very core of his being. It made him think of long-gone summers and of the sour tang of early apples stolen from the gnarled trees up at Springer Farm. It made him think of Lucy – cold and dead and too deep in the soil ever to feel the sun on her face again, however brightly it shone for him.

He had dropped behind the others. He picked up his pace.

The only woman in their group – a slim, outdoorsy brunette who wore proper walking trousers with zip-off legs – offered every-one a piece of chocolate, and people chatted idly as they walked. Whenever Courier got confused by stiles or forks, Jonas put him back on the right course.

As it got warmer, the adrenaline of the morning dissipated, and they hiked doggedly from outbuilding to distant shed, speaking only when it was necessary.

The Reverend Chard was not a fit man or a young man and by lunchtime was plainly beginning to flag. Jonas had a quiet word with their leader, who suggested to the Reverend that he had done enough for one day. The vicar made a token protest and then set off gratefully back to Wheddon Cross for his car and, no doubt, a pint of cold cider at the Rest And Be Thankful.

Jonas watched him go with relief but also some envy. He had started out with the confidence of memory, but over a year of sitting and staring meant his lungs no longer had the capacity to fuel such exertions comfortably, and his legs ached. The sun, which had been so welcome at the start of the day, further sapped his strength, and he felt as hungry and tetchy as a toddler at teatime.

He had a sudden flash of a baby opening its rosebud mouth for a spoon-train, and of Lucy scooping the drips off its smooth chin. The baby had his eyes, and Lucy turned to smile at him, radiating happiness.

Jim Courier came over and pointed at something on the map. Jonas kept his head low and nodded, although he could see nothing but the man's blurred finger.

They moved on and Jonas emptied his mind and watched his own feet as they pointed his way across the fragrant hills.

Over the three days, not a single volunteer dropped out.

As his men reported to him by radio, the helicopter team crackled and Stourbridge called on variable phone lines from across the moor, Reynolds placed crosses over the satellite images of tumbledown barns and stands of trees, and watched the area left to search shrink by the hour.

At first he was delighted by the methodical way the ground was being covered. Then as they ran out of barns and copses and the children had still not been found, the relentless march of crosses denoting that a search had been completed in a particular grid took on a whole new complexion. Instead of triumphant, each cross made Reynolds feel more desperate.

The volunteers were thorough and reliable, and – as Stourbridge had promised – the hunt covered the ground faster than anyone else.

But all that meant was that it took them less time to discover absolutely nothing.

*

Startling, in't it, the amount of fuss what's made when it's all too late? All them people hunting all across the moor. And all for nothing.

I took no pleasure in searching with them; just had to be done, that's all – to keep things looking right. If I didn't do that, people might talk. Ask.

Inquire.

Some of them, though . . . I had to stop myself looking at the stupid hurt in their eyes, just in case they seen something back in mine. But being there and hearing them bleat about the children and the maniac what's got 'em made me want to kick all their arses – them careless bastards.

No one appreciates a single thing nowadays. No one values what they got. Not until it's gone, at least.

And them children's gone, that's for sure.

Gone for good.

12

It was night, and Mrs Paddon was in that warm, fluid state between sleep and wake when she heard a child crying.

She was a little deaf, and the walls of Honeysuckle Cottage were three feet thick and made of stone, but the sound was unmistakeable.

Mrs Paddon was nearing ninety and had never had children of her own, so the noise did not pull her from her slumber the way it might someone who had been a mother. Instead she kept her eyes closed, and allowed the faint sobs to take her back to the time when Jonas was a boy . . .

He'd been a sunny child, but too adventurous for her liking. There was always a tree to tumble from in the back garden, a bike to fall off on the steep lane, or a pony up at Springer Farm that bucked and bolted.

She'd heard him at times like that, sobbing just like this, and had always stopped whatever she was doing and stayed very still until she'd been sure someone was there to comfort him – until she'd heard Cath making soft cooing noises and kissing it better, or Desmond brushing him down and geeing him up. Moments later, she'd see Jonas back up the tree, back on his bike, Elastoplastered and ready for action. Only then had she resumed whatever she'd been doing.

Now, in her single bed, with most of her life behind her, Mrs Paddon drifted back to sleep to the sound of a child sobbing, and dreamed wonderfully of those balmy days when Cath and Desmond were still alive, when Jonas was sweetly innocent – and when she was young again.

When the old lady awoke the next morning, she could not even recall that her sleep had been interrupted; she only knew that it had been good.

*

Steven Lamb was on the skate ramp on the playing field the first time he saw Jonas Holly back on the beat. The shock was so great that he missed the lip and skidded to the bottom of the scuffed half-pipe on his chest and forearm – much to the amusement of Lalo Bryant.

'Twat!' Lalo chortled. He liked Steven, but he'd once broken his ankle on this very ramp and the memory of his own howling was always uncomfortably close. It had been nobody's fault but his own, but he was constantly looking for balances and paybacks.

Steven got up and said nothing, but his stomach was in turmoil.

It had been easy to forget Mr Holly while he was stuck in his house up the hill, being all hermity. But the sight of him walking calmly through the village in his uniform – and the knowledge that he would be doing that every day from now on – made Steven feel slightly panicky. He crossed the crisp grass to retrieve his skateboard, then tucked it under his arm and walked away.

'Don't be like that!' shouted Lalo.

But Steven hardly heard him.

Mr Holly was already passing the Red Lion by the time Steven reached the road. Barnstaple Road was the main – and very nearly only – road through Shipcott. Named in a simpler time when destinations were few.

Steven followed in Jonas Holly's footsteps. He didn't know what he was expecting. He didn't know why he was doing it. Part of him – a *big* part – was embarrassed by the childish notion of keeping watch on Mr Holly. A teenaged boy keeping tabs on a policeman; it was silly and it was pointless and it was unsustainable. But still, he kept pace with the tall figure up ahead, never getting closer, stopping to tie his shoelace when Mr Holly lingered to read the notices in the window of Mr Jacoby's shop, moving on again when he did.

The school was at the end of the village and Steven paused to tie his laces *again* while Mr Holly crossed the road and started back down the opposite pavement.

Now they were walking towards each other.

Steven didn't know where to look. He didn't want to have to say hello to Mr Holly but it seemed inevitable.

Steven turned his head to look into the windows of the houses he was passing. Some had nets, but many did not. Here were the dusty cacti in matching blue ceramic pots that lined the sill of Mr Peach, his PE teacher; here was the duck collection – including a plastic Donald – which Mrs Tithecott doted on and displayed proudly. Chris and Mark Tithecott had been getting into fights over those ducks ever since they'd started school – they made the twins a target just as surely as if they'd had red hair, glasses, or no-name trainers. Steven had witnessed them pleading with their mother to take the ducks out of the window on at least two occasions, but she'd been collecting them since she was a girl and was intransigent. Steven didn't think the ducks were as bad as the twins did, but had some sympathy anyway, because of the years his nan had stood in their own front window, staring like a loon, watching for her dead son to come home from the shop, making targets of them all.

Steven realized that while he'd been remembering stuff, Mr Holly had passed by on the other side without having to be acknowledged.

Result.

Still, Steven knew that now Jonas Holly was back at work in Shipcott, he would never feel easy again.

13

There was a car in the woods. It idled deep in the dapple, on a spring sea of bluebells and starry white garlic. About three years ago, Ronnie Trewell had driven it there and, in a moment of panic, set fire to it. That was before he grew up a bit and learned that stealing a car and driving it fast was only the beginning of what could be a beautiful friendship.

After watching in misery as that first car burned, Ronnie had vowed never to waste another one. From then on, he kept the cars he stole. If the bodywork was shoddy, he'd mask off, refill and re-spray. If the engine ran rough he'd take it apart and work on it until it was hard to tell whether the ignition was on or off. If the performance fell short of what the internet told him it should be, Ronnie invested in air filters and new plugs and synthetic oil. In short, he stole good cars and made them better.

And each time Jonas Holly finally called at his door to ask him to open the garage and hand over his latest illicit prize, Ronnie got a lump in his throat the size of a locking wheel nut.

He didn't blame Jonas; didn't hate him. He knew that that was the way things were. People lost stuff; eventually they wanted it back. Jonas was just the middleman.

And he was a good middleman. He seemed to understand that Ronnie was more than just a thief. He seemed to understand that he *cared*.

Once, as Ronnie stood misty-eyed, watching a powder-blue Triumph Stag (with freshly re-chromed wire wheels) driven away on a low-loader, Jonas had patted his shoulder kindly. 'This has got to stop, Ronnie,' he'd sighed – and Ronnie had thought bitterly that Jonas was finally showing his true blue police colours. Then Jonas had added, 'All this hard work going down the drain.'

He'd managed to get Ronnie on to a police-subsidized karting course, where his twin talents of mechanics and driving very fast led to him shining, instead of shaming his family.

The Stag was the last car Ronnie Trewell ever stole.

But this had been the first. This half-burned-out once-red Mazda MX5 convertible.

Ronnie had never gone back to the woods to see it, so it was left to Davey and Shane, among others, to find it and play in it. Although 'play' was not a word they would ever have used – even in their own heads.

Rally Crash was their favourite game – where one would sit behind the wheel, on a cushion stolen from Shane's mother's bedroom, and pretend to mow down the other, who was a hapless spectator at a hypothetical rally. This game involved much loud verbal gear-changing and last-minute shouts of warning from the driver, and cries of terror plus spectacular dives into the undergrowth from the victim. Then the driver would get out and pronounce the spectator dead, or the spectator would use his last breath to reach out and strangle the driver in the ferns.

Just depended how they felt.

The other game was Getaway, where both Shane and Davey robbed a bank – which was the big stump about fifty yards off – then had to dodge police snipers and gas grenades to make it to their getaway car, all the while spraying bullets from their AK-47s. The roof was burned off the Mazda so this game allowed them both to devise ever-more dangerous methods of getting into the car – the ultimate being a spectacular, testicle-threatening slide across the blistered boot.

If Davey and Shane weren't at Springer Farm, they could almost always be found deep in the woods in Ronnie Trewell's burned-out car.

Today they were bored and fractious. Things had started well. They'd robbed the bank two or three times – each time stealing the five £20 notes they'd found but not yet settled on how to spend. But after that things had gone awry when Davey had mown Shane down into a patch of nettles, for which he quite unfairly blamed Davey, given that – at the end of the day – the car *was* stationary.

They'd fought briefly over that and told each other to piss off, then sat together in the Mazda in bolshy silence.

Out of nowhere, Davey's mouth dropped open. 'I have an *awesome* game!'

Shane was on board instantly – everything forgiven – before he'd even heard the idea.

'Kidnap,' said Davey. 'Like those kids.'

'Cool! How does it work?' said Shane.

'One of us sits in the car and the other has to creep up and kidnap him.'

A slow smile spread across Shane's features. 'That *is* awesome.'

'I know,' said Davey, getting out of the driver's seat. 'I'll be the kidnapper first.'

'OK,' said Shane. 'But if I see you coming, I win.'

Davey frowned deeply at this amendment to the non-existent rules of the un-played game, but finally nodded his approval.

'OK, but don't *lie*.'

'OK,' agreed Shane, because he often did lie, so that was fair comment.

Davey ran into the woods and then carefully circled around until he was about forty yards behind the Mazda. He knelt in the ferns and found a couple of sticks.

Keeping trees between himself and his target, he moved quietly towards the car. There was a point where he had to move across an open patch of ground to get to another tree big enough to give him cover. He hurled a stick above the Mazda and was gratified to see Shane's head turn sharply away at the sound of it landing. Quickly he crept to the new tree. Only fifteen yards to go now, and Shane's head was still turned away from him, seeking any glimpse of his friend on the opposite side of the car.

Davey didn't even need the second stick. He crossed the last few yards like a cat and grabbed Shane's neck in the crook of his elbow.

'This is a kidnap,' he said harshly. 'Move and you're dead.'

'Shit,' said Shane.

Davey started to manhandle Shane out of the car.

'You're hurting!' yelled Shane.

'It's a *kidnap*. It's got to be realistic,' panted Davey.

Shane made it more realistic by struggling and trying to punch Davey in the face, while Davey hauled Shane out of the door, pushed him down into the wild garlic, pulled a length of twine from his jeans pocket and tried to tie his hands behind him.

'Owwww! Shit, Davey!' Shane wriggled free and knelt up, flushed and angry. 'You always go too far.' His mother sometimes said that about *him*, and it had a wonderfully self-righteous ring to it.

'Oh, bullshit,' said Davey dismissively. 'It's no fun if it's not real. Anyway, I win.'

'My turn,' said Shane, and they swapped places.

Davey didn't like being the victim half as much as being the kidnapper. Once Shane had disappeared, the sudden silence of the woods was unnerving and wherever he looked the back of his neck always felt exposed. It was as if the trees themselves were watching him. He became aware of his heart beating and didn't like it. He kept craning round to see where Shane was, but couldn't see him or even hear him.

Shit. If Shane was going to be better at Kidnap than he was, then they wouldn't play it again.

He scanned the woods methodically but without luck.

It was creepy, this vast silence under the green canopy. A gentle breeze whispered through the leaves and, from somewhere beyond his vision, a tree creaked and groaned as if in pain. Far above his head, he heard the mechanical drill of a woodpecker.

'Shane?' he said tentatively. 'Hey, Shane! Come out, I just noticed the time. We'd better go.' It was only five o'clock, but he could say he'd promised to weed the garden or something.

'Shane?'

Davey wriggled up into a kneeling position and looked out across the back of the car into the darkening woods. He strained his eyes and tried to hear any movement that would give his friend away – but all he could hear was his own shallow breathing and his heart beating in his ears.

'Shane, you div!'

Something grabbed him so hard from behind that it made him grunt, then yanked him sideways and over the door of the car so that he fell headfirst to the ground. A knee in his back and a mouthful of fern.

'I win!' yelled Shane, and pushed Davey's face once more into the cool leaves for good measure, before standing up, laughing.

Davey was so relieved it was only Shane that for a moment he just lay there, face down, pulling himself together again. Then he arced his fist out to the side and slammed it into Shane's knee so hard that his friend joined him on the forest floor with a shout of pain.

Davey got up and stood over him. 'You *cheat*.'

'I didn't cheat.' Shane sat up, holding his knee. 'You almost broke my leg, you *tosser*.'

Davey was about to come back at him, but suddenly the idea of falling out with Shane and having to walk home alone through the forest made him bite back his own insult.

'Sorry, mate,' he said instead, and extended his hand. Shane looked at it suspiciously, then allowed himself to be helped up.

'You OK?' said Davey, and his friend's unusual deference made Shane similarly noble.

'Yeah, it's fine,' he said.

'You want to lean on me?'

'Yeah, OK.'

Their games over for the day, Shane and Davey walked home, Shane making a meal of hobbling and leaning on Davey's shoulder once they reached the village, and Davey happy to let him show off his injury. He'd have done the same.

'Awesome game though,' said Shane as he reached his own house.

'Yeah,' said Davey. 'Awesome.'

14

They were in English class when Emily said, 'Do you want to go to the show on Saturday?'

'OK,' said Steven, then was forced to ask, 'What show?'

Emily smiled, but in a good way. 'The hunt show. At Deepwater Farm.'

Steven had never been to a horse show before. He knew they went on, of course, just as he vaguely knew farming and hunting and sheep-trialling and jam-making went on around him – all without the benefit of his active involvement.

He had no idea where Deepwater Farm was, nor any concept of what going to the show might be like, but those were trifles – and no bar to his feeling a little thrill that Emily had asked him. He was low-key about it though, because others were watching.

'OK,' he said. 'Sure.'

*

The Midmoor Hunt had cancelled its annual show out of deference to its Master's loss.

Joint Master, several disgruntled members had pointed out at a meeting where John Took was not present. Charles Stourbridge stood up for John Took, but in an arthritic kind of way, and the motion to cancel only survived by six votes.

The old Blacklands Hunt had been subsumed by the Midmoor last winter after years of decline. The rot had started years before, when it was discovered that the serial killer Arnold Avery had turned the hunt's patch of moorland into his own personal cemetery. It was an uneasy thing – galloping across the graves of murdered children – and many hunt supporters had lost their taste for it.

Later, in the wake of the hunting ban, saboteurs had stepped up their campaigns of harassment. Not all of them were incomers and professional agitators – some were local people who finally felt able to make their feelings known now that they had the law – albeit pallid – on their side. There had been clashes. Angry clashes. At Edgcott, a local sab named Frank Munk had his foot run over and crushed by a hunt follower's Land Rover, and in retaliation young David Lodge was pulled from his horse and broke his collar bone. His horse had bolted into a bog and died of exhaustion before they could get it out. Hunting stopped being fun and started being dangerous for more than the fox. Devout hunt followers were suddenly reluctant to bring their children out with them, and turn-out – and vital subscriptions – dipped alarmingly. Some members saw the writing on the wall and deserted to the bigger Dulverton West or the Exmoor Foxhounds on the basis that there was safety in numbers.

It only hastened the end for the Blacklands. As the smaller of the two beleaguered hunts, the Blacklands had come off worst. Jobs had been lost, horses sold and hounds disposed of. Sad but necessary. The Blacklands Master, John Took, had been made joint Master of the Midmoor, but it was clear to all just who the poor relations were within the new hunt.

Now – a mere six months into the uneasy alliance – many original Midmoor members blamed Took's crisis for the loss of their traditional summer show. To add insult to injury, the Exmoor Foxhounds had been indecently hasty to offer to run the show instead. After all, their secretary had reasoned, the field was booked, the jumps and tents paid for, the date publicized and the entries received.

'I mean,' she'd told Charles Stourbridge on the phone, 'the kidnapper's already taken poor Jess Took and that other boy. We shouldn't let him ruin a good day out into the bargain.'

When this fuzzy logic was relayed to them, the Midmoor members prayed for rain on Saturday, but an unusually reliable summer let them all down.

*

Saturday morning. Exactly two weeks since Jess Took had been taken.

She had not called home from a boyfriend's mobile or a London phone box. And no farmer had been surprised to find Pete Knox in his hay barn.

The two children had simply gone.

And every minute they remained gone was a minute when DI Reynolds's frustration quotient rose another notch.

It was the memory of his previous failure on Exmoor that haunted him as much as this new one unfolding. Of course, DCI Marvel had been in charge of that investigation, not him. And two children stolen from parked cars across the moor didn't compare with a rampage that had left eight people dead.

But Reynolds had a very bad feeling that it might yet.

It wasn't a hunch. Reynolds would have put his own eyes out before admitting to a hunch. Marvel had lived by his instincts, his hunches, his gut – and Reynolds had despised him with a passion worthy of opera. It was an embarrassment to base investigative decisions on whimsy and prejudice. This was the twenty-first century, for God's sake; Reynolds hadn't got two degrees – a first in Criminology and a 2:1 in Law – so he could lynch monkeys and burn witches. But now – when the searches and the lab had yielded next to nothing – DI Reynolds had a *theory* that things might get worse before they got better.

This theory was substantiated by all the cars that were going to be parked on Exmoor on a daily basis now that it was tourist season. In villages, on verges, behind pubs, in gravel lay-bys, in beauty-spot car parks, at flower shows and steam rallies and village fêtes. Most of them would be empty, of course, in the wake of the publicity about Jess Took and Pete Knox, but if simply being alive for thirty-seven years had taught DI Reynolds anything, it had taught him this:

People. Are. Stupid.

Reynolds tried never to underestimate how dumb his fellow human beings could be. How ignorant, how reckless, how cruel. Despite an avalanche of warnings, people still drank and drove, still thought trying crack just once might be fun . . . Still wouldn't bother taking their kids with them when they popped into the post office or bought a pint of milk at the corner shop.

Some people just never thought it would happen to them, even when it was happening all *around* them to people just *like* them.

Of course, thought Reynolds with a mental sniff, those were probably the same stupid people who were going into the corner shop for a lottery ticket – never considering the bleak maths that showed they were more likely to lose their child to a passing pervert than they were to win the jackpot.

No, if the kidnapper desired more victims, Reynolds was sure there'd be no great shortage of potential prey. All he could do was deploy his men as cleverly as possible in an attempt to get through what he hoped would be a weekend operation of prevention, nothing more.

At least Jonas Holly's reappearance meant he had another body on the ground, and Reynolds assigned him to the hunt show at Deepwater Farm.

*

Steven watched Em plait the horse's pale mane, and wondered why he felt so strange. A little short of breath. A little worried; a little excited; his mouth the wrong shape to say words.

Maybe he was allergic to horses.

Skip. That was the horse's name, and it stood with its eyes half closed and its lower lip loose as Em's fingers separated the creamy hairs, then started to weave them into plaits. Steven watched her hands twist this way and that, the braid growing magically between them. Her face was set with concentration. He watched her secure the plait with a needle and thread and then deftly roll it into a little knot on the horse's neck and sew it into place like a shiny gold button.

Then she started on the next one.

The silence in the stable had worried him at first. He should really be saying stuff. Entertaining stuff. Stuff that would impress her.

But after a while he was relieved. The more he watched her, the more he realized how little he knew about anything that was happening: Em, the horse, the show – *anything*. If he'd spoken, it would only have been empty noise. So he just sat there and watched, with barely a word passing between them.

Everything she did was right. The horse knew it and, even in his ignorance, Steven could see it too. She was so deft and quietly confident that all the two of *them* could do to help was to let her get on with it and not get in the way. When she clicked at Skip and touched his chest, the pony stepped backwards obligingly to let her duck under his throat. She asked Steven to pass her a little wooden box so that she could stand on it to reach the mane more easily. He placed it as carefully as he could, trying to gauge exactly how close she'd like to be – then was pleased when she stepped on to it without adjustment.

He looked into Skip's drowsy brown eye and felt they were on the same team.

Em saddled the horse with gleaming black leather that smelled of money, then led him on to the concrete yard to the pantomime echo of coconut shells.

She stripped off her mucky blue overalls to reveal dazzling white jodhpurs and sleeveless cotton shirt, like an angel appearing in a Sunday-school story.

'Do you ride?' she asked, and Steven shook his head dumbly. 'Want a go?'

He wondered what the right response would be. He didn't want to look scared, but he also didn't want to fall off.

'I'm scared I'll fall off,' he said, immediately stunned by his own stupidity.

But Em only nodded in understanding. 'Yeah. Falling off is crap.'

She put on a flared jacket with a blue velvet collar and swung into the saddle. 'You can ride home,' she said. 'Then if you fall off it won't ruin the whole day.'

When he looked up in surprise, she was showing him her little white teeth.

'Deal,' he laughed.

The black gates clicked shut behind them and they meandered through the lanes, the air buzzing with summer and her polished boot nudging his arm. Em cooed to the horse and flicked flies off his twitching skin with her whip. Or she just left the silence to settle, reflective and clear, until one of them felt like throwing a little pebble of conversation into it. The ripples seemed effortless, and the closer they came to the show, the better Steven's allergy got.

15

Charlie Peach was used to sitting and waiting in the minibus. He didn't mind it. In fact, he liked it. Charlie liked things just the way they were. He liked things not to change. When his dad put him to bed, he liked being in bed; when his dad got him up, he liked being up. So whenever he was in the minibus, he preferred not to get out.

He *would* get out, of course. Not like Robbie or Miranda. Always kicking and shouting and falling on the ground if they didn't get their way. *Making a fuss*, Mrs Johnson called it.

But Charlie never made a fuss. When the time came to get out, he would sit still while Mrs Johnson or Mr King unbuckled his harness, and let them help him from the minibus.

This minibus was new. It was much more comfy than the old one, which had ripped vinyl seats and smelled of toilets. Charlie would happily sit here all day – even though it was hot.

Robbie and Miranda had gone ahead because they always went first, so that just left him and Teddy and Beth. Teddy was the cleverest of all of them. He couldn't speak right but everyone knew he was clever. He even wrote stuff using a proper computer.

'Teddy?' said Charlie, and the boy beside him jerked his head awkwardly and pointed his shiny, spit-covered chin at Charlie.

Cocking his head to keep eye-contact, Charlie sang:

One man went to MOW
Went to mow a medal

Charlie waited for Teddy to join in, but he didn't, so he looked at Beth. He couldn't tell whether she was looking back because her eyes were so squinty, but she said 'Shut up, retard' – so he just continued quietly by himself.

One man went to MOW
Went to mow a medal

Teddy Loosemore turned his head away and looked out through the windscreen at the rows of cars reflecting the high sun in the middle of the field. They were parked a little distance from the other cars – closer to the tents and the toilets. Beth always needed to be close to the toilets.

They were late. They were always late wherever they went in the minibus. Teddy hated it but he had no control over it. He tried to look at the watch his mother had bought him for his birthday, but couldn't make his wrist turn the right way. He gripped it with his other hand and turned the watch face towards him. Almost 11am. The day was half over. The other kids didn't care, but Teddy did. When he had a day out, he wanted it to start when it did for normal people. The others probably didn't even know they were at a horse show.

In his head, Teddy sighed. In his mouth, it sounded like a weird grunt.

In a minute Mrs Johnson, whose name was Mary, and Mr King, whose name was Michael, would come back for him and Beth. The other two volunteers would stay with Robbie and Miranda. Teddy wished they would hurry up. It was hot and he wanted to see the horses. He was glad he was next off the bus. Charlie would be last, as usual, because he never made a fuss.

Poor Charlie.

Teddy knew what had happened to Charlie, although nobody had ever told him. Because he was twisted and couldn't get his words out and was usually covered in drool, people talked about private things right in front of Teddy. So he knew that the umbilical cord had got stuck around Charlie's neck when he was being born, and that was why he had the brain of a four-year-old, even though he was fourteen.

Teddy knew all kinds of things that people didn't know he knew. He heard things and remembered them. He knew that Mrs Johnson's daughter-in-law drank too much and then drove the children to school; he knew Mr King's wife had left him for a man twice his size and with half his IQ. And he knew that Beth's mother had been in prison for soliciting, although he was hazy on why being a solicitor was a crime.

Teddy also knew things he'd read in books and online – stories of heroes and inventors and soldiers and spacemen – and when he read those things he was *there* and he was free and whole, and he felt as if he were flying. In reality, he couldn't even walk. At least Charlie had that. At least Charlie could propel himself about the planet on his own two feet. Go where he pleased – even upstairs – run across a field in his bare feet if he felt like it, however damaged he was in the head.

Teddy's mother always told him how lucky he was. Lucky to be living in England instead of India, where he'd be begging in a gutter; lucky to have the internet when children in Africa didn't even have books or electric lights to read them by. Lucky to be alive.

Teddy's head jerked angrily. Sometimes it was hard to feel lucky.

Charlie sang quietly beside him. As usual. He only knew three songs. 'One Man Went to Mow', 'Ten Green Bottles' and 'Waltzing Matilda'. He didn't know all the right words and couldn't count up past ten or back down at all, which made his song choices unfortunate. Sometimes Teddy imagined that baby cord squeezing Charlie's tiny neck like a cruel python. What could Charlie have been without that cord? What songs might he have sung then? But it wasn't all bad. That fouled cord may have squeezed most of the IQ clean out of Charlie's head, but it had also squeezed out all the bad things – leaving only sunshine and smiles and a breathy, tuneful little-boy voice.

Teddy suddenly felt guilty for not singing along with Charlie.

'They're coming,' said Beth, and Teddy saw Mr King and Mrs Johnson walking back to them across the lush meadow, both wearing dark glasses that made them look like spies. He thought how amazing it would be to be a spy, and then realized that he almost was one – the way he picked up information while nobody thought he knew what they were saying. In his head he *was* a spy.

In his head he could be anything.

It made him happy, and when Charlie counted down from four men to one man – via nine men – he suddenly joined him:

. . . and his dog, Spot! Bottle of pop!

Charlie giggled. Only Teddy knew that bit, although when he sang it, it sounded like 'da, Spa! Oddey o pa!'

Went to mow a ME–DAL!

'Warm enough for you, Charlie?' Mr King took off his sunglasses and winked at Charlie, and Charlie laughed and nodded.

Mr King smiled and ruffled the boy's wispy yellow hair. 'Be back for you in a mo, OK, big man?'

'OK, Mr King.' He loved it when Mr King called him big man.

Beth and Teddy got out – Teddy in his wheelchair on the lift that Charlie liked to ride on when everyone was in a good mood – and he said goodbye and watched them cross the grass towards the tents and the horses and the flags and the fun.

*

Jonas eyed the horses from the safety of the refreshment tent. Now and then a child would amble over with a pony in tow like a saddled dog, and fumble change out of her jodhpurs for an ice cream, but mostly the horses stayed on the other side of the blue nylon rope that divided the middle of the field into three square rings – two for showing and one for jumping.

It was years since he'd been to a horse show. Not since he was a boy. He couldn't remember the name of the pony he'd borrowed from Springer Farm, but he remembered the sun beating down on his back, and the same smells of leather, hot grass and manure.

For some reason, they made him feel uneasy.

In a minute he'd have to make another circuit through the car park. The first two had been fraught with contact. Everyone wanted to say hello and shake his hand and ask how he was. Now Jonas was lingering over the dregs of his tea before venturing out into the open again.

The Exmoor foxhounds were in the showing ring. All tongues and tails, crowded around the huntsman with his red coat, white whip and gleaming britches. Children had been invited in to pet the big brown and white dogs, in a get-'em-early PR exercise for the hunt. There was even a boy in an electric wheelchair, flapping his crooked arms and looking at the sky, while a hound pissed on his wheel.

Now and then a hound would detach itself from the pack and lope across the ring after a scent. A sharp call of its name would bring it back in an instant. It had always amazed Jonas that the huntsman knew each of his forty or so dogs by name, when they all looked so similar.

'Daisy!'

'Dandy!'

'Milo!'

And the errant dog would lope back to the pack and join the patchwork mayhem.

In the nearest ring a fat grey pony put in a dirty stop and launched a tiny child over a shin-high fence. The girl's mother ducked under the nylon and hurried over. She stood the sobbing five-year-old on her feet, brushed her down, wiped her face and plonked her back on the grazing beast, with the usual instructions about heels and hands and showing him who was boss. The pigtailed tot sniffed, nodded fiercely and flapped her skinny peach legs up and down, before trotting a circle and performing a perfect action replay. The bell rang to say they'd been disqualified, and the judge in the caravan asked for a round of applause for a brave try. The mother picked up the pieces and left, leading the girl by one hand and the devious pony by the other – apparently far crosser with the former than the latter.

Astonishing, thought Jonas. People won't let their kids cycle to school, but they'll put them on half a ton of stupid muscle, then slap its arse to make it go faster.

Lucy would have loved this.

The thought came from nowhere and made his throat ache.

He put his tea down with a clatter of spoon and saucer, and headed for the car park.

The sun was already very warm but Charlie didn't mind. He turned his face towards it and closed his eyes and felt the lids heat up like little blankets.

There was a big voice from somewhere – like Mr King at sports day – saying things that Charlie couldn't quite catch, drifting in and out with the breeze. Whenever the voice stopped it was as quiet as bedtime.

He almost dozed.

There was a sharp, crunchy sound and he opened his eyes.

At first he saw nothing. Then, squinting into the sun, he saw a man between the parked cars draw back his hand with a stick in it, and hit a car window. Charlie jumped at the sound of glass breaking.

'Oh!' said Charlie. 'Oh!'

Bad man! He broke the window! Bad bad man! Nicola Park had broken a window in the school greenhouse and Mrs Johnson had been *sooooo* cross!

As Charlie watched, the man moved a few rows away, peering into cars. Then – first glancing left and right – he stopped and did the same thing again.

Charlie looked up towards the tents.

'Mr King!' he shouted. 'Mr *King!*'

The man looked up and saw him. Charlie shrank back against his seat.

The man turned and walked quickly towards the minibus. As he came closer, Charlie saw his big green gloves and strangely flattened, featureless face. The man looked like the Guy they'd made at the school last Bonfire Night – but alive and walking.

Charlie had never been so scared in his life. Worse than lights out.

'MR KING!' he squealed into his own chest as he tried to stop the man unbuckling his safety harness. 'MR KING!'

But the big voice was talking and then people were clapping too.

Charlie Peach continued to shout for someone to come and save him, but his terrified cries were quickly muffled by a strong woollen hand that smelled of hospitals.

*

Jonas was stopped half a dozen times on his way to the cars.

People meant well. He knew that. So he was polite and pleasant – and resisted the urge to tell them all to just go away and leave him alone.

A man in sunglasses and shirtsleeves shouted something he didn't catch and started jogging towards him, and even before the man reached him, something told Jonas that this was bad news . . .

16

Shut the gate. Shut the gate shutthegate shutthegateshutthegate . . .
Jonas ran in time to the words in his head. Ran for the first
time in over a year. Ran to the gate and swung it shut with a clang
that reverberated like a giant bell. A BMW X5 turning in from the
lane lurched to a halt to avoid being hit by all five bars.

'What the *shit*!' said the driver angrily, and then saw Jonas's
uniform and downgraded his protest to 'What's going on?'

'We've got a missing child,' panted Jonas, not even looking at
him – already scanning the field for Charlie Peach. He raised his
voice and said it again: 'We've got a missing child!'

The words were like a fire alarm going off. People moved to
him as if magnetized.

The gateman in a hi-vis vest was Graham Nash from the Red
Lion.

'Has anyone left?' Jonas demanded.

'A few.'

'Who?'

Nash looked defensive. 'I don't know. I'm busy getting people in. People going out aren't my job.'

'You notice anyone in particular? Strangers?'

'Shit, Jonas, I don't bloody know. I can't know everyone. The kid's probably getting an ice cream.'

Jonas knew Charlie Peach – he lived in Shipcott – and he knew that was not the case. He put Graham Nash on the road to direct traffic away from the show.

'But it's not even lunchtime,' Nash protested. 'People are going to be very pissed off if they've paid their entries and I won't let them in.'

'This gate stays shut until we find the boy,' said Jonas coldly, then he looked hopefully at his phone. Finding he was within range of a signal, he stood stock still so as not to lose it and called DI Reynolds.

Reynolds said he'd be right there and told him not to let anybody leave. Jonas didn't waste time explaining that he'd already done that – just said 'Yes' and hung up.

He and Mike King jogged back to the judges' caravan and commandeered the PA system. Through shards of feedback, Jonas asked all judges in all rings to halt their classes while they searched for Charlie Peach, then handed the microphone to the boy's carer to give a description of him.

The moment the announcement was over, the mood of the show changed as if a switch had been thrown. The urgency and purpose were palpable. Horses were dismounted and hitched to horseboxes, people left their deckchairs and put down their cups of tea and swarmed through the tents and the cars, crawling underneath, opening boots, checking the Portaloos.

Horse people, thought Jonas. Good or bad, they really get things done.

Steven heard Jonas Holly's voice on the PA system and flinched hard enough for Em to notice.

'What's up?'

'Nothing. Just made me jump, that's all.'

She smiled at him and he tried to smile back but it didn't feel right on his face. He was suddenly tense.

They listened to the announcement, sitting on the grass with Skip dozing over their heads. Another voice boomed out, describing a boy with pale hair and a Dr Who T-shirt.

'His name is Charlie,' the voice said. 'Charlie? If you can hear this, come on back to the minibus, all right, big man? I'll wait for you there.'

Steven and Em looked around them.

'He's probably getting an ice cream,' said Em.

'Mm.' Steven hoped she was right.

He sat for a minute more, inwardly twitching.

He couldn't do nothing; he stood up. 'I'm going to help look,' he told her.

Em scrambled to her feet. 'I'll come too.'

She tied Skip to a piece of twine attached to a random horsebox and draped her jacket across the mudguard. 'We won't be long,' she shrugged.

Steven watched the crowds looking in and under cars and around the tents and toilets. If the boy were there, someone else would find him. Instead, Steven led Em to the edge of the meadow, which was bounded by thick hawthorn hedges run through with old man's beard, bindweed and the occasional wild clematis.

'Do you know the kids who have gone missing?' asked Em.

'Nah.' He shrugged. 'The girl, Jess, went to our school but I didn't know her.'

'You must be the only one,' said Em wryly.

Steven shrugged and added, 'The boy wasn't from round here.'

They walked clockwise around the meadow. In most places the hedge was so thick they couldn't even see the field on the other side. Elsewhere it was thinner, but still made impassable by thorns.

The field sloped away at the far end, and the show disappeared over the close horizon. The sound of it disappeared along with the sight. Deep in the second corner, close to a single oak tree, Em noticed a break in the hedge. They couldn't get close to it because of waist-high nettles, but by walking on a little way and looking back, they could see the posts of a stile, disused and almost hidden by the surrounding foliage.

'You think he could have got through there?' said Em.

Steven examined the nettles, then shook his head. 'They'd be broken if anyone had gone through them.'

They walked on. Even though they were only a hundred yards from where people were searching desperately for the missing boy, it was quiet here. The loudest sound was the chirrup of crickets in the long grass, and the occasional thump and rustle of rabbits as they warned each other and ran away. One baby, too young to understand danger, sat in the open as they approached. They were less than ten feet away before it gave a playful binky and hopped into the hedge, making them both laugh.

The ensuing silence was such that they could hear the rain-starved grass crackle underfoot.

'Thanks for bringing back the trailer,' said Em suddenly.

Steven's stomach lurched. 'I didn't take it.'

'It doesn't matter who took it,' said Em with a shrug.

Steven stopped her with a hand on her arm. He felt a little thrill at touching her skin and took his hand back hurriedly as she turned to him.

'I promise,' he said urgently. 'I didn't take it.'

Em nodded her understanding that the distinction was important to him. 'But *you* brought it back,' she said. 'You remembered the code.' She looked at him until he broke eye-contact.

When they walked on this time, she took his hand.

A tingle ran up Steven's arm and spread across his chest, kick-starting his allergy again.

He stole a glance at her. She seemed unaffected. Their arms formed a V between them, his wiry and too long, hers bare and slim and perfect. At the point of the V, their hands tied a knot that swung easily – as if they'd been holding hands for years.

She said something and he didn't hear her, so she said it again.

'We should let that policeman know about the stile, just in case.'

Steven saw she was leading him back up the hill to the rows of cars. Even from this low angle, he could see Mr Holly towering above the roofs. Following him was one thing; initiating a conversation with him was another thing entirely.

'No,' he said, and stopped walking.

She stopped too and their hands slid apart.

'Why?'

Steven floundered. 'Just. No. Just because. He's busy. And we shouldn't walk over their . . . Over the . . . you know, crime scene and stuff.'

'Crime scene? Kids go missing all the time at shows. They always find them and everything goes on the same.' She spoke a little sharply – as if saying it would make it happen, and Steven took his uneasy cue from that.

'Yeah,' he said. 'They'll probably find him in a minute.'

But the genie was out of the bottle, and Em looked worried.

'I'm going to tell him. You coming?'

She started walking. He didn't follow her.

As Em spoke to Jonas Holly, the policeman looked across the roofs of the cars towards the corner of the field and made fleeting eye-contact with Steven.

Em returned to him. 'He said he'd check it out.'

'OK. Good.'

As they walked away, she looked at him quizzically. 'Are you in trouble with the police?'

'No. Of course not.'

'Then why are you being so weird?'

What could he say? Explaining that he alone suspected that the village policeman had murdered his wife would make him sound crazy.

And now there was another suspicion as well. A new feeling just starting to take shape in Steven's mind. Mr Holly had re-emerged, just as three children went missing. Steven didn't have strong views on the validity of coincidence, but he had learned to trust his gut, and it rarely lied to him.

He could tell Em nothing of this, of course. Trying to justify odd behaviour by revealing insanity was unlikely to impress her. He knew this instinctively, too, and was relieved that that, at least, implied *some* sort of normality.

She was still looking at him, waiting for an answer.

'Sorry,' he said finally.

She stared at him for a long moment, then turned away.

He trailed behind her to where Skip was dozing in the sunshine.

*

You don't love him.

Jonas stared at the yellow note on the wheel and still hoped it was a hoax. A joke. Maybe Charlie was an attention-seeker – or another child had put him up to it. Charlie could be hiding in a Portaloo right now, giggling at the mayhem he'd caused, Jonas thought.

He hoped.

Because if it wasn't a hoax, Jonas had an awful sinking feeling that Charlie Peach was already beyond their help.

All around the showground, people were searching. Maybe three hundred people in a single large field. If Charlie were still on the site, he'd have been found by now, surely?

If he weren't, that meant that the gate had been shut too late.

At this time of day, the priority was to get people *into* the show, not to keep tabs on those few who were leaving after early classes or drop-offs. He couldn't blame Graham Nash. The man on the gate was expected to do nothing more than make sure cars leaving didn't crash into cars coming in. He was not there to check whether they were leaving with a stolen child stuffed in the boot or hog-tied on the back seat . . .

No, that was *his* job.

Jonas wandered up the hill a little so he would have a better view of the whole site. He looked across the rows of cars and horseboxes that covered the side of the sloping field like bright scales. His eye was caught by a dot of darkness on the window of a car a few rows in. He frowned and walked over to it. As he got closer he could see that the darkness was a neat hole in the rear passenger window of a silver Renault Megane. He cupped his hands and peered through the window into the dark interior, expecting to see something worth stealing on the back seat. There was a ripped map book, a scattering of wax crayons, a little girl's cardigan. He noticed a similar hole in the opposite rear window and walked around the car to look at that too. It was not big enough to put even a child's hand through and he noticed that the Megane's doors were still locked. If someone had attempted to feed some kind of instrument through the window to pull open the locks, they'd been interrupted.

Interrupted in their quest to steal wax crayons.

Jonas looked over his shoulder and could see the minibus. He stepped away from the Megane and started to make his way back to it. As he passed a Ford Focus he saw that it, too, had a broken window – a small, neat hole surrounded by a mosaic of cracked safety glass. He peered through the two-inch hole and saw a large, tubby chocolate Labrador draped awkwardly across the rear seat. It raised its head and gave a token bark, but looked too hot to do any more.

Before he even thought about it, Jonas tried to open the door but it was locked.

Shit.

Now his prints would be on the handle. Bollocks and shit. Reynolds would be justifiably furious with him – especially after the debacle during the last case, when his prints and hair had been found at more than one scene. Even though Jonas had been there in an official capacity, Marvel had made a song and dance about it and had been gunning for him from then on. He didn't want to alienate Reynolds in the same way.

Instead he needed to glean as much information as possible that might help them to find Charlie Peach.

Jonas looked towards the minibus again; it was easily visible, maybe sixty yards away. Had the kidnapper broken this window and then had his eye caught by Charlie? Maybe his ear? Jonas bent at the knees a little to reduce his six-foot-four to more average proportions. Even from six inches lower he could see the minibus clearly.

Inside the car, the dog heaved itself to its feet and pressed its snout to the hole. A few blocks of safety glass tinkled free of the window.

Jonas heard the whoop of police sirens and walked back to the minibus to meet Reynolds.

Charlie Peach was not hiding or playing a joke. Charlie Peach had just plain vanished.

Reynolds blamed Jonas Holly. One hundred per cent. His only task had been to stop anyone leaving the show ground through the single exit with a child that was not his own – and he'd failed miserably.

The man was a jinx.

Reynolds looked again at the note stuck to the steering wheel. Even without touching it he could see a tiny fibre of greenish wool clinging to its gummed edge.

The man they were hunting had been right here, in the confines of a field that also contained a policeman who had been specifically assigned to look for him.

The more Reynolds thought about it, the worse it got.

Jonas appeared at his shoulder and Reynolds was suddenly uncomfortably aware that, at his height, Jonas probably had a bird's eye view of his plugs. He hunched away from him angrily, then bitterly slapped the roof of the minibus where Charlie Peach used to be.

'Welcome back, Holly,' he said.

Reynolds's words would sting Jonas later, but right now he ignored them and told the DI what he knew so far. Reynolds asked follow-up questions while Rice made notes. Reynolds handed Jonas a roll of police tape and told him to secure the scene, then he and Rice went to look at the other cars.

Someone fetched Jonas some metal stakes and helped him to hammer them into the firm ground around the minibus, then Jonas unwound the tape, watched by a wide-eyed audience of children in jodhpurs and ribbons.

When he'd done that, Jonas stood by the minibus and stared at the empty seats. In his mind's eye he saw Charlie Peach, left there, maybe scared, maybe just interested, as the man approached. Had he followed him on a promise of sweets or an Xbox? Had he been dragged from his harness kicking and biting? Had he shouted for help? Would he even have understood what was going on? A mental age of four, the carers had said. Jonas felt a surge of anger at whoever had stolen such a child.

You have to save the boy, Jonas.

Lucy's voice was so clear in his head that his heart leaped, and he had to stop himself turning to find her.

She wasn't there. Lucy was dead. She wasn't there.

She never was.

After the initial shock, the echo of her voice calmed him – just as it always had.

Jonas stared sightlessly at the little yellow note. 'I'll save him,' he whispered fiercely. 'I promise.'

*

Steven and Em had been allowed out soon after the police arrived, and walked the two miles home in silence broken only by the pony's metallic hoofs scraping the tarmac. Em was distracted and hadn't offered to let him ride. He hoped she was thinking about the missing boy, but he feared she was bored – or irritated by his weirdness over Jonas Holly.

At the entrance to Old Barn Farm she said, 'Bye then.'

She wasn't even going to let him back through the gates. He was crushed.

'Bye then,' he said awkwardly, then added 'Thanks,' because he meant it.

'See you at school.'

'See you at school.'

He patted Skip's warm neck and turned towards home, hearing the gates opening behind him.

'Do you . . . want to go out again some time?'

He looked back in surprise.

Em looked uncharacteristically nervous. 'Only if you want to.'

'I want to.'

'Good.' She smiled. 'Me too.'

She waved.

'Bye,' he said again, and held his hand up in return.

She pointed Skip down the driveway, and Steven walked home. At least, he assumed later that he *must* have walked home, but only because home was where he found himself when he finally stopped running in circles, laughing and shouting with joy, inside his own head.

*

There were 127 cars and horseboxes on the site, and by 6pm all but three had been searched as they left through the gate, past a yawning Graham Nash and an industrious Elizabeth Rice.

Only the minibus and the Focus and Megane that had suffered broken windows remained, with three men from the forensics lab at Portishead poring over them.

Their disgorged occupants, with assorted children and dogs, got more and more hungry, tired and fractious until finally Jonas offered to drive them all home himself, just for some peace and quiet. He took them in two shifts – first Alison Marks, the chatty owner of the Focus, along with her family, who lived in Exford. There was no conversation to be had with Barbara Moorcroft on their way to Loxhore. Her two hysterical Patterdales barked relentlessly and her three children sat in pained silence throughout the ride, apparently used to being yapped into submission.

On his way home, Jonas stopped at the highest point of the road that draped across Withypool Common. He cut the engine and listened to the silence swell around him like a balm.

He'd become so used to silence since Lucy had died that he'd forgotten how stressful noise could be. How stressful talking and people could be. The thought that he'd once talked to people every day seemed impossible to him now. And the idea that he would have to get used to it again was sobering.

He wasn't sure he could.

Jonas expelled a long, shuddering breath that he felt he might have drawn in hours ago when Charlie Peach first went missing. Everything after that point was hazy to him – a fairground blur of panic and shouting and movement and guilt.

But now – here atop the moor, with the window down and the summer evening breeze soothing his mind – he could start to think again. He drank in the stillness, even as he started to recognize its separate components: a blackbird somewhere close by, the swish of the long grass and the dry rattle of gorse; the ebb and flow of the air itself against his ear – a coded whisper in breathy Morse.

Jonas sat and allowed the moor to clear his head.

He didn't want to think about the day just gone, but the broken windows nagged him.

He was sure a couple of cars at Tarr Steps, where Pete Knox was taken, had also been vandalized. He would have to ask Reynolds about Dunkery Beacon. If windows had been broken there too, the connection with the kidnapper would be undeniable.

But it still begged the question: *why*?

The answer stayed in the shadows like a wolf skirting a campfire.

17

Three children gone in the space of a fortnight.

The *Sun* called him the Pied Piper, this man who was spiriting the children of Exmoor away, right under the noses of their guardians, and the other tabloids fell on the name with glee. Even the broadsheets picked up on it, although they sniffily referred to it as 'the case some are calling the Pied Piper', which meant they could *use* the name while somehow maintaining a dignified distance *from* it.

Either way, Reynolds found it unhelpful. The name conjured up a damning image of the police stupidly failing to spot an endless crocodile of children being danced away across the moor by a man in a jester's outfit playing a tin whistle.

The tabloids also seemed to imply that the kidnapper of three children must be an awful lot easier to catch than the kidnapper of one, and with the national media spotlight turned so brightly on the case, he was now at risk of failing far more publicly.

Reynolds could only hope that his hair would stand the strain.

He was assigned three more officers and held a press conference where he announced – teeth slightly on edge – that the *Sun* had offered a £10,000 reward for information leading to the recovery of the missing children or the identification of their abductor. When he watched it on the news, he was relieved to see that his plugs looked pretty damned good, even under the harsh TV lights.

Everyone was talking about it.

Not his hair – the reward.

*

That evening, Kate Gulliver called DI Reynolds to ask how Jonas Holly was doing.

She got Elizabeth Rice instead.

'Oh hi, this is DC Rice. DI Reynolds isn't here right now.'

'Can you ask him to call me?'

'Sure,' said Rice. 'What's it about?'

Kate prickled. She didn't know Rice, but Rice must know she was a force-approved psychologist. For all she knew, Kate could be calling to speak to Reynolds about his own personal issues. It was rude of her to ask. Bloody rude.

But Rice *was* a woman, and Kate hated to be rude to any woman in a man's world, from tea ladies up. There was always a sense that they were in this together, like sisters, and to be rude to a sister would only get one a reputation as a bitch.

So instead of telling Rice that it was confidential, she told her she was calling about Jonas Holly.

'Just wondered how he was coping being back at work, that's all.'

It wasn't all, of course. If Kate Gulliver had been confident that Jonas was equipped to be doing just fine, she'd never have called.

'OK, I think,' said Rice, sounding a little surprised. 'He seems OK.'

Kate said 'Good,' and cursed the sisterhood that meant that now she'd had an answer from Rice, she could no longer ask to speak to

Reynolds. She trusted Reynolds's judgement, whereas she didn't know Rice from a bar of soap. But sisterly manners now dictated that she had to accept the opinion of some underling, thank her, and say goodbye.

Which she did.

Rice hung up and frowned into the middle distance of the Red Lion bar. She did not share Reynolds's erudition, it was true. But she had more common sense in her little finger than any man she'd ever known, and something told her that Kate Gulliver was unusually concerned about Jonas Holly.

It wasn't intuition, it was just logical.

Jonas had been through a horrendous, life-altering experience. Rice herself had suffered nightmares for months after their last trip to Shipcott. The memory of Jonas holding the still-warm body of his dead wife at the foot of the bloodied stairs would be with her for ever. Even now – here in the bonhomie of the Red Lion bar – Elizabeth Rice shivered as she remembered the slide of warm blood against her lips as she'd tried to keep Lucy Holly alive; the smell of iron and – somehow – burning rubber; Jonas's eyes never leaving his wife's face, but growing darker and darker as his own blood drained away through the deep wounds in his stomach.

Some time later that day, she'd showered and cried as the water turned pink around her ankles. She'd had to scrub the dried blood off her knees. Only her fear of being seen as a weak woman had kept her from going to see one of the force shrinks herself.

So Gulliver's call might have been routine, but Rice's logic said it was not.

For a start, it was after 6pm. That implied that Gulliver had wanted to have a proper chat with Reynolds, not just a quick check on a former patient as part of the working day. Then Rice had noticed the irritation in Gulliver's voice when she'd answered Reynolds's phone. Fleetingly, she considered that they might have a more-than-professional relationship, but quickly discounted that. Reynolds was not a man she could imagine having sex with anyone – not even himself. So Gulliver was irritated because her enquiry was more than casual; it was important; she really wanted to *know* how Jonas Holly was doing. And that must mean she was not 100 per cent sure he'd be doing OK – even though making sure was her job.

Reynolds approached with a half of Thatchers for her, and a white wine.

Rice quickly took the decision to tell him to call Gulliver and leave it at that. If there was something wrong with Jonas Holly, Reynolds would pick it up. He already seemed to dislike Holly for some reason Rice couldn't quite fathom, but which she felt instinctively wasn't quite fair. She had no desire to feed her boss's irrational dislike of a man who was a victim and deserved only sympathy.

But if Jonas's own psychologist – the person who'd signed him off to return to work – was worried about Jonas, then Rice decided there and then that *she'd* better be worried about him too.

18

It was almost strange – how Exmoor could remain as hot and sunny as it did, with such a black cloud hanging over it. An uneasy feeling hung there with it, and the children suffered most. Those who had considered the moor their personal playground were suddenly confined to tiny back gardens. Despite the brilliant summer, parents did an unprecedented one-eighty and actively encouraged the playing of video games in darkened rooms.

There was an upturn in sightings of toddlers on old-fashioned reins, and people whose offspring were too old to fit into reins eyed the contraptions wistfully. Tourists who couldn't cancel their bookings without losing their deposits stocked up on jigsaws and Swingballs, and when they were forced by the superb weather into hiking, were seen in lay-bys and car parks across the moor giving stern briefings to unimpressed-looking youngsters about the dangers of wandering off alone.

When they did get into their cars and venture out across the hills or towards the beaches, they were likely to be stopped and questioned at police roadblocks, and asked to open their boots, so that their deckchairs and windbreaks and kites and spare toilet rolls could spill on to the road – all without revealing a single missing child.

Shops suffered too. Exmoor survived its winters and thrived on its summers, when the population swelled fifty-fold. Within a fortnight of Jess Took being taken, it felt the difference. Summer stock aimed at tourists and outdoor pursuits hardly sold, but disappeared reasonably fast anyway, as sulky kids required to trail into shops behind their mothers instead of waiting in cars retaliated with an outrageous spree of petty theft. In Dulverton twelve-year-old James Meldrum enjoyed brief popularity by brazenly walking out of Field & Stream with a brand-new fishing rod for every boy in his class, before going back the next day and stupidly getting caught stuffing an 80p bag of No.1 hooks into his pocket.

But such light relief was the exception.

Shopkeepers were grim-faced, and B&B owners sat and waited for the phone to ring. Publicans' eyes rarely left the door, even as they served halves and the occasional ploughman's lunch to locals. Prices were slashed; sales brought forward. Old Bob Moat drove his tractor all the way from Exford to Lynton and didn't have to pull over for a single caravan. It was an anecdote worth repeating – as rare as heather flowers in April.

Basically, tourists stayed away from Exmoor in droves, and chose other areas of outstanding natural beauty in which to leave their children in cars.

*

Davey and Shane still hadn't spent the money.

It was simply too much. If they'd found a fiver, they'd have blown it in a single trip to Mr Jacoby's shop. If they'd found a tenner, they'd have asked Dougie Trewell to get them some cans so they could see what getting drunk was all about.

But a hundred pounds was serious money, and although there were many false starts, it stuck to their fingers like glue.

The simple solution, of course, would have been to split the cash, but having grown accustomed to thinking of the possession of an entire hundred pounds, it was too much of a comedown now to consider spending a mere fifty.

Davey volunteered to take care of the money, but Shane was immediately suspicious. Davey was offended by his suspicion, but then baulked at allowing Shane to keep it at *his* house. They came to an arrangement: one of them would take the cash home one night, then hand it over in a corner of the school playground the next day, so that the other could take his turn at keeping it safe.

It was during one of these increasingly casual playground handovers that Mark Trumbull solved the problem for them by relieving them of the lot in a single transaction.

'Gimme your money,' he said simply, and held out his hand.

'Piss off,' said Davey, even though Mark Trumbull was a foot taller, thirty pounds heavier and had previous form as a bully. The money in his pocket made Davey feisty.

'Yeah, piss off,' said Shane, taking a step backwards.

Mark Trumbull didn't bother with any gangster threats or clever conversation. He simply punched Davey so hard in the chest that he knocked him flat and left him gasping, then rummaged in his pocket for the notes, while Shane shouted at him from a safe distance. Then he walked away.

'I'll tell Mr Peach on you!' yelled Shane, and then remembered that Mr Peach was on leave 'cos of Charlie being kidnapped, and realized that the threat was therefore even emptier than it had sounded.

Shit.

19

Steven had never had a girlfriend before, and now that he did, he wasn't quite sure what to do with her.

'Shag her, of course,' Lewis advised, when Steven revealed his dilemma. 'Absolute minimum, she owes you a blowjob.'

Steven rolled his eyes.

They were babysitting, which was what they often did on Friday nights when Chantelle Cox went to Cheeky's in Minehead with her mother and her cousin.

Lewis had started the babysitting thing and roped Steven in with promises of a well-stocked fridge and porn on the TV. In fact, the Coxes' fridge was as dull as his mother's and the porn channel was a myth, even though Lewis insisted that he'd watched it 'loads' – and tried to maintain the lie by spending at least ten minutes of their regular Friday nights prodding the remote control and complaining about signals.

Plus, they didn't even get paid. Steven had assumed that he'd get a cut of whatever Lewis earned – or at least benefit in trickledown.

But when he'd finally raised the issue during a tantrum by the baby that had lasted right through *Top Gear*, Lewis had laughed and told him, 'I don't get *paid*, idiot!'

Only then had Steven realized that the baby they were sitting for was actually half Lewis's. Once *that* penny dropped, Steven looked at little Jake with new – more wary – eyes. Steven had never had sex, and had never seen any upside to that situation until now. But the ghastly light-of-day connection between sex and babies was suddenly very real and immensely sobering. Especially as the half of the baby that belonged to Lewis always seemed to be the bottom half – and watching him gag while unwrapping a shit-filled nappy was better contraception than Durex.

So he didn't shag Em.

Instead they just hung out together. Sometimes at the bus stop with the other kids, sometimes in the woods or up on the moor, where they once saw a kite take off with a snake in its grasp, knotting itself into a frenzy.

Sometimes he helped her groom Skip, and other times she watched him rebuild his motorbike. At the stable, he handed her brushes and filled buckets. He was quite sure that Em could groom Skip a lot faster without him, but she never said so. And having her with him at Ronnie Trewell's garage was great. She never got fed up and talked about shopping; she watched him and made encouraging noises. It made him feel that he knew what he was doing, and he was surprised to find that his bike actually started to seem less like junk and more like a bike while she was around. Once she spent a whole afternoon rubbing Autosol into the pitted chrome front mudguard, until they could see themselves grinning in it.

Steven and Em held hands when they were alone, and often he thought about kissing her, although he always chickened out at the last moment – even when it looked as if she was expecting it. The idea of getting it wrong was awful. Of leaning in and missing her mouth, or hitting her mouth just as she started to say something, or of his lips being too dry or too wet. It was just too important to ruin. Every time they said goodbye, he lingered – then kicked himself for not being man enough to kiss his own girlfriend.

He thought about other things too, of course. It was only natural. But even his sexual fantasies were short-lived things because he needed so little of her to fuel them. A kiss, a touch – sometimes just an imaginary whisper was enough.

Every time he saw Em, Steven's heart skipped a beat. He knew now that he was not allergic to horses or to anything else. He knew it was love, even though he'd never felt it before. He told no one, and barely allowed himself to think it. The idea of loving her was so huge that his brain skirted the edges of it and never faced it head-on. If he confessed it – even to himself – he was afraid it might lose its magic.

Because the journey took her past Rose Cottage, Steven always walked Em home. He was disturbed by the idea of Jonas Holly watching her walk past his house, but he didn't tell her that – just that he wanted her to be safe.

'I'll be fine,' Em told him. 'I'm fit. I can run fast.'

'Still,' he shrugged, 'things happen.'

'Only to other people,' she laughed.

He hesitated, and then told her, 'Then you'll be there if someone tries to kidnap *me*.'

Her parents knew his name. Her mother offered him tea and cake. Not Spar-shop cakes, but real cake she'd made herself and which he was expected to eat off a plate with a fork. Em's father was polite but wary. He'd shake Steven's hand and ask him how he was, but when he was at home he always seemed to be lurking nearby, frowning and watchful.

Steven was slightly insulted, but couldn't blame him.

They went to Steven's house only once, for tea. His mother kept apologizing for serving white bread and Nan showed Em photos of Steven as a small boy.

In one of them he was naked.

So mostly they went to hers.

They studied together at the kitchen table, or listened to music in her room, or watched TV in her lounge, which was bigger than his whole downstairs. They patted foals on the moor; they caught the bus to Barnstaple and he helped her choose CDs or strappy tops that made his head swim.

His friends took the piss, of course.

'She's new,' said Lalo Bryant. 'She'll learn.' And they all laughed.

'If you're not having sex with her, she's not really your girlfriend,' said Dougie Trewell with absolute authority. Steven hadn't *said* they weren't having sex, but they'd all assumed as much, given he wasn't boasting about it. *They* were always boasting about having sex. Everyone was doing it, apparently. All the boys, anyway. It made him nervous that if they didn't have sex soon, Em would think he was an idiot and move on to someone who knew what he was doing.

But the killer blow came from Lewis, who sighed heavily and patted Steven's back. 'She's too good for you, mate. No offence.'

Steven wanted to punch him.

Because he knew it was true.

Em was special. His friends all knew it and even the other girls in their school could see it. Some of them were already wearing velvet ribbons instead of letting their loose hair blow into their mouths.

Steven wasn't special.

It had never bothered him before, but suddenly it was critical. It raised painful questions: Why was Em going out with him? What did she see in him? Was it a joke? Was she secretly laughing behind his back, just as his friends were laughing to his face? His chest hurt at the thought.

At night he spent ages staring at himself in the bathroom mirror, worrying at spots and wishing his ears didn't stick out.

'Mu-um! Stevie won't get out the bathroom!'

'Shut up.'

'*You* shut up.'

'*Both* of you shut up! Steven, get out of the bathroom!'

He stopped saving for a bike jacket, and bought Clearasil and a Gillette Mach 3, which he scraped across his chin and cheeks every morning to encourage stubble.

Nan came back from a trip to Barnstaple with a can of Lynx.

'How's your girlfriend?' she said bluntly. The deodorant had given her asking rights.

Dougie's pronouncement rang in Steven's ears, and he hedged, 'She's not my *girl*friend. Just a friend.'

Nan snorted and stared at him until he blushed.

'I thought so!' she said triumphantly, and marched downstairs.

He was half-happy to think his nan knew that he was now a boy who had a girlfriend, but the fact that it had been acknowledged made him fearful too; the more people who knew, the greater would be the humiliation if – when – Em fulfilled his friends' cheerful predictions and dumped him.

While he waited for that to happen, he smelled of Lynx Instinct.

20

Jonas was back on his beat.

He was out by 8am every day and by 6.30pm, when he drove back to Shipcott, he was exhausted. He was no longer used to the physical exertion of a working day, and had eaten too little for too long to have any reserves of energy.

Now he parked outside the Red Lion and looked across at the Sunset Lodge retirement home.

He should go in; he always used to.

It used to be a regular part of his beat – sitting in that sauna of a garden room with a cup of tea balanced on one knee and a custard cream going soggy in his saucer.

Reassuring the old folk.

That had worked well, hadn't it? Keeping the killer at bay armed with cheap biscuits and empty promises. But the killer had paid a visit anyway – forcing a knife against the window latch, and leaving a bloody trail of tragedy through the home before disappearing into the night. No, he didn't have the bare-faced cheek to go into

Sunset Lodge again. The Reverend Chard may be bound by his faith to forgive, but Jonas expected no such thing from anyone else.

A few houses up he saw Steven Lamb watching him from the front window of his home – one in a long line of gaily painted terraced cottages that opened straight on to the narrow slate pavement. He raised a hand in greeting, but the boy merely stepped slowly back into the dark interior.

He sighed. It would take him years to rebuild the trust he'd once taken for granted in the village.

He got out of the Land Rover and locked it, and went into the pub.

Reynolds took a sip of white Merlot and scanned Jos Reeves's lab report. Working in the Red Lion was so much more pleasant than being stuck in that glorified shoebox in the car park – especially after hours.

'The white residue on the glass from the broken windows is PVC tape—'

'Like insulation tape?' Rice emptied a third of her glass of cider and sighed in enjoyment.

Reynolds nodded. 'And the green threads are a poor-quality synthetic wool mix, dyed using Malachite green, most commonly used during manufacturing processes in China.'

'So we're looking for a Chinese electrician in cheap green mittens.'

Reynolds looked at her over his Merlot like a disapproving schoolmaster over half-moon spectacles.

'Sorry,' she said.

'Could be gloves. Could be a blanket he throws over them. A scarf he was wearing . . .' He shrugged, then continued, 'Here's the thing. The green fibres at the Pete Knox and Charlie Peach scenes were impregnated with butane while the fibres at the Jess Took scene were not.'

'Weird,' she said. 'Maybe she put up more of a struggle than he liked. Forced him to change his tactics.'

'Anything's possible.' Reynolds sighed.

It was true, thought Rice. They knew so little about anything connected with the kidnapper that right now anything *was* possible.

Jonas found Reynolds and Rice in the bar, poring over what looked like lab reports.

She smiled; he didn't.

'Hi Jonas, have a seat,' said Rice, and Reynolds shifted a little way around the table to make space for him. Jonas perched uncomfortably on a low chair.

'The cars that were vandalized at the show,' he started hesitantly. 'Nothing was reported stolen from them, right?'

'No,' said Reynolds.

'Why?' asked Rice.

But Jonas didn't really have a theory to satisfy that question. Instead he asked another.

'I think you said windows were also broken at Tarr Steps.'

'That's right.'

'Was anything stolen there?'

'Apart from Pete Knox?' said Reynolds sarcastically.

'Nothing was stolen,' Rice supplied, giving Reynolds a slightly disapproving look.

Reynolds sighed. 'We're busy trying to find three missing children here. We're not so big on petty vandalism right now.'

'Yeah, sorry. Of course,' said Jonas. 'I just thought that maybe if nothing was taken, then the windows being broken were about something else. Some kind of message, maybe. I mean, who kidnaps a child and then hangs around to break windows? It must mean *something*. Maybe.'

Rice looked at Reynolds, who shrugged and said, 'Except that there were no windows broken at the Jess Took scene.'

'Oh.' Jonas hadn't known that. It was a dent in his theory. He wondered how big that dent was.

'Have a drink, Jonas?' asked Rice, then looked him up and down. 'Or something to eat?'

'No, thanks.'

He stood up, and Reynolds turned away to pick up a map. Jonas noticed that his brown hair sprouted from his scalp in doll-like tufts. He knew the conversation was at an end. But if he walked away now, he wouldn't be able to bring it up again.

'Do we have the names of the owners of the damaged cars at Tarr Steps?' He hated saying 'we' when he knew he was barely included. It was a poorly disguised attempt to remind Reynolds that he was also a policeman.

Reynolds looked up at him again. 'Of course.'

'Maybe I could ask them a few questions.'

'Such as?'

'I'm not really sure yet.'

Reynolds pursed his lips and Jonas could see him trying to think of a reason to say no. But eventually he said, 'Of course. Do you mind, Elizabeth?' and turned back to the papers.

Rice got up and motioned Jonas to follow her, which he did, through the creaking passages and stairways of the old pub to her room.

''Scuse the mess,' she said, although the only thing he could see out of place was a pair of black lacy panties over the back of the armchair.

She took a box file from the wardrobe and put it on the bed. Jonas stood silently just inside the door while she rummaged through it, until she smiled and held up a clear A4 folder.

'Here it is. I'll write the names and contact details down for you.'

'Thanks.'

She turned her back on him and sat at the small scratched desk in the chair that didn't match – or stand square on the floor.

When Rice turned round and held out a sheet of paper for him, she asked, 'How are you, Jonas?'

'Fine, thanks,' he said automatically, as he took the paper.

'How is it being back at work? Must be strange.'

'A bit.' He shrugged.

He didn't know why Elizabeth Rice was taking an interest in his wellbeing. Didn't know if it was genuine concern or keeping tabs on him.

'Take it slowly, won't you?'

Jonas wasn't sure if she was being sarcastic, so he didn't answer her. Instead he looked at the notes she'd made. 'Thanks for these.'

'Sure. Let us know what you find.'

'Will do.'

He put a hand on the door knob; he couldn't wait to leave.

'Jonas?'

He turned in the doorway and she walked over to him.

'If you need someone to talk to, make it me.'

He looked at her, a little bemused, then mumbled 'thank you' or something like it, and left.

Rice watched the door close behind Jonas and squirmed with embarrassment.

Make it me. She had no idea where she'd come up with the B-movie dialogue. She might as well have invited Jonas Holly to come up and see her some time.

Mind you, she thought, it would be nice if *some* bastard came up to see her some time. She'd broken up with Eric six months before and missed a man in her life. Of course, she worked with men every day, but that wasn't the same thing. They were cops, and the last thing Elizabeth Rice wanted was to work with cops all day and sleep with one at night, too. And now she'd gone all Mae West on poor Jonas Holly – who'd surely suffered enough already – when all she'd meant to do was let him know she was someone he could talk to if he needed it.

Not that he was unattractive, she thought suddenly. He was too thin, of course, but he was at least symmetrical, which she'd started to value around here. He had nice eyes and short, dark hair. Plus he had that solemn, guarded air about him that she found appealing. Still, she didn't know why she'd said something so suggestive. Rice prided herself on being professional – not the *oldest* professional . . .

She sighed. What the hell. She was probably worrying needlessly. Eric had never taken a hint unless it was dropped on his head like an anvil. Men were like that. Jonas Holly probably hadn't even noticed her accidental come-on.

She turned to put the file back in the wardrobe.

Oh *bollocks!*

She'd left yesterday's knickers on the back of the chair.

21

It was Shane's idea to ask Steven for help in getting their money back.

'*Steven?*' said Davey in astonishment. 'My *brother* Steven?'

'Yeah,' said Shane. 'He's taller than Mark bloody Trumbull.'

'Only a bit. And he can't fight.'

'Maybe he wouldn't have to fight. Maybe being taller and older would be enough. Maybe all he'd have to do is ask and he'd give him our money back.'

Davey shrugged. 'He wouldn't do it. He's a right chicken.'

'Aw, c'*mon*, Davey! If I had a brother, you know I'd ask him. But I don't.' Shane only had a big sister, Davina, and she cried at chick-flicks, so there was no way they could set her on Mark Trumbull with any expectation of success.

'He's probably spent the money already,' said Davey gloomily, which, in fact, was very nearly true. Mark Trumbull had got Ronnie Trewell to buy four cans of Dry Blackthorn from Mr Jacoby's shop, then vomited near the swings. He'd done the same thing four days running until Mr Jacoby got suspicious and Ronnie stopped playing ball. That was twenty quid gone. After that, he'd bought a skateboard from Lalo Bryant for £12, and two porn mags – *Big Jugs* and *Beaver Patrol*. Thirty-eight quid's worth of ill-gotten bliss.

'Yeah, but maybe he hasn't,' wheedled Shane. 'Can't hurt to ask!'

It can always *hurt to ask.*

Shane is an idiot.

Those were the two truths that crystallized instantly in Davey's brain the very second he explained to his older brother that they needed his help in getting their stolen money back from Mark Trumbull.

Instead of just saying 'No' or simply carrying out the task as requested, Steven immediately asked questions. Awkward questions that Davey had not foreseen, but which – now they were being asked – seemed blindingly obvious.

How much money?

Where did you get it?

Davey was a pretty good liar, but even as he spun a web woven from Shane's birthday, Shane's rich uncle, and Shane's unprecedented generosity in deciding to split the windfall, he could tell it was full of holes. And Steven saw all those holes instantly, and repeated his questions with a quiet persistence until finally Davey felt the unaccustomed taste of truth on his tongue.

One hundred pounds in twenties, found in the hedge near the old witch's house halfway up the hill.

Davey rolled that truth around his mouth and found it was not so unpalatable after all. He should try it more often. He also noticed that the moment he *told* the truth, it was obvious that Steven believed it. How did he know? Davey was perplexed, but also pleased that they had got the truth out of the way and could now move on to the question of Mark Trumbull.

But Steven's idea of moving on was very different from his.

Instead of leaping immediately off his bed and into action, Steven went very quiet. So quiet that Davey could hear the alarm clock ticking on his bedside table, even though it ran on batteries.

Davey let him think. In the meantime he looked around Steven's bedroom. It was smaller than the one they used to share, and darker, too. He wondered why Steven preferred it when he could almost certainly have pulled rank and demanded the big room. This one had blue curtains and a new carpet. For years – when they were not allowed in here because of Uncle Billy being dead and all – there was an ugly brown carpet on the floor, but a while back Nan had bought this one. It was pale blue and so cheap and thin that in places Davey could make out the shape of the uneven floorboards underneath, but it was still better.

Uncle Billy's stuff was no longer here. There used to be a Lego thing gathering dust on the floor, a few tattered paperbacks on the shelf, and a photo of Billy on the bedside table. Only the photo was still there, but up high on the bookshelf, almost hidden behind some Batman action figures that Davey used to covet. Now Steven's things filled the room: socks balled up behind the door; his iPod on the bedside table; his skateboard leaning against the wardrobe.

Davey wasn't allowed to touch Steven's stuff generally, but he'd had a go on the skateboard when Steven had first bought it. He'd thought he'd be great on it – it looked pretty simple and Steven was encouraging – but in fact he'd been hopeless. Steven had persevered despite falls, but Davey had quickly lost patience with pain, and rejected the skateboard, the ramp and Steven himself as a big waste of time. As time had gone on and Steven had got better and better – and further and further beyond him – Davey's animosity towards the skateboard had grown. He'd infected Shane and a few other uncoordinated classmates with his disdain, and 'bloody skater' had become a stock insult, whether their target partook or not.

'What were you doing up the hill? You're not allowed to go to Springer Farm.'

It wasn't what Davey had been expecting and he had no pat answer for his brother, so he said he hadn't been to Springer Farm.

Once more, Steven seemed to know he was lying. 'If you go up there again I'll tell Mum on you.'

'It's only an old ruin. Nobody cares.'

'You don't understand. Going up there is dangerous.'

Davey rolled his eyes. 'OK, Granny.'

Steven grabbed his upper arm so hard and so fast that Davey yelped. 'I'm serious! Don't go up that hill, OK?'

Davey twisted away from him. 'OK! Shit. I said OK, didn't I?' He rubbed his arm. 'You going to get our money back or not?'

'Yes,' said Steven quietly.

'Really?' said Davey suspiciously.

Steven didn't answer – just got off the bed and pulled on his trainers.

Mark Trumbull was reading *Beaver Patrol* in the bus shelter when Steven Lamb walked up to him and snatched it out of his hands.

'Hey!' he said and stood up. He was two years younger than Steven, but only a bit shorter and far heavier – and he wasn't used to taking shit from anyone.

'Where's the money?' said Steven coldly.

'What money?' said Mark Trumbull. 'Gimme back my magazine.'

'I'm Davey Lamb's brother.'

'Yeah? So what?'

'So where's the money?' said Steven again.

'I haven't got his money. Gimme back my *magazine*.'

Steven looked down at the magazine for the first time and then back at Mark Trumbull.

'I know where you live,' he said, and started walking.

'No you fucking don't.'

'Number seventy-two.'

Mark Trumbull hurried after him. His right hand was in a fist, but he wasn't sure whether he should actually hit Davey's brother or not. Some vague notion he'd picked up about Steven Lamb from the collective consciousness of school made him unusually cautious. 'You gimme my magazine or I'll fuck you up, shithead.'

Steven Lamb said nothing and kept walking. Mark Trumbull looked nervously up the street. His house was only fifty yards away and his parents were home.

'Hey!' he said angrily and clutched the back of Steven's T-shirt.

Steven turned and slapped him so hard with the rolled-up copy of *Beaver Patrol* that Mark Trumbull staggered off the pavement and into the road, clutching the side of his head.

Steven kept walking.

He was at the front door.

'Where's the money?'

Mark Trumbull stood a few feet away – panic-stricken. He didn't know how to stop Steven knocking. Maybe he was bluffing. He'd never knock.

Steven knocked. 'Where's the money?' he said again.

'Shit! Here!' hissed Mark Trumbull. 'Here! Just don't . . . Just come away from the bloody door! Here!' He dug in his jeans pockets and shoved money at Steven – crumpled notes, and coins spilling on to the pavement.

'It's not all here,' said Steven.

'I spent some. That's all there is. I swear. I fucking *swear!*' Mark Trumbull was sweating and almost weeping with panic. Steven wasn't moving away from the front door of his house. Why wasn't he *moving away?*

Steven glanced at the magazine. 'What else did you buy?'

'Some cider. Another magazine. A skateboard. *Please*, mate . . .'

'Bring the skateboard to school tomorrow and give it to Davey.'

'OK! I will. I swear. Please . . .!'

The door opened and Mark Trumbull's mother stood there, looking irritated.

'Yes, what?' she said to Steven, then noticed her son. 'What's going on, Mark?'

The bully looked pleadingly at Steven Lamb, who handed Mark Trumbull's mother the curled copy of *Beaver Patrol* and walked away.

As he approached home, Davey and Shane were waiting on the doorstep.

'Did you get it?' Davey yelled from twenty houses away.

Davey asked three more times before Steven pushed past him and Shane, went inside and up to his bedroom, and shut the door.

'He didn't get it,' said Shane flatly, and followed Davey inside.

Davey slapped the bedroom door with the flat of his hand. 'Steven! Did you *get* it?'

'What's all the noise up there?' said Nan from the front room. 'I'm watching the War.'

After a brief pause, Steven opened the door. 'I got what was left of it. About sixty quid.'

Davey and Shane exchanged shrugs.

'That's better than nothing,' said Shane. 'Thanks, Steven.'

'You're *awesome*, bro!' said Davey. 'Where is it then?'

'It's not yours.'

'It *is* ours!' Davey flared immediately.

'You found it. That doesn't mean it's yours,' said Steven. 'Mark Trumbull owes you a skateboard. If he doesn't give it to you tomorrow, let me know.' He closed the door again and turned the key in the lock.

Shane was open-mouthed with injustice, while the anger rose higher and higher in Davey. He kicked the door.

'Bastard!' he yelled. 'I don't want a skateboard! I want my fucking *money*!'

He kicked the door three more times – hard enough to splinter the wood around the lock.

Davey was so angry with his brother that he never even heard Lettie coming up the stairs. Shane stepped swiftly aside, so she could get a clear run at her younger son.

22

Only two of the three people on the list Elizabeth Rice had given Jonas actually lived within the force area. The third, Stanley Cotton, lived in Cumbria. Jonas had been to the Lakes once as a boy and was mystified by the idea that anyone who lived there would bother coming all the way to Exmoor on holiday.

There wasn't much to see at David Tedworthy's immaculate Dunster home. He'd already had the broken window in his Mercedes repaired.

'Got photos if you want to see, though,' he said helpfully. He and his wife had been nothing *but* helpful since Jonas had arrived. Mary Tedworthy had made him have a cup of tea and a rock-hard home-baked scone before he'd even been allowed to view the car. He'd nibbled at the scone slowly, and managed to slip the last few bites to an ancient and smelly Golden Retriever that had been drooling on his trouser leg since he'd sat down. Then the gleaming three-month-old Merc had been ready and waiting for him, still dripping from a wash – as if he were a prospective purchaser, not a policeman.

He looked through the digital photos on their state-of-the-art Apple computer. They showed a single smallish hole in the rear passenger window.

'Were these taken at the scene?' he asked.

'No – when we got home. For the insurance.'

Jonas nodded at the pictures. Through the windows he could see only that the car was neat and clean. There didn't appear to be any marks or fingerprints on the surrounding glass, but it was hard to be sure from photos. The lab would have found any prints anyway.

'Did you notice anything at all out of the ordinary that day?'

'No,' said Mr Tedworthy. 'We only wish we had. That poor boy.'

Mrs Tedworthy nodded in agreement. 'Our granddaughter's the same age.' She handed Jonas a photo of the ugliest child he had ever seen.

'Chloe,' she said, as if it mattered – or improved things.

'Lovely,' he managed.

'If anything happened to her, well—' She glanced at her husband and he put a reassuring hand on hers, as if he'd taken care of things so that they'd never have to suffer something so awful, so she should stop worrying her pretty little head about it.

You're wrong, thought Jonas sadly. No child was ever completely safe. To imagine that it was possible was a delusion. Lucy had wanted children, but Jonas had known better. Not that it gave him any satisfaction to have been proven right once again. Lucy just hadn't understood how dangerous the world could be.

And never would now.

It was small comfort, but it was something.

He stood up to go.

'There was one thing, though,' said Mrs Tedworthy. 'It struck us both as strange, didn't it?' she said, looking at her husband, who nodded.

'What was that?' said Jonas, suddenly alert.

'Well, I had some embroidery supplies on the parcel shelf. Quite a lot, and they're not cheap, you know. Right there in plain sight. And yet . . . they didn't steal them.'

Jonas waited for a beat, in case she was joking.

'Isn't that strange, Mr Holly?' she insisted.

'Well,' he said. 'Maybe the kidnapper wasn't the needlework type.'

*

Tamzin Skinner sat on the metal steps of her mobile home, showing off her dirty toenails in pink flip-flops.

'So though I've got insurance, it's not worth claiming. They really screw you, these insurance companies, don't they?'

'They certainly do,' Jonas said as he peered into the hole punched in the rear window of her rustbucket 1987 Nissan Sunny. Even though the hole was only the size of a ping-pong ball, Jonas guessed that the cost of repairing it would probably be more than the car was worth. Which was virtually nothing.

Skinner – a stick-thin forty-year-old with the dusty complexion and lip wrinkles of a lifelong smoker – was the only one of the three people on the list who had a police record. Low-level drugs and one caution for soliciting.

'Not worth fixing then, is it?' She shrugged, leaning further back than was necessary to get a tobacco pouch from the front pocket of her cut-off jeans – and treating Jonas to a view of her belly ring and very nearly her Brazilian.

'Probably not,' he agreed.

She snorted 'Typical' and rolled a fag.

'Did you see anything or anyone strange or noteworthy around the car park that day, Miss Skinner?'

She sucked smoke deep into her lungs and held it there while she shook her head. 'I already told the police everything I know,' she said with smoke curling out of her nose and mouth. 'Saw nothing, heard nothing, noticed nothing. Nothing like *that*, anyway. You know.'

Jonas nodded. He had nothing else to ask, but given that he was unlikely to be able to go to Cumbria to interview Stanley Cotton or to see his car, he was reluctant to leave Tamzin Skinner's meagre home with nothing to show for his day's work.

There was a long silence between them, which became a little uncomfortable when it was plain that his visit should really be at an end. Mrs Tedworthy would have offered him another scone; Tamzin Skinner leaned backwards on her elbows and stuck out her tits.

Jonas turned away and did another circuit of the car. He seriously doubted that it was insured. She'd probably just said that to throw him off track. Certainly the tax was out of date by two months.

'You need tax,' he said – but not with any real intent to do anything about it.

She dropped her chest a little and said, 'Yeah?' as if it were a surprise.

He got back to the hole in the window and bent to look at it again.

'You married?' she said, out of the blue.

'Yes,' he told her.

'All the good ones are.'

'So they say,' he said neutrally.

He didn't want to look up and catch her eye, in case this conversation got awkward. Instead he pretended to be intensely interested in the hole with its surround of crazed glass, looking at it from every angle.

As he did, he saw something he hadn't noticed before.

Halfway in and halfway out of the window – trapped by the broken glass – was a black hair about two inches long. Instantly he thought of Reynolds and his tufts, but this was darker than Reynolds's hair.

He looked around at Tamzin Skinner, who was a bottle blonde, and whose parting was brown, not black.

A seed of excitement sprouted in Jonas's belly. If this hair belonged to the kidnapper then they could have DNA within the week; mass testing across the moor; an arrest within the month. Maybe Jess and Pete and Charlie would still be alive in a month. Maybe they could be saved. Was that possible? The bumping of his heart was a response to the injection of pure hope – a sensation he hadn't known for years. Literally years.

'There's a hair here,' he said, and turned to point it out to the woman. She got up and came over with a little sway of the hips, and stood too close to him – her arm rubbing his as she peered at the hair.

She nodded. 'That'll be Jack's.'

'Who's Jack?' he said, feeling his hope teetering on the brink.

'My dog.'

'You have a dog,' he said. Less a question than a statement.

'Sure,' she said. 'Lurcher.'

'Oh,' said Jonas, looking around. 'Where is it, then?'

'At the pub,' she said. And then, when Jonas looked at her for more, she added defensively, 'With my boyfriend.'

'Oh,' said Jonas again. He plucked the hair from the window and dropped it, wishing it were something heavy that he could throw hard into the scrub behind the caravan, to satisfy his disappointment. No hair from the kidnapper. No DNA and no arrest, and no found and rescued children.

Nothing.

He'd been so sure that the broken windows meant *something*.

But it was just a hair from a dog.

A dog.

It hit Jonas like something physical.

Dogs in the cars.

'Did you have your dog with you that day at Tarr Steps?'

'Yeah, we take Jack pretty much everywhere. If we leave him here he chews shit up.'

'Was he in the car when the window was broken?'

'Yeah. Why?'

'Excuse me a minute.' Jonas pulled his phone from his pocket and walked slightly away from the woman.

He asked David Tedworthy the same question.

They'd walked Gus down to Tarr Steps and back, then left him in the car while they did an hour-long hike. 'He's old and wobbly, you see. He can't do long walks any more. He's happier in the car.'

He called Directory Inquiries and had them connect him to Barbara Moorcroft. He asked whether she'd left her dogs in the car at any point while at the show.

'Yes,' she said, and Jonas could hear faint yapping in the background. 'Just while I got the kids settled with the picnic and things. Then I went back and got them. That's when I noticed the windows had been broken. Then the whole thing kicked off with the missing boy and I just grabbed the dogs and went back to make sure the kids were OK before seeing you near the cars. But by then you'd already seen it.'

Jonas hung up, his head spinning with new hope that made the old hope seem small and tawdry.

'Is that important?' said Skinner.

Jonas didn't answer her. He barely heard her question. He mumbled something about having to go, and something else about getting new tax, and got back into the Land Rover.

At Tarr Steps Tamzin Skinner had left her dog in her car, and so had David Tedworthy. Both cars vandalized at the show had had dogs left in them. And here was the clincher: Barbara Moorcroft had left *two* dogs in the car – and there had been holes punched through *two* windows of her Renault Megane.

One for each dog.

With unsteady hands, he called Stanley Cotton. He mis-dialled three times and then, when he finally got it right, the phone rang endlessly and Jonas almost groaned with frustration in expectation of an answer machine. Instead a man finally answered impatiently. Jonas explained briefly who he was.

'I spoke to the police already. They kept me there half the day. It wasn't even a big hole. Big hole in my bloody pocket though.'

'Did you have a dog in the car when the window was broken, Mr Cotton?'

'Jesus! What kind of waste of time is this? Aren't you supposed to be finding that little boy who was taken?'

'*Did* you?' said Jonas forcefully.

'Yes. What of it?'

Jonas hung up, feeling dizzy. It was all about the dogs. He didn't know *why*, or what the hell it meant, or how it was connected to the disappearance of three children, but he was sure that was why the kidnapper had made holes in the car windows.

And Dunkery Beacon, where Jess Took was taken? Reynolds had told him no windows had been broken there. *That* was the piece of the puzzle that didn't fit.

Jonas frowned at his own hands trembling on the steering wheel until the answer hit him with blinding ease.

The only dogs at Dunkery Beacon that early in the day would have been connected to the hunt – taken there to work.

No dogs left in cars. No windows broken.

He'd cracked it.

He wasn't quite sure *what* he'd cracked, but Jonas felt instinctively that this brought him closer to keeping his promise to Lucy to save Charlie Peach.

23

DI Reynolds didn't think Jonas Holly had cracked it at all.
'Dogs?' he said, with a lemon-sucking face.

'Maybe,' said Jonas, not so sure himself now.

He was confused by Reynolds. He had seemed such a reasonable, friendly man when he'd been here before, but Jonas was starting to understand that in the company of DCI Marvel, Josef Stalin might have appeared similarly blessed with social graces, so he was having to re-evaluate Reynolds from the ground up.

'I think that maybe he breaks the windows because the dogs are left in hot cars.'

Reynolds grunted, his arms crossed on his chest, and leaned on the door of the unmarked Peugeot.

'I don't know, Jonas,' said Rice doubtfully. 'Why would he bother doing that if he's there to kidnap a child? If he's that concerned, why not take the dogs instead? Or as well? Or just smash the whole window and let them out to run about?'

'I don't know. All I know is that when I saw that dog in the car at the show, even *my* first instinct was to pull open the door and get it some air.'

'But breaking the windows only increases his chances of being caught,' Reynolds pointed out. 'There must be more to it than that. And what about Dunkery Beacon?'

'No dogs there,' said Jonas. 'Only the hounds and maybe a few terriers, but they would all have been working. None would have been left in cars or horseboxes.'

Reynolds made another sour mouth. 'Even if it's true – even if the kidnapper has a sideline in . . . dog paramedics . . . how does that help us catch him?'

'I don't know,' admitted Jonas. 'But it's *something*, isn't it?'

'At least it means he cares,' said Rice.

'Cares about *dogs*,' said Reynolds. He was a cat person himself.

'Caring is caring,' she retorted. 'If he has empathy then it shows he's not a total psychopath.'

'Myra Hindley had a poodle,' said Reynolds. 'Look, if he cared about those children he wouldn't have taken them from their parents at all.'

Jonas shrugged. 'You mean the parents who weren't doing such a great job of looking after them in the first place?'

Reynolds and Rice both stared at him.

'I'm just saying,' said Jonas, showing his palms defensively, 'maybe it's not only about *him* and *his* desires. Maybe all he sees is kids left alone in cars and he thinks he could do a better job of protecting them. That's what the notes imply, isn't it?'

'You just want to believe that they're still alive,' said Reynolds.

'Yes, I do,' Jonas shot back.

'Me too,' said Rice quietly.

'So where's he keeping them?' demanded Reynolds. 'Tell me that, if you know so much about him.'

Jones spread his arms in a hopeless gesture. 'I don't know. I suppose somewhere isolated. Somewhere on the moor—'

'Somewhere like all the places a hundred people and a helicopter spent three days searching?'

Jonas chewed his lip by way of an answer. Reynolds sighed and said more gently, 'Look, we'd all love to think that Jess and Pete and Charlie are all alive and happy and being well cared for, but we have to face facts, and that's not likely to be the case.'

Jonas felt defeated. 'I'm just trying to think about things from his point of view.'

'That's fine,' said Reynolds briskly. 'Let's just try to keep it realistic.'

He pulled open the passenger door.

'Good thinking though, Jonas,' Rice said, and got behind the wheel.

Jonas watched them drive away.

'You were a bit hard on him, weren't you?' said Rice, not taking her eyes off the road.

Reynolds looked at her in surprise. 'I thought I was very tolerant, considering.'

'Considering what?'

'Considering all that rubbish about dogs.'

'I thought it was interesting.'

'Hmm.'

'What does that mean?'

'Nothing.'

She looked at him. 'What does *hmm* mean?'

He shrugged and she clicked at him and stared at the road.

'Look,' he said at last, 'I spoke to Kate Gulliver about Holly.'

'Oh yes?'

'She wanted to know how he was.'

Rice nodded and pretended she hadn't known that. 'What did you tell her?'

'That he seems OK to me. Doesn't he to you?'

'I suppose so. Is she worried about him?'

'I don't think so,' he said. 'But when she heard what we were working on, she did say that she thought he had issues with children.'

'Issues with children? What does that mean?'

Reynolds wasn't sure because he hadn't asked – so he told Rice that Gulliver wasn't sure. 'Just said she thought he had unresolved issues about children.'

'But what does that *mean*?' said Rice in exasperation.

'Look, I don't want to go into this too deeply. Obviously it's confidential stuff. All I'm saying is that Holly's been through a tough time, and he may not be the most objective or reliable person to have on this case or *any* case. I think we should treat anything he comes up with with a certain degree of caution.'

*

This is better. Much better. One was good and served a purpose, but it weren't enough. Now it's like I'm back in the swing of things. I missed the work, see? I missed the work; the routine; I missed the *love*. Now it's starting to feel like I'm doing something useful again.

Three is good.

Four would be better.

24

The bus bumped into a pothole, and Ken Beard nearly wet his pants. He squeezed down hard and gritted his teeth.

That was close.

Cancer. Cancer. Cancer. Cancer. Ken felt sweat break out on his temples as the word pulsed in his head.

He had a lump.

Down there.

He hadn't felt it – hadn't had the guts to do that. The *balls*, if you will. But he knew the lump was there, somewhere, swelling in his prostate or jostling his bladder. At night he got up three or four times to pass a stinging trickle. By day he went before and immediately after starting the school run, but there were still times – like right now – when the need to pee became desperate. The nearest public convenience was at Tarr Steps, and that was two miles away and not on his route. The children would be late home and he might be reported to the school board.

Ken looked in his mirror. There were only two children left on the bus – Kylie Martin and Maisie Cook, both from Withypool. They were about eight, he guessed. They sat facing each other across the aisle, swinging their bare legs and sandals, and giggling about God knew what. They were nice kids. Most of them were, he'd found – contrary to popular myth.

As he looked at the girls, the bus hit another rut, almost making him groan with the need to pee. His bladder was going to burst, he knew it – whatever experience had taught him about straining and waiting over the toilet bowl in the small hours.

He had to go. He couldn't hold on any more.

As soon as he thought it, Ken steered the bus into a shallow layby at the top of a hill and stopped.

In the mirror, Maisie and Kylie looked up at him questioningly.

'You girls wait here, OK? Don't get off the bus. I just need to check something out.'

''K,' said Maisie.

'Promise me you won't get off the bus, all right?'

'Promise,' said Kylie.

'Promise, Mr Beard,' said Maisie.

'Good girls.'

Ken hurried down the steps, crossed the narrow strip of tarmac and set off down the hill towards a stand of gorse. The going was steep and uneven and his bladder almost let go twice more before he made it to the cover.

Ken Beard unzipped, then stood with his back to the road and enjoyed one of the most glorious views in Britain as he tried to pee.

Nothing.

His bladder felt like a beach ball and his penis tingled with anticipation, but it wasn't happening. Now that it had permission to piss up a storm, his urinary tract had stalled like Middle Eastern peace talks.

The pain. The humiliation. The embarrassment. The edges of Ken's own personal Exmoor blurred as tears sprung to his eyes. When had something as simple as pissing become so traumatic? Every time he couldn't go, he imagined a doctor's finger up his arse, probing his prostate. Probably with a crowd of medical students watching.

Nightmare.

He couldn't mess about here; he didn't have the time. He grimaced and squeezed the base of his penis – *willing* the urine to come forth, and not caring if it hurt.

He had to get back to the bus.

But he couldn't until he'd *peed*, for God's sake! Was it too much to *ask*? Ken glanced over his shoulder. He could just see the cream roof of his bus. He trusted the girls would stay put. They were good girls. Not like his Karen, who'd gone off the rails at sixteen and moved into a squat with a boyfriend who wore eye make-up. But you couldn't be too careful, with those other children being taken. It wouldn't happen to *him*, of course, but maybe he should have peed somewhere that actually had a view of Kylie and Maisie, just for peace of mind. Of course, that would have meant *them* having a view of *him*, too – and that would hardly have helped him relax enough to pass water.

They'd be fine. They were together. It was a bright summer afternoon and he was only fifty yards away.

He heard another car approach. A diesel, by the sound of the engine.

Come *on*!

A few more drops.

Above him, the car slowed and stopped. He looked up the hill but he couldn't see it. The engine idled noisily.

Why? Ken frowned. He was sure he'd pulled over far enough for another car to pass. Maybe it was someone who'd stopped to see if the bus had broken down. People did things like that out here on the moor. Isolation brought out the best in people.

Most people.

Ken hoped it wasn't someone who would report him for leaving the children alone while he took a piss. He reckoned cancer was a good enough excuse, but once it was voiced aloud and was out there in the ether, he'd have to go to the doctor and listen to him confirm that he had only months to live. Maybe weeks.

The distraction of his own mortality worked. A halting flow, and Ken started to feel the blessed relief in his bladder. It was going to be OK. He was going to make it. Maybe it wasn't even cancer. Maybe he'd live to see Karen with an accountant, and a baby of her own—

Maisie screamed, high and reedy.

Or was it Kylie?

Ken Beard wasn't sure, but he was suddenly scrambling back up the hill to the road, stones giving way beneath his Hush Puppies, knees hitting rocks, hands grasping clumps of brittle grass and thorny gorse.

Another short shriek.

'*WHO'S THERE?!*' he shouted. Or maybe that was just in his head, along with the terrible sound of panting and fear that made his brain feel as full to bursting as his bladder had recently been.

Were they just messing about? He'd read them the bloody riot act if they were. But they were good girls who'd never given him any trouble. He could see the maroon frames of the bus windows emerge, the dark glass, the struts, the cream lower paint, the neat lettering EXMOOR COACHES – CONTRACT OR HIRE.

The clatter of the diesel engine rose and Ken missed his footing and fell flat on his face. He got up to a sharp pain in his right knee but kept going.

He staggered up to the road, half on his hands and knees.

It was empty apart from the bus and the unmistakeable smell of diesel fumes. He hobbled to the steps and hauled himself up on the handrails.

The girls were gone.

Or hiding! Please God they were hiding! He limped down the aisle, looking madly from side to side at the seats, at the floor, even at the overhead luggage racks.

'Maisie! Kylie!'

This couldn't be happening. Not to *him*. The cancer was nothing compared to this hollow horror in his heart. He *wished* he had cancer instead of two missing children. Cancer would be a blessing.

He ran up and down outside the bus, looking underneath, then shouted the girls' names furiously from the top of the steps.

'It's not funny!' he yelled. 'You get back here! It's not funny! I'll leave you! I'll bloody well *leave* you and you can walk home and tell your mothers why you're late! You get back here *right now!*' His voice cracked.

He limped up and down the aisle compulsively. He could have missed them. They might be sitting very still, or curled into balls on the back seat, winding him up. He was close to crying, he was so scared. He had to call Karen and tell her he loved her, *whatever* she did, and to please come back home and everything would be OK, just like it was when she was little. Please, please, please come back. *Please.*

Frank Tithecott pulled his Royal Mail van over behind the school bus and got out. There was a curious thumping from inside the bus, and it rocked ever so slightly from side to side.

The postman climbed the steps cautiously, and was met by the disturbing sight of Ken Beard lurching down the aisle towards him, babbling about two children and a diesel car, and with his limp penis bobbing from side to side through his open slacks.

Frank took charge. He got Ken Beard to zip up and sit down, then called the police to tell them that it seemed two children had gone missing from the school bus.

That the driver was mazed.

And that there was a square yellow note on the steering wheel that read: *You don't love them.*

*

The postman who'd stopped behind the school bus had told Reynolds that Ken Beard had been exposing himself at the scene. What he'd actually said was, 'Come at me pretty as you please, bawling and babbling and with his dongle out.' So Reynolds had quizzed the driver until he cried so hard he was no longer coherent, whereupon the local doctor was called to give him a sedative, and his nephew – a small-town solicitor who was there at short notice to safeguard his Uncle Ken's legal rights – hurriedly removed himself from the case and called a proper criminal lawyer from Bristol.

Reynolds would have loved it if having your dongle out was conclusive evidence of serial kidnap, but life just wasn't that simple. As it was, he was not even suspicious enough of Ken Beard to hold him in custody overnight.

The Bristol lawyer was turned back on the M5 and still charged the family £285.

A mobile incident room arrived from HQ – although this one was less grotty than the one they'd been assigned two winters back. Graham Nash allowed them to put it in the Red Lion car park, which was handy.

Reynolds now had twelve officers assigned specifically to the case, and could call on another dozen or so from the Exmoor team, in the form of men volunteering their days off, or beat officers like Holly and PC Walters, who could be seconded from regular duties as and when they were needed.

With most of Exmoor's manpower concentrated on the abductions, other crimes on the moor took a back seat. Theft from garden sheds soared – doubling over the next two weeks from four to eight, and prompting one police-control-room officer to sigh without irony, 'It's all gone Chicago out there.'

Despite all the hustle and bustle and the new men and the new incident room and the new publicity and the new thermal-imaging search and the new Google maps Reynolds kept sticking on the whiteboard, in the hunt for five missing children there were no new leads.

25

Kate Gulliver knew she'd done the wrong thing.

Even if it all turned out all right – which it surely would – nothing could change that.

Her conscience had wrestled with her instincts ever since she'd rubber-stamped Jonas Holly and cleared him for going back to work. While other clients were infinitely more troublesome by day, it was Jonas Holly who invaded her night-time thoughts and kept her from sleep.

A dozen times, lying in bed, she'd resolved to call him for a chat, and then failed to do so the next morning. And every day she put it off, she felt her initial knee-jerk decision swelling like a trick flower dropped in water, until she couldn't sleep, couldn't eat, couldn't *think* about anything other than Jonas Holly and that strange cold fear that had left her so weak that she'd sidestepped her own ethics.

Finally she called him.

The ring tone sounded old-fashioned. She'd never been to

Exmoor but her imagination was not a bad facsimile of the reality of the little stone cottage where Jonas lived.

He picked up on the fifth ring and she found herself unprepared, even though she'd been thinking about what to say for weeks.

'Hello Jonas, it's Kate.'

There was a silence, so she added, 'Gulliver.'

A tentative 'Hello.'

'How are you?'

'Fine,' he said.

'Good. That's good. I just wanted to know . . . I just wondered how you've been. Back at work.'

There was another long pause. Christ! It was like pulling teeth!

'Fine, thanks.'

His voice was flat. Kate wished she'd just got into her car and gone to see him; she was getting nothing from this. Worse than that, she felt that she was on the back foot. Instead of feeling like the professional – cool, calm and in control – she felt as if she was scrabbling for a foothold on the conversation, jostling for firm ground. She wished she hadn't called, but it was too late now. She just needed to get this over with.

'I'd like to see you for a follow-up session, Jonas.'

There. No beating about the bush. The moment the words were out of her mouth, Kate started to feel better. Braver.

'Why?'

'It's standard practice,' she said, although that wasn't strictly true. 'Just to help smooth the transition back into work. We don't like to leave people high and dry.'

'I'm not . . . high and dry,' he said.

'I'm glad, Jonas,' she soothed. 'But I wouldn't be doing my job if I didn't see you again. Shall we say next Thursday?'

This was *much* better. Now she had her pen poised over her diary, Kate felt she had the upper hand once more. This was how things were supposed to be. He'd agree to next Thursday and she'd write it in her diary with the gold Waterman fountain pen her father had given her upon her graduation from Cambridge. Then, next Thursday, Jonas Holly would come to her office and she could work on him some more. Be *sure*, this time. And if she *wasn't* sure, she would then have the power to remove him from the duty roster once more, and her initial, panicky mistake would seem smaller and smaller every step of the way. Once that pen touched down, it was a done deal.

'I'm busy next Thursday,' he said. 'I'm busy right now. And I'm fine.'

Damn.

'This is important, Jonas.' The panic inside her gave a little edge to her voice.

He must have heard it. There was an interminable silence during which Kate Gulliver had to literally bite her lip to keep from begging.

'Do I have to?' he said flatly.

Never in her life had she been so close to a barefaced lie.

'No,' she said tightly. 'Once I've signed off on a client, they are not obliged to undergo further therapy unless circumstances change.'

'Then I'd rather not.'

'Very well,' she said like a humourless headmistress.

'Thank you anyway,' said Jonas, who didn't sound as if he meant it.

'Of course,' she said. 'Please remember I am here whenever you need me. Any time at all, OK?'

'OK.'

She hung up and saw that she had dug a blue-ink hole right through next Thursday with the golden nib of her graduation pen.

As he put it back in its cradle, Jonas noticed that the phone was covered in blood.

Because his hand was covered in blood.

His arm didn't sting until he noticed the two long shallow slits running down it, from bicep to wrist. The blood was all over the flagstones of the hallway, so he crooked his elbow and walked back into the kitchen, where the sink looked like a Francis Bacon. The fruit knife lay where he must have left it on the draining board. Blood droplets had hit the floor and splattered there like little red sunshines.

Jonas rinsed his arm under the cold tap.

He wrapped it in a tea towel and fell asleep on the couch.

*

Reynolds puzzled over the notes.

You don't love her for Jess Took; *You don't love him* for Peter Knox; *You don't love them* for Maisie and Kylie.

He sat at the Formica desk in the mobile unit, with the door open to try to create a breeze that would dry the sweat on the back of his neck. Through the doorway he could see an obelisk of yellow-brown moorland dotted with gorse and heather and topped with a slice of Wedgwood sky.

'Do you think the notes were written at the scenes?' he asked.

'Hmm?' said Rice. She was looking at the computer screen. Reynolds had checked the history and *someone* had already visited Match.com. He wasn't necessarily blaming Rice, but it did make him wonder what boxes her perfect man would have to tick. He'd bet none of them said 'Balding' and thanked God he'd taken action.

'I said, do you think the notes were written at the scenes?'

'Why?'

'Because they're tailored to the children abducted. *You don't love her. Him. Them.* Either he took the time to write them at the scenes, or he chose his victims beforehand and had the notes prepared.'

Rice pouted in thought and then nodded. 'Yes,' she said. 'I agree.'

'Thank you,' he told her with a sarcastic eyebrow.

'But taking Kylie and Maisie off the bus was pretty random,' mused Rice. 'He can't have planned that. Maybe he just carries notes around with him and leaves whichever one suits the situation.'

Reynolds frowned and made a noise with his tongue that drove her nuts. *Tu-tu-tu.* Then he shook his head. 'I don't think that sounds right. It seems a bit *organized.*'

'He's only scribbling a note, not icing it on a birthday cake.'

'Regardless,' said Reynolds, 'we should consider both scenarios. If he writes them at the scene, or has them prepared for any eventuality, that's one thing. But if he wrote them in anticipation of abducting particular children, then that's another thing entirely. It means he chose those children. Maybe watched them.'

Rice nodded. 'We've already asked the parents about anyone who might have been hanging around before the abductions. Nobody remembers anything.'

'That doesn't mean he wasn't there,' shrugged Reynolds. 'My point is, if he *did* watch them, then maybe he watched them for a reason. Maybe the children *were* being abused or neglected. Maybe he felt they really *weren't* loved. It could be a link.'

'And it's a link they'd hardly reveal.'

'Exactly.' Reynolds nodded. 'Would you mind having a little dig, Elizabeth?'

Of course she didn't mind. How could she? He was the inspector and she was the sergeant.

26

L ucy Holly had been buried without him.
Her body had been retained for more than a month for
forensic examination as part of the investigation into the murders
in Shipcott that winter, but Jonas had still been in hospital by the
time it was finally released for interment. Her parents had arranged
and paid for the funeral, but had been kind enough to have her
buried in Shipcott, even though they lived in Surrey. They had
always liked Jonas, and he had no other family of his own. When
he eventually got home and realized what had been done in his
absence, he was overwhelmed with gratitude. They still called him
now and then – Lucy's mother encouraging and practical, and her
father quietly useless but no less kind.

Six months after the burial, the undertaker had called Jonas
to let him know that the grave had 'settled' and that a headstone
could now be erected in the little churchyard of St Mary's, where
his parents were also buried. For weeks after the call, Jonas had
nightmares – and sometimes horrific daytime visions – of what

the 'settling' of the grave really meant: that the flesh that had been Lucy had decomposed and liquefied and was now leaking from the crushed coffin into the Exmoor sod.

He'd thought of a thousand words to be carved on her stone, but in his shattered state the poetic always ran away from him and into maudlin doggerel, and so finally he'd kept it simple:

LUCY JANE HOLLY
Born April 21, 1982
Died January 29, 2011
Missed Every Day

The undertaker had provided an ugly stainless-steel jar with holes in the lid for flowers, which Jones never used and generally hid behind the headstone. Instead he'd installed two bird feeders – one filled with nyjer seeds and the other with peanuts – which attracted the blue tits and goldfinches to Lucy's grave for most of the year. In the winter he'd hung a coconut shell filled with fat, and had often seen a robin there too.

From Lucy's grave, it was fewer than twenty paces to the church door where they'd stood for their wedding photos.

Till death do us part.

Today Jonas had brought new peanuts.

But as soon as he got to the wooden gate of the churchyard, he saw there was someone already at Lucy's grave.

Jonas immediately took his hand off the heavy iron handle and stayed within the shadow of the stone-built arbour.

People *did* leave flowers on her grave. Not often, but often enough to show that she'd made an impression on the village in the few short years she'd lived here with him. Probably once a month he'd come here to find the ugly jar gainfully employed by wilting poppies or a spray of heather and cow parsley. He knew that Mrs Paddon from next door left daffodils in spring and roses in the autumn, and he was pretty sure Alan Marsh sometimes left flowers on Lucy's grave, because they were the same as the ones he left on the nearby graves of his wife and son.

From his slightly obscured viewpoint, it was only when the figure stood up that Jonas recognized Steven Lamb.

The paperboy picked his school bag out of the summer daisies, slung it over his shoulder and walked towards the gate.

Jonas slid quietly behind one side of the arbour and listened to Steven lift the heavy iron latch, then drop it behind him with a little squeak and a clunk. He passed within three feet of Jonas and never knew he was there.

Jonas went over to Lucy's grave. The nasty jar was back in its place, but there were no new flowers. Strange. Jonas replenished the nut feeder, then moved the jar to behind the headstone once more.

As he did, something shifted within it with a dull metallic sound. Imagining a stone, Jonas unscrewed the lid.

Inside was £62.30 in three twenties and change.

＊

The parents formed a support group. Find Exmoor's Children, they called themselves – although the papers quickly dubbed them the Piper Parents, which stuck, of course. Even Marcie Meyrick had had to come into line on that one.

John Took was the spokesman, naturally, and they met once a week in each other's homes to have a good cry.

At least, that's how Rice saw it.

DC Paul Berry was the family liaison officer. Rice had been one herself in a previous incarnation, and could see he was hopelessly overwhelmed. As a beneficiary of the relaxation of force height restrictions, the over-keen, rosy-cheeked Berry looked like a child who'd found a police uniform in a dressing-up box, and

John Took could look straight over his head, which made it even easier to ignore him. Sometimes the families told him when they were meeting and sometimes they didn't. When they did, they expected him to make the tea.

Reynolds had gone to the first meeting at John Took's, hoping that having all the parents in the same place at the same time might throw up the kind of case-busting coincidence so routinely seen in television cop shows. A common handyman; a sudden recognition of old college mates; a memory of all having been witness to a pivotal moment at a local hog-roast.

But nothing.

Once they had all spent an uncomfortable half-hour sipping tea while John Took and David Peach tried to establish a Skype connection to Jeff and Denise Knox in Swindon, the only consensus seemed to be that the broadband on Exmoor was an embarrassment.

Nobody had had anything useful to offer the investigation, and Reynolds had sat and tried not to look at his watch until nine o'clock, when they'd all got up. The men had shaken hands purposefully while the women exchanged stilted hugs and nose-bumping air-kisses, like old foes on a red carpet.

After that, Reynolds didn't go again.

This Friday they were in Withypool in Maisie Cook's home.

Maisie Cook's parents had expressed their grief by not tidying up, even for guests, and Rice had to move an armful of newspapers and dirty washing before she could sit down.

John Took had brought his laptop and opened it to welcome the Knoxes, but the Cooks had just looked blank when he asked about broadband, so he hadn't bothered trying to connect. The laptop sat there throughout with revolving screensavers showing Took with various women, horses and dogs, instead of the Knoxes. Rice imagined Jeff and Denise, shoulder to shoulder in Swindon, staring at their PC and wondering when they'd be included; finally trailing miserably to bed when it became apparent that they'd lost their son, *and* any meaningful support from the only people who really understood what they were going through.

Over the next two hours, Rice assessed the parents. John Took was loudest, David Peach most reasonable, Kylie's mother Jenny the quickest to tears. Took's ex, Barbara, was the most efficient – making the tea when it was plain Mrs Cook wasn't about to – and Took's girlfriend, Rachel, the most cloying.

None of them looked like the kind of people who would abuse their children, but she knew that that was no guarantee. Child abuse was the most egalitarian of crimes. Her discreet inquiries with Social Services had yielded nothing, and with nothing else to go on, Rice mentally sorted the Piper Parents into order for future interview, based on nothing more than gut feeling.

John Took was top of the list, just because she didn't like him, but Jeff Knox was second, even though she did. The way his wife had turned on him in the car park at Tarr Steps was either very unfair or rooted in some history. History of *what*, she had no idea. After that came Mr Cook, because there were several Steven Seagal DVDs on his shelf, which Rice considered tantamount to calling your dog Rambo on the psycho scale.

She readily admitted to herself that her methods were neither scientific, nor likely to yield fruit. But she'd been asked to dig, and dig she would. It didn't really matter where she started – what counted was what she might find.

Staying on topic was tough for the Piper Parents when they'd run out of helpful things to say in the first ten minutes of the very first FEC meeting. As usual, it degenerated into a maudlin memorial of the missing children, crossed with a non-debate about bringing back hanging. Her list completed, Rice raised her head now and then to say something temperate or technical, but she had nothing new to tell them. That she was allowed to tell, that is.

For the moment, the secrecy over the green fibres and the white plastic tape outweighed even the parents' need to know.

Rice let out a sigh of relief when it was all over. She was usually pretty lax about what she considered overtime, but she always made a meticulous note of the FEC meetings, during which she could feel her life draining away like sand in an hourglass.

Way to spend a Friday night, Lizzie, she thought to herself as she swung the Peugeot around in a neat loop at the end of the road and headed back towards Shipcott.

She thought she might have a drink in the bar before going upstairs in the Red Lion, then quickly discounted the idea. Reynolds would be sure to come and join her and want to talk shop. And she'd long since lost faith in finding anyone else to chat to who wanted to talk about anything but cricket, the price of milk, or the upcoming North Devon Show.

She drove down the hill into Shipcott, past Jonas Holly's house. A light was on downstairs.

Rice stood on the brake, thought for less than two seconds, then reversed back up the hill and parked the car in front of Jonas's police Land Rover.

Kate Gulliver was concerned about him, wasn't she? She was just making sure he was OK.

Wasn't she?

A security light guided her up the uneven slate path to the front door. She knocked, then got an uncomfortable flashback: slithering on the ice, watching the back of Reynolds's snow-covered jacket as he pushed open the door.

The horror inside.

Rice shivered.

Jonas Holly opened the door and looked at her as if he didn't quite recognize her.

That wasn't flattering.

'Hi, Jonas,' she said brightly anyway.

His eyes cleared. 'Oh,' he said. 'Hello.'

'I was just passing and wondered if you fancied a drink.'

'No, thanks,' he said so fast that for a second she thought he'd said 'Yes, please.'

'Oh.' She felt deflated and stupid – and then slightly angry at his lack of fake manners. He didn't soften the blow by saying anything else or inviting her in, and her slight anger grew into a defiant decision to have a drink with Jonas Holly, whether he liked it or not.

'We don't have to go out. I could just come in for a cuppa.'

This was tougher for him to reject – she could see that – although he still didn't look keen.

'Don't make me beg, Jonas!'

'Sorry,' he said, and held the door open.

They bypassed the living room and went straight into the kitchen. The table was cluttered – keys, paperwork, unopened mail – but the rest of the room was reasonably tidy. She'd expected the mayhem of a bachelor.

He put the kettle on, then said, 'I think we have some wine.'

'God yes, please. I've just come from the bloody Piper Parents' meeting. I need booze.'

He clinked about behind some cooking oil and then opened a bottle of red. Good. Reynolds was a white-wine drinker. She cleared a space at the kitchen table and took a seat.

Jonas poured himself a glass too, but didn't join her at the table or raise his glass in answer to her salute, just leaned against a counter.

There was a long silence as she sipped her wine, which was rough and Spanish. He just held his, looking into the glass.

'Nice,' she said. 'Thanks.'

He nodded. The clock ticked. He wasn't going to say anything. She'd have to start.

'This case is driving us nuts.'

He nodded slowly. 'It's a tough one,' he said. '*You don't love him.*'

'What does that *mean*?' Rice was relieved that Jonas had finally allowed himself to become engaged in conversation – even if it *was* shoptalk.

He shrugged. 'I guess it means something to *him*.'

'The kidnapper?'

'Yes.'

'But what?' said Rice, and took another sip. Encouraging Jonas to fill the gap.

'I think . . .' he started and then stopped. She nodded at him, letting him know she was ready to listen. He put his glass down and put his hands in the pockets of his jeans, then took them out again. Nervous.

'I mean, I can understand in one way.'

'Understand what?'

'His anger.'

Rice hid her surprise and sipped her wine while giving another supportive nod.

Jonas continued without further prodding. 'People. You know.'

She thought that was all she was going to get, but then he sighed and went on.

'They put their shopping in the boot, the satnavs under the seats. They hide their stereos in the glovebox. Then they leave their children on display like old umbrellas. I mean – their fucking *children*!'

She blinked in surprise. Jonas picked up his glass and took a mouthful of wine.

'Sorry,' he said.

'Not at all. I know what you mean.'

She was surprised to find that she actually did. Jonas was right, wasn't he? If people's Christmas presents had been pinched off the back seat instead of their children, she would have shaken her head and asked them what the hell else they had expected. She was pleased he'd trusted her enough to speak his mind. Plus, Jonas looked good when he got fired up like that. When he got *passionate*. The slightly distant expression he wore most of the time was replaced by a dark intensity. And he'd looked at her properly for the first time. She emptied her glass and felt the warmth of the wine relaxing her and making her feel that they had something in common, although she wasn't quite sure yet what it was.

'Shall we go in the other room?' she said impulsively, then stood up and picked up the bottle before he could demur.

The front room was cold, despite the summer. It had the feel of a closed-up place. When Jonas turned on the light, she noticed the TV wasn't even plugged in. This time *he* sat down while she stood. She replenished her glass and put the bottle on the mantelpiece beside a photo of Lucy Holly doing the garden. It seemed rude not to say anything about it.

'She was very beautiful.'

Jonas nodded briefly but said nothing. She'd expected him to agree and expand. His unusual response made Rice feel self-conscious. It was all she could do to stop herself babbling – asking how he was coping alone, whether he'd thought of anyone new, all the clichéd crap.

To hide her discomfort she picked up a slim gold letter knife with an engraving of Weston pier on the handle, and studied it as if it held great interest for her.

He sat on the couch, elbows on his knees, glass held loosely, and watched her as she turned the little fake dagger over in her hands. She was conscious of his eyes on her and felt her stomach fluttering. So silly! Part of it was the wine – she knew. But part of it wasn't. Absently, she ran a neatly clipped nail across the engraved hilt of the knife, and tiny brown flecks flaked from the shiny surface.

She wondered what he'd be like in bed. She doubted he'd had sex since his wife's death. That would be exciting. Maybe moving, too. It was a very long time since Elizabeth Rice had had sex that was exciting and she wasn't sure she'd *ever* been moved by it.

The idea and the wine made her bold. What did she have to lose? What did *either* of them have to lose?

She looked up to ask Jonas Holly if he'd like to take the bottle and the conversation upstairs.

It was only then that Rice realized that he wasn't staring at her at all, but at the letter knife in her hand. He had a curious expression on his face – as if he'd woken suddenly, and in a strange place.

'You OK?' she said.

He got up and nodded and put down his wine before saying 'Yes' like a really bad liar.

Rice sighed and put the knife and her half-glass of wine back on the mantel.

She'd be driving tonight, after all.

27

Mark Trumbull had given Davey the skateboard he'd bought from Lalo Bryant. It was a Renner Blood Tattoo, which Davey had denounced as 'crap'.

'I'll have it if you don't want it,' said Shane, and having poured such scorn on it, Davey had been forced to surrender the deck.

Now Shane rode it down the street to the playing field in a series of erratic little skids and wobbling rolls, as Davey eyed him with a mixture of contempt and envy. 'Have a go,' said Shane. 'It's not that hard.' Davey shook his head. He had Steven's skateboard under his arm, but held on to it.

They reached the field at the edge of the village. The last house in the row had been boarded up for ages with a For Sale sign, and its side windows stared blindly across the gradually sloping field where the home team never seemed to have the advantage. Shane picked up his board and they set off across the yellowing grass.

Chantelle Cox was pushing her baby on a rusty swing, her hair scraped and parted to within an inch of its life and fastened on top of her head with the precision of an SAS kitbag.

'Got a fag?' Davey asked her.

'No,' she said, even though she was tipping a fresh one out of a soft pack.

He didn't care. He didn't smoke. It just sounded good.

They walked on past the skate ramp to the far edge of the field, where a narrow stream defined the border between the village and the steep yellow moor behind it. The lack of recent rain had left the stream sluggish and shallow.

Davey leaned out and dropped Steven's skateboard into the water. It entered with a smacky little splash, sank below the surface and was carried only half a dozen yards before it nose-dived gently into the mud at the bottom. He was disappointed. He'd imagined the board being tossed and turned on white-water rapids all the way to Tiverton. Still, beggars can't be choosers – as his mum had said when he'd asked for an Xbox for his birthday and got a second-hand PlayStation 2 with a wobbly lead that meant he could never save his high score.

'What do you think he'll do?' asked Shane.

'Don't give a shit *what* he does. Serves him right.'

'He's going to kick your arse.'

'I'd like to see him try,' said Davey. Although really he'd rather *not* see Steven try. Steven's grip on his arm had been unexpectedly strong, and he guessed he couldn't outrun him either.

They trudged back across the grass to the ramp, where Shane dropped the deck that had briefly belonged to Davey, and started to push himself tentatively up one side of the half-pipe. Almost immediately the board skidded away from him and he fell heavily on to his elbow. He clutched it and groaned.

'Shit bollocks shit and bollocks!'

'Thought you said it wasn't hard?'

'Shut up.'

Seeing Shane fail on the board made Davey feel better disposed towards him, and he helped him to his feet, hoping that was the end of it. But Shane simply retrieved the board and tried again.

Davey sighed and went to sit on a swing to watch Shane. He hadn't been on the swings for years. The last time, his feet hadn't even reached the ground. Now the toes of his trainers dragged through the dust as he pushed himself gently to and fro.

The toddler in the baby swing beside him kept looking at him and saying something he didn't understand.

'He likes you,' said Chantelle Cox.

'Yeah?' Davey didn't care for babies, but hearing that this one liked him still made him feel good.

'His name's Jake,' she offered, although he hadn't asked.

Jake reached out a chubby hand towards him and pitched forward in the rubber-coated cradle.

'Hold on, mate,' Davey advised, and took the child's hand and replaced it on the chain. Jake laughed and Davey couldn't help smiling back.

There was a rattle and a thump and a yelp of pain and Davey turned to see Shane lying face up, back arched, rubbing his backside.

'Nice one!' he called.

'Piss off,' Shane groaned back.

'Only place to play now,' said Chantelle, waving her cigarette vaguely at the field behind Davey.

'Why?' He didn't understand.

''Cos of the kidnapper, of course! Got to stay near people and places, see? Can't go off on the moor or anything now.'

'We do,' said Davey with a shrug. 'We go everywhere.'

'Well, you be careful,' she said, 'or he'll have you too.'

'Nah, there's two of us. We'd kick his butt.'

'Took those two girls off the bus, didn't he?'

'Two *girls*,' Davey pointed out.

'I'm just saying, that's all.'

He only grunted a reply. Chantelle Cox was OK, but she was only as old as Steven and she was acting like she was his mother or something.

Chantelle hauled Jake out of the swing, which was his cue to turn from a happy, chuckling toddler into a screaming red ball of fury. Davey actually winced at the volume, but Chantelle didn't seem to notice, even though it was happening right next to her face as she bundled the baby into his pushchair.

She straightened up. 'Going now,' she said.

'Right then.'

She shook another cigarette out of the pack and lit it. She took a long drag, then impulsively handed it to a surprised Davey.

'Bye then,' she said.

'See ya,' he said. 'Thanks.'

He didn't even know how to hold it. He touched it to his lips and was surprised to feel the little core of heat at the filter tip. He sucked tentatively and blew the smoke out of his mouth without inhaling. It tasted rubbish. Still, it was a lit cigarette and it made him feel ten years older. He swung lazily, puffing the smoke out of his mouth almost before it had got in there.

He could still hear the baby wailing as Chantelle Cox disappeared. He thought about the kidnapper stealing Jake and having to put up with that terrible noise. If he was the kidnapper he'd bring him back in a heartbeat. Chantelle Cox sometimes probably *wished* Jake would be kidnapped when he was making that noise.

The notion hit him like lightning.

'*Hey!*' he said. He threw the cigarette into the dust at his feet, hopped off the swing and hurried over to the ramp.

'What?' said Shane, stumbling off the deck and pretending he'd meant to. He turned to Davey, who was wide-eyed with his own sudden genius.

'*What?*' said Shane again – more excited this time.

'I know where we can get all the money we'll ever need.'

'Bloody brilliant!' said Shane. 'Where?'

'The reward money, idiot! Ten thousand pounds for finding those kids!'

Shane's mouth dropped open in excitement, then snapped shut again in a reality check. His rolling eyes said this plan was too speculative, even for him. He picked his deck up. 'But *everyone's* looking for them. How are *we* gonna find them?'

'*We* catch the *kidnapper!*'

'How?' said Shane.

Davey could hardly bear to tell. His idea was so simple and yet so outrageous that he didn't want to say it out loud. He kept running through it in his head in case he had missed anything. He didn't want Shane poking a big hole in his plan the moment he told him. But at the same time, he was *bursting* to tell his friend.

'*How* can we catch him?' Shane asked insistently.

Davey grinned and mimed an angler reeling in a catch.

'Like a fish.'

28

The moment Davey had told him the truth about where they'd found the money, Steven had known who it belonged to.

Strictly speaking, he supposed it belonged to *him*.

But really it still belonged to Lucy Holly.

She had given it to him the night she'd died. With the split on her lip still fresh and her eyes still red from crying, she'd fetched a tin from the back of the cupboard and taken out a wodge of bound notes. She'd handed them to him as if she would never need money again.

Then she'd hugged him goodbye.

As he'd walked home in the blizzard he'd thrown the money into the wind. No doubt the rest of it – around £500, he'd guessed – was still in the hedges and fields close to the joined cottages of Mr Holly and Mrs Paddon.

Steven had never once thought of going back to retrieve it – even when he'd wanted the motorbike – and the thought of Mark Trumbull spending it now on cider and *Beaver Patrol* had made him shake with anger.

Maybe he should have explained these things to Davey. But how could he open *that* can of worms? So instead Steven had lain on his bed and listened to his mother lay into Davey for breaking the door and saying 'Fuck' in the house. He'd felt bad about it, but he'd had no option.

So when Steven came home from school and found his skateboard was missing, there was no doubt in his mind who had taken it.

'DAVEY!'

He banged through his brother's bedroom door. Davey wasn't there, so Steven searched the room. It was in its usual chaotic state, and looked no worse after he'd spent fifteen minutes turning it upside down and inside out, but at least he was sure his skateboard was not there.

He searched the back garden, making threats inside his head to kill Davey if he had left it out to be warped by dew or rain. Inside the coal bunker, behind the bins, under the wigwams of beans that he and Uncle Jude planted each spring. He even took a careful garden fork to the compost heap, just in case Davey had buried it there among the dirt and weeds and potato peelings. He'd kill him if he had. The skateboard had Bones Swiss bearings and had cost him £95 – and he only earned twelve quid a week.

Nothing.

'Little *shit!*' he shouted, and didn't even say sorry to Mr Randall when his head popped up over the garden fence.

Steven ran back through the house, yelling for his brother.

'What's wrong?' shouted his mother from upstairs. 'He's at Shane's house!'

Steven knew *that* wasn't true.

He slammed the front door behind him.

Davey saw Steven coming at the exact same moment that Shane managed to perform his first turn at the lip of the ramp without falling.

'Yes!' shouted Shane, with his fists in the air, and promptly fell off.

'Shit!' said Davey and jumped off the swing before it had stopped, giving himself a running start across the football field. Just as he'd suspected, Steven was faster. And worse than that, Steven was *angry*. Angrier than Davey had ever seen him. Shane shouted something from behind him, but he didn't know what. Davey had never been scared of Steven, but all that changed in an instant. For the first time in his short life, Davey experienced complete and utter regret. He'd thought he was being so clever. He'd thought he was getting Steven back *but good*. Now he realized that all he had been doing was signing his own death warrant, and fear speeded him so much that for a brief moment he actually thought he might outrun his brother.

He raced away from the village and towards the stile at the far edge of the field, arms pumping, knees flashing, but twenty yards off, he knew he'd never make it. He threw a desperate look over his shoulder and yelped at how close Steven was.

He stopped and turned – hands out defensively.

'I'm sorry!' he yelled. 'Don't hit me!'

Steven ran right through him, knocking him backwards straight off his feet, and landing on top of him with a force that made Davey howl.

'*Where is it?! Where is it, you little shit?*' He drew back his clenched fist.

Davey covered his face with raised arms. 'Don't hurt me, Stevie! I'm sorry! Please don't hurt me!'

Steven hesitated, straddling his brother's chest.

'Where *is* it?' he yelled again.

'In the river!' shouted a panicky Shane from beside them. 'It's in the river!'

'Fuck!' Steven got to his feet, dragging Davey up with him by the front of his T-shirt and one skinny arm. 'Show me,' he said, and started to haul his brother towards the stream at the edge of the field.

'I don't know, Stevie . . .'

Steven half pushed, half dragged Davey to the top of the steep, bramble-strewn bank. 'Show me!' he demanded again.

They followed the stream – Davey stumbling and twisting in Steven's grip, trying not to cry.

'There,' he pointed.

Through the shallow water, Steven saw the tail of his skateboard sticking out of the mud and was seized with new fury.

'Go get it!' he told Davey, and shoved him hard down the bank. Davey tumbled through the thorns and the prickles and skidded into the water with a solid splash.

'Shit,' said Shane.

Davey scrambled to his feet, crying now, spluttering and choking as his sobs sucked water close to his lungs. 'Bastard!'

'Just get it,' Steven demanded coldly.

Davey felt about with his hands and feet in the mud. Hitching with sobs and choked by tears, he staggered about and fell over half a dozen times, and finally stood up with the skateboard in his hands. He held it up to Steven like a sacrificial baby. 'Here!' he shouted. 'I *hate* you!'

'I hate you too, you spoiled little shit!'

Steven spat at Davey's upturned face. The gob missed, but even as he did it, Steven felt ashamed. He wiped his mouth and walked away.

Davey hurled the ruined deck at his back. It nearly hit Shane. 'I wish you were *dead*! I wish you'd *died*. I hate you, you big fucking *pig*!'

Steven said nothing and didn't look back.

29

I'm just pissing people off, thought Rice. Not just any old people either – she was pissing off the Piper Parents. It was embarrassing.

As agreed with Reynolds, she'd probed John Took and his ex-wife for information about their relationship with their daughter, while she sipped tea on the sofa. Took had suddenly realized what Rice was getting at and blown a fuse.

'It's just routine, Mr Took,' she soothed. 'We're asking everybody the same questions.'

'Why start with me?'

'I'm going in order,' she lied swiftly.

'Fine,' he said, pulling his phone from his pocket. 'Let me tell the others they can expect you.'

He dialled a number, while Barbara Took watched them in concern.

'Look, Mr Took,' said Rice, trying to sound professional instead of simply annoyed with him, 'this is an official line of inquiry. I would hope you'd be happy to help if it meant shedding any light on what might have happened to Jess.'

'No *bloody* signal,' muttered Took, and started walking around the room with his phone above his head.

'Miss Rice,' said Barbara Took. 'I absolutely understand why you're asking these questions, but I can also understand why my h— Why John is so upset by it. Can't *you*? I mean, you're treating us like suspects, when he knows and I know that we both love Jess very much and would never harm her. It's insulting.'

'It *is*,' shouted Took from the fireplace. '*Bloody* insulting.'

'I'm not saying either of you harmed her, Mrs Took, I'm just saying that if somebody else *thought* she was being harmed or neglected, then that might be a motive. And a motive would really help us at this stage.'

'John, do stop waving that phone around and sit down.'

To Rice's surprise, John Took did just that. Barbara topped up his tea and offered her a refill too. She'd been trained to accept tea whenever possible in this kind of situation – it established a rapport.

Once they were all sipping from the delicate china, everything seemed better. More civilized. The windows were open, and from somewhere, Rice could hear Rachel say 'Oh hell!' and a young man's voice answer, 'That's what happens if you don't keep your leg on!'

Took made a noise of extreme irritation and muttered, 'Fucking leg on. I'm paying eighty quid an hour for that pony-club shit.'

Barbara sighed and put down her cup. 'John, I think we're agreed that this line of questioning is pointless.'

'Too bloody right.'

'But it's just as clear that Miss Rice needs to ask these questions as part of the investigation.'

Took was grumpily silent.

'So let her ask them and we'll answer them, and then Miss Rice can go off and ask them of somebody else. Really, John, as the leader of the FEC, I think it's up to you to set an example to the other parents. They look to you for things like that.'

Took put his cup down noisily on the coffee table and glared at the carpet. Then finally grunted, 'Fine.'

'Good,' said Barbara. '*We* both know that you and I have never abused or neglected Jess, and I dare say Miss Rice knows that's true, too?'

Rice nodded eagerly, because it wouldn't make any difference to the questions she would ask.

'So let's not waste her time.'

Barbara patted Took's knee and, briefly, he put a hand over hers.

Ten minutes later, Rice left with all her questions answered exactly the way she thought they would be, and with the feeling that what had seemed like a good idea at the time was actually going to be a time-consuming, alienating dead end.

30

The Suzuki had really taken shape.

Now, whenever Steven opened the garage door, he got a little thrill to see his bike upright and with the wheels on. The contents of the boxes had lessened to the point where every time he worked on the bike, there was a tiny feeling that *this* might be the time he'd finish. But the final bits in the box were like the blue sky on a jigsaw – frustratingly slow, and keeping him from completing the whole.

Still, the experience was an end in itself. Sitting under the cold fluorescent strip lights with Em, their voices echoing just a little, the sound of metal tools on the cement floor, the warm silk of the visiting greyhound, and the puckering tang of the Super-Sours that Em bought in quarters from Mr Jacoby's shop.

Best of all, Em seemed to have supreme confidence that he knew what he was doing, and it actually made Steven attempt things he might otherwise have left to Ronnie.

Dismantling and cleaning the carburettor was one of those things. He'd been putting it off for a while, afraid of messing it up.

But because of Em's faith in him, Steven finally announced that it had to be done, and on Thursday night they took their usual places – he on an upturned bucket and she on a plastic milk crate.

Steven soon found that the carburettor was like so much in life: looked difficult; was easy.

With the Haynes manual open on the floor at his feet, and Em passing him bits and making helpful comments ('I'll find it . . . I also thought it was upside-down . . . That looks brilliant . . .'), he cleaned the jets, inserted the needle and dropped the float and filter into place, then methodically screwed it all back together with a happy flourish, and grinned at Em.

'Finished!'

'Woo-hoo!' she laughed, and threw her arms around him. 'Well done, Stevie,' she said into his shoulder.

Steven entirely lost his breath. He sat on his bucket, twisted sideways, with his arms held out away from her like stiff wings.

'Don't,' he said shakily. 'I'm all oily.'

'Don't care,' she mumbled into his neck, and he shivered.

So he put his arms around her, which was *so different* from holding her hand. Under her cotton T-shirt he could feel the warm skin sliding across the bones of her spine and ribcage, and the thin straps of her bra.

His first.

'You're shaking,' she said, looking up into his face. 'Are you cold?'

'Yes,' he croaked, although he thought he might burst into flames.

He looked at her lips, and she kissed him.

Just like that.

It was perfect. Every single little thing about it was perfect. She tasted of Super-Sours and smelled like fresh hay and Persil and motor oil. Or maybe that was him. He didn't care. He *didn't care*. It was all too perfect to care about anything else.

Looked difficult; was easy.

They parted, then sat up on the bucket and the crate and just looked at each other and smiled.

'I love you.' The words burst out of him like champagne.

'I love you too.' She didn't even hesitate, and Steven felt a surge through his veins that made his whole body tingle.

By silent agreement, they got up and packed away. They barely spoke, apart from the mundane 'Where does this go?' and 'Should we leave this out for Ronnie?' But the air in the garage had changed. It was warmer, and charged with some kind of magnetism that meant that whenever he looked at her, she was looking at him too, and a strange sort of physics that dictated that when their eyes met, their lips smiled – as if they held an independent memory of the contact they had shared.

In the fading light, they walked up the hill, hands intertwined with new frisson. They didn't talk about the kiss, but only because they didn't have to; they didn't talk about anything else, because only the kiss was important.

Steven didn't even notice Rose Cottage pass them.

At the black iron gates they kissed again. This time he started it, and by the time she finished it, it was dark.

'I'd better go,' she said.

'OK,' he said, and kissed her again.

'I'd better go,' she said.

'Me too,' he said.

She kissed him.

'It's late,' she said. 'I've got to go.'

They separated everywhere except their pinky fingers.

'Your T-shirt has dirty handmarks all over it,' he said.

'OK,' she said. 'Bye then.' But she didn't let go.

'Bye then,' he agreed.

'I'm going now,' she warned.

'Go,' he said. 'See if I care.'

She slowly stuck out her tongue, then squeezed his little finger.
'Aren't you going to kiss me goodnight?'

Steven might have thought of a dozen clever, funny answers. But it spoke well for his future happiness that he simply did what she asked.

As the gates slid shut behind Em, Steven looked at his watch. It was gone 11pm and his mother would kill him.

It seemed a very small price to pay.

He walked through the moonless summer night feeling . . . *chosen*. Em loved him. She *loved* him. Him with the sticky-out ears. Him with no moves and no money. *Him!* She loved *him*. He played their kisses over and over and over in his mind – the thrill of touching her lips with his; her breath in his mouth, her lashes on his cheek. Nothing had ever felt like this. Nothing, nothing, *nothing* was like this – or ever could be.

With a sense of wonder, Steven Lamb felt one part of his life end and another part begin. This was the part where he loved a girl and she loved him back – and he felt instinctively that nothing that had gone before would ever seem quite as important as it once had.

An enormous feeling of goodwill swept through him. The skateboard meant nothing. He would apologize to Davey and explain about the money. Maybe even give him some cash. Maybe. For the first time in his life, Steven felt so much like a grown-up that he knew he could lose a battle without losing face. It was a good feeling.

Without the moon, the Milky Way seemed closer – touchable – like stars stuck on a blue velvet ceiling. He smiled up at Orion, and reached a single finger out into the universe to darken the mighty Mars. Em loved him and he could do anything.

Anything.

'Hello, Steven.'

Steven's heart jerked in his chest.

He dropped his arm and looked around.

It took him a couple of turns. Then, in the blackness a few yards down the hill, he saw the vague form of Jonas Holly sitting on the stone steps that led from his garden gate into the lane.

'What are you doing?' The fright made him blunt.

'Waiting for you,' said Jonas Holly.

Steven's neck prickled like a dog's. He didn't want to ask why. Not here in the darkness between the towering hedges that made the lane feel like a funnel.

During the silence, Mr Holly just sat there, forearms on his knees, hands clasped loosely in front of him. Steven wondered how long he'd been there. Wondered whether he'd watched him and Em walk up the hill. He didn't like that idea.

'I wanted to ask you something.'

Again, Steven gave him no encouragement.

'Why did you put the money on Lucy's grave?'

The question took Steven by surprise.

'What money?' he stalled.

'This money,' said Mr Holly, and leaned to one side until Steven heard the chink of coins and the rustle of notes coming out of his pocket. 'Sixty-two pounds thirty.'

Steven was quiet again. The dark let him be so, when in daylight he would have felt compelled to answer immediately.

Mr Holly said nothing for a long while. And when he did speak again, it was not about the money.

'People hurt children, you know,' he said softly.

Steven's heart began to beat hard. 'I know.'

He started to edge down the hill until he was level with the policeman. Another few yards and he'd be beyond him, and then he could run if he had to. He thought he might have to, however stupid that would look.

'Of course you do,' said Mr Holly, nodding his head slowly. 'We *both* know that.'

'I have to get home now, Mr Holly,' said Steven. He took the few paces that meant he was past the gate.

The man crossed the distance between them silently and with disturbing speed.

Steven retreated but found the sharp hedge at his back. He flinched at the contact he knew was coming. 'What do you *want*?' Jonas Holly stopped, as if aware for the first time that Steven might be scared. He stood still and spoke softly. 'Are you in trouble, Steven? Do you owe someone money?'

Steven was confused. His mind had to catch up.

Mr Holly seemed to take his silence as an admission. 'Is it drugs? If someone's threatening you I can help you; that's my job.'

Steven said nothing. Mr Holly was the last person in the world he would go to for help.

As if reading that thought, the policeman continued, 'I know I let people down before, but it won't happen again. If you're in danger, Steven—'

'No! I'm *fine*. Leave me *alone*.' Steven waved an arm in front of him in a subconscious attempt to clear himself some space. His knuckles grazed Jonas Holly's chest.

'Then why leave the money there?'

'Because it's *hers*.'

Steven held his breath.

Jonas Holly stood absolutely motionless, arms at his sides. 'What do you mean?'

'I have to go home now.'

'What do you *mean*?'

Steven tried to edge around him and Mr Holly grabbed his arm in an iron grip. '*Tell me*.'

Steven hitched in a breath of shock. The voice was Mr Holly's, but *not*. It was flat and harsh and inky black, and Steven felt a change in the warm night air as if somewhere God had left a door open and the cold had rushed in.

He started to shake. Brief seconds ago he'd felt like a man. Now he felt like a man about to die, without refuge or defence, a crab without a shell, scuttling in a bucket and with nothing to protect him from the looming threat that Mr Holly had suddenly become.

Shame burned Steven's eyes. If Em could see him now – so small and frightened – she would never kiss him again. In the dark, Steven could not see the man's eyes – only the faint twin glimmers where he knew his eyes to be. He couldn't even pretend to be brave under that invisible gaze.

'It's *hers*,' he whispered. 'She gave it to me but I didn't want it, so I was giving it back. My mum is waiting for me. And my nan.'

'Why would she do that?'

'I don't know. I don't *know*! I didn't ask. You're hurting me.'

'When did she give it to you?'

Steven's voice cracked. 'I have to *go*!'

'*When?*'

Steven was scared but suddenly he was angry too. Angry that Mr Holly had stolen his joy over the kiss. Angry that he'd murdered his wife, when she'd been so kind and pretty and funny. So angry that for one terrible second he lost all sense of self-preservation . . .

'The night you killed her.'

The darkness between the two of them became a slow vacuum that sucked the last of the bravado out of Steven, the tears from his eyes, the scream from his lips, the anger from his belly; he felt them all being extracted by the silent black shape before him, leaving him filled only with numb terror.

Right now, if Mr Holly had told him to stay there while he went to fetch a knife to kill him with, Steven would have sat down in the road and waited. Snivelling.

Instead Jonas let go of Steven's arm.

He took a slow step backwards.

He tilted his head at the escape route down the hill.

'You can run now,' he said.

So Steven did.

31

Elizabeth Rice had just got out of the shower when her phone rang. It was Reynolds.

'There's someone downstairs who wants to talk to the police. I've just got out of the shower, so would you mind, Elizabeth?'

Would you mind, Elizabeth?

Rice was getting pretty sick of those four words.

'Sure,' she said tightly.

Her hair was still dripping, so she wrapped it in a towel and piled it on her head, then pulled on a skirt, shirt and low, practical heels and was about to leave her room. Then she thought that there was an outside chance – about 0.5 per cent, but a chance none the less – that the person downstairs might be a handsome young farmer, so she quickly applied mascara and a swipe of lipstick. It was only on her way down the rickety staircase that she remembered the towel. She was about to take it off, but then wondered at her own optimism, when she'd long ago noticed that any phrase containing the words 'handsome', 'young' and 'farmer' was a kind of triple oxymoron, held together only by expectations nurtured by a Mills & Boon adolescence.

Her dimmed mood and wet towel were both vindicated when she saw that the visitor was not even a man but a schoolboy – a gangly, dark-eyed youth with jutting ears, a jagged haircut, and that crazily transient combination of fair, boyish complexion and shaving stubble.

'Hi,' she said. 'I'm Detective Sergeant Rice. How can I help you?'

The boy glanced at her makeshift turban, then looked away. 'Um,' he said. 'I don't know.'

Rice sighed inwardly. Children were a mystery to her. She couldn't really remember what it was like to be one, and the children of her friends and sisters always made her slightly uncomfortable. She would smile at them and they would stare solemnly back at her, as if they knew what she was thinking.

Babies cried on contact.

She didn't *dislike* children, but they bored her. She even got impatient with cute children in Hollywood movies, with their curls and their adenoids and their smart-arse comebacks.

Before she could catch it, she sighed outwardly too, which made the boy in front of her blush. This made her feel bad enough to make an effort with him, even though she knew her hair was going to look like total shit for the rest of the day.

'What's your name?'

'Steven,' he said. 'Lamb.'

The name rang a faint bell, but she didn't waste time wondering why. She softened her tone consciously.

'What did you want to tell me, Steven?'

Steven wished he hadn't come. He hadn't thought things through, and didn't have the words ready to explain. He'd once played one of Fagin's boys in a school production of *Oliver!* He'd only had one line – 'Kill you as soon as look at you, he would' – but had been astonished by the sheer number of ways he could get that line wrong. Either he forgot the words entirely, or remembered them but all in the wrong order. Even when he got the line right he sounded like Yoda.

That was how he felt now. As if saying the words he'd come to say would only complicate things that were already fuzzy and fleeting in his own head. Still, he couldn't go without saying *something*. He didn't know much about women, but he knew that they were always more grumpy when they had wet hair, so he'd better make an effort.

'It's about Mr Holly,' he said.

The woman – DS Rice – looked slightly more interested than she had a second ago, but Steven was lost again. How could he tell her all the stuff that was in his head?

He killed his wife! I think he did; I saw him hit her. He grabbed my arm. He said something about hurting children. Maybe he took those children. He could do it. If he could kill his wife he could murder children, couldn't he? People hurt children – that's what he said. People hurt children. And he scared me. I thought he was going to kill me. His voice wasn't his voice and his eyes were like nothing. He could kill children. He could kill anyone. I know he could.

Here, in daylight, in the stale-beer bar of the Red Lion, talking to a policewoman with a towel on her head, it sounded like a case for Scooby-Doo.

DS Rice glanced at her watch.

'I don't think he likes children,' Steven said carefully.

'Why do you think that? Did he say something?'

'Kind of. He told me people hurt children.'

'But that's true. Sadly. Isn't it? People sometimes *do* hurt children.'

'Yes. But . . .' He struggled to explain and finally couldn't. 'It was just the *way* he said it.' He paused and then finished in a rush: 'I think maybe he took those children. And I think he could hurt someone. I *know* he could.'

'That's a serious allegation, Steven. Do you have any proof of that?' DS Rice was looking at him sharply now, as if she was about to get angry with him.

Did he have proof? He knew it was true – he'd seen Mr Holly slap his wife – but did he have *proof*? He knew what proof was, what evidence was, and it wasn't just saying you'd seen something when there was nobody else there to back you up. That was just his word against the word of a policeman.

'Not really,' he said finally.

'And what reason do you have to think he might have taken the children?'

'Just . . . I don't know.' That was never going to be enough, he knew. 'Just a feeling really.'

DS Rice looked at her watch quite openly this time. 'OK, Steven. Is there anything else?'

He shook his head. He knew he'd failed. She'd already lost interest.

'Well, thanks for coming in to speak to us, all right?'

'OK,' he said. 'But I'm not making it up.'

'I didn't say you were.'

He thought she kind of *had*, but let it go.

Then she glanced down at his scuffed school bag. 'You off to school now?'

'Yes.'

'OK,' she said. 'Anything else you want to tell us, you just come to the mobile unit in the car park, all right? Anything you think could help with finding the children. OK? After nine.'

'OK,' he said.

'Thanks, Steven.'

Elizabeth Rice watched Steven Lamb leave the bar, hoisting his backpack on to his shoulders as he went. She didn't remember what it was to be a child, but one thing he'd said *had* made her remember something.

It was just the WAY he said it.

It made her think of being sixteen and telling her mother that a neighbour, Mr Craddock, had made suggestive remarks to her at the bus stop on her way to school one day. She'd known Mr Craddock since she was small, and always thought he was a nice man. In the summer he would let Elizabeth walk his dog, Fuzzy, because her parents wouldn't let her have one. Once he'd shouted at some boys who'd been teasing her. He always waved and smiled, and his wife did too.

And then that day at the bus stop – when she was sixteen years old – he'd asked her if they spanked her at school.

'No!' She'd laughed. The idea was silly. Nobody got spanked at school any more. Even the word was laughable. 'They just give us detention.'

'What about at home?' Mr Craddock had said. 'Does your daddy spank you?'

'No,' said Elizabeth, and hadn't laughed, because suddenly this was making her feel uncomfortable.

They'd got on the bus together and she remembered how she'd hated the fact that he'd come up the steps behind her, knowing that he must be looking at her bare legs under the school skirt she'd always insisted on wearing just a little too short. Feeling that Mr Craddock had moved from the column marked 'Nice Man' to the one marked 'Pervert' in the mental list she kept. A list that seemed to be growing in direct proportion to her breasts.

It had been a week before she'd told her mother about it.

'I'm sure he was just joking,' her mother had said.

'He wasn't,' Rice could hear herself saying now. 'It was the *way* he said it.'

Now the grown-up Elizabeth Rice watched the boy pass the small leaded window, head down, frowning.

She went upstairs and dried her hair – which *was* shit – and mentioned the conversation to Reynolds over breakfast.

'Steven Lamb?' he said, prissily rubbing his fingers and thumb together to dislodge crumbs.

'Yes,' said Rice. She thought that Reynolds might be a lot more attractive if he didn't always have the continental breakfast. Croissants weren't manly.

'He's that kid who nearly got killed by Arnold Avery.'

'I *thought* it rang a bell.'

'Interesting,' mused Reynolds, raising a Roger Moore eyebrow.

Rice didn't ask why. That was what Reynolds wanted and she hated playing silly games, in or out of a relationship. If it really *was* interesting she had no doubt that he would tell her anyway. His ego wouldn't be able to resist it.

It only took a moment . . .

'It makes you wonder what effect that might have on a child.'

'What do you mean?'

Reynolds leaned back away from his croissant – torn, never sliced – and put his splayed fingers together under his nose.

He thinks he's Sherlock bloody Holmes. Rice had to take a mouthful of bacon to keep from laughing.

'I don't know,' said Reynolds slowly, but in a tone that said he *did* know – he just wasn't telling *you*.

Rice *was* interested in the fact that Steven Lamb had almost been murdered. Who wouldn't be interested in that? She wished now that she'd known that at the time. But right now she'd rather drop down dead with curiosity than give Reynolds the satisfaction of pleading for information he should be sharing as a matter of course.

So she took a piece of toast from the rack and mopped up her bean juice with it.

'Maybe I'll call Kate Gulliver,' he said sharply. 'Discuss it with her.'

Oh shut up, thought Rice.

32

June the second – exactly four weeks after Jess Took had been stolen from her father's horsebox – Nan's birthday dawned early and bright, the chill night warming quickly as the sun cleared the top of the moor.

Steven and Davey still hadn't made up. Steven had tried a few times but Davey was a grudge-bearer, and after a week of grunts and monosyllables, Lettie had told them they weren't welcome on the birthday trip to Barnstaple.

'They should go through a war together,' Nan had decreed. 'That'd sort them out.' Her default position was that there was no problem so big that it could not be resolved by going through a war together. It was her solution for everything from family spats to inflation. Steven had once pointed out that the Israelis and Palestinians had been going through a war together for years and it didn't seem to be sorting much out, and Nan had told him not to be cheeky.

Steven was slightly disappointed with the weather, because he had bought his nan an umbrella. It sounded boring as hell, but it was so small and light that it could be carried in her pocket, let alone her handbag. And the best thing about it – the absolute best – was that when raised, the canopy was covered with old family photos.

Once he'd accepted the truth about the porn channel, Steven had put his Friday evenings at Chantelle Cox's to good use. He didn't have a computer of his own, so he'd used hers – scanning old pictures and emailing them to the company he'd found online that would print photos on to almost any object he cared to pay over the odds for.

Steven had used the box of photos from the cupboard under the stairs and had picked a dozen of the best. They were all old; he couldn't remember the last time family photos had been taken, or who had taken most of these. He and Davey under Weston pier with ice creams; a young Lettie with her hair up, looking sparkly; Nan squinting, with Davey in a buggy.

A dozen times since it had arrived, Steven had opened the umbrella in his room to admire it. He was sure Nan would love it, combining as it did the two things she was most interested in – the past and the weather.

Steven folded the umbrella carefully down to its smallest size, clipped it tightly in place and pulled on the little cover it was supplied with. Then he wrapped it in a sheet of flowered paper he'd bought specially from Mr Jacoby's shop. The paper came with two little tags in matching colours. He wrote 'To Nan, with love from Steven' on one, and taped it to the parcel.

Despite the lack of rain, his good mood had returned. Friday at school had seen to that. Em hadn't changed her mind; she still loved him. The relief had been tremendous. His fledgling self-confidence – shaken by the encounter with Jonas Holly – had been quickly rebuilt by Em's smile as he'd walked into the classroom. He could tell she'd been watching the door for him.

'Have you had sex?' Lewis had said suspiciously.

'No.' Steven had smiled, because that no longer mattered.

'Didn't think so,' Lewis had snorted, when he so obviously *had* thought so that it made Steven laugh.

'Breakfast!' Lettie yelled up the stairs. It was early today, because of her and Nan getting the bus to Barnstaple. Even so, Steven heard Davey thundering down the stairs as if he hadn't eaten for a week.

Davey had had no money to buy Nan a gift with. He'd revealed this with a meaningful glare in Steven's direction, which was wasted on Lettie.

'Then make her something,' she'd shrugged.

Davey had screwed up his face. '*Make* something?! I'm not a Chinese, you know!'

'I can see that, thank you, Mr Smartypants.'

'Make *what*? All the stuff I make falls apart.'

That was true; he was a craftwork dunce.

'Then try harder,' Lettie said unsympathetically. 'It's not like you don't know your nan's birthday. It's the same date every year, you know.'

So Davey had made Nan a bird out of a cereal packet and assorted feathers he'd found up in the woods. It looked like cardboard road-kill and – true to Davey's skill level – was already starting to moult.

Now Steven stopped with his hand on his bedroom door handle. He felt bad for Davey. Even though the little shit had ruined his skateboard, he felt bad that his brother only had a sticky clump of kindergarten crap to give to Nan for her birthday. Felt bad for Davey *and* Nan.

'Steven! Breakfast! I'm not saying again!'

Quickly, he picked up a pen and added 'and Davey' to the tag, then ran downstairs.

Nan made a fuss of the cardboard bird, although a couple of feathers fell out of it before she'd even finished hugging Davey. Lettie had bought her the *Bumper Book of Daily Mail Crosswords*, which Nan loved, of course. Then she turned to Steven's present and admired the wrapping paper.

'I'll save that,' she said, and he knew she would. Nan had quite the collection of carefully folded wrapping paper and a similar stash of used paper bags. She didn't exactly iron them, but it was close. 'With love from Steven and Davey,' she read over the top of her glasses.

Davey gave Steven a puzzled look.

Nan opened the gift. 'Oooh, a lovely umbrella.'

'Open it, Nan,' said Steven.

'Not indoors! Bad luck to open a brolly indoors.'

Steven didn't tell her that he'd already extended repeated invitations to bad luck while admiring the umbrella in his room. Instead he left his fake Weetabix to go soggy and took the umbrella from Nan. He stepped outside the back door and opened it so she could see the canopy.

'Well!' she said. 'Well, do you see that? Pictures of everyone! Look at that! Isn't that clever! Me squinting away, and you boys on the beach. I remember that day. Both got covered in tar off the pier. Charming. And Lettie! All pretty! Turn it round a bit, Steven. Did you make it?'

'Got it online.'

Nan leaned in to Lettie, looking confused. 'He got it where?'

'Online, Mum. On the computer.'

Nan flapped a hand at technology, but couldn't hide her pleasure. 'Well, you boys are chocolate. Thank you.'

She hugged them both.

'Welcome,' said Steven.

'Welcome,' said Davey.

But Steven noticed that for some reason Davey still didn't look happy.

Lettie ran through the rules of non-engagement one last time: no fighting; no leaving the house; no mess; no touching the stove until Uncle Jude had had a chance to fix it. There was bread, and they knew where the toaster was. Then she and Nan left at 9.25 to catch the 9.32 bus to Barnstaple. Nan made a show of taking the umbrella, even though the sun was already scorching the sky.

Twenty minutes after they left, Shane arrived with a bag of coconut mushrooms, and he and Davey switched on the TV and hooked up the PS2.

Steven took up his nan's old station at the window, but for a very different purpose. His heart recognized the shape of Em while she was still a blur, and he smiled. As she got closer he saw she was wearing cut-off jeans with a white vest top and her favourite shoes. Flip-flops, his nan would have called them, but they went far beyond seaside plastic. They were soft leather and had turquoise beads and little shells sewn on to them. She'd got them on holiday in Spain. Steven had never been on holiday anywhere, let alone somewhere foreign. Weston-super-Mare was the furthest from home he'd ever been and that had only been day trips. When he'd told Em that, she'd laughed and hadn't believed him. She lived in a different world half a mile away.

Em looked up and saw him, and smiled and raised a hand in brief greeting.

He grinned and hurdled the PS2 control cables on his way to the front door.

'What's with him?' Shane said.

'He thinks someone loves him,' he heard Davey say.

The words sliced a cruel edge off his happiness, so that by the time he opened the door, his smile had faded.

'What's up?' said Em.

'Nothing. Hi. Come in,' he said, and stood aside, wondering if he should be kissing Em hello. It seemed a bit . . . *familiar*, so he didn't.

They faced each other a little awkwardly in the narrow hallway.

'Thanks for coming,' he said. 'Sorry we can't – you know – go somewhere.'

'No problem,' said Em.

From the lounge they heard an overblown squeal of tyres and a crash.

'Bull*shit*!' yelled Shane, while Davey laughed and called him a twat.

'Shall we go upstairs?' said Steven, then realized how that sounded. 'I don't mean like that, I just mean . . . 'cos of *them*, you know . . .'

'Sure,' said Em, and reached out to touch his hand.

Reassured, he put his head round the front-room door. 'We'll be upstairs. Don't touch the stove, OK?'

'Fuck off,' said Davey quietly. Steven let it go.

Em had never seen his bedroom and suddenly he was aware of how small it was; how messy – and that it smelled of Lynx and dirty socks. He opened a window and sat on the bed, but Em wandered around the room, inspecting it. For the first time in his life he wished he'd tidied up. Em tilted her head to the shelf and ran her eyes over all the books he'd ever read. Steven let his eyes drift along the spines in time with hers. He should *definitely* have tidied *those* up. There were still Famous Five books up there. And *The Cucumber Pony* – a picture book about a green talking horse, for God's sake! She was going to think he was so gay.

But her eyes moved on without comment. 'Who's that boy?' she said when she noticed the photo.

'My Uncle Billy.'

'Why d'you have a picture of him?'

'He's dead,' he told her, and hoped that would be enough.

'Yeah? How'd he die?'

Steven hesitated momentarily while an entire conversation – an entire *future* – played out in his head; a future where Em viewed him as a curiosity instead of a boyfriend.

'He was run over.' He hated lying to her.

'How awful,' she said.

'It was before I was born.' He shrugged.

She turned away from the shelves and smiled at him and he was glad he'd lied instead of spoiling things.

He watched her examine his room like an exotic animal exploring a new cage. He resisted the temptation to justify his mess or to get up and hide stuff, and the longer the inspection went on, the more he realized that she wasn't judging him, just interested. Now and then she'd say something: 'I have one those. Did yours work? Nor mine; I don't know anyone whose did.' Or: 'Oh look, your Liverpool shirt has your name on the back! Cool! Oh, it's torn here, what a shame.' And: 'I can't believe you collect these things. You geek.'

Steven relaxed into being teased and soon he was enjoying her circuit as much as she obviously was.

As she ran out of room, she slowly approached the bed, and Steven stopped laughing and became acutely aware of his own body – and hers. Finally, she sat down a couple of feet away from him, then shifted along until their hips were touching.

They kissed again, as if not a second had passed between their last kiss and this one, two days later. As if Jonas Holly was a bad dream and Nan's birthday had yet to dawn.

This kiss was different in a whole 'nother way. They weren't in Ronnie's garage or outside a pair of iron gates; they were in his *bed*room and on his *bed*. That thought alone was exciting enough for him to kiss Em harder and to put his hand on her bare thigh.

Then it all got muddled in Steven's head. He touched Em; she touched him; she opened her mouth and there was a roaring in his ears; he slid his hand under the bottom of her little vest and touched the hot, smooth skin of her waist, and felt a bit faint.

She broke the kiss.

'Sorry,' he said. 'I'm sorry.'

'I'm not,' she said seriously.

Em slid her feet from her pretty shell-covered shoes and carefully lifted her legs on to Steven's bed. She took his hand.

'Can we lie down?'

He kicked off his trainers and the pair of them lay on their backs on the narrow bed, shoulders, arms, hands, hips touching, staring at the ceiling. He couldn't believe this was the same bedroom where he'd slept for the past five years. He was lying on his Liverpool cover with a girl he'd kissed. He had wonderful things to say to her, but he could barely breathe, let alone talk, his throat was so tight with desire and nerves. The kiss had been easy, but the thought of getting actual sex wrong made him feel dizzy with horror. He wanted it so badly he was shaking, but he'd rather never have it at all than get it all wrong and have to live with that shame. A shame that Em would know all about. A shame she might share with her friends. With *his* friends. He was so scared his jaw ached with clenching—

'I'm scared,' she said in a very small voice. 'I've never done this.'

Steven wanted to cry, he loved her so much.

He turned towards her.

'I want to,' she said. 'I love you. But I'm scared.'

Steven put an arm around her and she turned to face him, so close that he could feel her warm breath on his lips.

'We don't have to do anything,' he told her. 'I love you too.'

*

Davey was in the woods with Shane.

He'd left the PlayStation revving and crashing all by itself. They were going to catch the kidnapper and there was nothing Steven could do to stop them. Serve him right for making Davey's feather bird seem so crap that he'd needed the charity of his name on a stupid umbrella.

They hardly spoke; the plan was so simple.

The only discussion was who should be the bait. Right from the start, Shane had suspected it might be him. Even so, when they actually reached the car, he made a token protest as Davey started to unravel the reel of garden twine they'd stolen from Mr Randall's shed.

'Don't be such a chicken,' said Davey sharply. 'We're going to be tied together. No one can take you without me knowing.'

'I'm not a chicken,' said Shane crossly. 'I'm just saying we should take turns, that's all. Why should I *always* be the bait?'

'Because you're better at sitting still than I am.'

'But you're going to be sitting still in the woods.'

'Yeah, and you get the cushion, so what are you moaning about?'

'It's my cushion anyway. I *should* get it.'

'It's not yours, it's your mum's.'

'That still makes it more mine than yours.'

'Whatever. Stop making excuses and being a chicken.'

While they'd bickered, Davey had tied one end of the twine around Shane's wrist. 'Get in the car then.'

'I'm only doing this if we swap places every hour.'

'All right.'

'Promise?'

'Shitting bloody hell, Shane! How old are you? You sound like a baby! A baby *girl.*'

'Piss off.'

'I'm going,' said Davey, unfazed. 'Remember, two jerks if you see anyone, three if you're in danger, and then I'll come running in and we'll take the bastard *down.*'

'How far are you going?' said Shane nervously as he settled himself on his mother's cushion.

'Not far. I'll be out of sight in case he realizes I'm there, but close enough. OK?'

'I suppose so,' said Shane. 'Two for a stranger, three for danger.'

'Exactly. Don't worry. We're going to be rich *and* we're going to be heroes. It's going to be brilliant.'

'Yeah,' said Shane doubtfully.

Davey walked away from him into the woods, unravelling the twine through his fingers, lifting it around saplings and over branches.

Shane watched him become increasingly hard to see through the undergrowth, waiting for Davey to look at him and give him a last nod of joint enterprise, but he didn't. Instead his friend just stopped being visible, and soon stopped being audible too. Shane watched his hand jiggle on the steering wheel or jerk about like a puppet's as Davey continued to move through the woods. He willed it to stop, so that he would know that Davey had settled somewhere not too far away, but it went on for longer than he'd hoped.

Then his hand stilled, and he placed it on the blistered wheel. He looked around.

The sound of Davey had faded away or stopped – he couldn't tell which – and the forest seemed unsually quiet.

He'd sat in this car a hundred times, but had never felt so vulnerable. They'd talked in abstract terms about 'fishing' and 'bait', but now he realized that he really did feel as exposed as a worm on a hook. He kept eyeing the trees around him, even though he and Davey had agreed that the bait should not 'act all suspicious'. He wondered if Davey could see him acting all suspicious, but he couldn't help himself.

Every second took a week, and every leaf that trembled on the hot breath of summer was a killer in the dim greenish shade. There was a big beech tree behind his left ear – maybe fifteen metres off – wide enough to hide even a fat kidnapper. Shane tried to ignore it, but couldn't stop twisting his head to look. Once, when he turned suddenly, he caught movement behind the tree. He was sure. Just a shadow but it was there. He *knew* it was. He strained his eyes until they watered, but didn't see the dark motion again.

Sunlight stabbed through the trees in biblical rays, making the shade even darker, and turning the light into patterns that painted faces on the bark.

He looked at his watch. Fifteen minutes. *Only!* The watch was crap; his father had got it free with ten gallons of petrol. It must be wrong. It must be Davey's turn by now.

He fiddled with the dashboard controls. The clicks of the indicator and wiper switches sounded too loud – as if they might attract the wrong kind of attention – so he stopped and the thick silence fell about him once more.

Shane started to feel truly scared. He knew his job was to sit there and wait and make the kidnapper come to him. He understood that. But he just *couldn't*. Not with that shadow moving behind the big beech.

He sucked in his breath as he heard a rustle in the woods. A *proper* rustle this time – the big sound of somebody moving towards him. Or away from him. It was hard to tell. It was off in the direction of where Davey—

Shane let the breath go and laughed out loud with relief. *Shi–it!* It *was* Davey. Come to be the bait. He *knew* his watch must be wrong. He laughed out loud.

'Hey Davey! You sound like a hippo!'

Davey stopped.

'C'mon, you tosser. Your turn!' Shane gave two sharp jerks on the twine and felt Davey at the other end.

A twig cracked behind the beech and Shane scrambled out of the car. Fuck this for a game of soldiers, as he'd once heard his father say. His shift was *over* and it was Davey's turn to be the bait. See how *he* liked sitting there waiting to be snatched by a perv.

Shane hurried through the ferns and fallen logs towards Davey, winding up the twine as he went, casting nervous looks back at the big beech, grateful to be leaving it behind in the clearing. The Mazda disappeared behind him.

'Davey, you *tosser*!' How far had he bloody gone? There was no way he would have made it back to the car in time if Shane *had* been jumped by the kidnapper. No fucking way! He'd have been all on his own. The thought made Shane so angry that as he reeled in the twine he knew he was going to beat the shit out of Davey when he saw him. Bollocks to the reward. He was sick of always being the one doing the dirty work.

'Davey!'

No answer.

'It's not *funny*, you dickhead!'

Shane stopped dead and frowned. He'd run out of twine. His fingers followed it to the point where it had been wrapped several times around the branch of a silver birch sapling, before trailing down to the remainder of the reel, which lay at the foot of the tree. Shane picked it up.

Underneath it was a square yellow note.

*

Steven was watching Em's heart beat like a butterfly trapped under the pale skin of her left breast when Shane burst through the bedroom door.

They couldn't understand him at first. He was so hysterical and breathless and they were so flustered and cross. Even as Shane babbled and tugged at the length of green twine knotted around his wrist, Steven was aware of Em putting her feet back into her turquoise sandals, her perfect breasts hidden once more under her top. Under her top where his hands had just been . . .

But once they *did* understand what he was saying, Steven didn't think he'd ever moved so fast. He was running before he'd finished stamping his feet back into his still-laced trainers. Em's hand was in his so she could keep up, but he could have towed her trailer up the hill and not been slowed. Every time Shane flagged, Steven shoved him between the shoulder blades or pushed the back of his head.

'Run!' he yelled. 'Keep running!'

At Rose Cottage, Em stopped dead and their hands tore apart.

'The police!' she panted.

'No!' Steven yelled.

'Steven! Don't be so *stupid*!' Em ran up the little stone steps before he could stop her.

He heard her hammer on the door and shout.

He didn't want Mr Holly there. Pretending to help. Pretending to care. Taking charge.

Leading them away from where Davey might be?

He would have run on alone, but he couldn't leave Em here with *him*.

Torn between his brother and the girl he loved, Steven Lamb dithered on the narrow lane, to the sound of Shane's doubled-over wheezing.

Em came down the steps with Mr Holly behind her, wearing jeans and a T-shirt and thick green gardening gloves.

Steven yanked the protesting Shane upright and started to push him onwards up the hill.

When they finally stopped beside the burned-out Mazda, the silent heat of the woods was oppressive.

'I was in here,' Shane panted. 'He was over there.'

They followed him through the ferns and between the trees to the little silver birch and the yellow note.

Steven picked it off the forest floor.

'*You don't love him.*' The relief left him wobbly.

'Shit,' he said. 'He's just messing about! I'm gonna kill him! We had a fight and—'

'No,' said Jonas Holly harshly. 'It's not a joke.'

They were surprised into silence by his words. Now they all watched as he frowned at the trees to the north, as if trying to remember something – or to see something that nobody else could.

'Wait here,' he said calmly. 'Stay together. If I'm not back in ten minutes, go for help.'

And with that he ran into the woods.

'Shit!' Steven felt his little brother disappearing from him as fast and as surely as if he was falling down a well. If Mr Holly thought he knew where he was, then Steven needed to know too. And if the policeman was somehow *involved*, then what the *hell* was he doing letting him get away?

Doing nothing was not an option.

Steven grabbed Em's hands. 'You two go for help *right now*,' he said urgently. 'I have to go after him.'

'But Stevie, he said—'

'I don't care, Em! He murdered his wife. He might have killed those children too. Tell the police. I have to go *after* him. I have to find Davey!'

Em's open mouth held a million questions, but Steven let go of her and ran after Jonas Holly.

'Steven!' she shouted, but he never looked back and was soon swallowed up by the trees.

*

Davey Lamb wasn't a girl, he wasn't nine years old, and he wasn't special like Charlie Peach. Davey Lamb was fit and strong and tried to fight every bit as hard as he'd once boasted to Chantelle Cox that he would. Twice he'd even broken away and reeled into the woods – trying to outrun his attacker on rubbery legs that let him down and tripped him up. The trees spun around him and the floor of the forest was cool and rough against his cheek. And the arms that pulled him upwards once more were strong and relentless.

Davey tried to see a face, but it always eluded him, like something seen from the corner of his eye. Smooth and featureless and glimpsed only in snatches. His kidnapper seemed neither tall nor short, nor fat nor thin. He wore a big coat, but other than that, he was just a being with hands that gripped and legs that moved faster than Davey's own could. A dark voice muttered threats beside his ear, and Davey's T-shirt – a red one with a pointing finger over the words HE MADE ME DO IT – bunched up under his arms as he was propelled staggering through the trees.

Davey wondered whether Shane was still sitting in the Mazda, waiting to be captured by the same person who now held him hard by the arm and the scruff, and who occasionally helped him along with a knee under his buttocks.

Davey laughed at that idea, and immediately felt sick. He was drunk. He hadn't been drinking, but this was definitely what being drunk felt like. Last winter he and Shane had finished a bottle of Advocaat they'd found in Shane's mother's kitchen cupboard. They'd downed it like cough mixture, then had laughed until they'd cried at the sight of Shane's hamster, Anakin, quivering under his shavings.

This was like that, but without the fun. Sometimes Davey's mind drifted off, even while his legs went on working. Then he would snap back and remember he was in great danger, and shout and flail and twist in the kidnapper's grip.

It was pointless.

'I'll shoot you in the head,' the voice said in his ear, and for a moment Davey believed him and sobered up and did his best to walk by himself. Then he forgot all about being shot in the head and stopped cooperating again.

He was pushed and pulled and bumped and dragged through the trees for several days. It felt like several days; it might have been seconds. At last they came to a picnic area and a car and Davey was leaned against the back door and told harshly to *stay*, so he didn't, of course. As soon as the man walked away from him and opened the boot, he set off for the woods again.

The man caught him and Davey sat down and refused to move. The man grasped his wrists and dragged him across the clearing on his arse, back to the car. He was surprisingly strong.

The man dropped his arms and Davey simply rolled under the car, snatching his ankle away from the man's hand just in the nick of time. The man swore loudly and got on his knees to reach for him. Davey giggled and moved, giggled and moved as the man probed and groped and grunted four-letter words.

'Oh, fuck you too!' Davey laughed, although each time he avoided the grasping fingers, some part of him felt like pissing his pants in terror.

The man stood up and moved away.

Now the fear had time to settle on Davey's back like a stiff blanket left out in the frost, and his teeth started to chatter. He watched the man's workboots walk to the back of the car; he could hear him moving things about in the boot.

Davey listened to the sound of his own breath pumping through his mouth; the sound of something being shifted and lifted. Not knowing *what* was the scariest thing of all.

The boots came back. This time, when the man's silhouetted head dipped below the sill, it was not his hand that reached for Davey, but a white stick. And he did not attempt to pull Davey out – but started to jab and swipe at the boy, trying to drive him from his narrow hiding place.

The stick first hit Davey in the knee and he yelped and bumped his head on the exhaust. He put out his hands in self-defence and the stick rapped the fingers on his left hand as it arced past him. Then its point jabbed him hard in the ribs, and Davey thought he would pass out. He didn't feel drunk any more. He felt sick and terrified. He couldn't move. All he could do was lie there, drowning in tears, clutching his side and hoping that the pain would go away; that was what mattered. The pain and the helplessness.

He'd once seen Iestyn Lloyd, the terrier man, digging out a fox as his Jack Russells yipped and clawed and snapped at the earth around it. Now Davey knew how a fox must feel.

With his eyes tight shut and his ribs still burning, Davey felt the pull on the back of his shirt, the hand at the waistband of his jeans and the gravel sliding forwards under his hip as he was dragged from under the car.

He came out of the darkness and into the light, blinking through his tears. As he emerged, he was dimly aware that suddenly there were *two* shapes looming over him.

And one of them was Jonas Holly.

33

Nobody believed Em. Not at first, anyway. They eyed her with suspicion and asked her questions she had no hope of answering. Frankly, she was embarrassed to repeat Steven's accusations; even though she loved him, she found them hard to believe herself, and she relayed them almost apologetically to Detective Inspector Reynolds. Em was quick to notice the glances he exchanged with his colleague as she spoke, and she got the feeling that if Shane had not been both beside her *and* beside himself, DI Reynolds might have told her to run along and stop wasting his time. It seemed they were far more impressed by a blubbering, panic-stricken eleven-year-old than they were by her careful re-telling of events.

When she'd finished, Reynolds and Rice drove all three of them back to the woods and followed them first to the burned-out car and then to the little birch where the yellow note still lay.

'Did you write this?' said the Detective Inspector so sharply to Em that she flinched.

'Of course not!' she snapped back. 'Steven thought it was his brother having a joke, but then the policeman said it wasn't. Then he told us to stay here and he ran into the trees.'

Reynolds stared in the direction her finger indicated. But he didn't move. Didn't run into the trees. Why wasn't he running into the trees?

Em was a girl who respected authority. Why shouldn't she? Authority had always respected *her*. Until now. Now she saw only suspicion in DI Reynolds's sharp eyes – a suspicion that was making everything proceed too slowly. The little jet of anger that shot through her took her by surprise.

'You think I'm lying!'

'I didn't—'

'You do. You think I'm lying. I'm not. You need to stop wasting time and go and find them!'

'Now, now,' said DI Reynolds. 'We need to do this the right way.'

'You need to do it the *fast* way!

'Listen, Emma—'

'*Emily.*'

Reynolds pursed his lips disapprovingly and glanced at Rice, but Rice pretended to be looking into the woods.

And then she really *was* looking into the woods.

'Somebody's there,' she said softly.

They all turned to follow her gaze. In the straining silence that followed, they heard something moving quickly through the undergrowth. Getting louder.

'It's coming this way,' whispered Rice, and her hushed words in the cathedral of trees made life suddenly seem like an evil fairy tale.

'There!' hissed Em, at a brief flash of red.

'Davey!' shouted Shane.

*

Reynolds felt a rush of relief.

'See?' he couldn't resist saying to the girl, and had to make a conscious effort not to add 'I told you so.'

Davey Lamb stumbled out of the trees at an angle to them, as if he had only arrived by accident.

'Davey!' Shane said again, but in a more faltering voice. Reynolds could see why. The boy moved as if drunk, his legs stiff and rubbery by turn, and his arms loose and flapping by his sides, the elbows jerking this way and that. He turned his head at the sound of Shane's voice, but it was with the wobbly neck and the vacant eyes of an unstrung puppet.

Nobody moved; nobody ran to Davey and helped him. That alone made the scene even more disturbing. Instead the boy swung himself around in a doddering arc and came to them. Rice finally closed the few paces between them. 'Are you OK, Davey?' she said.

'What?' he said, screwing up his face in confusion. 'What?'

Drugs. Reynolds had seen enough of them to know. These rural communities were rife with them. An edge of anger made him want to slap the boy for wasting their time. Except, as he got closer he could see that Davey Lamb was also streaked with what looked like coal or grease.

'Where's Steven?' said Emily Carver urgently.

'Back there,' said Davey, waving a vague arm behind him. 'They tried to kill me, but I got away.'

'Who tried to kill you, Davey?' Rice had bent down a little now to get on to the same level as the boy. She spoke in her soothe-the-victim voice.

Davey stared at her, then turned and stared at the woods behind him, frowning deeply. 'I dunno,' he said. Vomit followed the last word out of his mouth and fell down his shirt in a lumpy coconut stream.

'Gross!' said Shane.

Reynolds looked soberly at Rice.

Davey sat down heavily on the forest floor, cross-legged, and with long strings of snotty fluid hanging from his nose. He started to cry.

'Davey, where's *Steven*?' the girl insisted, but Davey Lamb could only shake his head and sob.

PART TWO

LAST WINTER

34

The hocks, the hoofs, the hide, the head.
   The hocks, the hoofs, the hide, the head . . .

Funny, I never do this without singing that old song. In my head, mostly, but sometimes out loud, as my knife slips easy through the skin. No accident, that. Old Murton taught me well about knives. Meat likes a fresh blade, old Murton used to say – no point in sharpening a knife and then not using it. I sharpen my knives right before I use them, see? Right before I take the legs off at the hock, like *so*. They come off so clean and I pick them up. This is a calf, so it's easy to hold all four feet in one hand. Place them off to one side. Now a little slit here and *here*, a long slit *there* and all round the throat.

Now the chain goes round the head like that, to hold him in place, see? And the hook for the winch goes in the collar like *so*. When I started there weren't no electric up here and it were my job to turn the winch by hand. All right for a calf, but you try winding the hide off a bloody carthorse! It's different now. Press the button and away we go. The hide comes off lovely with a crackle and quiet little *sssssssss* and leaves neat pink muscles and tendons in the shape of a calf.

Taking off the head dulls the knife but I won't sharpen it until the next job – whether that's five minutes from now or five days. Old Murton taught me well. *Old!* Listen to me calling him old when he was likely younger than I am now. Just seemed old to me 'cos I was just a bay, see? Fourteen when I started here, and it took me a right good sweat to line out my first sheep. Up to my elbows in blood and shit and I still couldn't get the head off!

Not like now. One, two, three and it's gone. That's the only place that bleeds. Just drops out of the throat on to the concrete. Dark red and shiny but not much of it. Put the head beside the legs, with the fat pink tongue poking out all comical.

Hang the calf at the back of the flesh room and spray it blue so it can't go for people to eat. There's a dozen carcasses in here but we'll get through all those before they go bad. Easy. Cold, see? Even in midsummer it's always cold in the flesh room 'cos of the thick walls and turf roof.

Mostly it's horses this year. Been a bad winter and feeding an old horse is no way to spend money. There's a couple of late calves too small to make it by the time the snow come, a few ponies off the moor and Jack Biggins's best old milker, Bubbles. Brought her in himself, he did, and said she'd always liked to watch the hunt go by. Daft old bugger! But he didn't want her going off to Brown's, see, where they treat 'em so bad. Likely old Bubbles thought her was coming in to be milked! Down the concrete slope, a pat between the eyes, a kind word. No bother.

I go back into the big shed and collect the leftovers of the calf – *the hocks, the hoofs, the hide, the head* – and put 'em in the incinerator. Time was we'd sell the hides to the tanneries at Porlock or Swimbridge, but now everything that's leather comes from China or India ten times as cheap. We're nothing now, England.

All we got left now is our traditions, and there's those what would like to see them gone too, and us all living like Russians.

I hose down the shed, then sharpen up another knife and take down old Bubbles. The hounds know the sound of the second knife sharpening and start to sing, so I join 'em: *The hocks, the hoofs, the hide, the head, the hocks, the hoofs, the hide, the head* . . .

I put chunks of the old milker in a wheelbarrow and take her out to the yards and throw her over the gates. The hounds stop singing and start eating. The older ones eat first: the pups learn that fast. Only Milo tries it on, and I have to wade in there with the whip and pull his teeth out of General's shoulder. Him'll be a fine dog, Milo, but he needs a lot of arse-kicking. The whole litter's turned out a bit bolshy, as it happens. That's Rufus for you. Finest sire in four counties, but him do get some growlers and some nippers. Rick and Rosie like a sly nip when they're walked. That's why they go out coupled with Drifter and Sandy – them two'll put any pup in its place quick enough. Nothing like being bit hard by a bigger hound you're chained to, to teach you some manners. By next winter them'll be as good as anything the Blacklands ever had.

There's a car coming up the lane. Not expecting visitors.

John Took got out of his Range Rover and lit a cigarette against the biting wind. He wasn't looking forward to this.

He'd inherited Bob Coffin. The bow-legged huntsman had come in a package deal with the sixty-odd hounds that had become his when he'd taken on the role of Blacklands Master three years before. If John Took could have chosen, he'd have picked a huntsman with a bit more stature. Someone who looked well in a white coat and bowler hat at the county hound show. Possibly not quite so much like Neanderthal Ice-cream Man.

The kennelman, Nigel, would have fitted the bill, but what could he do? Nigel was only twenty-eight and Coffin had been the Blacklands huntsman for almost forty years. Even Took had known enough not to rock a forty-year-old boat. Not here on the moor, anyway.

At least he kept the place clean. Never a bit of straw out of place, never a speck of blood in the big shed, never a turd in the cement runs. And he never complained about the cottage that came with the job, even though the hunt hadn't spent money on it in thirty years. Took assumed Coffin did any repairs himself, and never asked about the cost.

He turned out good hounds, too, Took had to give him that. Hounds well bred for the idiosyncrasies of Exmoor, big and strong enough to fight their way through gorse, wire and flooded rivers, but light enough behind to keep going all day over hilly terrain.

It was a shame. Really it was. They were all going to suffer.

He heard a gate latch and Coffin emerged from the yards and touched his cap. It was feudal, but Took rather liked it.

'Bob,' he said.

'Mr Took.'

Took had a final drag and stamped on his cigarette.

'Bad news, I'm afraid, Bob.'

Bob Coffin's expression didn't change. Like a sheep's.

'We've worked out the merger with the Midmoor.'

Coffin nodded, waiting for more.

'We'll have joint Masters, and their whipper-in has agreed to go part-time with Alistair Farrell. But I'm afraid we'll lose the name.'

This was a bitter blow. Took could tell by the way Coffin almost blinked. There'd been a Blacklands Hunt on Exmoor for a hundred and forty-odd years. Never fashionable, but *there*.

'The good news,' Took continued more cheerfully, 'is that Malcolm Bidgood has room for one more in kennels—'

'Huntsman?'

'Assistant huntsman.'

No such thing. Coffin didn't say it, but they both knew it. Forty years and he was being demoted to kennelman. Like some work-experience boy up for the summer holidays from Bicton College.

'We'll be based at their kennels,' Took hurried on, relieved that the worst was over. 'But I don't want you to have to hurry out of here, Bob. This is your home, and I made sure it was part of the deal that it won't be sold until next season, so you've got plenty of time to sort things out. I was very clear about that.'

Bob Coffin didn't thank him, but nodded briefly and glanced at the cottage.

'Sorry to be the bearer of bad tidings.'

Coffin nodded once more. 'What of the pack?' he asked.

'Ah yes. The pack. Mr Stourbridge says we'll take three couple. He trusts you to pick the best of them, but they did say nothing over three years old, please.'

'What of Rufus?'

'Nothing over three. I did ask. And I've been calling round all week but nobody needs the others. Bloody shame.'

'Nobody needs 'em,' said Bob Coffin. It wasn't a question, but Took answered it anyway.

'That's right.'

'What'll I do with 'em then?'

Took looked surprised. Surely that was self-evident? But Bob Coffin just looked confused. He wasn't going to make him *say* it, was he?

Apparently he was. The passive-aggressive little caveman.

'Well, I'm afraid we'll have to dispose of them, Bob. Terrible shame, but there you go.'

'Shoot 'em, you mean?'

Took was surprised that Coffin was surprised. God, anyone would think he'd never shot an animal in his life. Like there wasn't a constant stream of ribby horses and broken-legged cows to dispatch in the big shed. Not to mention the old hounds – every season there were five or six who could no longer keep up and had to go to the happy hunting ground, courtesy of a .22 handgun. The old bugger wasn't going to get all weepy on him now, was he?

'Yes,' said Took. 'We're all going to suffer a bit, I'm afraid. I can ask Nigel to come up to help you, if you like.'

Coffin looked away across the meadow to where the pied backs of the sixty hounds could be seen through the chain-link, tails high and curved and waving like happy flags as they milled around the giant slabs of raw cow.

'Shoot 'em,' he said softly.

'That's right,' said Took briskly. 'Nothing you haven't done a thousand times before though, is it?'

'Not to fit dogs.'

'Look, they exist to do a job and now they're out of work. We have to be realistic about this, you know.'

'The whole pack,' said Coffin quietly.

Took started to lose patience. 'They're *hounds*, Bob, not *pets*, for fuck's sake! They're not bloody children! You don't *love* them.'

Coffin said nothing – he continued to look away towards the yards through the first stinging flakes of sleet.

Took collected himself and cleared his throat. 'Look, I did my best. Been calling round all week. Packs like to breed their own now, you know that.'

Coffin said nothing. Took decided to stop grovelling and treat him like the hunt servant he was. 'So you don't want me to send Nigel up?'

'No,' Coffin said.

'Right,' said Took, and strode back to the Range Rover, leaving his flattened cigarette butt to show where he'd been.

*

When Mr Took left, I chose the three couple for the Midmoor.

Connor, Dancer, Patch, Boatman, Rusty and Rumble.

The rest I shot.

Better to do it before I could think about it too much, see? Didn't take more than an hour. I took 'em to the big shed in their couples, so I'd have the chain to hold 'em still by, but they were all good dogs.

Rufus was a bit hard. Only natural, him being the best and all, and a favourite. But – strange to say – the worst was a little bitch called Frankie. Nice little maid with a funny way of wrinkling up her snout to smile at you. Got that from her mother, Bella, who got it from *her* mother, Fern. Frankie was almost the last to go. The pack was already piled up in a corner of the shed when her and Bumper followed me in. Both put their heads down and licked at the blood on the floor so I shot Bumper quick, then put the muzzle against Frankie's head next, as it was held low by the chain between them.

Before I could pull the trigger, Frankie twisted to look up at me, and smiled.

PART THREE

SUMMER

35

Jonas woke on a cold cement floor with the smell of dogs and disinfectant strong in his nose, and icy hands on his chest. It was dark, even though he wasn't blindfolded, and he was dimly aware of a man bending over him, tugging his clothes off. Jonas flailed weakly, hoping to connect, but found he couldn't feel his own arms – didn't know where they were or what they were doing.

The hands were firm but not hurtful. They quickly stripped him, and Jonas became sick and panicky at the thought that he couldn't stop what was happening to him, however bad it got . . . He felt his adult self dissolving around him like sugar in water. The terror in his chest was the terror of a small boy. The strength of a man drained from him and he knew once more the weakness of the very young and vulnerable.

Then the dark figure bent forward and looped something around Jonas's throat. Something to hold him. Something to hold him *down* . . .

He tried to cry out, tried to jerk away, tried to fight back, but he was a fish flopping about on dry land.

'Ssshh now,' said the man. 'Ssssshh. There's a good bay.'

Jonas was a child again, and he was helpless.

And then – right under his chin – he felt the click that locked the collar around his neck.

*

New roadblocks were set up. More officers were drafted in from other force areas and even from the neighbouring Devon & Cornwall Police, whose patch bled into Exmoor to the north-west. As they arrived, Reynolds sent them straight to the woods to join the hunt . . . for what and for whom he was not completely sure.

Davey Lamb was returned to the bosom of his family. His brother was not. Rice hoped she never again had to watch two human beings disintegrate in front of her eyes the way that Lettie Lamb and her mother did when they realized Steven was still missing.

Jonas Holly's home was searched. First to check on Em's claim that he had indeed disappeared along with Steven Lamb – a fact supported by the open back door and the abandoned wheelbarrow half-full of weeds and hedge-trimmings. Then a more careful search was made as a matter of procedure, because allegations had been made and should therefore be investigated. Emily Carver seemed like a sensible girl, but her secondhand accusations smacked more of grudge than fact. Rice reminded Reynolds that she had personally demanded proof from Steven Lamb of any wrongdoing by Jonas and he'd been unable to provide it.

'I know,' said Reynolds. 'But it does seem unlikely that someone has managed to snatch a teenaged boy *and* a good-sized police officer at the same time. I'm duty bound to take it somewhat seriously.'

'You don't really think Jonas killed his wife and kidnapped all these children, do you?' Rice asked him bluntly.

'No, but life has taught me to consider all possibilities,' said Reynolds.

But he was also a cautious man, and Rice was relieved when Reynolds told the search team that they were searching the home of a fellow officer who was more likely to have been a victim of a crime than the culprit. In that spirit they moved through Rose Cottage with a rare degree of consideration.

Even so, the search felt intrusive, and Rice was not inclined to turn the place upside down. As she went through the house she was struck by the curious mix of chaos and Spartan neatness – as if Jonas Holly never entered certain rooms any more, but lived in the others without thought of his surroundings. Rice didn't do a meticulous search; she didn't feel it was called for, or that Reynolds had meant her to. She went through the rooms upstairs with a careful hand and an experienced eye.

But she didn't need an experienced eye to see Lucy Holly everywhere. Her make-up bag was still on the bedroom dresser; her clothes were still in the wardrobe. A woman's bathrobe hung on the back of the door, her trainers were under the bed – a scruffy pair of pink Converse All Stars.

It was as if Lucy Holly had popped out to the shops and would be back any second, bearing pasta for dinner and maybe a bottle of red like the one Jonas had opened for *her*.

It was a little unsettling, but maybe that was how Jonas liked it. Maybe he liked to imagine that his wife was so close he could almost touch her. That she might walk into the bedroom one night and turn down the covers and climb in beside him as if she'd never been away.

Maybe that was how it was when you lost somebody you loved.

Rice didn't know. She'd never loved someone like that. She realized that now for the first time, standing at the foot of the Hollys' marital bed, and felt the lingering regret of breaking up with Eric leave her like a soft burp.

Staring at the old mascara gone dry on the dressing table, Rice was engulfed by a wave of sadness for Jonas, and another for herself.

Downstairs, the kitchen table was piled high with laundry and mail – most of it junk – while the sink was clean and bare and the draining board held only a single mug, bowl and spoon. A half-bottle of Spanish wine was going bad without a cork.

Reynolds opened the cupboards, which contained ingredients but barely a thing to eat. Herbs, condiments, flour, rice, dried lentils, noodles and split peas, old sauces with sticky lids, and cans of tomatoes.

The front room was dim and everything was covered in a film of grey dust, as if it was all made of television. A red tartan rug folded over the arm of the leather couch was the only touch of warmth.

Reynolds ran his eyes over the eclectic mix on the bookshelf: Stephen King, Philip K. Dick, sports biographies and psychology textbooks. He recognized university leftovers and wondered who had studied the subject. He tilted a copy of *Civilization and its Discontents* off the shelf but found no clue inside. On the mantelpiece was a clock stopped at 7.39, a blue vase without flowers in it, and a photo of Lucy Holly in a silver frame. She was kneeling beside a fresh flowerbed, smiling up into the sunlight with a trowel in one gloved hand.

Not lying at the foot of the stairs with blood bubbling out of her neck.

Reynolds met his own eyes through the mist of the over-mantel mirror. Hazy, and with the light from the window behind him, his hair looked great.

He sighed deeply. If it had only been Steven Lamb who had disappeared, he might have delayed the roadblocks and the imme-diate request for extra manpower. In the middle of a crisis there was always the chance that children – OK, *boys* – there was always a chance that *boys* would invent their own slice of the action. Pretend to fall down a well, pretend to be lost at sea, pretend to be kidnapped . . .

But with Jonas Holly apparently missing too, everything became even more serious. Either both of them had been abducted, which seemed bizarre, or Jonas had taken the boy and, by logical conclusion, the other children as well.

Which seemed bizarre.

Reynolds sighed again and stared gloomily into the mirror. Overhead the floorboards creaked as Rice searched Jonas's bedroom.

The answerphone flashed and Reynolds hit Play on a robot message telling Jonas he had won a holiday in Florida and needed only to call this number to claim his prize.

He moved away, then back again – and played the outgoing message:

Hi, you've reached Jonas and Lucy . . .

Shit.

He'd forgotten what a bloody weirdo Jonas Holly was. For the first time, the idea that he might have murdered his wife and stolen a slew of local children didn't even seem that far-fetched.

He ordered his team to go through the house and garden again. This time with far more rigour.

36

Jess Took watched the skin peel off a small brown pony like a flesh banana, and remembered the fruit bowl in her mother's kitchen. The way her mother polished each apple before it was allowed to take its place among the peaches and grapes; the way Jess was only allowed to take a piece of fruit if she rearranged the display so it didn't look unbalanced.

Nothing worse than lopsided fruit, her mother used to say.

Jess smiled wryly against the cold block wall. She wished her mother could see her now. See the straw she slept on, the cement she shat on and the filth she ate. See if her mother still thought there was *nothing worse* than a wonky apple.

Jess's mouth filled suddenly with tangy saliva as her body remembered the fresh, sweet, juicy crunch of a Braeburn.

Her eyes overflowed.

In the past six weeks, her mouth had almost forgotten what freshness was. Her tongue tasted fetid and her teeth were jagged traps for tiny shards of bone and frayed strands of flesh that resisted her constant probing. She tried never to close her mouth now; tried to keep the air circulating. Sometimes she drooled because of it, but it was better than closing her lips on that dank cavern.

The *sssssssss* sound rose like sticky tape coming off a roll; the pony's carcass jerked as the last of its skin left it and skidded across the floor attached to the winch. The huntsman filled his arms with the hide and hoofs and head, and walked from the big shed to the incinerator to create more stench of burning hair.

He sang as he went, like a madman.

Of course he did. He *was* a madman.

Jess sighed and turned away.

In the kennel next to hers was the new boy. She didn't know his name but she had seen him at school. He was in the sixth form. He wasn't one of the cool kids; he was just an average kid.

Now he was just an average dog.

Hound. Her father always hated it when she called the fox-hounds dogs.

The older boy stirred and Jess turned away from the breezeblock wall and hung her fingers through the chain link on the other side instead.

'Hey,' she said. 'Hey, you with the ears.'

He blinked and frowned and then opened his eyes and looked at the corrugated plastic sheeting over his head.

'Hey, what's your name?'

He turned towards her.

'I'm Jess.'

He closed his eyes again and ignored her. Jess let him. She'd done that plenty when she'd first woken up here: closed her eyes and tried to go back to sleep so she could wake from this lunatic dream in her own bed.

After a few moments, he opened his eyes and looked at her again. She laughed – a short humourless sound.

'Yeah, it's real,' she said. 'Crap, right?'

He propped himself on his elbows. 'Jess Took?'

'Yep.'

'You're alive.'

'You're a genius.'

He got slowly to his feet and stared stupidly down at his dark-blue briefs. 'Where are my clothes?'

'He took them. Don't worry about it. He takes all our clothes.'

'Who does?'

'The huntsman. I can't remember his name. But I know he's the huntsman. Don't worry, he's not a perv. Not yet, anyway.'

Steven looked at her as if for the first time, taking in her grubby bra and matching knickers. It was only the second time he'd ever seen a girl in a bra, but this was nothing like the first.

'I feel sick,' he said.

'It's just the drugs,' Jess told him. 'Everyone feels sick when they first get here.'

Everyone.

Steven peered through the chain link beyond Jess Took and saw a little blonde girl, staring at him with solemn eyes; beyond her was a brown-haired child of about the same size. Kylie someone, and the other girl whose name he couldn't remember – they'd been taken from the bus. In the furthest kennel of all was a thin, freckled boy with red hair. All the wire between them made the child he guessed must be Pete Knox indistinct and hazy in a block pattern, like a bad digital signal.

'Hi,' Pete said, and waved sombrely. Steven raised a slow hand.

'What's your name?' said the blonde girl.

'Steven,' he said.

'She's Kylie,' said Jess. 'And that's Maisie and Pete.' She flicked her filthy hair and Steven noticed her collar for the first time. Almost simultaneously he put his hand to his own throat and felt the thick, soft leather collar there. His fingers worked at the buckle.

'You can't take it off. It's locked on.'

His fingers found the little padlock. 'Why?'

She shrugged. ''Cos he's a loony, that's why.'

A loony. The childish tag was not enough to describe anyone who would do this.

'Hey!' The shout and a metallic rattle behind him made Steven spin round, heart in his mouth. Two kennels down a youngster with bright-yellow hair slapped the chain link with the flats of both palms, and grinned happily.

'Hey! Hello!'

'Hi,' said Steven cautiously.

'Are we going home? Are we going home for tea? Can I have biscuits when we get home?'

Charlie Peach.

Steven had seen him occasionally, trailing behind his father into Mr Jacoby's shop; once waiting for Mr Peach inside the secretary's office after school. But mostly Charlie lived in a separate world, away from the normality of Shipcott. An indoors world where it was safe, or at the special school he went to. Steven had seen a Sunshine coach parked outside Mr Peach's house on more than one occasion, waiting to take Charlie out for the day with the other vacant, smiling children packed inside.

Although once he'd met the eyes of a boy in that coach.

Above the boy's crooked hands and shiny, wagging chin, he'd met a pair of eyes that had glared at him as if it was all *his* fault. Steven had looked away and never looked into the coach again. It was a different world in that coach.

Now he and Charlie Peach were in the *same* world. That made his already uneasy stomach feel still more sour.

'Who's *he*?' demanded Charlie, waggling a finger through the diamonds.

Steven looked down and sucked in his breath.

In the cage between them lay Jonas Holly – a bruise painting one eye as black as a pirate's patch, and a three-foot chain leading from the metal hoop on his collar to a small brass padlock fed through the fence that separated him from Charlie.

Jonas Holly was a *victim* – just like *him*.

All the rules Steven had lived by for eighteen long months changed in an instant and he felt dizzy with the adjustment. What did it mean? If Jonas hadn't kidnapped the children, then had he still killed his wife? Steven felt the two notions warring within him. He'd been almost sure of *both* those things, and now his own eyes were telling him that at least one of them was not true.

He thought of the woods. The memories came in disjointed flashes – the smooth-faced man trying to heave a limp body on to the back seat of the old Ford; Davey's red shoulder just visible in the open boot; the fear of moving *towards* danger instead of *away* from it, the way his gut churned at him not to . . .

His brother in his arms – warm, and waking too loudly.

Ssssssh!

Davey hadn't shushed. Instead he'd shouted and lashed out and caught Steven a stunning blow on the nose. Steven sighed. It wasn't Davey's fault; he hadn't known what he was doing.

'Where's Davey?' he said to no one.

'Who's Davey?' said Jess.

Steven looked both ways through the wire and did not see his brother. He had made it! He smiled inside – then thought of Davey falling into his mother's arms instead of him, and his face tingled with imminent tears.

'Who's *he*?' Charlie asked again, more forcefully, still wiggling a finger at Jonas Holly.

'He's a policeman,' said Steven.

'Oh,' said Charlie. 'Do you know "Ten Green Bottles"?' He started to sing it without waiting for an answer.

'Mr Holly?' said Steven tentatively, but the man did not move. Steven frowned at his long flat body clad only in shorts. His abdomen was a shallow dish between his ribs and his hip bones, containing thick red scars that crawled and twisted across his pale skin like some strange delicacy that might require chopsticks.

The marks a killer had made.

'I feel sick,' Steven said again, and turned away.

✳

When he wasn't robbing banks, Davey had often fantasized about being a cop. As part of those fantasies he'd also imagined interrogating a suspect. In his fertile young mind – fed by television – chairs were scraped across concrete floors, fists were banged on Formica tables, and interviews were conducted in an atmosphere of such loud intensity that spittle landed on the used coffee cups between the adversaries.

So when Dr Evans asked if he felt up to speaking to the police, Davey – despite having passed a restless night at North Devon Hospital – was excited.

At first.

He'd imagined a cop who looked like Will Smith in *Men In Black*. Cool, wearing shades and a sharp suit, with a gun in his sock and a watch shaped like a Dairylea slice. The reality was more like being quizzed by his maths teacher, Mr Harris, who picked his nose when he thought no one was looking.

DI Reynolds asked the same boring questions over and over again, and wrote everything down in a little notebook. Then he flipped the pages of that notebook back and forth before he asked his next question. It made him seem like he'd lost his memory. Davey had told him *three times* that he hadn't seen the face of the man who had snatched him, and yet he kept asking about him, but in another way – as if he could trap Davey into remembering who it was.

'Did you see him coming?'

'No. I told you that already. He came up behind me.'

'Tell me about the car.'

'I don't remember.'

'What colour was it?'

'I *told* you.'

'Can you tell me again?'

'Dark. Blue or black. Or green maybe.'

'Was the man wearing anything on his hands?'

'I can't *remember*.'

'Did he tie your hands or mouth at any time?'

'No.'

'Not with rope?'

'No.'

'Or tape of any kind?'

'*No!*'

'But you did see Constable Holly?'

'Yes, when they dragged me out from under the car.'

'*They* dragged you?'

'Someone dragged me. I was backwards.'

'But Mr Holly and this *smooth* man were two different people?'

Davey rolled his eyes and didn't bother answering.

Lettie gave him a look. 'Don't be rude, Davey.'

'Yes,' sang Davey. 'They were two different people.'

'What happened then?'

'I dunno. I was all . . . whirly.'

'And then you remember being in the boot—'

'Yes.'

'And that's when you saw Steven.'

'Yes.'

'And what happened then?'

Davey hesitated. There were things he couldn't remember. Lots of them. But there were other things he *could* remember that he'd rather not tell. Specially not with his mother and Dr Evans hovering anxiously at the foot of his bed, listening to everything. His mother clutched the metal rail with both hands, as if DI Reynolds might carry him *and* his bed off, just for a laugh.

He remembered being jostled and opening his eyes to see Steven's face so close . . .

'*Sssssh!*'

'*What? Go away.*'

'*Davey, shush!*'

Hands under his shoulders and knees, lifting him out of the boot of the car; the sky and the treetops above him, and sweat rolling off a spiky fringe.

His feet hitting the ground.

'*Go AWAY! I'll tell my brother!*'

'*Davey, shut up! It's me. Sssssh!*'

But he hadn't shushed. He *could* remember *that*. With shame coating his innards like hot syrup, Davey remembered fighting instead – fighting *Steven*! Waving his fists blindly and shouting so loud that it echoed. He couldn't remember what. He'd connected with one fist. Hard. And then he'd just run – all wobbly and tumbly and knee-scrapey through the stumps and the ferns.

He hadn't even looked back . . .

'Yes?' said DI Reynolds.

'And he helped me out and we ran away.'

'And where was Mr Holly while you were running away?'

'Dunno.' Davey shrugged.

'And where was the other man?'

'Dunno.'

A tiny, elderly Pakistani woman pushed a filthy mop shaped like a V into the ward and past the end of his bed while nodding into a mobile phone, and Davey longed for a life like that, where he didn't have to think, and nobody asked him difficult questions.

'They just let you run away? Didn't try to catch you?'

'I ran *fast*,' said Davey. Then, without prompting, he added hurriedly, 'Steven was right behind me; he must have got lost or something.'

DI Reynolds said nothing but flipped back several pages,

clicking his pen and making a small *tu-tu-tu* sound through his pursed lips, like a tiny train.

Why do I always get the retard? thought Davey. This guy was such a loser. Plus, there was something weird about DI Reynolds's hair, although Davey couldn't say quite what.

'We ran away *together*,' he provided for free.

'After he helped you out of the car, did your brother say anything to you?'

Sssssssh!

'I can't remember.'

Davey's mother bit her lip and blinked out of the window.

DI Reynolds didn't sigh, but Davey could tell he wanted to. Maybe the policeman was as disappointed with the interview as he was.

'Try,' said DI Reynolds.

'OK,' Davey said, and put on a trying face, but all the time his mind squirmed with the dawning awfulness of it all. Steven had come to help him, but he hadn't helped Steven back. Instead he'd punched him; he'd shouted when Steven had told him to shush; he'd given them both away and then only saved himself. This was not the kind of cop or bank robber he'd ever imagined being. The kind who abandoned a friend to his fate. A *brother*.

'What's wrong, Davey?' said DI Reynolds.

Davey shook his head. His mother gazed at him with eyes like a cartoon puppy in a rainstorm, and Davey could barely look at her straight.

'He *did* say something!'

The sudden hope in his mother's eyes triggered a tumble of words. 'He said . . . Steven said . . . "Run, Davey! I'm right behind you! Run home to Mum." And so I did.'

At the foot of the bed, Lettie clutched her mouth and nodded hard as tears rolled down her cheeks.

DI Reynolds clicked his pen, but did not write it down.

37

There was a sharp hiss and the children got up as one and moved towards the gates of their kennels. The hiss came again, and again, a slow metallic scraping of the knife being sharpened.

They clung to the chain link, waiting expectantly. Finally there was the dull thump of something hitting metal, and the low rumble of an approach on wheels across the rutted concrete walkway.

A low flatbed trolley emerged from the back door of the big shed. The huntsman propelled it, his legs bowed but sturdy, his face smoothed and distorted by a stocking mask, like a bad fabric puppet.

Steven got a flash of the clearing in the woods, of Davey curled in the boot of the old blue saloon while the man with the smooth head held Jonas Holly's legs; the slow stagger towards the trees; the grip on his arm; the kick to the backs of his knees. He remembered the hot chemical wool over his face and the way everything swam away from him like fish spiralling away through the tops of the trees . . .

Something heavy dropped into Pete's kennel and Steven flinched. The huntsman moved down the line.

It wasn't until he got to Jess's kennel that Steven could see clearly what he was throwing over the gates . . .

Bones.

As if they were dogs!

And Jess Took picked one up and started to chew on it as if no one had told her she *wasn't* a dog.

'All right, bay?' the huntsman said to Steven without looking at him and not waiting for an answer.

'Why am I here? What do you want?'

'Good lad,' said the huntsman, and leaned up to drop a couple of big bones over the fence. Steven looked down at the crude grey-pink chunks, with shiny white knobs protruding.

'I'm not eating that,' he said firmly.

The huntsman ignored him and moved on.

'He doesn't listen,' said Jess sadly. 'He only talks.'

The huntsman dropped bones into Jonas Holly's kennel and then into Charlie's.

Charlie picked up a rack of ribs and said, 'Thank you.'

The huntsman turned his trolley and wheeled it back down the line. It made a different sound when it was empty.

As he passed her kennel, Jess Took bared her teeth at him and said, 'Woof!'

*

Kate Gulliver also thought that it was 'very interesting' that Steven Lamb had implicated Jonas in the abductions – and then disappeared himself.

Reynolds was delighted. He'd rung Kate – who'd always encouraged him to call her that – and told her of Elizabeth Rice's conversation with the boy.

Very interesting, she'd said – and Reynolds wished he could turn back time and put her call on speakerphone just so he could give Rice a triumphant look.

'That's what *I* said,' he told Kate in Rice's hearing instead, but Rice gave no indication she had heard anything – triumphant or otherwise. She was rummaging in a bag from the Spar shop they were parked outside.

Kate continued, 'The trauma of Steven's experiences at a formative age could have damaged him in countless ways. He might have paranoid tendencies which make him focus his suspicions on an innocent party.'

She sounded quite enthusiastic about the idea. 'I can even see a scenario where he might visit similar experiences on other children. Abuse begets abuse; it's not unusual.'

'Exactly,' Reynolds nodded, hoping Rice was getting this: that he'd been *right* and that Kate Gulliver *said* so.

Increasingly he got the impression that Elizabeth Rice resented his superior intellect. It was a shame, because she was no slouch herself, but lately – since he'd been the boss – she hovered between two standpoints: questioning him or ignoring him. Both got under his skin. Today she'd been in a particularly bad mood because her digging into the background of the Piper Parents had turned up nothing and made everybody hate her. Reynolds had told her that it went with the territory and she'd replied, 'Maybe *your* territory,' in a tone he would have corrected if she'd been a man.

Reynolds had always felt he had a great kinship with women. Men were threatened by his brains and often responded with hostility. DCI Marvel had been a case in point. But women were generally far happier to let him do the thinking for them, while he encouraged them to shine in supporting roles.

'There's no *I* in *team*,' he was fond of telling them. It went down terribly well.

Most of the time.

Lately Elizabeth Rice had greeted the homily with stony silence.

Pity. There'd been a time a few years back when he'd thought Rice might be girlfriend material. Even wife. But then they'd spent time together on cases and he'd seen all the things that were wrong with her. It wasn't just the toast and the baked-bean juice. She often wore jeans, she laughed too loudly, and she sang in the shower. She didn't have a bad voice but she had no taste in music – or consideration for those who did, and who might be trying to work just the other side of the Travelodge wall.

Slowly those faults had eroded any ideas he might once have harboured about a possible future together, and her burgeoning intellectual jealousy was very unattractive.

Kate said she would contact Steven Lamb's old therapist.

'Excellent,' said Reynolds. 'Keep me informed.' He hung up and turned to Rice, who immediately held up two thin, white-bread sandwiches in plastic boxes – a barrier to his victory.

'Chicken or ham?' she said.

They both looked like the antithesis of nutrition. He thought of DCI Marvel and felt a single solitary pang of guilt. No, not guilt – *empathy*. It was tough at the top.

'Chicken.'

They ate in the hot car. He was halfway through his sandwich before he realized it was, in fact, ham. He grimaced and sighed loudly but Rice didn't ask him what was wrong.

Reynolds hoped his new hair made her realize just how badly she'd blown it.

*

The big one's not eating, but the youngster's settling in. Didn't want either of 'em, but what's to be done? The big one come sneaking up on me just as I'm winkling the first bay out from under the car. Grabs me hard and so I hit him with the stick. I know him too – and he knows me – so I had to bring him with. And right when I'm getting *him* in the car, here come another one trying to steal the first! It were Piccadilly Circus in the middle of Landacre Wood. Lucky they're both scrawny.

But it fills up the yard again. That's the main thing. Bin empty too long; made me *itch* with the emptiness. Every one I filled made the others look even emptier. Now I look at the runs, all full of life, and it's like a sigh of relief in my head.

They're still searching, but I'm not bothered. Let 'em come. I got my hiding places. Serves all them folk right. Teach 'em to value what they got, be it children or traditions. You can't get 'em back. Once they're gone they're gone for good.

Still, I don't like the big one. Something not right with that one, I always thought. Reminds me of a hound I had once off the Beaufort – Bosun. Huge brute, he were. A demon in the field, Jim Wetherall said when he offloaded him, but the wily old bastard never mentioned him were mazed in the yard. Bit a horse once. Imagine that – a bloody foxhound biting a horse! Not a nip either – a right proper chunk out the belly and I had to whip him raw before him let go.

Only dog I were ever wary of, Bosun, and the only one I ever shot and was happy to do it. Mostly him was as waggy as the rest, and that's what made him so dangerous, see – the way he'd turn, sudden like.

The big one's like that, I reckon – pretending to be weak, not eating, not moving. But I never had a hound fool me twice and I won't be starting now.

So the big one's chained up. Because of Bosun.

The others are free in the runs, like the old ones. They get hungry when they hear the knife like the old ones too! Already come running to the gates, slavering – specially the smallest bay – he's a hungry one! The maids are little charmers, too. Make daisy chains in the meadow! Like a storybook.

They're not as noisy as the old ones, but maybe that'll come with time. They can make all the noise they like up here and no one to hear 'em for miles.

I miss the noise. That quiet made me mazed.

Maybe I can walk 'em too, some time. At night maybe, and coupled up like pups to keep 'em from darting off all over. It would be good for 'em, and good for me. Watching 'em get fit and strong and biddable.

Don't know if I were happy before. Never rightly thought of it. But this makes me feel something like happy again.

It's good to get back in the old routine.

Good to have something to love.

38

The incinerator ignited with a soft *whump* and made Steven's mouth fill with saliva. It angered him, and he resisted the urge to rise and move to the front of the kennel to await feeding like the other children did. It made him think of the polar bears he'd once seen at Bristol Zoo – pacing tirelessly, staring up at the crowds, waiting for feeding time.

Instead he lay on the straw that was his bed and looked up through the yellowing corrugated plastic. Strips of dead flies and bird shit and little bits of grit. That had been his sky for six days now. His new horizons were close and diamond-meshed.

Steven wiped the drool off his lips and got to his knees.

The crumbling grey block wall at the back of the kennel had chinks that allowed him to see straight across the yard to the row of empty stables. If he leaned to one side, a chink showed him the ramp and partly inside the big shed – and the huntsman going about his work.

Today his work was a cow.

Steven watched the black-and-white beast walk cautiously off the trailer. It stopped at the bottom and gazed around with empty eyes. Steven had been to the new supermarket in Barnstaple once and seen old people doing the same thing, standing in the cheese aisle, looking for the tea.

'Hup! Hup!'

The huntsman touched her hip and the cow moved down the rutted ramp into the big shed, skidding a little and leaning back to maintain her balance, her giant udders swinging.

The huntsman followed her down in his green overalls, boots and flat cap. He didn't wear his stocking mask in the big shed and Steven could see the years of wrinkles and creases, the small blue eyes, the lipless mouth and the yellowing teeth.

'He doesn't know we can see him,' whispered Jess beside him, and he nodded. It was a small thing, but it was worth noting. Maybe they could use it one day. He didn't know how, but most things were useful, he'd always found.

The gunshot cracked loudly in the shed, and Steven jumped. Two cages away, Charlie sucked in a shocked breath and then started to howl like a child who's fallen off a bicycle – with a wide mouth and uninhibited lungs.

Jess turned away and sat down on her raised straw bed. 'It's hot,' she said dully.

Steven didn't answer. They all knew it was hot. It hadn't rained for ever.

He felt the collar around his neck. It was not uncomfortable, but it was annoying and confusing. The little padlock that held it shut lay in the hollow at the base of his throat like a cold pendant, but if he lay too long in the sun it grew hot enough to hurt. The collar itself was old leather, soft and tactile. There was a flat metal strip on it, perhaps two inches long; Steven imagined that it was where a dog's name might be engraved. He ran his fingernail over it carefully but could feel nothing that might indicate that his own name – or another's – had been marked there. He took some comfort in that; the collar had not been waiting for him. He was not chosen for this. Not special.

He thought of Em, who *was*.

Too special for him.

She probably would have realized it soon anyway, but now that he was gone, what was there to keep her true?

Was she already with someone else? Maybe even one of his friends? Lewis or Lalo Bryant. Lewis was definitely capable of turning comfort into copping a feel. The thought made Steven's lips thin, and he thumped the wall with the side of his fist.

'What's up?' said Jess Took.

'Nothing,' he said. 'Shut up.'

She stuck her tongue out at him but not with any great feeling.

Steven put his eye back to the best chink in the wall. He watched the huntsman sharpen his knife in a series of sibilant swipes, and swallowed the resulting saliva. His stomach rumbled. He turned away before the cuts were made but soon there was the clink of chains as the winch was attached, and then the rising *sssssssss* that was the hide separating from the flesh it had protected since birth.

'Sorry, Jess,' said Steven.

She stuck her tongue out at him again – but this time she smiled.

Down the row, Maisie and Kylie and Pete were playing I Spy. The game had limited scope – I spy a fence; I spy a gate; I spy concrete – but the three youngest children often played it anyway. Sometimes they played 'Shout for Help', in which one of them counted down from three and they all screamed 'Help.' Charlie usually joined in, but Jess never did; when Steven asked why, she just shrugged and said, 'They build kennels where people won't be bothered by the dogs howling. Nobody's going to hear us.'

'Somebody might,' said Steven, and shouted with the rest of them. But the huntsman never seemed perturbed by the game, so Steven guessed Jess was probably right.

Steven squinted through the wall again. The cow's carcass was being winched through a dark doorway within the big shed now, giant, pink and stripped of skin. The hide lay in a black-and-white pile along with the feet and the tail and the head, with eyes gone milky and its rude blue tongue lapping at a little ooze of blood on the floor.

Soon the air would stink of hair and horn. Something in the incinerator always popped loudly; Steven didn't know what it was, but imagined the eyes, and was relieved every time it was over.

'What do you think he wants?' he said.

Jess shrugged. 'Money, I suppose.'

'My mum doesn't have any money,' said Steven.

'Nor does my dad,' said Jess. 'The horses take it all.'

39

Davey saw the story in the paper on the rack outside Mr Jacoby's shop as he walked to Shane's house.

THE ONE THAT GOT AWAY

Davey stopped dead. He almost didn't recognize the blurred photo of his own mother, one hand over her mouth, the other clutching the end of his hospital bed. There *he* was, propped against pillows and looking disappointingly eleven, and there was DI Reynolds, leaning back in his chair and frowning.

Davey picked up the *Sunday Mirror*. The story was labelled 'Exclusive' and had been written by someone called Marcie Meyrick. As he read it, Davey felt his whole body go hot and cold and squirmy.

The mother of kidnapped brothers weeps as her younger son reveals the gruelling details of their ordeal at the hands of the infamous Pied Piper.

Speaking from his hospital bed, little Davey Lamb—

'*Little Davey Lamb*'? Davey's heart plummeted. Shit, they were going to have him for *breakfast* at school.

> *. . . little Davey Lamb told police he and Steven had managed a daring escape from the serial kidnapper.*
>
> *But, in a cruel twist of fate, Steven then got lost in the woods where they were both taken more than a week ago, and is presumed to have been recaptured.*
>
> *'We ran away together,' a sobbing Davey told his distraught mum, Lettie Lamb, 39, of Shipcott.*

Sobbing?! He hadn't *sobbed*! Shit! Davey wanted to *punch* someone. Who the hell was Marcie Meyrick? What a fucking *liar*! He read on:

> *But the last little Davey heard of his big brother was Steven shouting at him to run home to his mother – and then they lost touch in the deep Landacre Woods in the middle of the moor.*
>
> *The child snatcher has terrorized Exmoor for weeks, stealing children from parked cars, and cunningly eluding police.*
>
> *Detectives leading the manhunt now presume that Steven Lamb is being held with six other captives – five children and police constable Jonas Holly, who was apparently abducted while trying to rescue young Davey.*
>
> *The kidnaps are only the latest in a horrific series of crimes visited on the moor over the past thirty years.*
>
> *Between 1980 and 1983, serial killer Arnold Avery buried six young victims on Exmoor, and two years ago another murderous spree left eight people dead in the small town of Shipcott. The killer has never been caught.*
>
> *'Exmoor is cursed,' said one elderly resident who didn't want to be named . . .*

Davey threw the paper down furiously.

'Steady now,' said Mr Jacoby, who'd appeared in the doorway.

'They're writing lies!' shouted Davey.

'That's what newspapers do.'

'It shouldn't be allowed!'

'It's not,' said Mr Jacoby. 'If they've lied and you can prove it, you can sue them.'

'I'm *going* to! It said I cried and I didn't cry! Shit!'

'How's your mum doing, Davey?' asked Mr Jacoby soothingly.

Davey looked confused, then shrugged. 'Fine.'

Mr Jacoby sighed and withdrew, then reappeared a moment later and handed Davey a Mr Kipling Dundee cake and a Mars bar.

'Here you are. For teatime. I hope they find your brother soon. You give my best to your mother and gran, all right?'

Davey had pilfered industriously from Mr Jacoby's shop for years and now felt a bit embarrassed as he took the offerings and mumbled his thanks.

Life had been so simple and suddenly everything was just so *wrong*. How had it happened? Davey had no idea, but as he walked away with the Mars bar melting in his jeans pocket, images kept crowding into his head. Images of the money he and Shane had failed to spend, of the piece-of-shit cardboard bird he'd made for Nan – and of Steven's skateboard nose-diving gently into the silt.

He never had any luck, however hard he tried.

He carried on to Shane's, where they ate the Dundee cake with their fingers in the back garden and threw what was left into Shane's neighbour's pond.

40

'How do you do?' Charlie asked Jonas through the chain link. 'How old are you? I've got a mouse in my house. He's white. His name is Mickey. You can play with him if you want. Have you got any biscuits? I'm hungry.'

Charlie wiggled his fingers through the fence and touched Jonas, resting his pinkie on his shoulder, or stroking his hair like a child with a loved toy.

Jonas ignored him, just as he ignored Steven and the bones that thudded over the gate. It was food and he was hungry. But the thought of eating meat made him feel sick. He thought about Sunday lunchtimes, staring at the bloodied flesh on his plate while his mother cleared the table around him and his father became increasingly red-faced at the waste.

You liked meat a month ago.

But he didn't like it now.

There are children starving in Africa.

Jonas didn't care. Africa was welcome to his meat.

Every day the faceless man came into the kennel to clean it, and Jonas squeezed his eyes shut and curled up small so the man wouldn't notice him.

It worked.

Since that first night of those cold hands, the huntsman hadn't even come close to him. He carried a single key in his pocket that opened every padlock. He let himself into the kennel each day, scraped up shit with a short-handled shovel and sluiced the cement with milky disinfectant. Then he unwound a thick brick-coloured hose and sprayed any remaining mess into the little drain hole, refilled the water bucket and moved on.

Once he'd finished, Jonas could breathe again. Feel his ribs press down on to the ground again like long chill fingers cupping his torso, reminding him that he was still alive.

He was not let out into the meadow with the children. He could not even stand upright because he was never let off the short chain. He didn't know why, but he also didn't care about the lack of movement. Moving would only draw attention to himself, when he wanted to be invisible.

Only his stomach seemed aware of the time that had passed.

'I heard your tummy!' Charlie said beside him. 'Grrrrrrr. Grrrrrrr. Like that.' His smile faded and he added a plaintive, 'I'm hungry.'

'Give him your meat if you're not going to eat it,' said Steven Lamb.

Jonas didn't look at Steven and tried not to look at anything else either.

Cages filled with children, with no one to protect them.

This problem was too big and he was too small to do anything about it.

People hurt children. He'd had no answer when he was a child up at Springer Farm and he had no answer now that he was a child again.

All he could do was to close his eyes curl up tight, and hope it was all over quickly.

*

'Hey,' said Steven. 'Mr Holly?'

No answer. The man had barely moved since they arrived. He hadn't eaten at all. A few times Steven had seen him drink from the steel bucket, and he had pissed into the drain at the front of the cage. Once he'd cried in the night, like a baby.

It was embarrassing and it was bloody annoying.

Mr Holly was an adult. And a policeman. And he was doing nothing to help them – or even himself.

Unless he was playing some sick game. Trying to *pretend* to be one of them, when really he was in on it with the huntsman . . . Steven knew it was unlikely but he was still loathe to give the man the benefit of any doubt.

'Hey!' he said more sharply. 'Charlie's talking to you.'

Jonas Holly slowly closed his eyes.

Steven kicked the fence. 'Hey!'

Nothing.

Behind him, Jess started to sing quietly. '*Waltzing Matilda, waltzing Matilda . . .*'

Charlie twisted his fist back through the fence.

'C'mon, Charlie!' said Kylie, and she and Maisie started to sing along. '*You'll come a waltzing Matilda with me . . .*'

Charlie clapped and joined in. '*We all sing Matilda, we all sing Matilda . . .*'

Steven got up and ran his eyes and his fingers around his tiny prison, seeking escape.

Not for the first time.

The ends of the wire that folded over the steel struts were too stiff to unwind by hand; he could climb up and poke his head through the twelve-inch gap between the plastic roof and the top of the gate, but it was too narrow to do more. And although the grey block wall at the back of the kennel was crumbling around the edges, it was solid in all the important places. He had sat and kicked it repeatedly with his heel – and achieved nothing but a blister.

'You can't get out,' Jess Took had told him the first time he'd made this circuit, but he was still reluctant to concede the point. He'd had to concede every *other* point. He'd had to sleep on the straw bed, drink from the steel bucket, pee down the drain, and – after three agonizing days desperate for rescue – he had finally shat on the cold cement floor. The full house of humiliation.

They were exercised every morning and every afternoon. Everyone but Jonas Holly was led out of their cages and clipped to each other by short coupling chains that meant they could walk but not run or climb – although ballroom dancing would probably have been an option, as long as it was a slow tune. The huntsman led them to a small fenced meadow in pairs roughly according to height, which meant that Steven was always with Charlie, who often forgot that he was restrained and would wander off to pick up grit or stop suddenly to watch a cloud – each time jerking on Steven's neck.

While the other children walked or sat together, Steven ran a hand along the perimeter. The fence was high – maybe twelve feet – and its base was sunk in a kerb of concrete, so there was no burrowing under it. The gate was secured with a large, rusted padlock. Beyond the meadow was a small cottage. Once it had been whitewashed, but now it was grey-green with age. While they were locked in the meadow, the huntsman went to the cottage. Sometimes – like now – Steven could see him standing a little way back from the window with a mug of tea, watching them.

Always watching them.

Steven was a resourceful boy but, dogged though he was, he could see no way of escape – especially with Charlie hanging off his neck.

He stood for a moment and watched the huntsman, who shuffled backwards into the darkness where Steven could no longer see him.

He was a rubbish kidnapper.

But a good enough guard.

'Butterfly!' shouted Charlie, and yanked Steven sideways.

41

Em couldn't believe what was happening.

Steven had disappeared before her eyes and yet for a week her mother insisted that she get up every day and continue to go to school.

As if the sky hadn't fallen.

At first she refused. At first she wanted to saddle up Skip and spend the rest of the summer – the rest of her *life* – searching for Steven. Instead she was expected to put on her uniform, pick up her sandwiches and get in the car to be driven to school like a five-year-old.

'But I *love* him!' she'd told her mother, who'd looked at her father, who'd raised his eyebrows the same way he had when she'd said she wanted to do Chemistry instead of History. As if he didn't believe she was capable of such a thing.

She'd got an A in Chemistry though – and it was the thought of that which made her get out of the Range Rover at the school gates every day, wave her mother goodbye, then – once she'd been to registration – walk back down Barnstaple Road to Steven's house.

His nan was in a terrible state. Who could blame her? The doctor came often and gave her pills to add to the pills she already had for angina. He was a young, modern doctor who wore chinos, deck shoes and a pale-pink Ralph Lauren polo shirt, and his tanned presence made the Lambs' little front room seem even dingier than it was. It took a good half-hour after he'd gone for it all to seem quite cosy again.

Steven's mother, Lettie, took pills too. She sat on the sofa next to Nan, crying at *Homes under the Hammer*, with an old Spiderman pyjama top crumpled in her hands. Once – when Lettie left it on the sofa while she went to the bathroom – Em picked it up and pressed it to her nose. To her it smelled only of sleep, but then she was not Steven's mother.

Ten times a day, Nan would cover Lettie's hand with hers and say, 'God will take care of him.' And Lettie would swear and make a cup of tea, or nod and burst into fresh tears.

Steven's Uncle Jude came often. He weeded the garden and brought in shopping and left with the unopened bills. He sat on the sofa with his arm around Lettie, and kissed Nan's cheek when he arrived and when he left. Em gathered he was the kind of uncle who slept with your mother – not the kind you were related to by blood.

Davey got himself up and he made himself toast. He did his homework and made his own sandwiches and left the house quietly – sometimes before Lettie and Nan were even out of bed. Em usually passed him on his way to school, but when she tried to ask whether he was OK, Davey avoided her eyes and sidled around her. When Shane came round now, they made little noise, and Davey quickly tired of the PlayStation. At the ramp, Em had seen Davey frowning while Shane skated. It was as though Davey had become an older person swapped into a boy's body, and Em imagined that somewhere in this universe or the next, there might be a middle-aged woman wondering why her husband had suddenly become obsessed with *Grand Theft Auto* and laughed at his own farts.

Em cooked and washed up, she cleaned the bathroom. She answered the door to the doctor or reporters or police or neighbours with flowers and cakes, and she made sure there was always change for the electricity meter. The Piper Parents came round and Em made tea for everyone while they broke down in relays.

While her own family wouldn't acknowledge her loss, nobody here questioned it. It was assumed.

She learned to ignore the photographers calling her name as she arrived each day, and to say 'No comment, thanks' to reporters who asked outrageous questions to try to provoke her. 'Are you and Steven lovers?', 'Are you pregnant?', 'Do you pray for Steven?', 'Do you think he's dead?'.

School was a forgotten past and her own home was a mere interruption to her industrious vigil. Sometimes she went upstairs and lay on Steven's bed and thought about being there together. How scared she'd been; how excited. It was hard to remember, when being there now was just so sad. Sometimes she went through his things. She pulled on the Liverpool shirt with his name on the back; she didn't know why he kept it, it was way too small for him. She went through his school bag and read his essays – neatly written and neatly constructed. She browsed his odd collection of books – *Five Have Plenty of Fun*, *The Cucumber Pony* and *The Methodology of Serial Killing*. Talking animals and psychopaths nestling side by side on the shelf.

Sometimes Lettie and Nan mentioned Uncle Billy – the boy whose picture was in Steven's room.

He hadn't been hit by a car; he had been murdered.

At first Em was angry that Steven had lied to her. But by asking nothing and listening to everything, she learned the family's story. A story of loss, terror and survival. A story where Steven had very nearly been a victim, but was instead the hero, and which made sense of his bookshelf. It made her own family's stories – a great-grandfather's medal on the beaches, an aunt who'd met the Queen – seem hopelessly humdrum.

For no reason she could have verbalized, Em had always believed Steven was special.

In his absence she learned how right she was.

*

Steven came out of sleep through a rushing tunnel of noise and fear. He awoke sitting bolt upright, with one hand clutching his chest like an old man having an attack.

The screaming was coming from Charlie Peach. Usually so calm and easygoing, Charlie was hurling himself around his cage in a blind panic.

Even Jonas Holly was watching Charlie – his eyes wide and wary.

Charlie knew he was making a fuss and that making a fuss was a bad thing to do, but for once he didn't care. He covered his ears, squeezed shut his eyes and tried to run away from the sound, hurling himself blindly against the mesh of his cage, staggering back to his feet and running headlong into the wire once more. Again and again, his mouth wide, hardly drawing breath between raw, high-pitched howls.

'No meat! No meat!'

Steven pointed at the bones in Charlie's cage and tried to draw his attention. 'There's your meat, Charlie. It's OK. It's right there.'

Charlie was too upset to hear him.

The huntsman ran down the walkway with the flatbed trolley rumbling and clunking before him, and fumbled for the key – his green woollen gloves making it harder than usual. Pressed by the stocking, his face was as blank as always, but his body gave away his urgency.

He strode into the kennel and Charlie shrank back on his bed. The huntsman grabbed him, and Charlie kicked and flailed.

'Leave him alone!' Steven hammered his fist against the chain link. 'Bastard!'

Jonas scrambled to his feet, although the short chain jerked him back to his knees at once. He hooked his fingers through the fence and watched.

Everything went quiet very fast. One moment Charlie was screaming and struggling, the next the huntsman was hauling his limp body from the kennel with his green hand over the boy's mouth and nose.

'Where are you taking him?' Steven yelled. 'Leave him alone!'

The huntsman ignored him. In a series of jerks – and with a strength that belied his stature – he dumped Charlie on to the trolley, then hurried him up the walkway and around the corner.

Steven turned to Jess. 'What happened? Did you see what happened?'

She stared at him, her lower lip trembling.

'What?' he said. 'What's wrong?'

'Helicopter,' said Jess.

It was only then that Steven heard the noise. It was distant but it was unmistakable. He rushed to the front of his cage to peer up through the gap in the roof.

'They're looking for us!' said Steven excitedly.

The other children didn't move.

'Yes,' said Jess Took dully. In the cage at the end, Pete Knox started to cry, which set Maisie off.

'What's wrong?' said Steven, but before anyone could answer, the huntsman came back.

He took Jess next. She shrieked and tried to cover her face but he easily pushed her hands aside and clapped his glove over her nose and mouth. She went limp.

Then the others, one by one.

Pete kicked and howled and then succumbed like a kitten in a bucket of water. Steven shouted his name even after he disappeared from view – one arm dangling off the trolley. He fought panic.

The helicopter was closer now. The sound of the blades came to him in waves. It was criss-crossing the moor. Searching. For *them*.

'One, two, three – Help!' he shouted. 'One, two, three!' Maisie and Kylie just looked at him.

He had to give the helicopter a sign. He looked about his cage desperately. There was nothing to use. Steven gripped the top of the gate and hauled himself up. He pushed his head through the gap where the huntsman dropped the meat, swearing as his right ear tore. He tried to get his arm through as well, but couldn't. His shoulder was too lumpy. He pulled his head back down, scraping his bloody ear again, then waved his right hand in the air until the fingers of his left gave way and he fell back to the floor.

'Don't! You'll make him angry.'

Steven turned on Jonas Holly. The policeman hugged his knees to his chest, visibly trembling, his eyes huge and full of tears. Steven slapped the fence between them, making Jonas flinch.

'What's *wrong* with you?' yelled Steven. 'Get up and *fight*, you *baby!*'

Jonas closed his eyes and put his hands over his ears.

Steven kicked the fence once more, then turned around. The huntsman was right there – his green hand already reaching for him. Steven threw an arm up but he was too late.

There was barely a struggle. The fumes filled his head and he staggered and scraped his knees. He tried to get up and the huntsman helped him.

Helped him to his traitor's feet.

Helped him on to the trolley and rolled him up the walkway and through the big shed to the flesh room.

*

Reynolds had asked to go with the chopper crew. They'd had several flights across the moor already, but he felt sure that his being there would make all the difference to the success of the operation.

Now they'd get things done.

The helmet they gave him smelled of sweat, and he grimaced as he tugged it down over his well-shampooed hair.

The co-pilot, whose name was Lee, shouted instructions at his face as though the blades were already whirring. They weren't.

Reynolds made the mistake of asking about parachutes and everybody laughed so hard that he had to pretend it had been a joke.

He was no expert in aerodynamics, but as he approached the chopper he thought it looked too big for its rotor, and highly unlikely to take off. The closer he got, the more unsettled he felt. The paintwork was scratched all around the door as if it had been bumped in a car park; the vinyl seats were cracked and torn in places. The floor was grimy and utilitarian, with strips of wood screwed to it for grip – like the wooden slats in the changing rooms at the old public pool he'd been taken to as a child. Verruca city. He couldn't help thinking he'd have more confidence in the whole aircraft if it had only been carpeted, the way an airliner was. Reynolds didn't like to see the inner workings of things. It made him too conscious of how much there was to go wrong.

His seatbelt was frayed.

He should have sent Rice. Too late.

Leaving the ground was like climbing a rope ladder – a dizzy, lurching ascent. Lee and the pilot, whose name he hadn't caught, were up front. He was behind them with a jolly, overweight air-support officer who had been introduced as Tuckshop. Reynolds couldn't bring himself to use the name, but tried to sit as close to his own door as possible to stop the chopper yawing to one side.

They had barely left the big H before they were over Exmoor – the neat fields and Toytown cows giving way to brown patches and yellow and purple swathes of gorse and heather.

They passed over ponies, which did not look up, and deer that scattered. Reynolds peered between the seats at the thermal-imaging screen and watched a small group of them explode in a fountain of bright dots, like Pong gone mad.

The other three men shouted at each other and laughed, but Reynolds couldn't make out a thing they were saying. If they were looking at him when they laughed, he just smiled and nodded and hoped they weren't calling him a wanker. He seemed to be the only one who was taking this seriously. No wonder they hadn't found anyone on their previous sorties.

The children could have been taken a long way off, of course. They could be dead. But if they weren't on Exmoor, then there were no clues as to *where* they were. Exmoor was their only lead and it made a dull kind of sense to keep searching it.

Now, up ahead, on the top of a hill, Reynolds could see a small grey collection of utilitarian buildings. He consulted his map but couldn't tell what he was looking at until Tuckshop's nailbitten finger jabbed the paper and he shouted, 'Hunt kennels!' at full volume.

Reynolds nodded. It made him think of Jonas Holly and his dog theory.

The huntsman came back.

Jonas let it happen. He was so small, what else could he do? He kept his eyes closed and smelled that smell, and felt himself getting sick and wobbly.

'Get up.' The voice was in charge and Jonas tried to obey, but the chain pulled him back and he sagged against the fence with his long legs folded under him like a faun's.

'Get up.'

He tried again. The sound of the helicopter was louder now. 'Get *up*!' The huntsman gripped the tether chain and pulled. Jonas staggered out of the safety of the kennel.

The ride on the trolley was brief. Then the sun on his back winked out and the cold was so sudden that he opened his eyes on blackness.

'*Stay.*'

He stayed. There was the sound of chains and metal and the grunt of the huntsman moving something heavy. A squeal of something not oiled. Jonas wasn't sure whether his eyes were open or shut, but then started to make out shapes in the dark. Long, pale shapes, swaying gently.

He was tugged off the trolley and fell to his knees. Strong fingers bound his wrists before him, and a cloth that tasted of dirt was wound around his mouth, pulling his lips painfully against his teeth. He flinched as cold chain was looped around his chest and suddenly there was a mechanical whine and he was being raised from the floor. He half staggered into a standing position just as the chain went slack, and he fell on to his side on a stone floor that was wet with cold.

'Shit,' said the huntsman. 'You're too big.'

Jonas tried to stand but something heavy and cold bumped his face and he nearly fell again. The huntsman steadied him by the collar.

Jonas was dragged and jerked – feeling smaller all the time – back out into the warmth, but on his feet now. He closed his eyes against the brightness.

The helicopter was close. Close and low. It brought no hope to Jonas. Nothing could save him, not even the police. Even as a child he'd known that.

The huntsman pulled harder and Jonas stumbled across the concrete in his bare feet, until his knees hit something metal.

'Get in,' said the huntsman.

Jonas looked down at the horse trough, its deep green water as smooth as marble. Getting in seemed a foolish thing to do.

The helicopter beat so close that Jonas raised his head, but he couldn't see it. The very act made him dizzy.

'*In!*' said the huntsman, and pushed him roughly. The metal edge of the trough caught the side of his knee and he twisted awkwardly.

Off balance.

The huntsman shoved again and this time Jonas felt himself falling.

It took for ever. Falling and trying not to.

He splashed into the trough on his back – one leg still over the sharp metal side. He flopped back in the water and he saw the sky was cool green then cold olive then freezing brown, before the back of his head finally clunked on contact with metal.

He kicked and flailed for the edge of the trough. The water was up his nose and he needed to breathe. He pulled himself up from the brown through the green, towards the clattering roar . . .

Something pressed into his chest and pushed him back down where it was coldest. His groping hands felt the wiry bristles of a yard broom, pricking and pressing his naked skin. He was desperate to breathe. His chest hurt inside and out. His head might explode. He looked up at the dim sky pulsating in time to the whirring arms of the rotor blades.

Lucy looked down on him.

Lucy!

He'd found her at last, here in the water.

Or she had found him.

Her hair swayed on the surface like kelp, her lips moved – trying to tell him something he couldn't hear because the helicopter and his heart were pounding so hard and his lungs hurt so badly.

With the last of his strength, Jonas reached out to hold her, just like in his dreams.

But before he could touch her, everything went black.

Steven opened his eyes but it was still dark.

The sound of the helicopter was disorientating.

He was freezing.

At first he thought he was underwater, but when he tried to swim he found he was compressed by something tight and cold.

Had he been rescued? Was this what it was like to be strapped into a cradle and airlifted across the moor? Cold, cold air and the blades clattering overhead?

But something that was not fresh air stank so badly that his stomach rolled and his mouth filled with thin saliva. He tried to spit and found that he was gagged. He panicked for a moment, and struggled as he worked to swallow without choking. Some of whatever was wrapped tightly around him yielded, some was hard and sharp. His knees were drawn up; he couldn't feel his left leg at all. When he turned his face half an inch one way or the other he felt something slimy press against his cheek. He thought his left leg must be trapped under him and he guessed he was upright, although whatever his right foot was pressing against was far from solid.

Steven had a sudden mental image of a chrysalis hanging from a twig and felt his bowels contract sharply. He'd been captured by a giant insect, bound in sticky thread, and could only wait helplessly to be liquefied and sucked out through a sharp proboscis—

Proboscis was a good word.

That thought calmed him. Brought him back from the edge of panic. Allowed him to become aware of his own breathing again and to work on bringing it under control.

Yes, he was hanging up inside something disgusting, but a giant insect was major bollocks. He wasn't a child; he mustn't let childish fears stop him thinking straight. As his breathing slowed, he became aware once more of the stink that surrounded him. It was the same stink that came from the bones Jonas Holly never ate. That were left to lie in the sun for the flies to shit on . . .

He was inside meat.

Instantly he knew he was right. *This* was why Charlie had screamed about meat. *This* was what had scared him so. Steven had seen the huntsman skin the animals – the shaggy Exmoor pony, the cow with the empty eyes. He'd seen him drag the pink-and-grey carcasses through the dark door at the back of the big shed. He'd heard the clank of chains and the brief sounds of an electric winch.

Meat.

That was what he'd become.

What they'd all become.

The kennels were empty. Reynolds saw that with his own eyes, and the little grey screen was proof. There were only two bright blobs of warmth below them, and one was in the shape of the man standing over a water trough in the yard, leaning on a pole and squinting up into the sunshine. The other was an intensely white star in a small building near by.

Unwilling to shout loudly enough to make himself heard, Reynolds leaned between the seats and jabbed a finger at the white point on the screen.

'Incinerator!' Lee hollered into his ear.

Reynolds nodded and sat back.

Slowly the man below them raised a hand in greeting, and Tuckshop returned a half-wave, half-salute, like a fighter pilot in a black-and-white war film.

As the helicopter tilted away from the Blacklands hunt kennels, Reynolds did the same – and felt like the guardian of the entire world.

42

It's true, thought Lettie Lamb. *We're all cursed.*

She had never believed in curses; curses were for old folk and stupid people. But here, lying in a fast-cooling bath, watching condensation drip off the peeling ceiling, she could find no more logical reason for the miseries visited on her family than that which the *Sunday Mirror* had proposed.

Steven was gone.

Lettie's mouth distorted with sudden emotion and she squeezed her eyes shut to stop herself crying. Crying helped nobody. She'd learned that a long, long time ago.

She waited until her breathing was normal again, concentrating on her breasts, which sat like little islands on the water – the warm meniscus of the tide rising and falling on the beaches of pale skin, where faint blue rivers ran from the puckered peaks.

He'd been gone for a week and just today her mother had put down her knitting and walked to the front window. She'd stood in her old place – the one she'd worn bare over the twenty years when she'd waited for Billy to come home. Jude had replaced the carpet. Not all of it, but that piece in the window. It wasn't a perfect match with the rest of the room but it was close enough. Now the thought of her mother wearing a new path to the window to wait for Steven made Lettie shiver. Would *she* follow in time, however hard she tried to resist? Would the pair of them wear out the carpet together, lumbering back and forth like buffalo at a watering hole? Would Davey suffer the way *she* had suffered when Billy had gone? Was Steven suffering now? Or was he already dead?

This time her mouth would not obey her when she tried to pull it back into shape. This time her tears reheated the water around her temples.

She thought of all the times she'd snapped at him; all the times she'd been unfair; all the times she'd taken Davey's side for no reason other than that Davey was adorable and 'You're the oldest. You should know better.'

She thought of the time she'd slapped his face.

I can't, thought Lettie. *I can't do this. It hurts too much.*

She had to stop thinking. Thinking of Steven was like having a head full of thorns.

I'm cursed.

And suddenly – the revelation: all of the bad things had happened on her watch. Maybe all that was needed was to take herself out of the equation. The ultimate horror required the ultimate sacrifice. If it didn't actually help Steven, at least she wouldn't be around to know about it. Stopping everything meant stopping the agony of thinking about him every second of the day. It all made sense. A *kind* of sense. Sense enough for now.

Lettie opened her eyes. Without turning her head, she thought about what was in the bathroom that she might use.

Not much.

The water itself was tempting – just a tilt of the head would cover her face – but she guessed it would be almost impossible without something to keep her under while she drowned. There was the razor she used to shave her legs when Jude stayed over. It was a white Bic safety razor, and the blades were firmly encased in plastic that defied removal. Jude used an electric one that pushed his skin about his face in stubbled wavelets.

Lettie had a sudden bright memory of the razor her father had used. A steel-headed Gillette that held a proper blade in a canopy so smooth and shiny that it tempted tiny hands to pick it up and gaze into it like a mirror. He'd had a brush too, with coarse bristles that were black at the bottom and white at the tips. She and Billy used to squabble for the right to stir the solid shaving soap into a thick cream of suds and paint it on their father's face with 'the badger'. That's what they'd called it, she remembered now with a pang. Then they'd watch in awed silence as the Gillette left broad, smooth trails through the snowy lather on her father's tanned face.

She could smell her father now – that clean soapy smell of his cheek and his chin, and the Old Spice she'd bought him relentlessly for every birthday and every Christmas until he'd died when she was ten.

Cursed.

Someone pounded on the door and Lettie jolted upright with a splash, gripping the side of the bath with both hands, ready to leap out of it, scared of why.

Was he found?

Was he dead?

Was this the moment when her life shattered into a million pieces or started slowly to mend? She could feel her heart beating against the cold plastic of the tub in excitement and terror.

'*What is it?*' she croaked.

'Where are my socks?' yelled Davey.

Lettie sat there, frozen, for a few seconds that stretched to fill her entire future. Then she hauled herself from the water and went on living for a bit longer so she could find her son's socks.

43

Jonas knew the huntsman's name.

He wasn't sure when he'd remembered it, just as he wasn't sure where he'd got the bruises. Bruises down his arms, sharp black welts across his calves, ridges on his ribs that hurt to touch, and an odd raw abrasion on his chest.

He remembered Lucy in water – that was all.

Then he'd woken up just now, when a chunk of bone came over the gate with a soft thud.

Bob Coffin. That was his name.

He'd been the huntsman for years – even when Jonas was a boy, working for rides up at Springer Farm and galloping about the moors with his friends on a pony called Taffy. They'd seen him, walking the hounds or resplendent in scarlet. The huntsman had touched his cap at Jonas and led him to the Red Lion car park the day they'd all searched for Pete and Jess.

Jonas looked through the wire. There was Jess Took. Beyond

her were Kylie Martin and Maisie Cook and – at the end of the row – Pete Knox. He'd seen their pictures in the *Bugle*.

Bob Coffin. Jonas's skimpy memory was of a much younger man, treating hounds, horses and children with the same efficient confidence that he would be obeyed.

And these were the Blacklands hunt kennels – although the hunt was no more. Jonas hadn't sought its demise, but some locals had – and even more incomers. Incomers resented the red coats; they admired the foxes; they could afford the chickens.

The kennels had been searched at least once – Jonas was sure of it.

How did we miss them?

'I don't eat meat,' he said as a second slab slapped on to the concrete, but the man ignored him, as if the stocking mask he wore made him deaf as well as smooth.

'He doesn't listen,' said Steven Lamb to himself. 'He only talks.'

Jonas stood up, then winced as something tugged him back down. He put a hand to his throat and felt the collar.

Steven watched the way Jonas Holly touched the collar and chain; the bemused look on his face; the way he'd stood up as though he thought he could.

It was as if he'd only just arrived. Didn't know the ropes.

'Hey,' Steven said. 'How long have we been here?'

Jonas opened his mouth to answer, but then frowned.

'Five six nine elleventy years!' said Charlie behind him.

'Ten days,' said Steven, and Jonas Holly stared at him in blank confusion.

44

For a week, no child was taken. Then a week and a day. A week and *two* days.

A week and a half.

Exmoor held its breath.

Even the flash bulbs seemed more subdued, and the reporters more inclined to drift away from their vigils outside the homes of the Piper Parents to revisit the scenes of the abductions, to survey the local pubs, or to vox-pop market-day farmers about the curse of Exmoor. Several were even recalled and reassigned to stories that had a more tangible conclusion.

It was dull stuff. No new abductions meant no new news.

Marcie Meyrick took a view and stayed put, along with four die-hard freelance photographers who had stationed themselves outside the school in Shipcott which hosted children from several villages around. She was her own boss and had a feeling in her water that the Pied Piper story may yet pay for her to have that cruise to the fjords that she'd dreamed of for years.

So every morning she parked her only indulgence – a four-year-old Subaru Impreza – close to the school, and kept true to her vigil.

Three times a day she popped quickly into the Spar shop for a Cornish pasty or a bottle of water, or a pee. She'd flattered and cajoled Mr Jacoby into letting her use his toilet, and made sure he always saw her put a pound in the Guide Dogs box by way of thanks. So far she was right up there at the head of the hack pack with her single exclusive. She wasn't about to languish over lunch in the Red Lion and let some pampered expense-accounted *bimbo* catch up while she was gone. It could happen in an instant and suddenly she'd have to start all over again. It had happened before and she'd started all over before. Not once but many times; and each time it got harder.

For the first time in her life, Marcie Meyrick wondered when it was going to end. Not the story, the *job*. There was always another tragedy, another paedophile, another house fire, another pit bull, another car crash. And she was always clawing and fighting to be first in line. Just once, *just once*, thought Marcie, it would be so good to be ahead of the game. To know exactly how things were going to go, and to be confident of being there when they went.

Suddenly, while watching children spill out of the school gates, Marcie Meyrick had a brainwave. She told the photographers her plan.

'If we get pics of every single kid *now*, then when one of them's snatched we've got a head start! Got their pic, their name, age, address – everything! Screw running round kissing the cops' arses just to squeeze a bit of info out of them and a crappy old snap from the kid's third birthday party!'

The men looked at each other – interested but nervous.

'Is that legal?' said one.

'As long as we don't approach them on school property, where's the harm?' Marcie said. 'They have the right to say no.'

'What's the catch?' asked Rob Clarke for all of them.

'No catch,' shrugged Marcie. 'You're all freelance. The more kids you get, the better chance you have of hitting the jackpot. You just gotta promise to use my words, that's all. It's a package deal.'

Within minutes they were all approaching children, taking their pictures, and logging their names, ages and addresses. Most children were excited about having their picture in the paper, and those who declined were generally girls who declared their hair looked a mess and to ask again tomorrow.

Marcie and Rob jogged after two boys who were already heading up the street.

When they turned around, Marcie realized one of them was Davey Lamb.

Shane smiled for a photo and gave his name to Rob, but Davey was more wary.

'Who are *you*?' he asked.

'My name's Marcie. You're Davey Lamb, right?'

He said nothing.

'How's your mum doing, Davey?'

The boy looked up the street towards home and kept his mouth shut.

'I really am praying for Steven to come home. We all are. You know that, right?'

He fixed her with a steady gaze that would have wilted anyone less Australian.

'Can we take your photo quickly, Davey?' She smiled. 'Maybe one of you and Shane together?'

'You already have my photo,' he said, and walked away.

*

Reynolds let the water pummel his head into submission.

He should have been happy, but he wasn't. Nobody else had been kidnapped. It should have been a cause for relief, if not celebration, but all Reynolds could think was: *Why has he stopped?*

He always did his best worrying in the shower – even one as small as this. The worry used to be inextricably linked with watching his hair swirl down the drain between his feet, and had become a Pavlovian response, even though his hair was now silkily anchored. The second the water burst from the shower-head, Reynolds started to doubt himself and those around him; began to wonder why he'd become a police officer in the first place, to debate whether he should call his mother more, and to question what the future could possibly hold for him if he were unable to solve the case/get a girlfriend/finish that day's *Times* crossword.

Like a metaphysical plumber, no job was too small for Reynolds to worry about once he'd stepped under the flow.

He had called Kate Gulliver and they'd had an interesting chat, but even she'd had no answers for him for this one – at least none he hadn't already postulated in his own mind with an increasing sense of helplessness.

The Pied Piper (God, even *he* was calling him that now!) must have stopped for a reason. He might be dead. The children might be dead. He might have moved house along with his adoring wife and tow-headed babies. He might simply have run out of storage or his car could have broken down; or perhaps he'd become a born-again Christian and was even now preparing to release his captives, citing divine intervention. The possibilities were endless.

All Reynolds knew was that *something* had changed.

Not knowing what was just another bitter pill to swallow. Something in DI Reynolds almost hoped for another abduction – anything that might add to his pool of knowledge and give them a fighting chance of catching the culprit.

Because if the Piper had stopped for good, they'd never catch him.

45

Hunger was a funny thing. Sometimes it hurt like a blade in Jonas's gut – and he should know. Other times it was almost wonderful.

When it hurt, the pain came in long spasms that rippled up his body like a tsunami, tearing and squeezing the beaches of his organs and leaving him breathless and flattened. When it was wonderful, it freed him from the confines of his wire-mesh prison and speeded up the tortuous process that turned each day into the next.

His mouth was dry or drooling by turn, his thoughts either repulsed by the idea of sustenance or filled with fruit and potatoes and – bizarrely – cupcakes. Cupcakes he'd seen on TV, with thick, soft, fairytale icing, sprinkled with chocolate and little silver balls.

Instead of sweet cakes, he was served stinking slabs of dead flesh. He told the huntsman every day that he couldn't eat meat, and every day he was ignored, so the children had taken it upon themselves to keep him alive. Maisie and Kylie had started it and the others had quickly joined in. They returned from the meadow twice a day with handfuls of grass, dandelions and clover. They carefully pushed the increasingly mushy handfuls through the fences down the line to Steven, who dropped them into Jonas's kennel.

At first the idea of eating such offerings seemed ridiculously over-dramatic to Jonas. Then he reminded himself that he was being held in a dog kennel by a crazy man – and eating grass didn't seem like such an outlandish response after all.

The grass was bitter and hard to swallow. The dandelions were strangely creamy and tickled his throat like yellow feathers, while the clover was stiff and tasted only of green. Once Kylie found some wild strawberries – each the size of a pea, and so sweet it made everything else taste foul again, just as he'd been getting used to it. He noticed little improvement in his hunger pangs, but chewing was good and he imagined that the children's offerings must contain *some* worthwhile calories, so he was grateful.

He noticed that Steven Lamb never brought anything back from the meadow for him. He collected the assembled green stuff from Jess and dutifully pushed it through the wire, but, while Jonas thanked him, Steven never said a word.

Jonas was confused. Steven used to be a friendly kid. Used to keep an eye on Lucy for him as her disease progressed. Jonas had tipped him a fiver a month, but he knew Steven would have done it for nothing, and he'd given far more than a fiver's worth of time and effort to the task. And Lucy had adored Steven. She'd never had a bad thing to say about him. Jonas had always got on with him just fine. But that night when Jonas had tried to talk to him about the money, he'd acted like a boy who had something to hide – or something to fear.

He frowned at Steven through the mesh, and tried to work out what he could have done to upset him.

*

Now that he'd stopped being a mental patient, the Jonas Holly that Steven feared and hated was back.

Except he wasn't. Not quite, anyway.

Seeing the scars that patterned Jonas's stomach had shaken Steven. The scars could not lie, however much he wished they could. He was a fair-minded boy, and now had to consider that he might have been wrong about Jonas Holly killing his wife, just as he'd been wrong about him stealing the children.

But although his suspicions had been reduced, Steven was reluctant to let them go entirely. He was curious about that *other* person. That cringing ball of child-like fear with the trembling lip and night-time tears, who seemed to have vacated the kennel next to his as suddenly and completely as a dog retrieved at the end of a family holiday. The Jonas he saw now bore no resemblance to that pathetic other, and seemed to have no recollection of his time in captivity so far. He asked stupid questions; he expected to be taken out for exercise. He asked about a bloody *vegetarian* option! It was as if he'd only just arrived.

It was all too weird, and so Steven determined to keep hold of his caution, even if his hatred was deserting him.

46

There was a fracas at the school. Nobody ever agreed on precisely who had called the parents, but whoever did had managed to pick the biggest, strongest and most belligerent. They descended on Marcie Meyrick and the photographers just as they were lining up the first of several immaculately made-up, blow-dried teenaged girls to have their photos taken.

By the time Reynolds and Rice got there, all the witnesses seemed to have gone to work, and the only people left at the scene had all apparently arrived too late to see anything but five journalists disappearing up Barnstaple Road.

'Running like hell,' laughed Ronnie Trewell, who was there *in loco parentis* for his brother, Dougie.

'Jogging,' corrected Mike Haddon, the blacksmith. 'I think they're from London.'

It seemed they had also dropped their cameras, which were smashed to pieces on the pavement. And at some point during what Reynolds gathered must have been a very confusing mêlée, someone had had the time to key the word LIER down both sides of a black Subaru Impreza with gold alloys which had been parked on the school-crossing zigzags.

Rice ran a quick check and found it was registered to Marcie Meyrick.

Reynolds walked twice around the car inspecting the damage. He shook his head in despair.

'Outrageous,' he said. 'Can't spell *or* park.' Then he told Rice to issue a ticket.

*

Because she'd been delayed by the fuss at the school gates, Emily Carver's mother was late driving back home along Barnstaple Road. But she was just in time to see her daughter – whom she had dropped off at school less than fifteen minutes before – knocking on the door of number 111.

She pulled over, demanded an explanation and called the school when Em's story didn't ring true. Then she hit the roof. Right there on the pavement outside the Lambs' house, complete with waving arms and crazy hair. At one point Em glanced over her mother's shoulder to see Lettie and Nan watching round-eyed from the front window, and gave a nervous giggle.

'It's not *funny!*' shouted Mrs Carver, and slapped Em's face. 'I want you to be *safe*. You could be lying dead in a ditch!'

Em held her cheek and fought back tears.

The drive back to Old Barn Farm was stuffed to the brim with cold silence, but the noise started again back at home, while Em started to feel detached from the people who'd made her and loved her, yet couldn't understand her.

'This is ridiculous,' her father snapped at her. 'You're ruining your life for a boy you hardly know!'

'I *do* know him. And I love him.'

Her mother shouted, 'You don't even know what love *is*.'

'Don't tell me how I feel,' said Em, tilting further and further towards calm on this see-saw of hysteria.

'I'm selling Skip!' her father yelled. 'If you're going to start running off after boys!'

'OK.' Em nodded sadly.

And that's when they finally shut up and stopped treating her like a baby.

47

As Steven watched Jonas Holly reach out for the dandelions like some kind of starved but gentle ape, he had to keep reminding himself that Jonas had murdered his wife.

He thought of Em, and wondered whether Jonas and Lucy Holly had ever been that happy, that in love. Did Jonas Holly remember the feel of his wife's back under his hands, or the first time he'd seen her breasts inside her bra?

Jonas's stomach squealed and he put his hand under his ribs and grimaced. It was a big hand but it didn't hide the scars completely. They still squirmed out from underneath like dark maggots escaping his fist. Steven had a scar in the middle of his back that matched the tear in his Liverpool shirt; it was where Arnold Avery had hit him with a spade. He could no longer remember the pain with his body, but he did remember that it had hurt and then itched and then become a fading ache that had lasted months. He had twisted to look at it in the bathroom mirror. It wasn't big – just a red mark on his back that had become pale pink over the years. Nothing like the jagged ridges that criss-crossed Jonas Holly's abdomen. He tried to imagine how much they must have hurt.

With an angry jolt, he hoped they still did.

'Why did you kill her?'

Jonas looked confused. 'Who?'

'Your wife, of course!'

Jonas swayed on his haunches. Somewhere a long way off, he could hear a plaintive cow. He looked at Steven's mouth as if to check that the boy had indeed spoken and this was not all in his head, along with his guilty heartbeat.

He hadn't killed Lucy. That was the truth.

He was *sure* of it.

He remembered the knife. He remembered the blood. Those things were confusing. There were some things he couldn't remember, and other things he didn't *want* to, but if he had lived a million lifetimes he could not have killed Lucy. Even denying it out loud seemed to be too much for him. His jaw worked but no words came out.

Steven leaned against the fence and asked coldly, 'Didn't you love her any more?'

'I *still* love her!' The words came out of Jonas so fast, it was as though they always lived there, at the back of his throat, crowding to be heard.

'But you hit her! You wouldn't hit her if you loved her.'

'That's a lie,' said Jonas. 'That's a lie.'

'I saw it with my own eyes,' said Steven.

Steven realized he was trembling at his own daring. Jonas stared at him. No, not *at* him – *through* him.

'You said Lucy gave you money the night she died.'

'So what?'

'Why would she do that?' Jonas spoke haltingly and with a little frown on his face – as if he was working things out as he was going along.

'I don't know,' said Steven warily. 'She never did before.'

'Maybe,' said Jonas, 'maybe . . . she *knew* she was going to die.'

Steven said nothing, but something in Jonas's words – or the *way* he said them – was making his heart fill up with sadness. Or horror. Or a combination of the two. Either way, he had the uncomfortable feeling that something beyond his control was about to unfold. He turned away from the fence, hoping that it would stop the man talking.

But it didn't.

'Who knows they're going to be murdered, Steven?' said Jonas, with a soft break in his voice. 'Did *you*?'

Gooseflesh rippled across Steven's warm skin.

He hadn't known Arnold Avery was going to kill him. If he'd known he wasn't coming back, he would have prepared better – he would have given Davey the fiver he'd kept hidden in the shed, told his mother he loved her.

Lucy Holly had given him £500.

She had hugged him in a fierce goodbye.

Those things meant she could not have been murdered.

Steven's mind tumbled and spun. Could *everything* he knew be wrong? Had Lewis been right? Had he been paranoid all along? Had he seen danger in Jonas Holly because of his *own* demons?

Now he searched Jonas's face, but saw only pain there. No deception, no anger. No threat.

Not like that night outside Rose Cottage.

Where was *that* face when Steven needed it?

Then Jonas's eyes had been holes in his head. Dead black wells, like the old mines up at Brendon Hills. You felt a give in the turf and looked behind to see you'd stepped over a hole that would have killed you – dropped you into blackness so deep and narrow that by the time you hit the bottom you'd be skinned as well as dead. You shivered and then laughed too loudly to show you weren't scared.

And small, dark places invaded your dreams.

Today Jonas Holly's eyes were brown. That was all. Brown with a sheen that looked disturbingly like tears.

He doesn't know what you're talking about. He really did love her.

Steven thought about someone hurting Em and found wild fury in his chest – there as if by dark magic – and knew that he would rather kill himself than watch her in pain. If Jonas Holly had loved his wife that same way, then he could *never* have killed her, whatever Steven thought he had seen.

With a horrible jag of remorse, Steven started to wonder whether he'd also imagined the danger he'd felt coming off Jonas Holly that night outside Rose Cottage.

The little vertical line between his eyes deepened.

That was impossible. He hadn't imagined it.

Had he?

Had he?

What else might his brain have invented? The slap that had knocked Lucy Holly to her knees? The money falling from a black-and-white sky? The hedge at his back with nowhere to run.

Em?

She was too good for him, wasn't she? Too good to be true. Her heart ticking under his hand, her Super-Sour sweetness. Had he imagined that? Had he imagined *her*?

Steven blinked and shuddered. How much was real? All of a sudden, he wasn't sure any more. The heat and the stink of the kennels was his only truth now. How long had he been here? A month? A year? He no longer knew. Jess and Charlie and Maisie and Kylie and Pete were all real. He knew *that*. Jonas was just Jonas and his eyes were just brown, and his stomach bore the marks that a killer had made. Of those things he was sure. Anything else could be in his head alone. All the fears.

Steven felt as if he were teetering on the edge of a deep, dark precipice, rock crumbling below him and spinning into the abyss.

He'd been through a lot.

He'd been through a *lot*.

What if the last five years existed only in his head? What if Arnold Avery had won after all, that misty morning up at Blacklands . . .

Tears filled Steven like water in a jug, and poured out of his eyes in what felt like a never-ending stream.

'I'm sorry,' he sobbed. 'I'm sorry.'

Through the blur, he saw Jonas's stricken face become surprised, and then concerned. He moved as close as his tether would allow him and reached out to touch the wire between them.

'What's wrong?' said Jonas.

'I think I might be dead,' said Steven, and kept on crying.

48

Kate Gulliver came to Shipcott and had dinner with Reynolds and Rice. Rice had never met her before and was taken aback by how attractive she was – with a mane of dark hair, Spanish eyes, and legs that were needlessly lengthened by spike-heeled patent-leather boots.

Rice felt *dowdy* drop over her like a potato sack.

The Red Lion only had one vegetarian option and it was always an omelette. Kate made a townie face and ordered two salad starters instead.

In a defiant countermeasure, Rice ordered pizza and a dessert. She could run it off in the morning. Or not.

Kate had spoken at length with Rose Hammond, the psychologist who had helped Steven in the year following his ordeal. She made little quote marks in the air around 'helped', leaving them in no doubt what a crappy therapist Kate considered her to be.

In his turn, Reynolds had spoken to the officer who'd dealt with the aftermath of the Arnold Avery case – a taciturn chief inspector, who seemed to hold Steven Lamb personally responsible for depriving the Avon and Somerset force of the pleasure of bringing Arnold Avery down in a hail of officially sanctioned bullets. Apart from that, he'd grudgingly conceded that the experience of being attacked by a psychopath must have been traumatic for a twelve-year-old boy.

Kate thought it was a trauma that might not necessarily have been resolved by a twice-monthly session with a country psychologist. Especially one who came cheap enough to be paid for by some Irish gardener who claimed to be the boy's uncle.

She put air-quotes around 'uncle', too, and Reynolds laughed as if she'd been witty.

Rice felt like a stupid spare part. She wished there was someone across the table for *her*. Someone she could cock a secret eyebrow at, and whose mouth would twitch in amused support. She imagined Eric, but he'd never got her humour. He'd preferred jokes – often ones that started with an Englishman, an Irishman and a Pakistani going into a massage parlour. She imagined Jonas Holly instead – a quiet counterbalance, unimpressed by Kate Gulliver with her air-quotes and her Spanish eyes. Watching his plate or watching her, with absolute focus.

Just thinking about it made her feel warm. Everywhere.

After a lot of psychobabble that Reynolds nodded at eagerly – and that Rice largely tuned out – Kate said, 'The legal system failed Steven and allowed a killer to track him down and almost kill him. I think any finger-pointing at a symbol of that system should be treated with the utmost caution.'

'I agree,' said Reynolds.

Big shock, thought Rice.

'There's another thing.' Kate's voice took on a sombre tone. She speared a cherry tomato before going on. 'A child so traumatized, so *damaged*. It is not beyond the realms of possibility that Steven might be somehow culpable, and trying to deflect suspicion.'

'Great minds!' said Reynolds, smiling at Kate like a smug puppy.

Rice didn't have the letters after her name to argue with them. But, although she was relieved that suspicion seemed to be falling further and further from Jonas, she hated the drama that Kate Gulliver had squeezed from the moment with her cherry-tomato pause. Triumph disguised as concern. Kate and Reynolds were peas in a bloody pod.

Unless she was very much mistaken, she was the only person at this table who'd ever actually *spoken* to Steven Lamb. And so, for what it was worth – which she realized wasn't much – she told them that, to her, Steven hadn't seemed the type to be a kidnapper, a killer – or even particularly resentful.

'Interesting,' said Kate. She put down her fork and clasped her elegant hands under her chin. 'On what basis do you make that assessment?'

Reynolds snorted. 'On the basis of a five-minute chat with a towel on your head, wasn't it, Elizabeth?'

He and Kate showed each other their teeth.

Rice took her cheesecake upstairs. She ate it with her fingers, sitting in the bath.

49

There was a reason why Davey Lamb got up before his alarm every morning and often slipped from the house before his mother had stirred. Davey's instincts told him that if he didn't get out of the house while his mother was all doped up and watching bad TV, she might never let him leave again.

Every now and then Lettie focused on him with clear eyes, and then reached out and held him in arms that were so tight and desperate it made him itch to throw her off and skip away across the room to freedom. But – in the first consciously selfless act of his young life – Davey stayed put and allowed her to crush him to her breast as if she might re-absorb him straight through her skin.

It wasn't that he wasn't afraid. He *was* afraid.

He and Shane didn't go to Springer Farm any more, or to the woods. Both now seemed like places where bad things had happened – and still might. Sometimes they went to the playing field and he watched Shane skate. That was all. He stopped bothering with homework or the fallout. Sometimes he didn't go to school at all, but sat on the swings and shared a fag with Chantelle Cox, or swung himself so high and so fast that the world seemed easy to leave behind.

Gravity always dragged him back.

The Piper Parents came round for a meeting and pawed him like zombies. They asked him how he was and made sympathetic faces, but he knew they really wanted to grab him and shake him to make him tell them something – *anything* – that might help them to find their missing children.

He couldn't. He had seen the kidnapper, heard his voice, been in his car, and yet his recollection was so patchy as to be useless. The only things he remembered for sure were the plan he and Shane had thought was so clever, and the way he'd shouted instead of shushed . . .

He went into Steven's room and touched all the stuff he'd never been allowed to. He took down the Batman action figures, but found the fantasy of crime had been made dull by the reality. He looked through Steven's school bag and read a story he'd written called 'A Day in the Life of a Tree', which sounded shit but was actually quite good, considering the tree never went anywhere or did anything. He searched for porn under the bed, but found only Steven's name carved into the wall, and the crumpled receipt for the umbrella they had given Nan for her birthday.

£13.99.

It made him so angry he felt like crying.

If Steven ever came back, he'd tell everyone how Davey had lied about them running away together. Then, instead of a hero, he would be a baddie, who'd hit his own brother and left him behind.

Davey wanted his brother back – of course he did.

But only if he shushed, not shouted.

*

Through the bright-blue gap in the roof, Jonas could see a buzzard circling over the moor. Now and then it cried out – a strangely puny sound for such a big bird. He waved away a fly. They were always there, because of the meat. This one landed on his face again, and Jonas left it; took the decision that unless it was on his mouth, he no longer had the energy.

The children came back from the meadow with hands full of grass and dandelions, and Jonas's stomach squealed in pathetic anticipation. This time, Steven had picked some too, and when Jonas thanked him, he said: ''s OK,' and went immediately to his post at the back of his kennel, eye pressed to the chink in the wall. He had barely spoken since he'd broken down – not even to Jess.

Charlie touched Jonas's arm. 'Hello, Jonas. How do you do?'

'How do *you* do, Charlie?'

'Do you have some peanut butter?'

Jonas's stomach wrenched at the mere words. 'Sorry, Charlie.'

The boy screwed up his face. 'I'm hungry,' he said forlornly.

'Why don't you eat your meat?' asked Jonas, pointing at the bones behind Charlie.

'Why don't *you* eat *yours*?'

'I don't eat meat,' Jonas told him patiently for the fiftieth time.

'I don't eat meat too,' said the boy. He kicked out at one of the bones, yelping at the pain in his toes. The bone drubbed across the floor and rattled the bottom of the gate.

Charlie sat down on the edge of his bed and sniffled. 'Hurt my toe,' he said in a tiny voice.

Steven turned away from the wall and nodded at Charlie. 'I think he's scared of eating it,' he said.

'Why?'

''Cos of the meat. You know?'

'No.'

Steven sighed. 'When the helicopter came over. He put us in the meat. Hanging up in the little room. You know?'

Jonas looked so confused that Steven asked, 'Where were you, then?'

Jonas frowned. Where *was* he?

The helicopter, the cold splash, the banging on his legs, the sharp pricks on his chest and Lucy floating above him . . .

'He held me underwater.'

Steven blinked. 'Why?'

Jonas shrugged. He had no idea.

But now that he'd remembered the shock of the water, Jonas also remembered other things. Not all of it, just bits. Being so small, his head swimming with that smell, his arm hurting from the huntsman's grip, concrete grazing his knees. He remembered the sudden bitter darkness, the loop of chain pulling him upwards, and the heavy things touching his face . . . heavy, *cold* things . . .

It was *obvious.*

'Cold!' he said. 'The flesh room is cold and so is the water.'

Steven still looked blank.

'Thermal-imaging cameras. On the chopper.'

Steven's mouth opened in understanding. They'd all seen thermal imaging on *Police Camera Action!* Bright white shapes with arms and legs, trying to hide in bushes or run across fields away from the scene of the crime, their own body heat a beacon to the hunters overhead.

Jonas saw it clearly now. When the helicopter or the searchers had come, the children were drugged and gagged and forced into the icy flesh room and stuffed inside dead cows and horses until the coast was clear. The idea made his stomach recoil. No wonder poor Charlie had freaked out when he'd heard the sound of the blades.

How many times had they suffered so? He thought of the long-ago day of the search, the dry grass whispering against his legs, the smell of heather and sunblock and the helicopter droning overhead, coming and going. Bob Coffin had searched with the rest of them. That meant Pete and Jess had been inside the cold, cloying carcasses all day long, as rescue passed by so close – with the police helicopter triggering a fresh ordeal every time it launched.

It astonished Jonas that those same children could be right here in front of him, playing 'I Spy', making daisy chains, singing, gathering leaves for him to eat, being kind to each other in the midst of a waking nightmare. How did they do it?

Only Charlie was coming apart at the seams. He didn't have the language or the understanding to cope with what was happening to him. Either he was bouncy, or in tears. Increasingly it was the latter. Right now he was grizzling the way a two-year-old does when it's missed a feed or a nap.

'Hey, Charlie,' called Pete. 'You want to sing?'

'No.'

'OK. *One man went to mow, went to mow a meadow. One man and his dog . . .*'

Kylie joined in, and then the others, but Charlie slumped listlessly against the shade of the back wall.

Jonas peered through the fence. 'Hey, Charlie. Do you want to try my meat? It's much better than yours.'

Charlie looked from Jonas to the untouched bones in Jonas's kennel and back again, lips pursed. 'You don't eat meat.'

'No, but if I *did* eat meat, this is the meat I'd eat.'

Behind him Jess said, 'OK, Dr Seuss!' and Steven laughed, which made Charlie laugh too.

'You want to try it?' Jonas asked.

Fresh from laughing, Charlie looked more malleable. He screwed up his face and twisted his hands in front of him while he decided. Finally he gave a huge melodramatic sigh and a shrug and said, 'No.'

They all laughed then, even Jonas. It was crazy – laughing at a starving boy refusing food while they were all being held hostage by a lunatic – but it still felt good.

Jonas got to the end of his chain and reached out for the closest bone. It was too far to touch with his hand. Aware of Charlie watching his every move, he turned and stretched out one long leg. His toes felt the meat. He rocked it and it tumbled towards him. He pulled it the rest of the way until he could pick it up in his hands. Just the touch of it made his skin crawl. The double-fist-sized hunk of greying flesh, marbled with clots of yellow fat. All wrapped around the smooth protrusion of bone . . .

He closed his eyes and brought the chunk of meat to his lips. The smell! He swallowed sick. He couldn't do this. He grimaced and opened his eyes. Charlie was watching him with interest. Without thinking about it again, Jonas sank his teeth into the meat.

It was like trying to bite the nose off a face. That horrible, that hard. And it wouldn't come off. He had to start chewing while it was still attached.

Like an animal.

He retched but kept going, tears streaming from his eyes, until at last he was able to tear a small gristly chunk away and swallow it whole. He panted with tension and disgust, saliva running over his lower lip and his stomach cramping, as his traitorous system suddenly readied itself on a promise of nourishment.

He wiped his mouth and composed his features into something he hoped resembled appreciation, before looking at Charlie. 'This is good,' he said. 'I feel a lot better now.'

Charlie seemed interested.

'You want some?'

Charlie looked from his own untouched bones to the one in Jonas's hands.

'OK then,' he said, and got up. Jonas once more stretched to the end of his chain and just managed to tip the joint of meat through the gap where the roof stopped.

Charlie looked doubtfully at it for a moment, then dug his teeth in close to the place where Jonas had.

'Yours is nicer,' he confirmed.

'I told you so,' said Jonas.

'You can have mine,' Charlie said magnanimously, and threw them over the fence. They tumbled wetly across the cement.

Steven gave a short humourless laugh.

Jonas looked at the gross chunks of old animal. His stomach clenched like a fist in desperation.

You have to save the boy, Jonas.

I will. I promise.

How could he save anyone if he were dead?

The nearest chunk had a tube of thick, pink vein sticking from it. Jonas shuffled forward on his arse until he could grip the vein under his curled toes, then drew the slab of dead horse towards him.

50

It was six weeks since Jess had been taken, and John Took couldn't sleep.

Part of him – the ever-decreasing part that was in denial – was still hoping that Jess's disappearance was a petulant teenaged prank. Even the thought of Jess running off with a much older boyfriend was preferable to the idea that she'd been abducted.

Since she'd started to get breasts a year earlier, John Took had lain awake on many a night worrying about the kind of boys who might lust after his daughter. Boys who were too old, boys with tattoos and nose-rings, boys without jobs, boys who were only after one thing.

Now, awake through the night again, he was astonished to find that he actually *hoped* she was off in some grubby B&B being ravished by an old lech or a pierced punk – if only it meant she wasn't being raped and murdered. Or was already lying dead in a field somewhere, waiting to be found by some random dog-walker.

Everything was relative.

Rachel stirred beside him and pulled even more of the covers on to her side.

She was going through the motions of support and sympathy and offering him tea at ridiculously short intervals, but he could tell her heart wasn't in it. Why should it be? Jess wasn't her daughter. Rachel was suitably sympathetic in his company, but she continued to have two dressage lessons a week with that young buck he'd got out of *Horse & Hound*, and he could hear them laughing from the house.

No, it was the helpless terror he saw reflected in his ex-wife's eyes that let him know he was not alone.

Like Jess was.

Took threw off the covers and sat on the side of the bed. This circularity of thought was nothing new. It was the same when he spoke to DC Berry, who was the ridiculous toddler of a family liaison officer assigned to the case. It was the same at those tortuous Piper Parents meetings. Everything went in circles. The same questions again and again: *Where? How? Who? Why?*

It was that last question that really plagued him. With every abduction after Jess, the idea that this was personal became less and less likely. He knew that. But still it tormented him. The notion that somebody had chosen her – or had chosen her *first* – because of him. Because of something he'd done. DC Berry and DS Rice reassured him that it was now far from likely but, for the first time, John Took had started to reflect.

At first it was hard. He'd led a life as reflective as a black hole. It took practice. At the beginning it was like learning to meditate at that dumb class Rachel had wanted to do in the village hall. Bored wives and benefit scroungers *Om*-ing on the badminton court, while he watched the second hand linger on the wire-clad clock.

At first he hadn't been able to think of any more enemies than the people on the list he'd given DI Reynolds. But because it was for Jess, John Took had made a giant effort to rummage around inside his own head for anyone he'd offended. It took him literally days to come up with Will Bishop, the milkman, who had left him a rude note demanding payment one too many times. Bishop had been threatening the residents of central Exmoor for years and one morning John Took had felt enough was enough. It was the same morning Scotty had thrown the shoe off his near fore for the third time in a week, and Rachel had told him that the trainer had told *her* that the £1,300 Stubben saddle he'd bought her didn't fit. So he'd called the dairy and shouted very loudly until someone said something would be done. The notes had stopped and the milk had not, and Will Bishop had retired shortly afterwards, after more than fifty years on the job, so he'd considered the problem solved.

Maybe he could have handled that better.

After he'd thought of Will Bishop, the floodgates had opened.

Over the next few days, John Took was first surprised, then shocked, then ashamed by the sheer number of people he'd wronged, offended or simply hurt. The clues were in the looks, the mutterings, the silences when he approached a group of people in the pub or at a show. All those things he'd declined to notice, or had interpreted as respect, suddenly sprang up in his mind like tin ducks he'd missed on a fairground rifle range.

Charles Stourbridge – for telling him his new horse wasn't worth a quarter of what he'd paid, when it plainly was; Mr Jacoby – for pointing out his man-boobs to Rachel; Linda Cobb – for telling her to keep her *fucking* dog under control when Blue Boy had just stepped on its paw during an ill-advised gallop across the playing field . . .

If DI Reynolds asked him for another list now, he'd be forced to create a database. Or get Rachel to, because he could never be bothered with the computer and she typed with more than one finger . . .

Did he have to add *her* to the list for that?

Or did she already hate him for something he had yet to remember?

How many others hated him? *That* was the question he always came back to.

Now Took sat on the edge of the bed and stared at the stars. He wondered whether Jess could see them from wherever she was now.

Wherever she was . . . was it because of him?

✳

Steven watched the huntsman through the crack in the wall. It had become an obsession. It was a strange comfort to know that he was still there – that he had not drifted away from this madness and into a new one which would see him forget all about them and leave them to die of thirst in their kennels. They hated him, but he was all they had – and they feared his absence even more than they feared his crazy presence.

Even so, staying alive was becoming increasingly difficult. Although the days were still hot and dry, the nights had turned suddenly from chilly to cold. Steven woke every morning aching and stiff as an old man, despite the straw on his bed. He felt sorry for Jonas – out there on the bare cement – and wondered how long someone could survive with only his own chemistry to keep him warm.

The meat that the huntsman tossed into their cages every day was no good. The pieces were smaller and some bones had barely any meat on them at all – just fat or gristle, and some of it tasted as if it was already going bad.

All the children now started to eat flowers and leaves when they went out for exercise, and always brought some back for Jonas. But it was not enough to sustain them, and they had to eat what they could off the bones.

Charlie got sick. He spent forty-eight hours writhing and moaning over the drain in the floor of his kennel, while the bad meat rushed to evacuate his shaking body.

After every violent expulsion he crawled across the cement and – instead of making for his straw bed – lay curled up against the fence beside Jonas, who stroked his hair and held the hand that Charlie wormed through the chain link to reach him. Jonas murmured soothing sounds and sang 'One Man Went to Mow' in a low, hypnotic loop.

Dog. Spot. Bottle of pop . . .

Bob Coffin came often – to clean up the mess and to try to feed Charlie chicken and rice, although the boy turned away from him and shook his cold, sweaty head.

'He's not a dog,' said Jonas. 'You know that, right? He needs a doctor, not chicken and rice.'

The huntsman ignored him. Of course.

He came back later with a bucket and a bundle under his arm, and pulled Charlie's stained underwear down and off his legs.

'What are you doing?' Jonas's voice was so tight with tension that he could hardly hear it himself. He squeezed Charlie's hand so hard that the boy squeaked.

Coffin said nothing. Using a sponge and a bottle of Hibiscrub, he washed Charlie down with the efficiency of a mortician, then opened a new pack of briefs and tugged a pair on to the sick boy. He flapped open an old blanket flecked with straw and tucked it around him.

Jonas watched his every movement like a hawk.

'Can *I* have a blanket?' asked Jess, but Coffin ignored her.

'Good bay, Charlie,' Coffin said, and Jonas felt tearful with relief as the huntsman patted the boy's bony shoulder and locked the gate behind him.

Coffin started to clean Jonas's kennel next; the now familiar sounds filled Jonas's ears of the shovel scraping the floor, the slosh of the disinfectant, the hose in the water bucket.

'You should let Charlie go,' he said quietly.

Bob Coffin gave no indication of having heard him, but he picked up the broom that had pressed stippled bruises into Jonas's chest and made an angry swishing noise with it on the wet cement beside him.

'He shouldn't be here.'

Jonas moved his legs but the broom banged his knee anyway. And again. It was rare for Bob Coffin to get close enough to touch him.

'He won't tell, if that's what you're worried about. He doesn't even know where he is.'

Swissh! SWISSH!

Jonas hoped the silence meant the huntsman *must* be hearing him, taking it in, digesting his words. Maybe his conscience was finally being pricked.

'Charlie needs to be at home with his dad.'

The broom swung through a short arc and smashed into Jonas's face. It knocked him sideways so fast that his head bounced off the fence with a rattle. Bob Coffin loomed over him.

'He don't love him!' he spat. Then he clanged out of the run and stormed up the walkway.

Jonas sat up and touched his jaw cautiously. The side of his face was numb and blood dripped slowly over his lower lip.

Charlie looked scared, so Jonas said, 'Don't worry, Charlie,' and held his hand again.

The other children had been stunned into silence by the outburst.

All except Steven.

He rattled the fence, his eyes wide with excitement.

'He heard you!' he hissed at Jonas. 'He *heard* you!'

51

Davey stopped hanging out with Shane and now spent most of his days holding his PS2 console loosely in his hand, while pimps crashed their cars pointlessly into whores without any help from him. Uncle Jude tried to get him to help in the garden but he was already exhausted. He slept a lot, although not at night when he was supposed to; *then* he lay and stared into the darkness and thought of the way his mother would look at him when Steven came home. When she knew what a coward he was. What a liar.

Em called him downstairs for tea. She only came after school now and always cooked for them. It was spaghetti hoops on toast, his favourite, but his mum and his nan didn't eat it, and that made everything taste crap.

'I don't like this,' he told Em.

'Oh,' she said. 'I thought you did.'

He dropped his fork with a clatter. 'Why do you keep coming here?'

Everyone looked at Davey.

'Well, why does she?' he demanded. 'Is she going to keep coming for ever?'

There was a short silence before Nan covered Em's hand with hers. 'She's here because she loves Steven. Like we all do.'

'I don't!' said Davey.

'Of course you do,' said Lettie. 'Don't be silly.'

Davey stood up sharply, with a loud scrape of his chair. 'I don't! I hate him! I hope he never comes home!'

Em bit her lip and Nan looked down at her toast.

Davey waited for his mother to get up and slap him hard. He didn't care. Let her! She'd slap him and he'd cry and then *she'd* feel bad instead of *him*.

Instead Lettie reached for his hand. He tried to pull it away from her but she held on to it.

'Leave me!'

She didn't. She tugged him gently towards her. With every grudging step he felt his shell of brittle anger crack and flake.

'*Leave* me!'

Lettie didn't again. Instead she turned him and eased him on to her lap, and started to rub his back in warm circles, as if he were a small child.

'Just leave me *alone!*' he shouted.

Then he put his face in her neck so no one could see him cry.

After tea, Lettie took Davey to the Red Lion to see DI Reynolds.

'I lied,' Davey muttered, examining his own trainers as if he'd never seen them before.

'I know,' said DI Reynolds.

Davey was confused. DI Reynolds didn't seem angry – or even surprised. In fact, he then answered the question Davey hadn't asked. 'We do come across our fair share of liars, you know.'

'He's not a liar,' said Lettie firmly. 'He just lied about this because he felt so bad about leaving Steven.'

'Of course,' said DI Reynolds.

Davey bit his lip and – to his amazement – DI Reynolds winked at him. Or maybe he just twitched. Davey looked away, uncertain of how he should respond and hoping his mother hadn't seen it.

They sat down in the lounge bar where children were allowed, and Detective Sergeant Rice agreed with DI Reynolds that she didn't mind buying Davey a Coke and his mother a white wine. Davey guessed she was DI Reynolds's secretary.

DI Reynolds got out the same notebook he'd used before and they went through everything again. This time Davey did his best, however annoying it was, and told him even those details he wasn't sure were real – those dreamlike snatches that had seemed too small and uncertain to bother with. A paper sack with a torn picture of a dog's back legs and tail on it; black boots; zig-zag tyres. DI Reynolds made careful notes of everything and asked him all the same questions over and over again and even made his little train noise, and suddenly – out of nowhere – Davey remembered that the car was navy blue!

DI Reynolds wrote it down and Davey grinned in delight.

'And he wore gloves!' he shocked himself by saying.

'What kind of gloves?'

'Green woolly ones. That's what smelled like medicine.'

DI Reynolds hissed something that sounded like 'Shit' to Davey. He got up abruptly and walked to the fireplace and back, and then walked there again and stared up at the shiny dead eyes of the big stuffed stag. DS Rice watched him eagerly and when he turned round they exchanged meaningful nods.

'Does that help?' said Davey.

'Tons,' said DS Rice.

Lettie gently twisted the little hairs at the back of Davey's neck, and he didn't even mind that people were watching.

DI Reynolds came back and they went through things again, but Davey had nothing more to offer. Even so, when the officer finally snapped a strip of black elastic around his notebook, it was with a satisfied air.

'Well done, Davey,' he said. 'Thank you.'

Davey was sorry it was over. He was high on the joy of true things.

DI Reynolds shook his hand and then his mother's. 'Don't you blame yourself about what happened with Steven either,' he told Davey. 'You were drugged. Not your fault.'

Davey nodded wholeheartedly, and thought DI Reynolds was a lot less disappointing this time round.

'Mum?' said Davey cautiously as they walked home. 'Sometimes I *have* lied about other stuff.'

'I know,' said Lettie.

52

Even a dog learns how to get what it wants – a bone, a pat on the head, a place by the fire – by watching and learning and licking the hand that feeds it.

Steven had said nothing, but Jonas could tell by his restless pacing that the boy was excited and filled with new hope that the huntsman might be starting to crack. His mood was infectious, and the younger children played games and giggled, while Jess sang fragments of pop songs.

And the next day – when his jaw had almost stopped hurting – Jonas screwed up his courage and simply went on talking to the huntsman as if he'd never been interrupted.

'You're wrong about the children. People *do* love them.'

Coffin gave no indication of having heard him. His face was stretched and blank. He skirted Jonas like a dangerous whirlpool, spraying the cement with the brick-coloured hose.

'They weren't abandoned. Not like the dogs.'

He didn't expect a response, but he got one, gruff and muffled.

'Dogs die in hot cars. Seen it with my own eyes.'

Jonas flicked a look at Steven, who nodded encouragingly.

'You only wanted to protect them. I understand that.'

Coffin dropped the hose into the water bucket, then picked up the broom. Jonas flinched, but Coffin just swept around him and said nothing more.

Jonas had to keep him engaged. If it was only dogs the huntsman would talk about, he'd start there. With a vague motion of his arm, he asked, 'What happened to all the hounds?'

There was a long pause, then: 'Had to go.'

'Go where?'

The huntsman stopped sweeping and picked at the wooden handle of the broom. Jonas looked at Steven, who gave a little shrug.

Coffin bent to his task again, but now his strokes were short and jerky.

'The Midmoor took a few. The others I had to get rid.'

Jonas said nothing, but pictures raced through his head like a flicker book. He had hunted as a boy, and he knew how hounds were 'got rid'. He thought of the sixty or so animals that had made up the Blacklands pack. All his life he'd seen them milling about outside pubs, moving as one through the village by night and loping muddily across the moor. A joyous jigsaw of pied coats, silken ears and lolling tongues – vital and vibrant and singing for fun. The thought of spending years whelping them, raising them, training them – and then shooting them all in the head made him feel ill.

The strokes of the broom got louder and the huntsman spoke without any further prompting. 'Had to be done, Mr Took said.'

He angrily thrust the broom at the wet cement, his voice rising rapidly. 'Well, I say *bollocks* to him. Bollocks to him and them fox-loving incomers driving down from London for the weekend and tell us how to live our lives! Take our lives *away* from us! After a hundred years! Take *everything* away and then tell me I don't fucking *love* them!'

He hurled the broom across the run. It bounced off the fence next to Jonas's head and Charlie started to wail. The children watched the huntsman, their eyes wide with the fear of uncertainty.

Coffin's open mouth stretched the stocking mask into a darker shadow that fluttered with vehemence.

'Now I've took everything away from *them*,' he said, low and vicious. 'See how *they* like it.' Then he slowly retrieved the broom and carried on sweeping as if nothing had happened.

Jonas felt everything falling into place in his head like a little Chinese puzzle box. He watched Coffin with unseeing eyes, and thought of the emptiness Lucy had left in Rose Cottage – that deep, sucking silence that tugged at his soul and lured him to follow as surely as a siren's lament from a jagged rock. If he could have filled that void, he would have. If he had been able to forget for one single second the sheer *absence* signalled by the quiet clock, the folded rug and the empty vase, he would have done anything – *anything* – to make that happen.

Revenge may have sparked Coffin's madness, but at some point, Jonas guessed, he had started to steal children simply to fill the runs left echoing bare by the loss of his hounds. What he had done was unpardonable, reprehensible and utterly insane – and Jonas understood it completely.

'You did the right thing,' he said quietly.

'What the *hell*!' said Steven.

Jonas didn't even glance at him. He looked only at the huntsman, who had cocked his unformed face towards him in rare attention.

'I know what you're trying to do here, Bob. I can understand it now. I can see how much you love them, and how much you want to take care of them.'

'Yes,' said the huntsman.

'You just want them to be safe.'

'That's right,' said the huntsman.

'And we're very grateful,' said Jonas gently.

The huntsman nodded. 'Good.'

'You're nuts!' shouted Steven. 'Both of you!'

Jonas looked calmly at Steven and the boy closed his mouth.

Jonas felt confidence coursing through him. Starving, half naked and chained at the feet of a maniac, he felt suddenly buoyant and completely sure of himself. Coffin's face was turned towards him. It was blank and stretched, but Jonas knew he had the man's attention.

'But *Charlie* doesn't understand it,' he said carefully. 'He's not clever like you. Look at him, Bob.'

To his surprise, Bob Coffin *did* look through the fence. Charlie sniffed miserably and said, 'My tooth is sore.'

Everything was suddenly very quiet, as if the sky itself was holding its breath while the huntsman stood there, motionless in the sun, the broom held loosely in his hand.

Loose and close to Jonas.

Loose enough and close enough for him to grab? Coffin *never* got this close to him. The man was always wary around him, even though *he* was the one who was chained to a fence. Jonas shifted position slowly and slightly, testing his wasting muscles, wondering how fast he could still move.

He licked his dry lips and went on, 'Look how sad he is. What's the point of keeping him here when it's not making him happy?'

Coffin raised his arm and Jonas's whole body seized in readiness. But the man only touched the bottom of his stocking mask, as if he might lift it.

Jonas watched Coffin walk a tightrope strung between compassion and craziness. The wind thrummed the high wire, and the huntsman wobbled – and Jonas swayed a little closer to the broom. From the corner of his eye he could see Steven gripping the fence, tense with anticipation. Jonas's hand twitched—

Coffin grunted. He dropped his hand from the stocking mask. He picked the hose out of the overflowing bucket, walked out, and locked the kennel gate behind him.

'Shit,' said Steven.

Jonas slumped back against the fence, sick with disappointment. He'd hesitated. On the off-chance that Coffin would be rational, he'd put all his eggs in one basket case.

Lucy, I blew it.

He covered his face with his hands and his body let go of the tension in a long, shuddering breath. He felt fingers in his hair, smoothing him like a loved pet.

'*One man went to mow,*' sang Charlie cautiously. '*Went to mow a medal. One man and his dog . . .*' He waited for one of the others to supply the part that Teddy had sometimes sung. Jess or Steven often did. But today there was only a yawning hole in the air.

And then Jonas felt his heart jolt as if he'd touched a live wire.

One man and his dog . . .

Bob Coffin had got rid of the hounds. That meant he had shot them.

And *that* meant he had a gun.

53

Reynolds held a press conference in the Red Lion's skittle alley, and released the information about the green woollen gloves. It wasn't huge, but any breakthrough was enough to keep the story in the news, and Davey swelled with pride as he heard DI Reynolds say that this latest information had come from him.

'Davey's memory of events is becoming clearer all the time,' he added, 'and he's making a tremendous effort to help his brother in whatever way he can.'

Lettie stroked his back and Nan said, 'Well done, Davey,' and Davey went to bed so excited about the green-woollen-glove breakthrough that he could hardly sleep. He was sure that by that night the police would have received a tip-off. Steven could be home by tomorrow!

But by the next evening Davey had learned another valuable lesson – that sometimes truth has to be its own reward.

✳

I love them.

Funny how it's the big un what understands that. Appreciates what I done. I always thought he was a bit mazed, but turns out he's the one with the brains, after all!

Anyway, it's good to know that someone's on my side. Made me happy when he said that.

But that poor little Charlie. Can't be having 'em sickly and shitting that way. That's not right. Them's my responsibility and I got to take better care of 'em. Else I'm as bad as them what left 'em alone.

Old Murton always told me, if you can't feed it, don't keep it. And he were right about most things.

So if I want to keep 'em, I got to try harder to feed 'em.

54

The huntsman was late.

There was no bang as he left the cottage in the morning, no squealing rumble as the big shed door was pushed aside on its metal runner, no soft explosion in the incinerator, no *sssssshh* of the knife that would separate bone from cartilage from tendon for them to eat.

Within minutes of his being overdue, the children grew restless, and before the hour was up they were nervous and fractious.

'Where *is* he?' Jess Took kept saying. 'He's *never* late.'

But he was.

Jonas and Steven exchanged worried looks.

Charlie sang 'Ten Green Bottles' quietly, while Pete clung to the chain link at the front of his kennel, craning to see up the walkway and occasionally murmuring, 'I thought that was him' under his breath.

'He's *never* late,' Jess said again, as if words alone would make it true.

Steven turned his back to her and spoke softly to Jonas. 'How long should we wait?'

Jonas frowned. 'Before what?'

Steven opened his mouth, then closed it again. Before what indeed? Before escaping? Before calling for help? If those things had been realistic options then they would have worked already.

'Maybe we should save our water a bit,' said Jonas.

Steven nodded and passed the message down the line. Then he did something he hadn't done for weeks – he started to test the boundaries of his prison, kicking at the wall, pushing a stalk of grass into the padlock, tugging at the ends of the wire fence as if he might unravel the chain link like an old jumper.

*

The .22 pistol was a waste of time.

What worked well when pressed between the eyes was completely useless when trying to hit a galloping pony at fifty paces. Bob Coffin thought he'd winged a couple but not even badly enough to be able to hunt them down and kill them. The deer didn't even let him get within firing distance.

Bob Coffin threw the pistol on to the passenger seat of his old diesel and slammed the door hard.

Time was there was a never-ending parade of old, broken-down livestock coming into the yard, and the Park Rangers would let him know when a pony or deer was dead on the moor. Then the flesh room was always packed with fresh meat.

Not now the hounds were gone.

He'd stolen the last cow. Just walked into Jack Biggins's field by night and taken the first one he'd come to. It was so easy it didn't even feel like theft.

But when he'd tried it again over at Deepwater, the herd had gone off like a bovine car alarm – mooing and lowing and milling about him until he'd feared they would knock him down and trample him. But he'd needed the meat, and clung on to the cow until a skin-and-bone collie with one white eye had scattered the beasts and then bitten his ankle as he scrambled back over the five-bar gate.

He had a sheep, but it would last no time.

After that, he didn't know what he would do.

*

Jonas saw Steven wince as a sharp point of wire pricked his finger. The boy didn't give up, though – he shook his hand, then bent to his task again, even though it was hopeless.

Jonas thought of the grim truth – that Bob Coffin was their captor and tormentor, but he was also their lifeline. If he fell down and broke his leg, they were all dead; if he had a car accident and was taken to hospital, they were all dead; if he simply lost interest or got scared, or took a long weekend by the seaside, they were *all dead*.

Now the huntsman was somewhere else and they were here.

Helpless as infants.

As he watched Steven, Jonas cursed himself. A strip of leather and a small padlock, and he'd simply resigned himself to his fate, along with the children he was sworn to protect. He should have remembered the gun and realized the danger they were in. He should have been planning an escape for weeks, not waited until there was a crisis like this one. He'd been afraid, and frozen by that fear, and it had stopped him thinking.

He'd better start again right now.

Jonas ran his fingers along the chain that tethered him to the fence. He examined every link minutely, tried their strength with his hands and his teeth. He picked a link in the middle of the tether, and scraped it repeatedly across the cement, making a graze in the grey of the floor, and a shiny new corner on the metal.

That might work. Although an escape plan that relied on the erosion of metal was an escape plan that should have been formulated long before they were each left with half a bucket of water and no food.

The link became shiny but it didn't get thin. It seemed hopeless, but Jonas beat down the feeling that he was wasting his time. Right now this was the most important thing in the world. The *only* thing left within his control.

The thought made him strangely optimistic, and he went at the task with new vigour.

Steven said 'Shitshitshit' and flapped his hand again.

'You OK?' said Jonas.

'Cut it,' said Steven, holding it up to the fence for Jonas to see.

Jonas reached out and wiped away the blood with his own thumb. Immediately it squeezed out again in a pretty red sphere.

'It's just a flesh wound,' said Jonas with a smile.

'Yeah,' said Steven. He smiled back, but it didn't last long. 'Jonas?' he said tentatively, 'do you think he's going to come back for us?'

'Of course,' said Jonas. 'He loves us, doesn't he?'

The sun was high in the sky before Pete said, 'I hear him!' and he was right.

Bob Coffin came down the walkway without meat, but with purpose, carrying a coil of thin cord. He wore his mask but no gloves. He strode past them all and unlocked Charlie's kennel, then shook an end out of the coil like a cowboy about to rope a calf. Charlie stood up and moved away, like that same calf.

Jonas knelt against the fence. 'What are you doing?'

Coffin ignored him and lunged at Charlie, who dodged him, then burst into tears.

Bob Coffin tried again, arms outstretched, and Charlie cowered, then darted away, bawling his lungs out.

'Hold still, bay!'

Charlie rattled the gate in blind panic and twisted out of Bob Coffin's grip once more. 'No meat! No meat!'

'Stay! Or I'll get the gloves.'

Charlie ran to Jonas at the fence, clutching at the wire. 'I don't want to go!' he cried. 'Jonas!'

The terrified boy fell to his knees as Bob Coffin tried to drag him away.

'Leave him alone! What are you doing?'

Charlie tried to feed his hand through the fence, but Bob Coffin yanked it backwards. 'Trying to let the little bugger go!' he grunted.

Jonas took a second to realize what he'd said. He looked at the man's face, distorted despite the smoothing stocking.

He couldn't see his eyes, but it felt like the truth.

I promise.

Jonas couldn't afford to disbelieve him.

'Charlie! Charlie, calm down!'

Charlie cried and struggled and clung to the wire while Coffin hauled on his arms.

'Let him go,' Jonas told the huntsman sharply. 'Let him go so I can talk to him.'

Coffin did. He stepped back from Charlie, leaving the boy gripping the fence, facing Jonas with his arms spread in an incomplete hug.

Jonas had to work fast. He touched Charlie's fingers with his. 'Charlie, listen to me. *Listen* to me. You're going home.'

Charlie's brimming eyes met his. 'Home?'

Jonas nodded vehemently. 'Yes, home. Today. Right now. You're going to go home and see your dad.'

Charlie nodded, bottom lip still wobbling.

'But you have to go with him, Charlie. Go with him and be a good boy.'

'Don't make a fuss,' said Charlie.

'That's right. Be a good boy and don't make a fuss.'

Charlie looked warily over his shoulder at the huntsman.

Jonas tugged his fingers to bring his attention back to him. 'You'll be fine, Charlie. He's not going to hurt you. I promise.'

Charlie nodded but still looked doubtful. Coffin moved towards them, hand out. Charlie leaned away.

'I *promise*, Charlie.'

Charlie knelt still, hitching with sobs, as Coffin pushed the end of the cord through the metal loop on his collar.

'Good bay,' said Coffin soothingly.

'Where are you going to take him?' Jonas asked.

'Back,' said Coffin.

'To his house?'

'I'll leave him where he'll be found.'

Jonas felt uneasy. 'Somewhere safe, right?'

Coffin's voice rose. 'He'll be found.'

'Somewhere close to—'

'I'm taking him *back*!' Coffin spat angrily.

Jonas bit his lip. He had to shut up. If he didn't, the huntsman might change his crazy mind.

Coffin helped Charlie to his feet.

Jonas rose with him, and his heart rose too. Charlie was going home. He was going to save the boy, after all. Then he was seized with sudden panic.

What about the others?

He'd told Coffin the truth – Charlie probably *didn't* know where he was and so was unlikely to be able to lead the police back to the kennels. He did not have the capacity to relay any whispered instructions. Too late, Jonas realized that Charlie was the *last* captive he should have been working to free. Steven or Jess would have had the police up here within the hour; even little Maisie could have given them enough information to bring this nightmare to a swift close.

He was saving the boy – and leaving the other children to their fates. In a second Charlie would be gone – along with any faint chance of help. He had to send a message *with* him somehow. A clue. Where they were, or at least that they were still alive.

As Coffin turned to lead Charlie from the run, Jonas pushed his hand through the wire. His hand was big and the diamond pattern was small. He grimaced and twisted and shoved brutally, and watched the skin curl off in a bloody strip between his thumb and his wrist.

He cupped Charlie's neck and held him there a moment longer at the end of his rope leash.

'Bye, Charlie.'

'Bye, Jonas,' said Charlie. '*Dog! Spot!*'

Jonas pressed his thumb firmly on to the brass nameplate on the boy's collar. It was all he could think of.

Charlie was led from the yard to a chorus of tearful farewells.

Jonas watched him waving until he disappeared, then gouged another strip of flesh out of his hand as he pulled it back through the wire.

'Brilliant!' said Steven. 'That was fucking brilliant!'

55

After the Deepwater show, Grant Farmer – who actually *was* a farmer – let the grass in the field grow for haylage.

The summer was hot and dry and by the end of July the field was packed with long well-mixed grass. Farmer usually took it off in the middle of August, but it was starting to look a little brittle and his wife, Jackie, who often knew best, suggested they cut it early and try to get another crop from the field before the weather turned. Jackie had to convince her husband. He didn't like change or the unexpected, and he was still unsettled by the incident a week ago when someone had tried to steal one of the cows. Number 23 had come in at milking with a dirty rope halter on her head. Jack Biggins at Uphill Farm had lost one a few weeks before. Just disappeared. Grant didn't like it.

His wife didn't like it either, but two crops of good haylage from a twelve-acre field would keep their small herd of Friesians in feed all winter, maybe with extra to sell.

Money never comes amiss to a farmer. *Or* a Farmer.

So on 23 July, Grant unhitched the muck-spreader, hitched the rotary mower to his tractor instead and drove the eight-hundred yards up the road to the show field, leaving a broad swathe of mud and dung along the entire length, to test the mettle of unwary motorcyclists.

He turned left inside the gate that Jonas Holly had once banged shut so hard, and lowered the blades. Like many farmers, he liked to cut his hay in concentric squares, rather than in stripes. It was how his father had always done it. So he rolled a cigarette, then trundled along the edge of the field in his old John Deere, high above the broad hedges and far away from responsibilities.

He turned right in the first corner. Three-quarters of the way along this side, the field sloped away to the corner where the stile and the oak tree were. This slope stopped the field being great. One corner dropping away like that was never good. The ground there got boggy in winter, and care had to be taken that the farmhand – a twenty-year-old fool named Stuart Clegg – did not roll the tractor down the camber and kill himself, leading to increased paperwork.

At least the slope hid the stile. And Grant Farmer always let the nettles grow around it to further discourage ramblers. He'd never actually *seen* a rambler in this particular field, but he always came over the brow of the hill half expecting there'd be a gaggle of them there, tramping across his livelihood.

He set his face to 'hostile' and the tractor nosed downwards.

There was someone under the oak tree. As he came over the brow, he caught a glimpse of summer clothing, which disappeared below the level of the grass as the tractor descended.

Picnickers. Even worse than ramblers. Vandals and litterbugs.

Grant resisted the urge to steer straight over there and ruin the line of his mowing. He drove to where the nettles started and then turned sharp right towards the oak.

As he got closer he could see the clothes again. White shorts and a blue T-shirt. Just one person, in fact. And by the time he was twenty yards away, he could see it was a youngster with yellow-blond hair, lying on his side.

Grant stopped the big green tractor and walked the last several yards through the long grass to where the boy lay curled on a flattened patch of hay, with his thumb in his mouth.

He was quite, quite dead.

Grant Farmer was used to death. Death was sad but that was just life.

This was different, though – and even he had to sit down for a moment and stare at the boy, who was tethered to the oak tree by a slim rope attached to a collar around his neck. Like a dog.

Grant pulled out his phone and dialled 999. There was no signal, so he put the phone away again. He'd have to drive back up the hill to find a signal. He walked to the tractor and climbed in. From here the body was at a slightly different angle. He started the engine, but let it idle.

He'd call the police. The police would come. *Lots* of police would come. Grant Farmer could see them now, driving across his hay in their four-by-fours, putting tape across the gate, and maybe a man there to bar access – maybe even to him. A long slow line of officers searching for clues, flattening the grass underfoot as they moved across the field like a human mangle. Grant was not the most imaginative man alive, but even he could see all this so clearly in his mind that it looked like a series of photographs in a book about crime.

He could certainly imagine what it would cost to feed his forty-two Friesians all winter.

Grant Farmer rolled another cigarette, then looked at his watch.

The boy wasn't getting any deader.

It took him two hours to finish cutting the hay, and then he called the police.

*

Charlie liked things just the way they were. So when the bone man had told him to wait under the tree, that's what he had done. He hadn't even tried to undo the knots that kept him there. It was just like waiting in the minibus. Jonas had promised him he'd be OK and told him to do what the man said. So he'd sat down, waved goodbye, and waited for his daddy to come and take him home.

He'd sung his songs to keep himself amused.

One man went to MOW
Went to mow a MEDAL.

He'd shouted 'Hello!' and 'Daddy!' a few times, but the little slope kept the sound close at hand.

He'd eaten grass when he'd got hungry. The heavy dew ensured he'd had water. But it also ensured he'd got wet and cold.

On the third night Charlie Peach had died of exposure.

He'd never made a fuss.

Elizabeth Rice didn't know all this as she stared down at Charlie's body.

She would know it later, once the pathologist had examined the knots and fingernails; once he'd opened Charlie's taut little stomach and found old meat and new grass inside it. Later she'd also know that Charlie hadn't been sexually abused, and that would be a small comfort.

All she knew right *now*, though, was that her throat ached from trying not to cry, here in the open, with Reynolds beside her and the forensic and medical teams unloading their vans and trucks and ambulances behind them.

It was the thumb in the mouth that had undone her – that little-boy gesture that betrayed the teenager for what he really was, and what he always would have been, if he weren't lying dead at her feet.

'We'll have to inform Mr Peach,' said Reynolds tentatively. 'Would you mind, Elizabeth?'

'Yes, I fucking *would*,' said Rice, and burst into loud sobs. She knelt down next to Charlie. There was a fly at the corner of his mouth and she flapped it away. It came straight back and danced on his lip.

'Don't touch him,' said Reynolds, but she put a hand on Charlie's head anyway, and stroked his fine yellow hair the way a mother would.

If she found the man who'd done this, she'd kill him the way a mother would too.

The doctor came over in white paper overalls. He set his bag down at Charlie's feet and cleared his throat.

Reynolds was at her back. Rice thought that if he tried to drag her away from Charlie she'd have to gouge his eyes out, and then her career would be over. Instead, he touched her shoulder and said gently, 'Come on, Elizabeth. We should leave him to the doctor now.'

The doctor who was going to saw the top of Charlie's soft blond head off. For a nanosecond Elizabeth Rice wanted to kill him too. Then all the anger left her and she felt limp without it to hold her up.

It was over. They were too late. For Charlie Peach the Pied Piper case had ended badly.

Rice nodded and wiped her eyes and thanked God for waterproof mascara. Reynolds helped her to her feet with a hand on her elbow.

'Sorry,' she said.

'Don't worry about it,' he said.

56

Reynolds knocked and then waited on the pavement outside David Peach's front door.

A dozen times in his head he'd run through a rota of other officers he could have sent, but had finally accepted that this was something he had to do himself. He'd done it a couple of times as a rookie and been appalled that he'd been allowed to inflict himself on the bereaved. But children were different. Reynolds recognized that, even though he'd never had one. Anyone who had lost a child deserved the most senior officer available to break the news, and that buck stopped with him. *All* the bucks seemed to stop with him now. It didn't make him feel any better. He kept clearing his throat, and was suddenly very aware of every single finger and what each was doing. He stilled them all by clasping his hands together like Prince Charles, and felt even more nervous.

How to say it? How to start? There was a right way and a wrong way – he remembered that much. Reynolds ran through it over and over in his head, like an Oscar speech.

Hello, Mr Peach. Can I come in? Get him away from the prying eyes of the neighbours and lingering press.

Can we sit down? Get him off his feet in case he faints and hits his head on the coffee table.

I'm here with bad news, I'm afraid. Too fast. But anything *less* fast only seemed like toying with the man when he needed to get to the point.

Charlie's dead. That was the point. There was no sugar-coating it. DCI Marvel would have just said it and moved on. But DCI Marvel was no role model.

Reynolds looked up at the wall of the house, which was painted pale blue like the sky beyond it. In the top window was a piece of paper taped to the glass. It was covered with stickers and glitter and the carefully coloured-in words CHARLIE LIVES HERE.

Tears sprang unexpectedly to his eyes. *Shit, shit, shit.* He wiped them away roughly but more leaked out. He thought of Charlie in the hay with his thumb in his mouth, of Elizabeth Rice stroking his hair as though he were sleeping, and he couldn't believe he'd asked her not to do that – or to do *this*.

Shameful.

He hoped David Peach wasn't home. *Please God, don't let him be home.*

Reynolds didn't believe in God and apparently God didn't believe in him either, because almost immediately he heard the sound of someone coming down the stairs, and then David Peach opened the door, took one look at his face, and said, 'He's dead, isn't he?'

✳

Bob Coffin opened the gate to Jonas's run with hands that shook with fury.

He wasn't wearing his mask. It was that that made Jonas's stomach clench with fear. The man was so angry he'd forgotten it.

Instead he had a white hunting whip.

Jonas didn't know what was happening, or why, but he scrambled to his feet. He was still tethered, but the animal in him wanted to be as upright as possible in the face of attack, and as Coffin came at him, he stuck out his hands in self-defence.

It made no difference. This was full-force, no-holds-barred fury, fuelled by madness. The blows landed everywhere – his hands, his head, his face, his back and ribs. Sometimes with the heavy stock of the whip, sometimes the stinging hide lash, sometimes with the huntsman's boots. The noise was overwhelming – the sound of the assault on his flesh, the rattle of the fence, grunts of pain and of effort, and the shouting and crying of the children.

Bob Coffin hit Jonas so hard and for so long that Jonas knew the man was going to kill him.

Why?

He didn't know if he had asked, or how, but the huntsman told him anyway – in short exhalations as his arm rose and fell.

'He's *dead*. He *died*. You said to let him go and now he's DEAD!'

The words went through Jonas's numbed mind like a railway spike.

Charlie was dead?

The huntsman kicked him in the stomach and he curled around the pain.

Charlie was dead? That couldn't be possible.

Fingers in his hair. Not Charlie's careful hands, but a gnarled fist, dragging him off the cement and to his knees. Something hard and cold dug so brutally into his temple that it pushed his head round to look at Steven. The boy was screaming and beating the fence, like a crazed zoo-ape. Jonas couldn't make out the words, just the shape of his mouth and the fear in his eyes. He couldn't hear anything. Couldn't feel anything. He watched Steven shouting and thought about Lucy in the water.

I promise.

Something hit the back of his head and the cement rushed towards him.

Bob Coffin's boots passed by his face; the whip was picked off the floor. Jonas's breath whined loudly in his head. His eyes followed the boots as they left the kennel. It was only when the huntsman locked the gate behind him that Jonas saw the small black gun in his hand.

Steven was talking at Jonas and looking urgent, but Jonas couldn't hear him and didn't care. He never knew what Steven had said to keep Bob Coffin from shooting him.

It wasn't important.

Charlie was dead.

He rolled to his side and vomited.

Then he lay, heaving for breath, with his cheek in the thin, warm puddle while his stomach creaked, and mourned the loss.

57

Kidnap had become murder.

It was a turning point and, despite the tragedy of Charlie's death, Reynolds couldn't help being energized by it. Until now they'd all been expecting to find the bodies of children who had been killed within hours or days of their abductions. It was the way things usually went. But Charlie Peach had been kept alive for almost two months – and that meant the other children could have been kept alive too, and suddenly they might all be Superman, swooping to the rescue. It was the first break they'd had in the case since . . . well, it was the first break they'd had, and the mobile incident room literally rocked with activity.

The children had not vanished into the side of a mountain in the wake of a pennywhistle tune. Charlie been taken from that very field, and returned there. Reynolds dispatched officers immediately to check on the other kidnap sites. It was unbearably tantalizing to think that *all* of the children could be alive and well, and within a half-hour drive of the Red Lion car park where this very trailer was parked.

Reynolds had to fight the urge to get in the Peugeot and race about the moor with the windows down, shouting their names, they seemed so close.

At the same time, he knew the clock was ticking. No longer just a normal clock that marked time on the wall, this new clock was bound to a bundle of dynamite in Reynolds's head, and ticked far more urgently. Kidnap had become murder – and that irreversibility increased the threat to the other captives a thousand-fold. Whether it had been cruel intention or bungled release, Charlie Peach had died – and that put all seven remaining captives in serious danger.

He didn't need Kate Gulliver to tell him the truth of that.

Having killed one, the kidnapper could kill them all. He might do it in a panic to cover up his crimes or he might do it out of rage or horror at a plan gone wrong. Or he might do it because he'd meant to all along, and now that he'd summoned up the courage to take the first life, things would get easier.

Or maybe he was killing them in order, and Jess Took and Pete Knox were already out there somewhere, rotting at the end of a rope.

Reynolds felt his good energy turn on him like a sly wolf, making him suddenly panicky.

'Time's running out.'

Reynolds jumped, then turned to Elizabeth Rice. 'What?' he snapped.

'Time's running out,' she said again.

He understood. The white plastic tape on the broken windows, the notes. The things they'd been holding back to trap a future suspect.

A suspect they didn't have.

Reynolds sighed. He hated to undermine his own forensic foundations. But kidnap had become murder and it was time for that evidence to earn its keep. The notes would get them most publicity, he knew. But there was the danger that they'd also get them copycats. There were crazies out there who had the capacity to hurt or kill, but lacked originality. They might be only too eager to copy the Piper's notes in an attempt to appear more prolific than they were – muddying already murky waters for the Exmoor team. Plus, the notes reflected unfairly on the families of the missing children.

You don't love them.

They passed judgement – even though that judgement was obviously made by someone with a screw loose, at the very least. Reynolds had no desire to expose the already suffering families to the torment of self-righteous blame from the same kind of idiots who wrote racist letters to the *Sun*, or launched hate-filled rants on MSN.

'We need all the help we can get.' Rice said it gently, as if she had read his mind.

She was right, of course.

Reynolds nodded. 'OK. The notes and the tape.'

'Shall I call the press?'

'Would you mind?' he said, as someone handed him a ringing phone.

It was Jos Reeves from the lab in Portishead.

Rice watched Reynolds's face anxiously for clues. She saw the surprise in his eyes and itched to know what he knew. If he didn't tell this time, she would ask.

After an eternity, Reynolds hung up. He sighed and ran his hand through his hair.

'They found Jonas Holly's thumbprint on Charlie's collar.'

Rice's heart leaped at the news. Jonas was alive!

'In blood,' Reynolds continued.

She caught her breath. Reynolds had more to say – and his sombre face told her she didn't want to hear it.

'The blood is Steven Lamb's.'

58

Charlie's death was a turning point for the children.

They all cried. They all held hands through the fences. Steven shouted 'Fucking pig!' at Bob Coffin as he walked away from Jonas's cage with the gun, and Jess Took threw her bones back over the gate into the walkway as he passed. She missed him, but made her point.

The beating left Jonas curled on the cement, bloodied and weak. But more than that, Steven could see that he was mentally emptied out by the news.

'It's not your fault,' he insisted.

'I promised him he'd be OK,' said Jonas with brutal honesty.

'The guy's a nut, Jonas. It's *his* fault, not *yours*.'

'I promised him he'd be OK.'

It was the only response Steven got from Jonas, whatever truths he told. And Steven understood his misery, because that was true too – he *had* promised Charlie, and if Charlie hadn't believed him and given in and gone with Bob Coffin, he might still be alive now.

He'd still be *here*, though.

Steven wondered what he'd do if the huntsman offered him freedom now. Take it, even if it meant he might die somehow before he reached his family, or remain where he was, in the same blue underpants he'd worn for a month.

'At least you gave him a chance,' he said finally.

Jonas gave no indication of having heard. He lay on his side and continued to scrape the link on the cement.

To Steven it now looked more like madness than hope.

✳

The press conference was going to be well attended. As before, it was being held in the skittle alley at the Red Lion – a cold, cavernous place with the acoustics of a canyon, which made the twenty or so journalists sound like a factory floor.

Reynolds and Rice stood just outside the door – still arguing.

She'd never argued with him before.

She'd disagreed, which was her right, of course. He liked to engender a spirit of debate in his team. As long as they understood that he was best equipped to make the final decisions.

But this was different. This had started almost immediately after the phone call from Jos Reeves, with Reynolds saying he would be appealing for Jonas Holly to get in touch so he could be eliminated from the investigation.

Before he'd got any further, Rice had gone off on one.

'Why?' she demanded, close to rudely.

'We'd be remiss in our duty not to consider the implications of this new evidence.'

'The print is evidence that Jonas was *with* Charlie and Steven – not evidence that he *took* them.'

'I know that.'

'He might be trying to send us a message.'

'A message in Steven's blood?' said Reynolds. 'Look, I'm not suggesting we release the thumbprint right now – we don't know enough about it, and it's too emotive. I'm not even telling Steven's family at this point.'

Rice nodded her grudging agreement.

Reynolds went on, 'Saying that we want to speak to Jonas is not saying that we think he did it, but—'

'That's *exactly* what it's saying.'

'I beg to differ. What it *will* do is open the door for anyone who has . . . *information* about him which they might hitherto have felt unable to share, to come forward.'

Rice snorted. 'You need a suspect and he's the closest thing you've got. It's a witch hunt.'

Bob Stripe from *Points West* came out of the Gents' toilets. 'Not interrupting, I hope?' he said, when it was quite clear to all present that he fervently hoped he *was*.

'Not at all,' said Reynolds as he squeezed between them.

Reynolds waited until he'd closed the skittle-alley door behind him. 'Steven Lamb raised a question—'

'Which was bollocks. Even Kate Gulliver said so.'

'Kate Gulliver's changed her mind.'

Rice's jaw dropped. 'Is she allowed to do that?'

Reynolds turned his face away from her for a moment. He looked through the little square window in the skittle-alley door at the noisy throng.

Rice could tell he was wondering whether or not to share.

To her surprise, he did.

'I spoke to her earlier. She told me that she was frightened by Jonas Holly during their final session. So frightened that she feels it might have influenced her decision to clear him for duty.'

Rice was stunned. She couldn't imagine the super-confident Kate Gulliver being frightened *or* admitting she might have made a mistake – especially to a by-the-book man like Reynolds.

'Jesus! What did he do?'

'Nothing. Or at least, nothing that sounds like anything. She said he brought up the abduction of Jess Took. Then he said that people hurt children.'

People hurt children. Jonas had said the same thing to Steven Lamb, Rice remembered.

Reynolds continued, 'She said she felt an overwhelming sense of threat and danger from him.'

'A *sense?*' Rice struggled to stick to her guns. 'Not much to base an accusation of kidnap and murder on, is it?'

'She says it was just the way he said it.'

Rice felt the sands of reality shift under her feet. With sudden clarity she remembered Jonas saying he understood the Piper's anger. What was it he'd said? That people left their children on display in their cars like old umbrellas. At the time it had sounded sane. Harmless.

Now she wasn't so sure.

She bit her lip and turned her face to stare through the little window in the door. Framed like a Hogarth, Bob Stripe spooned one, two, three sugars into his teacup. Marcie Meyrick frowned up into the dark toe of her own empty shoe, while Mike Armstrong from the *Bugle* set up the skittles.

'You don't believe he killed his wife, do you?' Rice said flatly.

'I don't know what to believe,' said Reynolds, more cautiously than she'd ever heard him.

'We were *there* . . .'

'I know.'

She nodded. She was all out of fight.

'I understand your concerns, Elizabeth. But we have to weigh the reputation of one man against the lives of six children.'

'Five now,' said Rice sombrely.

'Exactly,' said Reynolds.

✳

After the press conference, Rice went back to Rose Cottage with a sense of foreboding.

Mrs Paddon let her in and then stood in the hallway. 'What are you looking for?' she said suspiciously.

'I don't know.' Rice started in the kitchen, looking with different eyes this time.

'You're wasting your time.'

Rice ignored her.

The bottle of red wine that Jonas had opened for her was still on the counter; still half full. The bills were routine, the laundry still washed but un-ironed, the sink still empty. There was a glass of water on the table with faint dirty smears where the fingers would grip, and Rice remembered that Jonas had been gardening when he'd been interrupted by the children on their way to the woods.

She bent down and examined the glass. The smears were just that – no prints. She straightened up and started to look around her.

'What are you looking for?' said Mrs Paddon from the kitchen doorway.

'Gloves,' said Rice.

Mrs Paddon stared at her, unblinking.

'Maybe woollen or gardening gloves?' She made it a question but Mrs Paddon didn't give her any help. Rice wished she'd go back to her own house.

She went out into the garden. It was easy to see where Jonas had been. The beds there were clear and turned over, only the flowers remaining in the newly turned soil. Rice didn't know a lot about flowers – not even cut ones, which Eric had never bought her – but she enjoyed these blue delphiniums, the heady phlox and the great bushes of pink daisies.

No gloves.

There was a little wooden shed at the end of the garden. Inside was dark and stuffy and smelled of earth. The single window was festooned with cobwebs, heavy with dust. She reached to brush them aside, then saw a fat spider stretched out along the sill.

She would make do with the light that she had.

There were tools in the shed and a couple of mountain bikes with webs between the spokes. The single shelf that ran at head-height held countless cans and bottles and containers: slug pellets, weedkiller, rose food, fly spray. There was a plastic bin filled with birdseed. Rice dug into it, in case it concealed something incriminating, and kept her arm there for a bit, up to the elbow, because it felt so odd and interesting.

At the back of the shed was a stack of three cardboard boxes. The bottom one was collapsing due to being plundered for bedding by rats. The confetti-like results were spread all over the floor back here in the deep gloom. Rice had kept rats as a child, Roland and Ratty, and was not deterred.

The top box held paperwork: insurance for window repairs, old bank statements and endless warranties and manuals for fax machines, cameras, phones and electric sanders. The second box was filled with children's drawings, exercise books and home-made cards inscribed in careful but haphazard hands.

Good lucky in yor new howse.
Goodbye Mrs Holly. Weel miss you!
Love from Tiff. Love frim Linling. Luv from Toby.
XXX

Rice thought about Charlie Peach lying in the hay meadow and, for the first time, she thought she understood the kind of person who loved children, and who could elicit such love in return.

The third box was much older. At some stage it had been damp, which meant that all the photos inside it had stuck together or been damaged beyond repair. Solid sandwiches of photos, crimped and curled and covered in mildew. The rats had destroyed what was left. Rice could only make out a few faded and stained faces. From the

1980s, judging by the shoulder pads and poodle perms. There was a couple standing in the garden she had just walked through, with a little boy on a toy tractor – all in sunshine made even brighter for fading. She guessed it must be Jonas and his parents. She squinted at them, just as they squinted back at her across the years – all equally unaware of what their futures would bring.

It was sad. To hold these people in her hands. Their hopes, their dreams, their happiness.

All gone.

She re-stacked the boxes and went back inside.

'Did you find anything?' said Mrs Paddon.

'Yes,' said Rice, just to fuck with her.

She went into the living room.

In dusty daylight, she stared at the photo of Lucy Holly – also squinting into the sun; also ignorant. Rice wondered whether she or Jonas had planted the flowers that were blooming in the garden now, with neither of them here to see.

The clock was stopped at 7.39 as before; the blue vase was still empty of flowers.

The letter knife was gone.

Rice frowned and looked around the room. She went back into the kitchen and searched under the mail and the clothes. The jagged edges of the few open envelopes told her they had not been opened with a letter knife.

'What are you looking for?' said Mrs Paddon *again*. Rice wondered if she was a bit touched in the head. She was old enough.

'There was a letter knife on the mantelpiece.'

'Oh. I don't know about that.'

Neither did Rice. But the fact that it was gone suddenly seemed significant.

She remembered the cold feel of it in her hand while Jonas sat there, not drinking, just watching her; watching the knife. The brownish flecks that had come off it with a scrape of her nail.

The way old blood might.

Elizabeth Rice felt panic spurt into her chest. Had she held vital evidence in her hands? Had she missed something she should have spotted because she had been thinking of fucking Jonas Holly?

It had been *right here.*

She leaned in to get a close-up of the mantelpiece – certain that the flecks would still be here. Then she would know for sure.

There was nothing. She ran the pad of her forefinger slowly along the wooden mantel, then looked at it. Nothing. Here in the grey-tinged room, this shelf alone had been dusted.

A twinge of suspicion. *It was the way he said it.*

Rice went upstairs and made a methodical search, while Mrs Paddon watched silently from the door of each room.

The letter knife was nowhere to be found.

*

By six o'clock, the Pied Piper story was back at the top of every news bulletin. Every single news outlet rode roughshod over DI Reynolds's careful words about being eliminated from the investigation, and was reporting that Police Constable Jonas Holly was the number-one suspect.

For the first time, Elizabeth Rice thought it might be true.

*

Em heard the news on the radio and burst into tears.

Mr Holly was the Piper.

The same Mr Holly Steven had been so wary of, and the same one *she* had insisted on taking with them to the woods. The same Mr Holly who had probably killed his wife *and* Charlie Peach – and who might be killing Steven right this very minute, while she stood here in the yard, hoof-pick in her hand, and with Skip nudging her pockets for the Polo mints he knew were always there.

59

To his great surprise, Teddy had missed Charlie. Specifically, he missed his singing. Bus rides now were dulled by silence. Or the silence was fractured by Dean Peaceman's meaningless jabber about cowboys and custard and little plastic cups. Dean Peaceman drove Teddy crazy. Not only because he talked utter shit, but because every syllable of that utter shit was enunciated with complete perfection. Dean Peaceman – a fourteen-year-old who'd just moved to Simonsbath from Cheshire – had a head full of rubbish and the mouth to prove it, while Teddy had a head full of wonders and a tongue so cruelly disconnected from his brain that those wonders turned to baby talk as soon as he let them loose from his lips. As if he lived his life in a pram, not a wheelchair.

Teddy tried so hard. Not a day went by when he did not think a coherent, important thought and then imagine escorting that thought – perfectly formed – from his brain to his mouth. He imagined holding its hand as he led it down behind the orbs of his eyeballs, past the snotty black ovals of his nasal cavities, past the ridges of his palate to his spongy tongue. There he imagined checking the thought was still intact and sensible before brushing it down, pointing it in the direction of his lips and releasing it like a proud parent on the first day of big school.

And then that thought would kick off its shoes, tear off its clothes, ruffle its hair into lunatic spikes, and run babbling out of his mouth and into the confused ears of other people, who bent over his wheelchair as if proximity were a cure for gibberish.

Nobody had ever asked him about the day Charlie went missing. Nobody had thought he had anything to add.

And he hadn't. Right up until the day when the police in their desperation released certain details that they'd kept carefully guarded.

Including the white plastic tape.

Sitting at home in front of the wide-screen TV, where his mother always let him hold the remote, Teddy watched from the wobbling corner of his eye as the news report showed the field where the horse show had been and where Charlie had been lost and found.

With total recall, Teddy the Spy immediately thought of the sun that had made his headrest so hot against his ear, the waving tails of the foxhounds that had surrounded him like a shiny brown-and-white sea, the huntsman in his red coat and black velvet cap. And the handle of the huntsman's whip – which had been bound up its entire length in white plastic tape.

Teddy grunted loudly for his mother, who always knew exactly what he meant to say.

60

The sunshine had died along with Charlie Peach. Overnight the August air got heavy, grey and motionless – and the huntsman went mad.

Mad*der*.

He had spent the past two sultry days pacing the walkway, without his mask or gloves. Or he stood at the kennel gates, brooding over his charges, lips moving soundlessly and sweat trickling down the side of his face. He opened and closed the door of the big shed ten times a day, and from the flesh room the children heard the clanking of the chains that held the meat, although he brought them nothing to eat.

Fear hung over them all, as pendulous and dark as the thunderclouds that were gathering in the west. Maisie and Kylie cried in fits and starts, and Jess stayed at the wire on that side of her cage and tried to keep them calm. She started to sing 'Ten Green Bottles', but didn't get past the first line before her voice cracked and stopped. After that, Maisie and Kylie just cried uninterrupted.

There was a cartoon – a little yellow bird in a cage, tormented by a cat. Even as a small child, Steven had hated it. The bars of the cage were too widely spaced. The cat could have snaked its paw through them at any time and pinioned the bird with one needle-sharp claw. It never did, but Steven remembered the constant fear that it *would*.

Under the glittering eye of the huntsman, Steven felt like that bird.

Even after the man strode purposefully back to the big shed, Steven couldn't stop shaking.

Jonas lay on his broken ribs so that it didn't hurt so much to breathe. He scraped the link on the floor like a metronome. When he made too deep a groove in the cement, he moved his operations half an inch to the left. When he did sleep, he slept with that single thinning link in his fingers, and sometimes he woke to the sound of the soft scraping beside his ear. Because the link was small and hard to grip, his nails tore and the skin was grazed from his fingertips.

There was no point in it. He knew that logically, and yet still he did it.

His life had come down to this closed loop of galvanized steel, rubbed shiny in his dulled fingers. For the thousandth time, Jonas pressed it against the floor until his hand went white, but it didn't bend or break.

No food. No water. No escape.

He was a goat, tethered for a tiger.

'I think he's going to kill us,' Steven Lamb whispered.

Jonas looked at him with his one good eye.

'Don't tell the others,' was all he said.

*

The huntsman stared at the children, but instead of being prized possessions, each frail figure now only reflected his own failure.

He'd been here all his life.

This *was* all his life.

He'd spent forty years rearing the hounds of the Blacklands Hunt. More backbreaking hours than any mother would ever spend on raising her child. More cold, more shit, more sweat, more blood. More mud, more miles, more nipped fingers, more freezing ears.

His life stretched out behind him in one long harsh winter.

Sometimes at night – before the hounds were . . . *disposed of* – he would sit in the dark and recite the generations, like an Apache wise man gifting history to his braves. Robbie to Bumper to Rufus to Stanley to Marcus to Major to Patch to Scout. And so on, back through time.

Those nights had brought him comfort. A sense of place and of purpose. A knowledge that everything he'd done and everything he *would* do was part of a whole. There was old Murton before him, and Townend before that. Beyond that, Coffin barely knew, because it was not important. The *pack* was the history of his tribe. The pack was his legacy – the proof of his skill and his dedication. Of his love. There were ribbons and trophies in the cottage, and old photos too. The smiling men in bowler hats were strangers who'd once lived in his home, but he would have known the hounds anywhere. He knew Rupert '71 because Pitcher '97 had had the same three marks on his ear; Dipper '85 was one of the family because Daisy '09 had that same high hock. And there was Fern '91 – smiling for the camera just the way she'd taught all her pups, and the way *they*'d taught *theirs*, all the way to little Frankie.

Once the last shot had rung out, the kennels had been silent for the first time in 163 years. After that his night-time soliloquies brought no comfort or pleasure. There were no braves to listen in the darkness, nor history for them to be part of.

No wife, no children. He had never had the time.

His only legacy now was his own bitter memory of warm bodies piled high, and the undignified wrestle to feed the stiffened carcasses into the flames.

He had destroyed the only things he'd ever cared about.

The pain was overwhelming. He gripped the wire gate and focused.

The child before him looked like John Took. Something about the eyes and the shape of the mouth was very like her father. She held out her empty bucket and moved her father's lips.

You don't love them.

Unconsciously, Bob Coffin touched the warm cotton of his overalls and felt the weight of the cold gun beneath it.

Everything was coming to an end.

Again.

61

Reynolds couldn't understand a word Teddy said. Or even how he said it.

Every syllable appeared to be agony and took an eternity. His head wagged, his chin jerked, his eyes screwed up and his hands flapped.

And yet Teddy's mother nodded at Reynolds and Rice throughout each garbled passage and then translated it all into English. It was like watching a medium at work, cocking her ear at knocks and swaying curtains, and deciphering them into a message about Uncle Arthur's missing will.

Except that the message Mrs Loosemore received was far more interesting than one from a dead uncle.

Reynolds and Rice walked to the car in silence, but the looks they exchanged held a thing called hope that neither of them had experienced for quite some time.

Because he knew less than nothing about hunting, Reynolds called John Took and put him on speakerphone for Rice to hear. He asked him about the white tape.

Took said, 'Hunt servants use white tape on their whips so they can be identified easily in the field.'

'Hunt servants?' said Reynolds.

'Employees of the hunt.'

'And do you have any enemies among the ranks of hunt employees?'

'Not that I know of,' said Took.

Rice mouthed, 'Shit.'

Reynolds very nearly hung up. Then he remembered the man in the yard below the helicopter. Waving like a cannibal at the iron bird in the sky. Reynolds got a strange feeling in the pit of his stomach.

'Mr Took, we flew over the hunt kennels a few weeks back.'

'Yes,' said Took. 'They're empty now.'

'But we saw a man there,' said Reynolds carefully.

'That'll be Bob Coffin. Our old huntsman. He still lives in the cottage. For a bit. The place'll be sold off this winter.'

The feeling in Reynolds's gut splashed through his body like spilled milk. A sick, excited feeling that he'd never felt before. Never believed he *would* feel.

He tried to deny it. Tried to suppress it. But it defied him.

It was a hunch.

He was having a fucking hunch!

He tried to keep his voice from shaking. 'There's an incinerator there, right?'

'Yes. We've got an incinerator up there,' said John Took.

'What's it for?'

'For burning what's left of the fallen stock after it's been slaughtered for the dogs. Hoofs and hides and the like.'

'But why would the incinerator be in use if the kennels are empty?'

There was a silence on the line that seemed to last for the whole of Reynolds's life up to that moment.

'It shouldn't be,' said John Took.

*

The incinerator roared softly to life and the children pricked up their ears like Dobermanns.

Even Jonas felt the dull flames in his stomach as he scrape-scrape-scraped the link on the cement immediately in front of his face.

The knives started to sharpen, and saliva trickled into his mouth. It disgusted him, but he couldn't help it. It was a relief, in fact. He'd drunk the last of his water yesterday, and his tongue already felt too big, as if it were trying to crowd down his sticky throat.

The children pressed diamonds into their own meagre flesh as they squeezed themselves against the fence, their eyes fixed unwaveringly on the big shed. They waited for the rumble of the trolley piled with meat.

But it never came.

In the big shed Bob Coffin took the coupling chains from the hooks on the wall.

They would give him something to hold them still by.

62

R ice drove as fast as the roads allowed.
    At least.

Reynolds kept his right foot pressed hard on the brake he
didn't have and – now and then – slapped a steadying hand on
the dashboard.

'Sorry,' Rice said, after one particularly close shave with a
caravan.

'Not at all,' said Reynolds. He assumed Rice had done the
Advanced Driver course, but thought that now would be a poor
time to double-check.

He leaned forward and tilted his head to the left to peer into
the wing mirror. They'd lost the other three cars in the convoy
somewhere. They should really wait for them, but Reynolds wasn't
about to slow Rice down. His hunch had segued into a feeling of
such imminent disaster – such impending doom – that getting to
the hunt kennels as fast as humanly possible was the only thing
that mattered. He'd already summoned ambulances from Weston

and Minehead, and the police helicopter from Filton. He didn't care who got there first, as long as they got there fast.

He sat up straight again, and fake-braked through an S-bend.

'I was getting worried it was Jonas,' said Rice.

'Me too.' He nodded.

'I'm glad it's not.'

'Me too,' he admitted, and braced himself for a collision with a bank of trees that loomed across the road.

'Your hair looks good,' said Rice.

Reynolds was surprised. 'Thanks.' He touched his fringe self-consciously.

Rice swung around a hairpin, then stamped on the accelerator and picked up frightening speed on a rare straight.

We're going to make it, thought Reynolds, with hope unfurling in his heart.

They passed a group of deer so fast they didn't even have time to scatter, only to flinch and then stand and quiver post-fright. In his wing mirror, Reynolds saw the buck pointing after them, its dark nose raised and its antlers laid along its back in fury.

He wished he hadn't looked.

*

The first fat drops of rain fell on to the concrete, releasing the hot smell of dust. More rang slowly off the corrugated plastic roofs.

Bob Coffin padlocked one end of a coupling chain to Steven's collar and handed him the other end. He unlocked the gate next door, and pointed at Jonas.

'Put it on him, bay,' he said.

Steven walked slowly into Jonas's cage. It was strange to be so close to him after all the time they'd spent in separate spaces. It made everything seem brighter, more real. Jonas lay twisted on one side, like a dead fox in a ditch. His stretched skin was split in a dozen swollen yellow-purple places, the way a loaf cracks open as it rises. As Steven approached, Jonas stopped scraping the chain on the cement and watched him through one eye, the shallow rise of his ribs now the only thing that showed he was alive.

'Can you sit up?'

Slowly, Jonas put a flat hand on the cement, and Steven helped him to sit against the mesh.

Steven knelt and attached the other end of the coupling chain to his collar. Now they were harnessed to each other.

'Here.'

Steven looked round. The huntsman was leaning towards him with the key. He nodded at the padlock that held Jonas to the fence. Steven noticed that as soon as he took the key, the huntsman stepped quickly away, afraid of getting too close to Jonas.

Steven unlocked Jonas from the fence and helped him to his unsteady feet.

'Where are we going?' said Jonas.

'Exercise. Put your arm on my shoulder,' said Steven, and Jonas did, and together they left the stinking kennel. As they passed the huntsman, he held out his hand for the key and then slipped it into his pocket.

The others were already on the walkway, waiting for them: Pete and Jess linked together, and Kylie with Maisie.

Jonas was all bones. Steven guessed they all were, but to feel another man's bones against his own was strangely sad.

The rain got louder on the roofs, and the children turned their faces to it and opened their mouths.

'Hup!' said the huntsman.

They were facing the meadow, as usual, but the huntsman spread his arms and encouraged them to turn the other way – towards the big shed.

'Hup! Hup!'

Pete and the girls started to shuffle slowly round, but Steven stood his ground.

'Where are we going?'

'Hup!' said the huntsman.

Steven didn't move. This didn't feel right. Routine had kept them alive for so long and this was not routine. First Jonas had been let out, and now they were being herded towards the big shed instead of the meadow. Steven started to feel bad. He didn't exactly feel sick, but he thought he might quite soon.

'Why aren't we going to the meadow?'

'Hup!'

'Where are we going?' said Steven stubbornly.

The huntsman paused and then gestured vaguely at the sky. 'Helicopter.'

They all looked up, but saw nothing, heard nothing. Even so, Maisie began to sob loudly, which set Kylie off like a twin.

The younger children continued to move, searching the sky. Even Jonas moved his weight as if he expected Steven to start walking.

But Steven didn't.

Instinct had served Steven well in his short life, and every instinct he possessed now told him something was wrong.

'Hup!' said Bob Coffin, poking and pushing at Jonas and Steven to try to get them started. 'Get on now!'

'We're not cows,' said Steven, shaking him off angrily. 'We're not bloody *cows*.'

Bob Coffin calmly pulled the gun out of his pocket and pointed it at Steven's face. Steven ducked and Jess shrieked.

'Helicopter,' said the huntsman flatly.

There was no helicopter, but, galvanized by the gun, they all moved up the walkway made slippery by the rain.

Jonas wasn't leaning too heavily on Steven, but it was still awkward to walk without stumbling. They were bumpingly close – all sharp elbows and hips. The loose end of the yard-long chain that had tethered Jonas to the fence for so long swung between them, the padlock bouncing off their thighs. Steven thought he should have unlocked it at the collar end, but whatever – it didn't seem like a big problem after the gun.

They walked down the rutted concrete ramp into the big shed.

Steven looked around him at the room he'd only ever seen half of when fully conscious – and through a crack in a wall. It was bigger than he'd thought – big enough for a couple of tractors, at least – and almost empty. There was an old wooden bench on one side of the room, where he could see three knives laid out as if for supper at a grand house: neatly, and in order of length. There was a whetstone gripped in a shiny blue metal vice, a couple of lengths of heavy chain, some shackles and spring clips and a few rusting cans; Steven recognized 3-in-1 oil and Castrol grease from Ronnie's garage.

Em's arms around him, her warm breath on his neck . . . 'I don't care' . . .

His heart ached to think of it.

On one wall was the electric winch, its steel cable the only thing in the shed that glinted with newness. Bolted low on the wall directly opposite was a heavy curled hook. Directly between the two was a drain and a small dark patch – the only evidence, Stephen realized, of countless animals that had been butchered on the spot – the place where the head was severed from the neck and the blood leaked out.

Beside the hook was the half-open door to the flesh room, and Steven's stomach rolled at what was to come. The memory of being enclosed in the cold, fetid flesh was shockingly clear.

'I don't want to! I don't want to!' Maisie's continuing sobs echoed loudly in his head, joining forces with the rain beating on the iron roof.

Even if the helicopter were directly overhead, Steven doubted that any of them would hear it now. He wondered what they might look like through a thermal-imaging camera: an odd party of white blobs shuffling together across the shed, becoming greyer in the cold of the flesh room, and then disappearing altogether once they were inside the meat. Maybe a grey foot would protrude, or a charcoal elbow – but the crew overhead would have to know what they were looking for. What they were looking *at*.

Bob Coffin turned on a flickering fluorescent strip light and squealed the shed door shut on its un-oiled runners. As the yard and the kennels and the darkening sky disappeared behind them, Steven's instincts gifted him a powerful mental image of the stone lid of an ancient tomb closing over his head.

Jonas saw the same things they all did: the bench, the vice, the winch, the chains. But he truly *looked* at only one thing – the half-open door to the flesh room, where Bob Coffin would soon stuff the weeping, terrified children into the stinking carcasses like pimentos in olives. Already the huntsman had a hold of the chain between Jess and Pete. Already he was tugging them away from the others, the gun in his hand making things easy.

But there was something wrong . . .

Jonas frowned and strained his eyes, and leaned away from Steven to see as much of the small room as possible. It was dark but his eyes were adjusting, and it shouldn't be *that* hard to see . . .

When he realized what he was seeing – or what he wasn't seeing – Jonas felt the world tilt under him. He stumbled and Steven grabbed him before he could fall.

'You OK?'

Jonas shook his head.

He wasn't OK.

None of them were.

Jonas said something that Steven didn't catch.

'What?' said Steven.

'There's no meat,' said Jonas faintly. 'In the flesh room.'

No meat. Steven frowned. That must be wrong. No meat meant there was nowhere to hide them. Nowhere to hide their heat. If there was no meat, how would the huntsman conceal them from the thermal-imaging camera?

How would he make them all cold?

It took Steven for ever to understand. Time slowed to a virtual standstill. He blinked at Jonas with rusty eyelids, then turned his creaking head to stare into the infinite flesh room. The neurons in his brain fired up the message like a sputtering candle; it plodded slowly down axons, and connected to other neurons via two tin cans and a piece of string.

When the answer finally came, it hit him like a sledgehammer.

'*Steven!*'

He spun round at the sound of Jess's desperate cry.

She and Pete were on their hands and knees; Jess was trying to get back up, but the huntsman's right boot was on the coupling chain, holding it to the concrete floor. The muzzle of the small black gun banged and slid against Pete's thrashing head.

Steven and Jonas moved as one – the only way they could.

The gunshot was deafening.

They fell over Pete and on to Bob Coffin. Steven had the hand with the gun in it in both of his hands, pressing it to the floor like a snake, too scared to let go. The shot still rang inside his head like thunder in an iron bucket.

Jonas and the huntsman struggled beside him and under him, but Steven just focused on the gun. His only job was the gun. The huntsman fought like the insane thing he was, and Jonas's knees and elbows and head slammed into Steven repeatedly, like a boat tied to a dock in a storm.

Slowly the waves subsided but still Steven leaned on the wrist, trembling with effort, until he saw Coffin's grip on the gun start to slacken. Even then he was too frightened to let go and grab it. Instead he banged the hand against the cement until the gun fell from it, and then used the same slack hand to knock the gun across the floor, where Maisie and Kylie shuffled over to it.

'Leave it!' he yelled, and they left it, looking almost as frightened of him as they had been of Coffin.

For a long moment, Steven just lay there, gripping the still wrist, wondering if this could really be the end of it all, or whether Bob Coffin might suddenly throw them both off and murder them all – the way things happened in the movies.

He looked around. Jess was helping Pete to his feet; Pete had pissed himself and Steven didn't blame him.

Finally, *finally*, Steven looked over at the huntsman's face.

Jonas Holly had wrapped the long, loose end of his tether chain around Bob Coffin's neck. Coffin was puce, his small blue eyes wide and staring up into Jonas's, small bubbles of spit popping at the corners of his mouth.

'It's OK, Jonas! I got the gun!' panted Steven.

Jonas felt for the key in the huntsman's pocket and then sat up on his chest. He fumbled for the lock under his own chin, and the padlock clicked open. The chain snaked on to Bob Coffin's chest with a musical hiss.

Then Jonas rose to his feet, dragging Steven up with him, and hauled the slack-kneed Coffin across the shed. He seemed to have no regard for the fact that they were still chained together, and the movement hurt Steven's neck.

'Give me the key,' he gasped, but Jonas ignored him. Instead he looped the free end of the tether chain over the low hook bolted to the wall. Then he squatted down beside Coffin, whose hands now clawed desperately at the links biting into his flesh.

Jonas stared hard into Coffin's face and jerked the chain around his neck. 'This is not love,' he said softly.

Steven shuddered. He'd heard that voice before. He had not imagined it.

You can run now.

Jonas stood up and crossed the shed as if Steven wasn't lurching and stumbling beside him, and pulled the end of the cable from the winch. The huntsman was lying on the floor, barely moving, his hands at his throat and a faint whine coming from his bloodless lips. Jonas looped the cable around his boots.

'Stop!' croaked Steven. 'Stop!'

But Jonas walked right through him, knocking him off his feet once more. He kept going, pulling Steven along with him, backwards and in a crude headlock. The feeble hostage who had looked like roadkill now seemed to have the strength of ten men; the teenager hanging from his throat was a drag, not a bar to his progress. Steven clutched at Jonas's arm for support and looked up at the ceiling – at the curtains of cobwebs in the rafters, and the old-fashioned strip lighting like in Ronnie's garage. He arched his back and craned his head to see where they were going, and saw the buttons on the wall beside the winch.

Jonas Holly was going to tear Bob Coffin apart.

In his mind, Steven could already see the huntsman stretch, hear the shrieks and the ripping muscles, watch the neck lengthen and split, exposing red-liquorice veins and chewing-gum skin. He could already see the head jerk and pop off, and roll twitching into a corner, while the rest of Bob Coffin fishtailed across the floor, spraying fountains of blood, until the soles of his dead feet hit the wall.

Jonas stopped at the winch and Steven twisted to look up into his eyes.

They were as blank as a shark's – as cold and dark as the muzzle of the huntsman's gun – in a face Steven had seen before and would never make the mistake of forgetting again.

'You killed her,' he whispered. 'I know you did.'

Jonas said nothing. And – even over the battle-drum roar of the rain on the roof – Steven heard the winch whirr into life.

'Get out!' he shouted at the rafters. 'Jess, get them OUT!'

Then he squeezed his eyes shut and covered his ears, but he heard the screams anyway, as Bob Coffin started to die.

63

Rice beat the helicopter to the Blacklands Hunt kennels.

Reynolds knew she would.

The rain was biblical now and the second they stepped out of the car they were drenched. Reynolds ran through the yard – past the row of empty kennels on his left, stables on his right.

'Be careful!' yelled Rice behind him, but he wasn't. Irrational fear had gripped him and made him reckless for the first time in his life.

Ahead of him the concrete sloped down towards a large shed. Reynolds faltered as the huge door squealed open, then stopped dead as four children spilled out of the light and into the storm. They were half naked, weeping and terrified, but even through the driving rain Reynolds recognized them as if he'd fathered them.

'*Elizabeth!*' he yelled, and he ran down the ramp.

Jess Took pointed into the shed and cried, 'He's killing him.'

Reynolds burst through the door in time to see the final screaming agony of Bob Coffin.

Too late.

There was a loud crack and the chain wound around Coffin's neck snapped in two. It whipped up and hit the wall, sending a single broken link skittering past Reynolds's feet like money. The huntsman skidded across the concrete in the other direction, his boots hitting the opposite wall, his knees crumpling behind them.

'Christ!' Reynolds bounded across the room and hit the cut-off switch. Jonas Holly and Steven Lamb were right there and he turned to them now, fizzing with adrenaline.

The sight of them stopped him dead.

Jonas Holly was covered in blood and bruises, one eye was barely open and his chest and stomach ran with blood from fresh wounds. Beside him – *chained* to him – Steven Lamb emitted a high, whining noise. His eyes were tightly shut, his teeth gritted with the effort of remaining blind, his hands pressed against his ears.

'Steven?' said Reynolds, and touched his shoulder. 'Steven, you're safe.'

Steven opened his eyes. For a brief second Reynolds saw relief on his face – then panic hit, and he started to shout and flail.

'Get him off me! Get him *off me*! Please, just get him off me! *Please . . .*'

Jonas and Reynolds fended off what blows they could. Reynolds kept saying *You're safe* and *It's over*, but Steven was beyond sense. In the middle of it all, Jonas put his hands to Steven's throat – and opened the lock that had held them together. Steven grabbed the key from his hand and pushed himself off Jonas. He fell to the floor and crawled rapidly away, only stumbling to his feet again as he burst out of the shed door.

Reynolds was so full of questions that he asked none of them. And Jonas Holly just stood there blinking, as if he'd been surprised out of sleep. The brief silence was plugged by the rain and – at last – the *whup-whup-whup* of the chopper.

Reynolds knelt and unwound the chain from Coffin's neck as the ambulances approached. He was going to need one. Coffin was still breathing but not moving. Whatever the provocation, if Jonas Holly had done this to him, there was something wrong with the man. Something seriously wrong. Reynolds felt it in his guts and he didn't care if it was unscientific.

He saw a gun lying in the middle of the floor. Under normal circumstances he'd insist that it was left where it was, for the scenes-of-crime officers to photograph in situ. But these were not normal circumstances, and Reynolds stepped swiftly over Bob Coffin to pick it up. He felt safer with it in his hand, and realized just how *un*safe he'd felt until then.

God knows what the hell had happened here over the past two months *or* the past two minutes. He had an uneasy feeling that the Piper case had only just started giving up its secrets. He shivered. This hunch thing was like opening the window to a vampire – after letting the first one in, it seemed he had no choice in the matter.

Paramedics strode in, and he pointed at Bob Coffin. One of them put a blanket around Jonas's shoulders and led him out of the big shed.

Reynolds watched him all the way.

Close to the door, Jonas bent and picked up the broken link. He held it up to the light and turned it in his fingers – twisted and bent out of shape, and rubbed shiny in the corner where it had snapped.

Reynolds heard him ask, 'How did this get here?'

Rice was in one of the stables, in the dry, wrapping the children in blankets. They were all crying, but for once she felt blameless.

A medic moved among them with the key he'd taken from Steven, unlocking the collars they'd worn for so long.

Steven stood outside. When Rice tried to usher him out of the rain, he twisted away from her. 'I don't want to go inside!' he said. Then, more calmly, 'Thank you.'

She nodded and brought him a rough grey NHS blanket and he stood shivering against the wall of the stable block as, one by one, the other children were led to the waiting ambulances. Their tearful faces were freshly washed with rain and cautious hope as they waved goodbye. Jess Took hugged him as she left.

Two medics tried to lead him away, but Steven resisted.

'I don't want to go to hospital.'

'You need to be checked out,' said one medic.

'I'm fine.'

The man took hold of his arm – gentle but firm. Steven shook him off and pushed him away, panic rising within him—

Elizabeth Rice was suddenly at his side. Her hair was wet again, but this time she didn't look annoyed.

'He won't get in the ambulance,' said the medic, but she just waved him away and then turned to Steven.

'Shall we just go straight home?' she said.

Steven's eyes pricked and he felt joy cup his heart at the thought of his mother's arms open to greet him, Nan's eyes all big and shiny behind her glasses, Davey happy to see him, and Em's warm back under his hands. The images were so powerful that he felt the muscles in his arms twitch to embrace them all.

'Yes, please,' he said. And he put his arms around Elizabeth Rice and let her hold him until his mother could.

Over her shoulder, Jonas Holly limped past between two paramedics. He turned his brown eyes towards Steven and raised a hand.

Steven didn't raise one back. He watched the medics help Jonas into an ambulance and hoped that it crashed on the way to hospital.

Then he followed DS Rice to a car that still smelled of hot brakes.

64

Their homecomings were just as they'd expected – and more. Jess Took was clamped between her mother and her father so tight that she wondered how they could ever be prised apart. Rachel stood nearby – her smile and talons fixed – and wondered the same thing.

Pete Knox's parents put on a united front and their neighbours threw a street party to welcome him home, with bunting and cakes. The council even agreed to close the road so that they wouldn't all be mown down during the celebrations. Pete only managed half a cupcake and a sip of Coke before he began to feel queasy. It would take a while.

His mother followed him around like a mitten on a string, and his father watched her with a look on his face that suggested he could not forget what she'd said back in that early-morning car park, however hard he tried. Mercifully, Pete didn't notice that right then. He was just happy to be home.

Maisie and Kylie were submerged in love and protection, and never took the bus to school again.

A few days after their return, the driver Ken Beard sat in his car outside their homes and shook so badly that he couldn't do what he'd gone there for. Finally it was his daughter Karen and her boyfriend – whose name was simply Mark, despite the mascara – who encouraged him up the paths and knocked on the doors for him, so that he could beg the girls' forgiveness in person.

They and their families were in forgiving moods, and would be for a long time to come.

Steven was bruised from all the hugging, Lettie cried and laughed for days, Uncle Jude bought him an Xbox still in its original packaging, and Nan kept saying, 'I *told* you he'd be back!' when she hadn't at all.

Davey hugged him and almost cried, but then called him a wanker instead, which meant a lot, coming from him.

Physically Steven bounced back quickly. It took a few weeks to learn to eat right again, but that was hardly a chore. Mentally, he was . . . fine.

That surprised even him.

Sure, the smell of the bathroom disinfectant had the power to turn his stomach, and he often caught himself touching his own neck – feeling for the collar he'd worn for so long. But still, when DS Rice explained that Victim Support was arranging for all the children to see a psychologist to help them over the trauma, Steven politely declined.

He had survived, hadn't he? The past was the past and surviving it was the important thing. Now he had the rest of his life to live, and more important things to think about.

Some more important than others . . .

Em had not hooked up with Lewis or Lalo; she had waited for Steven.

'I would have waited for ever,' she told him fiercely, as they lay dizzy and breathless after their first time.

Steven held her close. He was a man now, but he felt like the same boy – only much happier. He wondered whether Lewis would guess he'd had sex and he hoped not. The only witnesses he needed to this moment were the silent ones gazing down at them from his walls. Uncle Billy, Angelina Jolie and the Liverpool first eleven.

'For ever is a long, long time,' he said carefully.

'Good,' said Em. 'Then we'll spend it together.'

The next day they walked up the hill to continue rebuilding their lives and the Suzuki, only to find that Ronnie and Dougie had finished the bike for him, and that all Steven had to do was turn the key and kick it over.

He would never have to walk past Rose Cottage again.

The newspapers and TV were all over the children – particularly Steven, who had cheated death twice before he was old enough to drink. Marcie Meyrick came to the door four times – each time with a higher offer. On the final visit, she actually cried.

Much to Davey's annoyance, his brother had no interest in getting free money, so he sold his own story to a rival reporter from the *Star*. It appeared under the headline MY BROTHER THE NUT MAGNET. Davey spent £115 of the proceeds on a new skateboard for Steven, and felt cleansed. And the next time he and Shane went up to Springer Farm, they took with them a can of black paint and obliterated *Mr PEach is a COCK* from the farmhouse wall.

They pretty much stopped going there after that, although for many years afterwards Davey would think about the blackened rafters, the dark chimney, and the box of gay junk that Shane hadn't wanted.

There was, of course, no homecoming to celebrate for David Peach. While the other children were being returned to their families, he watched Channel 4 Racing with DI Reynolds by his side. For some reason, the man who'd led the investigation had chosen to allow his sergeant to bask in the sunshine of the TV cameras and the grateful parents, while *they* worked their way through a bottle of Glenfiddich and pretended to give a shit about who won the 3.45 from Doncaster.

DI Reynolds was no drinker and almost choked on the first shot. But by the fourth he'd got the hang of it.

So they sat and got more and more slumped and slurred – surrounded by a bright sea of flowers and teddy bears that countless well-wishers had left on the doorstep of the little blue house where Charlie had lived . . .

For a while after his son's funeral David Peach did think of moving away, but finally he stayed among friends.

Among those he now counted John Took, who wasn't half the prick he used to be.

*

Jonas was the only person who was truly surprised by his homecoming.

After three days in hospital he took a taxi home. He arrived at Rose Cottage as the sun dipped below the moor, and found Elizabeth Rice on his doorstep with a bottle of Rioja.

'The hospital called. Said you'd discharged yourself.'

'I had things to do.'

'DI Reynolds wants a chat tomorrow morning.'

'But not tonight,' he said.

'No,' she agreed. 'Not tonight.'

They went inside and shared the wine at the kitchen table, where Mrs Paddon had left a vegetarian stew and a yellow Post-it note:

45 mins at 140 (Centigrade, Jonas!)

Jonas peeled off the note and rolled it into a tight tube between his fingers as they talked.

Actually *she* talked. He just listened, but he did it well enough.

They took the bottle into the living room in an action replay that she knew in her loins was going to have a different result this time.

They stood at the window and, as they watched the coming night turn the Exmoor sky as green as the sea, she kissed him properly.

For a moment there was a rush of hunger between them – then he stepped away awkwardly and looked at the rising moon.

'It's getting dark,' he said.

Rice nodded and felt like a fool. An unwanted fool.

From the mantel Lucy Holly watched her, trowel in hand, smiling in a place that was always warm.

'Where's that little gold letter knife you had here?' she said dully.

Jonas turned and looked at her, silhouetted against the oceanic sky, with the moon on one shoulder and Venus at the other.

'I don't remember,' he shrugged.

As Rice left Rose Cottage, Mrs Paddon opened her front door. 'I told you you were wasting your time,' she said.

Rice bit her lip.

But only as far as the gate. Then she turned. 'Why don't you just piss off, you nosey old bitch?'

Mrs Paddon closed her door quietly and Rice cried all the way back to the Red Lion.

*

Elizabeth Rice woke hours later because she was cold, and she was cold because the window was open.

She closed it and looked across the haphazard roofs below, and then up at the moon – a brilliant coin with dove-grey oceans. If she'd had a book, she could have read by this light alone, but her books were packed away now in the small bag by the bedroom door, awaiting tomorrow's departure. Instead, she held up her hand and looked at the lines criss-crossing her silver palm. She wondered whether her future really could be written in those lines, like music in the grooves of an old 45. She wondered what tunes they might play. Love songs or bitter country heartbreakers.

Rice sighed and dropped her hand, and rested her forehead against the cold glass.

The letter knife was on the window-sill.

She flinched as if burned. She failed to breathe.

She stepped gingerly away from the window, and went quickly into the bathroom – coming back with a few sheets of tissue paper. With that, she picked up the little gold dagger with the engraved handle.

By the light of the moon she could read *A Gift from Weston-super-Mare*.

Even though the window was now closed, Elizabeth Rice started to shiver.

65

Jonas should have been in Shipcott at the debrief with DI Reynolds, but instead he was walking across the vast flat sands of Weston-super-Mare beach, eating an ice cream.

He'd left his shoes and socks under the ice-cream van; he didn't think anyone would take them. Not until the van left for the night, at least – but that particular night was hours away.

It was another spectacular day, and he had to eat fast to keep the vanilla from rolling down his knuckles.

There were plenty of holidaymakers, but the beach was so wide, and they were all so close to the ice-cream van, that it seemed deserted.

He approached the new pier. The old one of his dreams had burned down, surrounded by water. He looked around as he passed between the pilings, even though he would not find Lucy here.

He knew that now.

The thought didn't make him sad. How could he be sad on a day like this? The sun was hot, the sand was cool, the ice cream was sweet, and he'd kept his promise.

He had saved the boy.

Not Charlie, sadly, but the boy that was himself.

People hurt children. Of course they did. That was the truth. But it was also true that children escaped, they recovered and they survived. Steven Lamb was proof of that twice over. Until Bob Coffin had shown him, Jonas had had no idea how *resilient* children were. How resilient *he* finally was.

Lucy had been right to want children and he had been wrong to prevent her. Jonas could see that now. But he knew she would forgive him; he had been a different person then. Now he felt complete. He had never felt so *whole*.

Jonas reached the water's edge and the flat waves cooled his bare feet. The wet sand shifted slightly under his toes as the outgoing tide tried to suck the beach back into the ocean. He couldn't help smiling, and excited butterflies filled his stomach.

He finished his ice cream, then leaned down to rinse his hands in the sea, before straightening up and squinting into the blue. Steep Holm island seemed very close, although it was miles away – high in the water and brilliant green in the sunshine. He'd never been there, but he'd heard it was covered in wild peonies. He'd like to see that some time. On the horizon was the hazy grey stripe of Wales.

Jonas stretched like a dog in the sun, and felt calm settle warmly into his bones.

Everything was going to be fine. Elizabeth Rice was smart; she would discover that the blood on the handle of the knife was not Lucy's.

Jonas hoped that Steven would learn of it somehow, and know that he had told him the truth about that.

There were other truths about himself that were more disturbing, and Bob Coffin on the winch had finally convinced him of those too.

Jonas took off his uniform, folding each item and leaving them in a neat pile. He looked around before removing his trousers, but there was nobody close by. They slipped off easily because of the missing button that he'd never got around to sewing back on.

A button was like a wife. They both held things together. He'd lost a button and he'd lost a wife. But at least he knew where to find one of them.

Wearing only his shorts, Jonas walked into the cold water until it covered his scars, and then he started to swim.

It was years since he'd swum in the ocean. It was easier than he'd remembered; the salt was his friend. He headed for Steep Holm, even though he wasn't planning to swim there. It gave him something to point at. He didn't want to go round in embarrassing circles like a broken motor-boat.

The further he went, the happier he got. He swam freestyle, breathing under his right arm, the way they'd been taught at school. Sometimes it worked and sometimes he got a noseful of brine. But he felt strong, and he felt clean and he felt *whole*, and nothing was going to stop him. Not ever.

Finally Jonas tired.

His arms barely cleared the surface, and his lungs seemed to have shrunk. His legs were far heavier than when he'd first launched himself into the waves. He trod water for a moment, then paddled himself around to look back at the beach.

He was surprised by how far he'd come. Weston-super-Mare was draped across his horizon like a toy village. As the sea swelled under him, he could pinpoint the Winter Gardens, and the new white pier glinting in the sunshine, but nothing else was recognizable from this distance. The broad beach was no more than a narrow brown line.

He wondered whether anyone had stolen his shoes yet, and remembered he'd only put an hour's parking ticket on the Land Rover.

He laughed. A short sound, which was all his burning lungs could spare him. He was too far out, and his arms were too tired and his legs were too heavy. But he didn't feel frightened and he didn't feel alone.

Jonas turned his back on the beach and kept swimming. He concentrated on lifting his weary arms and kicking his leaden legs and turning his mouth to suck in the sunshine.

Every weakening stroke pumped more joy into his heart.

He couldn't wait to tell Lucy all that he had learned.

ACKNOWLEDGMENTS

I could not have written this book without the kind help of hunt staff and members on Exmoor, who were so generous with their time and knowledge.

Many thanks to the editorial, design and marketing teams at Transworld for their insight, creativity and attention to detail. I'm particularly grateful for the support of Sarah Adams and Ben Willis.

Read on for the opening pages of
The Beautiful Dead,
the new novel from Belinda Bauer.

"[A] taut thriller. . . Readers will root for Bauer's
spunky heroine on this suspenseful slay ride
through a snow-globe London."
—*Publishers Weekly*

Available now

1

1 December

Layla Martin's shoes were killing her.

She had bought them on Thursday even though they rubbed her little toes.

A hundred and thirty pounds. A third of her weekly wage.

She'd worn them on Thursday night and again on Friday night while making cheese on toast for tea. And she had worn them to work on a Saturday even though she knew she'd be the only person on the eighth floor – quite possibly in the whole building. She'd wanted to break them in for Monday, when she was planning to walk past the glass-walled office of the new accounts manager at least twenty times, because he had a sports car and a great bum, and the ridiculously high heels made her calves look fabulous.

But now it was those very same heels that she was running in. Running for her life, she had to assume.

And, as the machine-gun clatter of her brand-new heels rang through the empty stairwell, any consciousness Layla Martin could spare from the terror of being chased by a madman was consumed by the desperate wish that she'd come to work in her usual weekend garb of jeans, jumper and Reeboks.

Because right here, right now, her shoes might mean the difference between life and death . . .

The man had appeared across the wide open-plan office. She had looked up from the ToppFlyte file and seen him standing at the lift. It had given her a little jolt of surprise and fear. Silly, really – in broad daylight in the middle of London. But she was alone on the eighth floor, and that made all the difference.

Still, he was an ordinary-looking man. Not weird. A delivery guy, most likely – or lost.

'Hi,' she'd said. 'Can I help you?'

'I am a friend,' he'd said. 'I am not fierce.'

She'd frowned. 'Say again?'

By way of an answer, the ordinary man had put his gloved hand inside his coat and drawn out a knife.

Layla Martin had never been in danger before, but she'd hesitated for only a second before leaping to her feet, grabbing her bag and running.

Because he'd been blocking her way to the lift, she'd headed for the stairs . . .

Layla didn't scream. The thought of the sound bouncing endlessly up and down the stairwell only frightened her more – and she was trying not to panic, trying to *think*. She ran as fast as she dared in those *bloody shoes*, clutching the black-plastic-covered handrail in case she lost her footing, watching the stairs blur underfoot with eyes that bulged in concentration, desperate not to fall, her long blonde hair swinging into her mouth, her bag bumping her ribs.

There would be someone on the fourth floor. She had once come halfway up in the lift with a woman who'd bitched about working at weekends.

Layla stopped above the fourth-floor landing, panting, gasping. She forced herself to be quiet so she could listen.

She heard nothing. No one.

Maybe he wasn't coming after her. Maybe he'd never planned to. Maybe he hadn't even had a knife.

He had though . . .

She started downstairs again – slowly this time – her knees like jelly and her toes on fire.

She pulled open the fire-escape door marked with a giant 4 and took a tentative step on to the carpet.

'Hello!'

The lift door slid open. The man was inside. Calm and still, and with the knife – it *was* a knife! – held casually by his side.

He smiled.

Layla gave a shriek of shock, fear and disbelief. She swung her bag at his head, hitting him a glancing blow, showering him with assorted bag-junk, seeing him flinch and duck. Then she turned back into the stairwell and ran downstairs again.

At the next landing she kicked off her heels and left them there. This was better.

Layla was not that fit, but she was young and slim and – without the killer heels – she was nimble. She started to get into a rhythm. She barely touched the stairs now, leaping from five or six treads up on to each landing, grabbing the rail as it turned, using it to slingshot around the blind concrete corners. Somewhere behind her she heard a door slam shut. But it was a long way back.

He wasn't catching her. *He wasn't catching her.* She was going to make it!

The sobs that had choked her became hysterical glee in her throat. Her stockinged feet skidded and slid but she *used* that. She worked it, baby! She had it all under control.

Run jump grab skid turn . . . Run jump grab skid turn . . .

It was a helter-skelter without the mats, but with added terror. But that was *good*, because it was all going to be OK in the end.

With manic laughter bubbling inside her, Layla burst through the door marked G and into the vast, bright lobby with its shiny polished floor. She turned towards the exit so fast that she skidded over on to her right side with a bang, but was on her feet again before the fall even registered.

The door was right there.

Escape was in sight. More than in sight . . .

Escape was panoramic.

Coldharbour was a new building and the lobby was a sleek and shiny glass-walled, marble-floored expanse that still smelled of stone dust, and not yet of people. The front wall was entirely glass – smoked grey and impenetrable from outside; but from inside Layla could see that, just thirty yards away, Oxford Street was teeming with Christmas shoppers beating a path through dirty snow.

She ran to the door, fumbling under her armpit and into her bag, her fingers spreading panic among the random objects, clutching and sifting with unaccustomed urgency.

The keys. The *keys*!

At weekends they had to let themselves in and keep the doors locked. Something about cutting security costs. The cheap bastards. She'd like to see what they thought about cutting costs after *this* little episode . . .

A door clicked behind her and she turned and saw the man standing at the entrance to the stairwell.

Not coming for her, not running; just standing, watching her escape.

She cackled at him like a witch.

'*FUCK* you!' she shrilled. 'Fuck *YOU!*'

She turned back to the door. Mentally she was already outside. Already safe.

Where were the *keys*?

Then she heard them – that wonderful chink of familiar metal – and for a glorious split second Layla was *on* Oxford Street in all its slushy glory. She was stepping out on to the crowded pavement alongside that bottle-blonde woman and her Goth daughter. She was brushing past that young man with the cheap bouquet, who had his back to the glass wall and who was looking up and down the road, waiting for someone special. She could already feel the wet city snowflakes melting on her hot cheeks . . .

And then she realized that her keys were jangling *behind* her.

With one clutching hand still in her bag, Layla looked around slowly.

The man had her keys.

Maybe they'd hit him in the head when she'd swung her bag; maybe she'd never put them *in* her bag and he'd picked them up off her desk.

It didn't matter how he had them.

He had them.

And she didn't.

He gave a half-smile and tossed the keys a few inches into the air again. They settled in his palm with a sound like money. From here Layla could see the key ring that her flatmate, Dougie, had bought her at the petrol station they used on the Old Kent Road. Lisa Simpson nestled snugly between the black-leather fingers of the man with the knife.

He had driven her down here.

Layla realized that now. Now that it was too late.

He could have killed her on the eighth floor; he could have killed her on the fourth. He could probably have caught her in the stairwell and killed her there. But instead he'd herded her to this very place – like a dumb sheep on that TV show with farmers and collies.

She could see it in his forgettable face: he had her right where he wanted her. Right here in this bright open space with people passing by.

'Be of good cheer,' he said. 'I am not fierce.' And although he did not speak loudly, his voice swelled to fill the marble lobby so that it came at her gently from all sides.

The man put her keys in his pocket and started to walk towards her, almost casually, the hand with the knife in it swinging gently by his side and his murmur caressing her like a breeze.

'I do not come to punish.'

She turned and beat the door with her fists. The building was new; nothing rattled, nothing budged, and the heartless glass swallowed the sound smoothly and burped nothing back.

Layla took the deepest breath since her very first, twenty-four years earlier, and screamed.

Nothing came out but a strangled squeak that scurried about the echoing lobby like a silly white mouse. She tried again, but her throat was so tight that air could barely get through in either direction.

Suddenly drowning in fear, Layla pressed her back against the cold glass – an infinite half-inch from where people were safe – and waited for the man to reach her.

He did.

'Softly shall you sleep in my arms,' he murmured kindly.

Right up until the very last second, Layla Martin didn't believe that she would – or could – be murdered. She knew that *something* would save her.

It didn't.

The knife had gone in; the blood had come out, warming the killer's hands with the joy of creation.

At first the girl had flip-flopped like a fish on the floor. But once she'd understood, she'd calmed down, and died as she should.

Beautifully.

Searching his face with her grateful eyes until they'd faded to ash.

And as she had emptied, so he had filled up.

For the first time in a long time, his heart had started to beat, and he had cried with relief.

Thank you, he'd sobbed against her clotted ear. *Thank you.*

And knew he would do this again.

Wanted to. *Needed* to.

Looked forward to it.